The Love

Caroline Khoury was born in Beirut to a Lebanese mother and Welsh father. Having grown up in the suburbs of London, she returned there after over ten years living in Hong Kong, Japan and the US. Single mother to two amazing teen girls and writer of armchair escapist romances.

Also by Caroline Khoury

Still Unwritten
The Love Intervention

THE
Love
INTERVENTION

CAROLINE KHOURY

CANELO

First published in the United Kingdom in 2025 by

Canelo
Unit 9, 5th Floor
Cargo Works, 1–2 Hatfields
London SE1 9PG
United Kingdom

A CIP catalogue record for this book is available from the British Library.

Print ISBN 978 1 83598 106 1
Ebook ISBN 978 1 83598 107 8

Cover design by Cherie Chapman. Cover illustration by Sophie Melissa

Look for more great books at www.canelo.co

Printed and bound in Great Britain by Clays Ltd, Elcograf S.p.A.

1

For anyone who needs a hug

Chapter 1

$C_8H_{11}NO_2$. The chemical formula for dopamine: an organic chemical of the catecholamine and phenethylamine families. Why I needed to know this, I had no idea. But if I nodded knowledgeably, then maybe my best friend Jena would get to the point.

'Dopamine is known as the feel-good neurotransmitter and it serves several important neurological functions essential for the survival of our species,' she said, reading the words off her laptop screen. 'Its existence helps with memory and learning and is very important for romantic attachments. Dopamine is released through' – she clicked a key – 'touch, when you are attracted to someone and when you—'

'Orgasm,' my other bestie – Samira – interjected, her face lighting up. Her deep voice reverberated around the bar, causing a few heads to turn.

We were sat around a high table in Simmons, a former historic pub between Warren Street and Euston Square stations. I was perched on a stool while Samira and Jena had camped on the leather banquette opposite. Neon quote signs were nailed to the brick walls and the whole place was bathed in a red light giving a burlesque feel. A disco ball featured in the centre of the ceiling for when the place would turn into a karaoke bar later on. But there was no way I would still be here for that transformation.

'Yes, orgasm,' Jena whispered, clicking the key again so the word appeared in dark pink.

I awaited the next slide and slurped my virgin daiquiri. Brain freeze. Rubbing my temples sadly didn't alleviate the numbing sensation in my head nor did it eradicate the thought that I needed to find a way to end this evening rapidly and get back to the lab. One of our senior cardiology surgeons at Royal London where I worked as a clinical scientist had slammed a report on my desk at five with questions surrounding my team's findings on a biopsy. The buck stopped with me, so it didn't matter that the rest of the team were clocking off when it had been handed over. I had to address his concerns and get back to him ASAP.

Jena had travelled over an hour to get to a bar close to Euston hoping that would make it easier for me to join them, and Samira had a babysitter booked for the whole night, as she reminded me when I had tried to bail a couple of hours ago. These end-of-the-working-week meet-ups had occurred religiously for almost ten years – ever since my return from my Master's at NYU. Work and our love lives (or lack of) usually dominated our conversations, but a PowerPoint presentation had never been a feature of our discussions and my interest had been piqued as soon as Jena lifted the laptop from her bag after I'd rushed in late.

She pressed the return key and another slide popped up. 'Low levels of dopamine can lead to a lack of motiv-ation, an inability to concentrate, depression, anxiety and disturbed sleep.'

As if on cue I yawned, my eyes watering. *Atchoo*. I sneezed into my jacket sleeve before leaning down and pulling out a pack of tissues from my rucksack nestled at my feet. An assortment of Lemsip sachets and paracetamol packets slipped out and I shoved them back in.

Samira tossed her balayage locks over her shoulder and leaned closer to Jena. 'When are we gonna hit her with the hot guy slides?' she whispered behind her hand.

'I think she'll be more amenable if we bamboozle her with the science first,' Jena replied, her voice even lower.

But I had heard every word.

'Guys, what's going on?' I asked. 'I told you I've only got an hour.' I fanned my face with a coaster. Thermals had been a good idea to shield me from the February arctic freeze and my sub-zero lab but not for this heated, crowded cocktail bar. Or was I sweating cobs thinking about the report on my desk? But if I bailed now, it would be the third week in a row I had cut one of our sacred evenings short.

'Laila?' Jena laid a cool hand over my warm one. It tempered the heat and was a comfort.

'Hmm?' I murmured.

'We're worried about you,' she continued. 'You've been clock-watching since the second you sat down, you haven't removed your suit jacket—'

'You're having a mocktail,' Samira interrupted, giving a slight shudder.

'Please, guys, cut me some slack.'

'We're not raising these points to be mean,' Jena said. 'We're commenting on them because we are your friends, and we thought you needed a proper break tonight.'

Samira raised a hand. 'Jena thinks that. I think you need to get laid. Can I move on to my half of the presentation now, *please*?' she said before I had a chance to comment on the middle part of what she had uttered.

I needed to take whatever it was they were plotting more seriously if I was going to slip away swiftly. 'OK,' I said, unbuttoning my jacket and placing it on the stool next to me, which was piled high with our winter coats. 'I am all ears.'

'Finally.' Samira grinned broadly, revelling in this minor victory.

'Can't we go back to my slides?' Jena asked.

'No!' Samira and I said in unison and laughed when our eyes met, knowing full well that once Jena started talking about anything she felt passionately about, we would be there all night.

'OK, OK,' Jena conceded, her jaw locked and nostrils flared. It was a look she usually saved for her Year Elevens when she had delivered a lecture on the importance of exams, but no one was listening. She taught biology at a state secondary school in south London, and it pained her that most of her students would give up the subject the second they had finished their GCSEs.

Jena rolled up the sleeves of her cardigan and clicked the mouse several times. Slides with the words 'oxytocin', 'serotonin' and 'endorphins' flashed by until she settled on one with a word flashing intermittently.

I spluttered my drink before wiping my mouth with a napkin and looking over my shoulder in case a camera crew was lurking and I was about to be Punk'd. 'You're kidding, right?'

'No, we are not kidding, Laila,' Samira said, her chin raised. 'This is an intervention. A…' She nudged Jena and another slide popped up with a neon heart pulsing.

'*Love* intervention,' they sang, harmonising the words.

I drew a deep breath. 'For the love of God,' I mumbled as I grabbed my suit jacket and slipped off the stool, shrugging my arms into the sleeves.

'Wait,' Jena said, a panicked look on her face. 'Please, hear us out.'

My earlier feelings of guilt evaporated and in its wake a surge of irritation bubbled beneath. 'I told you I couldn't come out tonight, but you kept badgering me. If I can't figure out why the findings from this biopsy are inconclusive, my job will be on the line and more importantly someone's life will be in my hands. And I have to work on this tonight before heading home and tending to my mum. Seriously. Grow up, the two of you. We are not back at school and life does *not* revolve around men.'

Jena gave me one of her deer-caught-in-the-headlights looks, the one that made me instantly regret those words I had uttered.

'I'm sorry, that was blunt.' I drained my drink and pushed it to the centre of the table, a shiver rippling up my spine at the sudden influx of cold liquid. 'I just need to get back to work.'

Jena clenched her fists. She was steeling herself to say something and knowing her it was going to be big.

'We know you've got a lot on your plate, Laila,' she began. 'We know you spend every waking moment working in the lab or looking after your mum, but we are your best friends in the whole wide world, have known you since you were sixteen and we wouldn't be doing all this' – she waved at her laptop screen – 'if we weren't genuinely worried about you. If you'd had the patience to listen to my slides, you would understand the detrimental effect the lack of these chemicals has on the nervous system and the long-term effects these damaged

5

neurological pathways can have on you if you don't get a dose of these molecules on a regular basis. You need to stop. Recalibrate. You have been working tirelessly the last ten years with very little time for much else.'

I continued buttoning up my jacket. Jena meant well, but I didn't need a lecture from her as if I had a second mother.

'OK, I can see Jena's words are having zero effect on you,' Samira said, standing up, 'so it's time for *me* to be blunt.' She laid a hand on my shoulder. 'You're heading for burnout, girl. And if you don't do something about it now, all this chasing of this promotion, that project and nursing your mum until she is back on her feet again will be impossible cos you will be shot to shit. I mean, look at you.' She gave me a not-so-subtle once-over with a flick of her hand up and down my body. 'You look a mess.'

I self-consciously tucked my shirt into my black work trousers, noticing a stain at the top of my left leg. Dabbing my finger with spit, I wetted the area but to no avail.

'No offence to women in their forties,' she continued, 'but you seriously look ten years older. Those bags under your eyes are *deep*… and when was the last time you went to the hairdresser's?'

I patted my dark brown hair, conscious of split ends and, even worse, the first sighting of a grey hair, which ordinarily shouldn't be an issue, but I was about to turn thirty-one soon and thought this was a little premature.

'Now,' Samira said, softening her tone and reclaiming her seat. 'You are going to sit down and hear us out. We won't take more than another twenty minutes of your time. Then you are going back to the lab to be a super-hero and figure out this' – she waved her hand around –

'inconclusiveness, while I use your keys to check in on your mum and get her what she needs. OK?'

A deep breath filled my lungs. The ache that had nestled on my chest dissolved instantly when I took in their sympathetic smiles. They knew me better than anyone in the world and something in my brain told me I had to sit and listen.

'Thanks, Samira. I'd appreciate that. I can message her and say you're stopping by.'

'I'm happy to do it. It's been a while since we caught up.'

'I think she'd love that.'

Samira's smile broadened. Mum and Samira had an unbreakable bond – more so than Mum and I had. I was sure Samira was the daughter Mum wished she'd had but I had never confided in either of them that this was a thought I had harboured for years.

'Right,' Samira said, shifting her scarlet boob-tube dress up a fraction. 'Sit down and listen up.'

Her tone came across as an order, as if she was up on the investment floor at the bank she worked for, issuing instructions at one of her minions. I took heed and settled back on my seat. Samira caught the eye of the bartender, throwing one of her winning smiles at him before raising her eyebrows and taking in a sweep of our drinks with her beautifully manicured hand. The gesture was met with a salute and a wink.

Taking charge of the laptop, Samira straightened. 'Sun, sea and sex,' she announced. 'When was the last time you experienced any of these three things?'

I chewed my bottom lip in concentration as I considered her question. 'Well...'

'Bzzz,' she trilled, causing me to lean back a fraction.

'If you have to even think about the answer to that question or even bore us with the reasons why you haven't had them in ages, then this needs changing.' She nodded at Jena, who clicked onto the next slide.

My eyes bulged at the image of the semi-naked man dominating the screen: all oiled muscles and bulging biceps. A memory scratched away at the back of my mind. 'Is that—'

'Paul Crossfield? Your first kiss? Yes, it is him. Major glow-up.'

I leaned in and studied the image more carefully.

'Gay,' she declared.

'Excuse me?'

'Came out five years ago.'

'My first boyfriend is gay?'

'Technically not a boyfriend but yes, 'fraid so. Next slide.'

A photo of me and Alex Benedictus popped up from a New Year's Eve party during lower sixth. My cheeks flushed at the memory of him. He was the guy I lost my virginity to, the one who happily took it and moved on to the next sacrificial victim a week later. Jena clicked again and an older version of Alex appeared – all chunky-cable-knit-jumper-wearing and floppy-haired, with two bright-eyed, blonde children at his feet.

'Married. Two kids. Though word on the street has it that he has some French girl on the side.' Samira winked.

'How do you know all this?' I asked. 'And more to the point, why are you telling me?'

'Jena and I have our sources and we have been working on this a long time, researching who from your past is single, separated or divorced and where everyone is living.' She began clicking on some other slides with a random selection of my previous hook-ups/guys I had briefly dated.

'You make it seem like I have dated every guy on the planet. My love life hasn't been that active. And you haven't answered my "why do I care?" question.'

She scrolled back to the start of the selection. 'You care because it has been a long time since you got laid or had anything that even resembled a relationship and look where all these guys are now…' She pointed at the words 'married', 'engaged' and 'off the market'. There was one major omission in this collection of men, but Samira knew he was a trigger and had obviously excluded him. Besides, I already knew where he was.

'You know why I haven't wanted anything serious. Nothing fits in with my career plan.'

'Correction. Nothing *has* fitted in with your plan up until now. You're a doctor for heaven's sake.'

'I have a doctorate. There's a difference.'

Samira rolled her eyes. 'Whatever. Semantics. You have the job you've always dreamed of and your mum is going to be back on her feet in no time. What then?'

'Then I have to get the next promotion, the one that will take me to the next level as supervisor. And I want my name on a cutting-edge piece of research. Listen, Samira. I appreciate the interest in my love life and when my next holiday is going to be, but it's February and life is hectic. There are other ways to get a shot of all these molecules. I'll, um… I'll join a running club.'

'You can't even make it to the bus stop without getting a cramp.'

'Then I'll join a yoga class.'

Jena shifted in her seat. 'What Samira is trying to say is, we think you not only need to have a break, you need to fall in love. There's nothing greater. The security and safety of two strong arms embracing you on a regular basis, the feeling of having someone in your corner, supporting you and—'

'Sex on tap.' Samira let her shoulders dance. 'The high of repeated orgasms.'

I folded my arms and decided to humour them. 'So, you have trawled through all my previous boyfriends, hook-ups, coffee dates and have come up with my ideal man who is going to fulfil all my sexual and loving needs and can fit in with my long hours in the lab and the fact that I still live at home and who is also the only guy from my past that is single?'

Samira scoffed. 'Laila, we have done more than that, we have come up with a plan – the Love Intervention plan. *Three* guys, who live in three different countries, offering you an abundance of sun, sea and… the rest is up to you. The guys in question are…'

I sat rigid, my focus on the laptop screen, as she paused to make the big reveal. Which three guys had they unearthed? In my mind, there was no one from my past that I had even given a second thought to. And I didn't need a man – or men in this case. My life was complete and fulfilling as it was. Love was a complication, and I had sworn off ever falling in love after wasting my mid-twenties thinking I had found it with the one guy that had been omitted from their presentation – Josh.

Whoever they had discovered, I wasn't interested.

Chapter 2

'Now, to be clear,' Samira said, her finger poised in the air. 'Jena and I weren't unanimous in choosing these guys, but they were the ones that fit the remit best. We had to take into account personal status obviously – no affairs here, thank you very much, Mr Benedictus.' She chuckled. Samira had had the measure of Alex the second we sat opposite him during maths class and he had flirted with me, and I had always regretted not listening to her. 'We also had to consider where they were located to ensure a winter sun offering.'

'Winter?' I questioned.

Samira clicked her fingers repeatedly in front of my face. 'Get with the programme, Laila. The Love Intervention has to be undertaken soon, like possibly this-month or next-month soon.'

'I can't up and leave and go on holiday, guys.' I gave Jena a pleading look. She was the organised one, the one who listened to me when I spoke about my upcoming schedule.

'Laila, I know for a fact that you have fifteen days' holiday that you are owed and have to take off by the end of March,' Jena said. 'It's use it or lose it, right? And I know in the past you have always been happy to book off the odd day here and there, but this last year has been brutal for you, with your mum's accident and doing all this extra overtime on that heart project and that's why you haven't used up your entitlement. Samira and I worked on the basis that you would tell your boss that you want to take it now.'

I loved how Jena referred to such an important piece of research as 'that heart project'. It made me wonder how much my friends listened when I talked about work.

'Speaking of my mum,' I said. 'I can't leave her. She still has another few weeks before the cast comes off.'

'Jena and I will cover you. It's an easy commute for me from your house to work and half term is coming up. Jena's school's break doesn't coincide with Rosie's and we will figure out the extra time.'

The sentiment was well meaning but I'm not sure Mum would approve of this plan in the slightest. I sneezed again and grabbed another tissue to blow my nose.

'Or…' Samira shuffled away. 'You could take sick leave. Seriously, Laila. You are run-down, picking up every winter bug out there. You've been sniffling for our last three meet-ups.'

Jena laid the back of her hand against my forehead. Her cool touch was a balm against my burning skin. 'Hmm,' she murmured, that line appearing above her nose as it did whenever she was concerned. 'You do feel quite warm.'

'I'll be fine once the last Lemsip kicks in.' I yawned and my eyes watered again. It happened every time.

'What you need is rest and relaxation,' Jena said.

I clocked the time again. This discussion had so far taken up ten minutes of the allotted time and my report was calling me. 'I appreciate your concern, guys, but I feel fine. A good night's sleep and I will bounce back.'

Jena narrowed her eyes at me. 'When was the last time you *had* a good night's sleep?'

Her question caught me off guard. The truth? I was on the back of a string of sleepless nights. Since taking on the management of a second team while the hospital tried to hire a replacement for one of our clinical scientists, I had been responsible for picking up the slack. The extra duties weighed heavily on my shoulders. And ever since Mum had slipped on a patch of ice and broken her ankle, she had been calling for me in the night when she was in need of a trip to the bathroom. Falling back asleep had begun to be a struggle – my brain suddenly wide awake, streams of data spinning in my mind. Life appeared to be spiralling, but I was sure once winter was over and the days grew longer my life would get back on track.

'A while ago. But who clocks a full night's sleep these days anyway?' I said, letting out another yawn. 'It's probably that late-afternoon caffeine fix I've recently adopted. I'll cut it out of my daily routine.'

'Or you could embrace our plan to get away somewhere warm?' Jena said. 'The guys are optional.'

Samira huffed. 'No, they are not. They are at the very centre of the plan, the very reason why we went to all this trouble to trawl through your Instagram, Facebook and every other social media platform you use, to uncover them. Intimacy is at the very heart of getting your fill of dopamine, oxytocin, serotonin and endorphins, or DOSE as we shall affectionately refer to them from here on in.'

'To recap, you want me to go on holiday and hook up with three guys I have been with before to get a dose of molecules that will restore my mental health and wellbeing?'

'Actually.' Samira pointed to her pursed lips. 'You have only been with one of them before, if by being with them, you mean in the biblical sense. We have no idea what you got up to with the other two.'

'What makes them candidates for the "Love Intervention" plan?' I air-quoted their ridiculous name for this whole idea.

'Can we stop with the nitty-gritty of why we chose them and do the big reveal?' Samira pleaded.

'By all means,' I said, my irritation gauge cranking up a notch. Samira was prickly tonight and I wondered what was bothering her.

The barman brought our next round of drinks. He lingered a little too long as he positioned Samira's porn-star martini in front of her. As he laid a folded napkin next to it, his fingers brushed hers. It was almost impossible not to notice her squeezing her arms together, forcing her cleavage up and out of her dress. She looked up at him, biting her bottom lip. He leaned in and whispered in her ear, and a coy smile broke on her face, before he retreated. Slipping the napkin into her handbag, she resumed her business-as-usual pose.

'What was that?' I asked.

'*That* was my weekend sorted.'

'Samira,' Jena gasped. 'What about Rosie?'

'My parents land tomorrow, so she's spending the weekend with them.'

'Again?'

'Don't be so judgy. I work a fifty-hour week and show up for parents' evenings, school events and the like. I deserve a night off or two now and again.'

'I'm sorry,' Jena said, tugging at the heart pendant around her neck, before slipping it beneath her high scooped black wool dress. 'I didn't mean to pass judgement. You're a great mum.'

Samira accepted Jena's apology but I could see in the depths of her eyes that the words had stung. Becoming a mum at twenty-two had not been part of her life plan. We had never met Rosie's father. Samira had told us she had no way of holding him accountable for his role in Rosie's upbringing as he had merely been a one-night stand and they hadn't stayed in touch. Samira had worked like a demon to support herself and her daughter for the last nine years, her parents having cut her off initially as they had told her how ashamed they were of her illicit affair. They had softened a little once Rosie was born but Samira was clear that men were of one use to her now: fulfilling sexual needs only.

Samira cleared her throat, finger hovering over the return key. 'Introducing eligible bachelor number one.'

The image on the screen came into focus and my brain took a second to catch up with the vision. Memories stirred of passionate nights in my grad room at NYU and heated discussions about the synthesis of small molecule organometallics over a few beers in the student bar – a subject on which he knew nothing because he was an engineering student.

'Edoardo Moretti,' I whispered, taking in the recent photo of him in a smart suit, standing at a lectern delivering a speech. His dark hair was a little shorter than I remembered, but he had those same intense eyes that I had fallen for all those years ago. 'He's still single?'

'We trawled his Instagram and Facebook accounts. No sign of a significant other. This involved extensive searches of women featured in photos of him to check out whether they had tagged him as a boyfriend or husband. He has had relationships but there's no one on the scene currently.' She clicked to another slide, which showed him wearing a hard hat, kneeling on the ground in what looked like a building site. There was a group of kids laughing around him, one with their arms wrapped tightly around his neck. That smile. It used to make my insides constrict every time he laughed.

I shook myself from that reverie. Had I forgotten how our relationship ended?

'Why have you included Edoardo? He and I broke up almost ten years ago.' A spasm of pain knocked my ribcage as I thought of that eventful afternoon when we had split up.

'Second-chance romance,' Jena declared, clasping her hands by her head, swooning.

'Look at him, Laila.' Samira had clicked onto the next slide. He was cradling a surfboard under his arm, the top part of his wetsuit hanging off his hips – his smooth abs wet and rippling, an unmistakable V shape pointing to the bulge below.

I leaned towards the screen. 'He looks good.'

'Yup.' Samira nodded. 'That's on some beach in Hawaii.'

'He lives in Hawaii?'

'No, he's currently working in Puerto Rico, helping with the country's reconstruction after that devastating hurricane a few years back. From his LinkedIn' – she clicked the key to show his profile picture – 'it appears he has been working for an Italian company as a structural engineer for the last few years with stints in Mexico and Brazil and currently undertaking a project in San Juan.'

I studied the photo a little more closely. He was decked out in a smart suit, a serious expression on his face, clean shaven. I had complained about his prickly stubble many times during our six months together, but he had always declared it made him more distinguished-looking.

'We identified that visiting Puerto Rico gives you the serotonin hit from the perfect weather they have at this time of year,' Jena said, locating the weather app on her phone and showing me the screen. 'Late twenties centigrade, and lower humidity than the height of the summer months. The state also has endless opportunities for adventures and sightseeing.'

'And more importantly, if you and Edoardo…' Samira winked and tilted her head before making it more obvious what she meant by making a circle with her left hand and sticking her right index finger in and out of it. 'Oodles of opportunities to get a fix of those other DOSE ingredients.'

There was no point in arguing with her that this was the worst idea I had ever heard, so I decided to move things along. 'Dare I ask who my second victim is?'

'We think you will like this one,' Jena said, a toothy grin plastered on her face.

'The one that got away,' Samira declared, the next slide popping up at the touch of a key.

'Mateo,' I said wistfully. 'Mateo Pérez,' I said, immediately recognising the guy in the picture. He was also on a beach with the beginning of a sunset in the background. 'How is he?'

'He was incredibly hard to track down. Off-radar for years.'

Flashbacks flicked to the front of my mind. Mateo and I had been good friends in our late teens, having first met on a school trip to Geneva. We had texted on and off after that until we chanced upon both being accepted to do a Master's at NYU. He had been my lab partner and confidante, and I realised suddenly that I had missed his friendship. We'd lost touch not long after graduation when his mum got sick and he had returned home to Madrid. But a heavy feeling sat in my chest thinking of an incident between me and Mateo that had caused Edoardo and I to end our relationship – an incident I had never confided to either Samira or Jena.

I took in the photo of Mateo again – his thick brown hair longer on top than I remembered, wet tendrils stuck to his face, which had a light beard. That broad smile I remembered so fondly was on full display as he was laughing at someone or something off camera. His board shorts sat low on his hips, his tanned chest had a smattering of hair. A thought came to my mind.

'But Mateo and I were friends. He isn't "the one that got away".' I looked from Jena back to Samira.

'Jena thinks otherwise,' Samira said, putting Jena on the spot.

Her cheeks pinkened. 'I thought you guys looked good together.'

'As friends,' I clarified. '*You* were the one that had a crush on him when we met him in Switzerland.'

Jena tutted. 'That was a lifetime ago. You and he were obviously the ones that had the connection. He never gave me a second thought. And besides, friendship is the most wonderful foundation of any solid relationship.'

'Call it "friends to lovers", then,' Samira huffed. 'I'm not on top of all these romance book tropes that Jena absorbs like a piece of litmus paper. The focus here is identifying possible scenarios where you could get laid—'

'Fall in love,' Jena interjected, a defiant look on her face.

Before I dissed their suggestion again, I had to remind myself that this was all hypothetical and that I was here to listen to their plan, be a grateful friend that they were so concerned about my mental wellbeing and get to the end of the presentation.

'Doesn't he look hot in this photo, though,' Jena said.

I didn't recall ever having seen Mateo with his shirt off. He did look good, there was no denying it. 'Where was the photo taken?'

'Costa Rica. He's volunteering out there, saving turtles,' Samira said.

'Major swoon.' Jena rolled her eyes skyward. She was a hopeless romantic.

'Right,' I said. 'So you want me to travel to Puerto Rico and Costa Rica. Where's the third hotspot you're suggesting I escape to?'

'California,' Samira said, folding her arms. 'But I'll let Jena announce this one.'

'Samira insists that once a bad boy always a bad boy, but I believe he was unfinished business and that bad boys can redeem themselves.' She straightened and tapped her finger on the return key. 'Austin Bradley.'

A slideshow of pictures began on the screen. Photo after photo of Austin in various poses: riding a horse, diving into the sea, picking a bunch of grapes, holding up a bottle of wine and one where he was standing next to a sign that had the word 'SOLD' obscuring the name. In every single photo, his blonde hair glistened, and pearly whites gleamed. He was the epitome of the all-American guy.

The room felt stuffy again, and I tugged at the neckline of my shirt. Austin was as attractive as I remembered. He had also been a grad student at NYU, after completing his undergraduate degree in physics. From the moment I arrived, he had been on my radar as he had been chosen to show around some of the incoming international students, which included me, Mateo and Edoardo. He was charming and ridiculously good-looking, and he knew it.

'How did you find him?'

'He was the easiest to find,' Jena said. 'He left the world of financial services a couple of years ago and has pretty much kept his Instagram up to date with his journey to creating his own wine. He cashed in his shares or stocks or... something like that and bought a vineyard. He finds peace in sunrises,' she said, reading the blurb beneath the picture, 'does yoga on the beach and occasionally helps out at a local food bank, volunteering his time and donating some of his produce.'

Jena leaned her chin on her hand and raised her eyes to the ceiling once more. She was swooning again.

'So... this is evidence of his reformation?' I asked.

'We don't know he was a bad boy.' Jena took a sip of her mojito. 'That was Samira's analysis.'

Analysis that I had taken to heart. The crush I had had on Austin Bradley had reached epic proportions a few weeks into my year at NYU, but something happened at the start of Christmas break that meant nothing ever developed between us and I couldn't deny I had thought of what might have been on more than one occasion.

'If you look at his Instagram prior to this epiphany of his where he sank his life's savings into some plot of land in the Californian Hills,' Samira said, 'there was woman after woman hanging off him, no single one appearing more than two or three times.'

'That doesn't necessarily mean they were all his exes,' Jena said. 'It means—'

'He's an F-boy.' Samira straightened and folded her arms, before catching the attention of the barman again and throwing him a wink.

'He was a pain in the arse, is what he was,' I countered.

'Perfect.' Jena clapped her hands together. 'This can be enemies to lovers.'

'Guys, we can speculate all we want about the merits or faults of Austin Bradley, but I have moved on, from him, from all of them.' I closed the lid of Jena's laptop. 'My time at NYU was ten years ago. What happened in the past should stay in the past.' I drained my drink and clenched my teeth as the iced beverage froze my brain again. 'I appreciate that you went to all this trouble to come up with this plan. Maybe you can send it to me, and I'll give it some thought over the weekend, and we can discuss it next Friday.'

'Yeah, right,' Samira mumbled under her breath.

I sighed audibly, picking up my jacket and coat from the stool and slipping off my seat. Samira was acting like a sulky teen. Confrontation never sat well with me and the tension behind my eyeballs was beginning to increase in intensity. But I wasn't going to be riled by her, especially as she was going to be spending the evening with my mother when she could be making out with the sexy barman.

Sexy barman? Where had that observation come from?

I stole a glance at him as he shook the cocktail shaker. The sleeves of his white shirt were rolled up tight on his forearms and his biceps pulsed at every movement. There were at least three or four women at the bar vying for his attention, but he only had eyes for Samira. Mid-twenties at a guess but clearly a magnet for older women judging by the age bracket of the fan club poised on barstools in front of him. Samira liked them younger and submissive. Dominant in the boardroom and bedroom was how she liked to live her life. Perhaps they were a good match.

I liked to have more of an emotional and intellectual connection with my men for the encounter to be even remotely satisfying. And for that to happen, time needed to be dedicated to any such blossoming relationship – time I did not have, time I swore I would never sacrifice again. That was why I had no intention of pursuing this plan of Samira and Jena's, especially with three guys from a time in my past that I had fought hard to suppress, as it was also laced with so much pain.

'The blood oath's honour,' I said finally, alluding to our decade-old pledge. 'I promise next week I won't bail on you and will have read through and considered your proposal. They're making a decision on Wednesday about the Henderson cardiovascular team, so maybe we can celebrate as well.'

This was the next level up for me, the reason behind all these increased hours and stepping forward to fill the gaps in the department. There was no one more qualified than me in our team to take on this advisory role that had been newly created at the hospital. My PhD had even involved an element of what the project was addressing – the impact on the heart of ischaemia-reperfusion injury. Call me cocky, but I knew it was in the bag. All the sleepless nights and hours in the lab would be worth it once I was on that team. The director was someone I looked up to enormously and having him notice me and my work would be life-changing. What did it matter that my love life had taken a nosedive as a result? There was an end game, and it was within reach.

Samira's eyes glazed over, and Jena had a wounded-deer look plastered over her face again. I dragged my mind back to why they might look so affronted.

'Oh, come on. You didn't seriously think I would accept this intervention challenge straight off the bat, did you?'

They both remained tight-lipped.

'How were you even proposing I got in contact? Did you think I would sit here and message them?'

Suddenly neither of them could make eye contact with me. My phone buzzed on the table, and something told me I didn't want to pick it up. *No, they haven't.*

'I have a confession,' Samira said, tapping her French-tipped nail on my mobile as if she was communicating a message in code. 'I did that for you.'

My mouth dropped open at the realisation that she wasn't joking. 'You hacked my phone and sent them each a message?'

She averted my boring eyes and nodded, pinching her lips tight.

'How? When?'

'Earlier on, when you went to the bathroom. We're not fucking around, Laila.' Samira's tone had turned serious. 'We knew you would shut this down so that's why we took matters into our own hands.'

This time she didn't break my glare and when I turned to Jena for support, she had a defiant expression on her face. I slid back down onto my stool, the weight of their concern pushing me down.

'We're not forcing you to do this, Laila,' Jena said, her tone softer. 'Ultimately, it has to be your decision. But we thought you might say cost as well as time might be an issue.' She reached into her handbag and pulled out an envelope. 'Consider this an early birthday present.'

Hesitantly, I opened it. A single sheet of paper was inside with the words 'E-ticket confirmation' at the top. My hand rose to my mouth as I took in the rest of the words.

'This will at least get you over the Atlantic,' Jena said. 'The other flights aren't too expensive. We thought we would leave it up to you to figure out the itinerary because we know how much you love to plan things. You have three months in which to fix the dates. We hoped that would give you some flexibility to organise it with your work. We're not monsters, Laila. We're your best friends. And we wouldn't have called this intervention unless we were genuinely worried about you.'

The enormity of what they had planned made my head throb even more. An overwhelming mix of feelings churned inside my brain, predominantly when I checked the airport destination again. New York.

How could I go back when I hadn't healed from the last time I was there?

My phone vibrated again on the table. Slowly I turned it over and I saw who the notification was from. One name. Two words. Austin Bradley.

Chapter 3

'Have some fun,' the assistant dean of academic affairs boomed through the microphone. They were three words I hadn't expected to hear during the New Master's Student Welcome talk.

'This is a great city,' he continued. 'Get up early, do your work and enjoy your weekends.'

I soaked up the speech, my fellow grad students seated around me nodding periodically, their laughter punctuating the air-conditioned auditorium when Dr Peterson told an anecdote.

Fun. I couldn't compute this word. Especially now that I was trebling my student loans to be here. But this had been the dream as soon as the opportunity had presented itself to me during my final year at UCL, when my senior tutor had said my grades were good enough to apply for a Master's programme at a top US school. And if I wanted to further my studies and land the job of my dreams, I had to think big. So I had aimed for Big Apple big. When the acceptance letter from NYU had landed in my inbox, I'd whooped and then had a good cry. Partly because of the student debt I would be accumulating but also something else. Coming to America would give me the opportunity to do something I had wanted to do for a long time.

This was it. A chance. A chance to find him. Dad.

Those thoughts were interrupted by a movement two rows in front of me in the auditorium. A head had turned and through the darkness I could see a face scanning the crowd before settling on me. I shifted in my seat as his eyes bored into mine. That stare pinned me to the spot and was a little unnerving. But then the corner of his mouth twitched at the same time an eyebrow raised. Like a signal. But I couldn't read it.

'He's *so* checking you out,' Alesha's voice whispered by my ear.

I turned to my roommate who was grinning like a Cheshire cat.

'No, he's not,' I whispered back, patting down my hair and smoothing the pleats of my skirt. I turned back to the stage as the next speaker came on – an administrator to talk about the Bobst Library – a place I would no doubt frequent regularly as my roommate appeared to have a very different work ethic to me. Her music had filled our two-bed dorm room over the last two days – Red Hot Chili Peppers and Foo Fighters on repeat – with no thought to the fact that I might want to do some pre-course work.

Alesha was also an international student – from Mumbai – but her course was fully funded by her parents, and she had told me on our first day that she planned to hone in on the nearest French or Spanish guy to help perfect her language skills. *That* was her method of study for her modern language Master's – textbooks be damned. How we were going to navigate the coming year sharing, I had no idea, but I hadn't wanted to splash out on a room in an apartment once I had seen the rates for ones in Manhattan. Brooklyn had been a relatively cheaper option, but I wasn't keen on schlepping on the A train every morning and evening, especially in a city I didn't know. But here were our faculty advisors actively encouraging exploring this incredible city and now I was wishing I had stretched my budget for a Lower East Side studio.

The guy two rows in front turned again and this time he smiled broadly, a dimple forming in his left cheek. I smiled back, idly wondering whether the 'have fun/explore the city' speech extended to exploring the local talent. I shook myself from that thought. Mum had given me the usual lecture before she left me at the departures gate of Heathrow Terminal 4 – studies first, internships second, societies third. Play wasn't even mentioned. It was advice I had lived by during my undergraduate degree, and I was sure the main reason why I had nailed a double first and secured a summer placement at a pharmaceutical company at the end of my second year. I had 'played' a bit, usually at the insistence of Samira, who loved to party, while Jena had been loved up the entire three years.

A pang of homesickness pulsed inside as I thought of my two best friends back home. Jena was now nursing a broken heart as her boyfriend had moved to Australia after dumping her. She was planning on throwing herself into her PGCE teaching course while Samira was beginning her first paid internship at a bank, bemoaning the long hours already. But they had both sworn that they would splurge on a trip to see me over the Christmas holidays. And I couldn't wait.

Another slide popped on the screen, the words 'intellectual exploration' appearing in bold, and I made an inward promise to myself: *that* was the only exploring I would be doing.

'Isn't this a riot?' Alesha said, sipping her glass of wine as we scanned the dining room packed with students, their chatter escalating as every new person entered the room. A long trestle table running down the length of the hall was filled with an assortment of drinks plus a spread of mini burgers, pizza and other appetisers.

We had headed back to our digs after the welcome speech, and Alesha had looked at me, horrified, when I began changing into a cozy tee and shorts combo, declaring I wanted to get stuck into some reading and have an early night. She had persuaded me to get changed and go with her to the school's Fall Fling, claiming she didn't want to walk into the first grad party of the semester alone.

I tugged at my H&M slip dress, conscious that it was a lot shorter than I remembered when I had bought it on a shopping spree with Samira. Taking a sip of my wine, the sharp earthy tones caught at the back of my throat. I coughed and set my glass down, wondering whether now was a good time to bail and get back to my studying.

And then I saw him.

Tall. Blonde. Chiselled cheekbones. All the girls turned as he cut a path through the room. Was he walking in slow motion? Or had the space-time continuum glitched? His eyes locked with mine and that grin that he had showcased in the auditorium began to erupt over his face.

Oh, God, he's coming this way.

I turned over my shoulder to check he wasn't making eye contact with someone else. When I turned back, he was there, standing about half a foot above me, those blue eyes piercing. Jena would no doubt have a much better descriptor lifted from one of her romance novels. Maybe aquamarine, cobalt, azure, ocean blue…

'Hey,' he said, his stance wide, one hand slipped in the back pocket of his grey khaki shorts as if he was posing for a model shoot. The collar of his navy-blue polo shirt was popped. He reminded me of one of those preppy boys I had gone to school with at Westminster – the ones with the trust funds and credit cards linked to Daddy's offshore account. Unlike them, I had been on a full scholarship, like Jena, and that was the only way both of us could afford to attend the eleven-thousand-pounds-a-term private-school fees.

'Hey,' I replied, my voice a little too flutey. *Jeez, Laila. Get a grip. You know the measure of these boys – the ones who know how good-looking they are.*

'It's Clarke?' His nose crinkled a little as he said that word and it was adorable.

Adorable? No guy is adorable. Teddy bears are adorable. Six-foot-four men are not adorable.

I then realised he had fallen silent. Crap. Had he asked me a question? I looked to Alesha for backup but she was simpering. Like, almost drooling on the spot.

'Excuse me?' I blinked up at him.

'Your last name. It's Clarke?'

'Oh yeah, sorry. Yes, it's Clarke. Laila Clarke.' I laid my plate down on the table, wiped my hand down the side of my dress and held it out in greeting, inwardly scolding myself for being rendered so tongue-tied and flustered. He took my hand and a gasp emanated from my mouth as a jolt of static electricity pulsed between our fingertips. No, this wasn't a scene straight out of one of Jena's novels, I reminded myself. This guy was merely carrying an extra surge of electrons – the result of the quick movement of a million of these particles upon contact with something oppositely charged. Though, this was a more common occurrence in colder months when the air was drier. I looked down at his feet. Rubber-soled shoes. There was my answer. As my eyes trailed back up, a smirk crossed his face. Oh, God, he thought I had been checking him out.

His hold tightened and the warmth was all-encompassing. The subtle strength in his grasp had me wondering if he could pick me up in his arms and carry me off out of the room. The feeling caught me off guard. *I am no damsel in distress needing to be rescued*, I thought, shaking myself.

'Umm, chemistry major,' I added for good measure, pulling my hand away and smoothing down my hair. Stating your major seemed the standard form of greeting I had noticed since I had arrived here and mingled with my new graduate cohort.

'It's a pleasure to meet you, Laila Clarke. I'm Austin Bradley. Physics. How you settling in?'

'I…' His question flustered me again. Wasn't he a grad student? 'Fine, I guess. It's a minefield of new information and endless paperwork. Right, Alesha?'

There was no reply. I nudged her.

'Hmm, what?' she said in a breathy voice.

I turned and noticed she was all doe-eyed and her mouth was gawping. 'And *this* is my roommate. Alesha Sharma. Modern Languages. We're both international students,' I said, stating the obvious considering our lack of American accents.

'It's a pleasure to meet you both, but it's actually you, Laila, that I came to find.'

'Me?' I pointed to my chest as if I hadn't heard him correctly.

'Yeah, I'm your buddy and…' He reached into his back pocket. 'I have your name listed here.' He showed me the sheet and there was my name at the top with a thumbnail of my student photo. 'I was an undergraduate here in the science faculty and know the lay of the land, so they chose me to buddy up with a few STEM grads for a mini orientation.'

'Oh, right.' I hoped the tone in my voice didn't show a hint of disappointment. How could someone like Austin Bradley be interested in me? Maybe it was the New York heat turning my brain to mush to even think such a thought. I simply wasn't used to these extreme temperatures, despite the periodic London heatwaves.

He tipped his head to the side. 'I'll meet you at the front of the Bobst Library tomorrow at two. That good for you? Sadly, I can't divert from the guidance they gave me, so we have to take in the library.'

This comment was lost on me. I loved libraries. All that research. All that knowledge waiting to be lapped up. Maybe he was nothing more than one of those pretty-boy jocks.

'You've pegged me as a dumb jock, right?' His arms crossed over his chest, and it had the effect of emphasising those muscles in his arms.

My cheeks flushed. 'I… How…' Words failed me.

'It's written all over your face. You're partly right. I *am* captain of the soccer team and have been known to dabble in a bit of volleyball, cross-country and ice hockey too, but I am far from dumb. Got a 4.0 GPA score for my undergraduate programme. I just don't like libraries. I'm allergic to dust.' That corner-of-his-mouth-and-eyebrow-raised smirk thing he had going for himself appeared again.

I swallowed away my embarrassment while Alesha giggled beside me as if he had told the joke of the century. 'I wasn't thinking that you were a dumb jock at all.' My skin colour no doubt betrayed me as the heat intensified in my cheeks.

'Sure. See you tomorrow, Clarke.'

And with those words he turned and I crumpled, inwardly scolding myself for being so judgemental. But then he looked over his shoulder before the crowd swallowed him up.

'Cute accent by the way,' he said and winked.

I turned away and grabbed the nearest soda bottle and pressed it to my cheeks. Alesha was sniggering beside me.

'Oh, Laila, Laila.' She laughed, a snort puncturing each giggle. 'I am going to have some fun with you.'

'What do you mean?'

'Your flirting skills could do with some refining.'

'I wasn't flirting.' Like a reflex, I lifted the neckline of my dress. It was cut way too low, I suddenly thought; my 'ample bust' – as Mum once referred to it when she caught me sneaking out to a sixth-form party with it visible – was noticeably on full display. 'Besides,' I said, slipping on my cardigan that was tied around my waist, 'I told you this year my focus is on my work.'

'Are you out of your mind? Look around the room. Hot talent everywhere. And you heard the assistant dean. Have. Some. Fun. I promise you will have time for all your studying but there is no way my roommate is going to be curling up with a book by nine p.m. We're going to work hard and play hard. Once I find my French or Spanish guy, that is.' She twisted on the balls of her feet, raising on tiptoes to get a better scan of the crowd.

A thought popped into my head. Maybe if she was distracted with a boyfriend, she would conveniently leave me out of her partying plans. That way I could not only focus on my work but also attempt to find my father. I had an address for him, but it was hours away in upstate New York. A handwritten letter was in my suitcase ready to be sent – an old-fashioned method of communication but he had left me with no other way to get in touch with him. It had been years since I had seen him, and I was aching to find him.

'I know someone who is Spanish,' I said suddenly. 'He's an old friend who I met on a school trip to Switzerland and he's on my course. Mateo Pérez is his name.'

'Is he fit?'

I pondered this question. I had never had the opportunity to look at Mateo in that way – the last time we had met was four years ago. 'I guess.'

'You mean you haven't road-tested him?'

I laughed. 'No, I haven't. If by road-tested, you mean—'

'Had sex with him.'

'That's what I thought you meant. No, we're friends. *Really* good friends.'

Chapter 4

Mateo Pérez. The notification from him sat unread on my phone along with Austin's and I hadn't dared open either of them. It would be a slippery slope into the past if I did, I told myself and I simply didn't need the distraction.

The Love Intervention.

Seriously?

What had Samira and Jena been thinking and for how long had they been planning this? A simple 'let's organise a spa weekend for the three of us' would have sufficed, though even that would have been a stretch. But love? I shivered beneath my lab coat at the thought. Love was a complication. It involved sacrifice and compromise, two words that weren't currently in my vocabulary.

The bulb from my desk lamp fizzed by my ear. A faulty fuse no doubt. I switched it off and the room plunged into darkness. I went over to turn the main lights on and the room was instantly bathed in fluorescent light, which made the pain in my head throb even more.

Sitting back down on my chair, I picked up the pages of the report the consultant had slammed down on my desk a few hours ago. I had read through it three times and I still couldn't find why the biopsy had shown no abnormalities and why it couldn't give us the cause of the patient's symptoms. I clicked on a few tabs on my laptop and identified the numbers the surgeon had questioned.

Why wasn't the answer jumping from the screen? This should be a no-brainer.

There was nothing else to do but run the tests again. After I slipped on my goggles and other protective gear, I took a pair of tweezers and picked up a sample of the heart muscle tissue the doctor had extracted during the biopsy. This was not something we did lightly; it was an invasive but necessary procedure, I had concluded. The patient had been presented to us with an increase in fatigue and slight shortness of breath six months after having a new valve put into his heart. Two major warning signs that things weren't right.

After running through the same tests we had carried out only yesterday, I peered into the microscope and looked at the cells but couldn't see the abnormalities that the data had picked up. My head was beginning to throb again, and beads of sweat pricked my forehead. A surge of dizziness forced me to sit back down again, and I mopped my brow with a tissue, defeated.

No. Laila Clarke was not a quitter. I peeled off my surgical gloves and ran the data through the computer again. The tick of the clock on the wall appeared to grow louder and more ominous.

My phone buzzing startled me. A quick glance showed it was a message from Samira saying all was well and that Mum had retired to bed. Samira said she was happy to stay until I got back. I sent her a reply saying how grateful I was for all she had done but that she could go home and place my keys under the doormat. I said that I would be leaving within the hour.

I laid out the original data from the echocardiogram and studied it a little more closely. Minutes ticked by, the click of the clock hands matching the throbbing in my head. Then…

No. It can't be.

The error was merely a transposition of two numbers. Two numbers that represented the reason why I had insisted the biopsy was a good idea.

No no no.

I double-checked and triple-checked but there it was in black and white. The report that I had produced based on my team's initial echocardiogram with the patient had a mistake. *My* mistake.

Sweat encased the back of my neck and my teeth began to chatter. My forehead was burning too. This was a fever, no question about it. Raiding my rucksack for my Lemsip pack proved fruitless. It was empty. I also couldn't remember when I had taken my last sachet.

I hugged myself tightly and willed the pain to go away, for the shaking to cease, to have something go my way.

But I knew there was nothing else I could do. I had to raise my hand up and admit my mistake. My fingers quivered over my laptop keys as I typed out an email to the consultant surgeon, cc'ing the rest of my team. *Mea culpa.*

An hour later, after clearing up all my papers and cleaning the medical equipment used, I headed to the Tube, horizontal rain hitting my face. The chill of the winter evening drizzle sent trembles along my aching limbs and I pulled my coat tightly to my chin, my back-pack weighed down with other reports I had to look over and review by Monday.

Crawling home, I unearthed my key from beneath the welcome mat, dropping it twice as my numb digits failed to get purchase of the metal.

After I stumbled in, doing my best to not make a noise and wake Mum, I tiptoed up our spiral staircase, having slipped off my shoes. The thought of changing out of my work clothes seemed like an almost impossible task. In my bedroom, I slipped my phone out of my pocket and put it on my bedside table then shrugged out of my winter coat, letting it hit the floor with no energy to even hang it over my desk chair. As I was about to crash and lay my head on my pillow, my mobile buzzed with a WhatsApp message from someone I hadn't had contact with in ten years. One name. Two words.

Edoardo Moretti.

Chapter 5

NYU – ten years ago – January

'Come back to bed.' The seductive tone of his Italian voice made it almost impossible to concentrate on the chemistry book that was grasped between my hands.

Sunlight spilled through the gaps in my blinds and bathed my desk with pools of sunshine. The window was frosty on the outside and I knew it would be another one of those achingly beautiful crisp winter mornings in the city. Nothing could beat the feeling of wrapping up in winter clothes and having the warmth of the sun on your face – misty breath mingling with the steam of a freshly purchased hot chocolate.

Yes, I had fallen in love. No, not with the Italian guy in my bed.

I had fallen in love with the city. New York City.

I shifted in my desk chair, trying not to peer over my shoulder and clock the naked Roman man lounging between my sheets. He wouldn't be if Alesha had decided to stay here last night, but she'd hung out in her French boyfriend's SoHo apartment instead. He was a fashion designer she had met last month and sparks had flown immediately.

'Laila, why you not listen to me?' Edoardo said, his voice pleading, that accent sending me over the edge to the other side where sensible Laila Clarke knew this had been a bad idea. Hadn't it?

A glance over my shoulder and I locked eyes with his deep-set hazel ones. 'Stop distracting me. I have a lecture starting in half an hour and I haven't finished the reading.'

He tutted and raised his hands behind his head. It had the effect of letting the sheet slip further down his torso and reveal a lot more of his naked skin. And it was almost impossible not to notice that he appeared ready for round three.

Last night had been wild. It was the first time I had seen Edoardo since our first drunken kiss during a Christmas grad party on the final day of last semester and the potential for more had been bubbling in the background ever since. We hadn't messaged over the holidays because Laila Clarke did not chase boys, but I had idly thought about that kiss throughout the Christmas break, dissecting it with Samira and Jena over many late-night drinking sessions in various bars across New York City. But I thought it had been a one-off and was a little taken aback when Edoardo appeared in my doorway last night having got off a flight from Rome. With a bottle of red and meal for two from my favourite Italian restaurant on West 9th Street and Fifth – which he had somehow known was my favourite spot in town – he had banked on me being in my room. I thought this made me a bit too predictable. When I challenged him, he had said the library would have been his next stop but he was wary that he wouldn't have been able to get the aroma of cannelloni past the alert nose of the security guard and the prominent sign forbidding food.

I had laughed. His determination was endearing and that twinkle in his eyes made my legs buckle a little. We had shared the wine and food and I was determined to play hard to get but the attraction that was fizzing beneath the surface had been impossible to ignore and once his lips had touched mine again there was only one way the interaction was heading.

No. Concentrate, Laila, I inwardly scolded myself and flipped the page. *I will not be seduced by this Italian any longer.*

A squeak signalled he was getting out of bed. Good. The sooner he put some clothes on, the better it was for me. But then I felt a touch. Soft fingers pulling my hair away from my neck and hot breath in their wake. Lips on my skin like molten liquid as his mouth laid kisses there.

By my ear he whispered words in his native tongue, and they had that same effect on me that they had last night and pretty much every time he'd opened his mouth since.

'What did you say?' I asked, my voice all breathy as he continued to torment me with his lips, finding that spot beneath my hairline that was oh so sensitive.

'I said, you look so sexy in my T-shirt.'

Sunk. I was sunk as I leaned back into him and his fingers roamed over the fabric, rubbing over my breasts, my nipples hardening beneath the cotton. He swivelled my chair around and dropped to a crouch, hands running up my thighs, catching the edge of his T-shirt before pulling it up over my head in one seamless move and dragging me up off the chair in one swoop. Those strong arms were around my waist, and he lifted me effortlessly before throwing me back onto my bed. I didn't think I had ever been thrown onto a bed before.

I moaned as his mouth roamed over every part of me, from the bottom of my leg up to the inside of my thigh: light feathery kisses. The second he pulled down my knickers and let his tongue get to work, I knew I wasn't making it to the lecture.

Chapter 6

'Wake up, Laila. *Habibti*, wake up.'

Mum's soothing voice stirred me and a coolness touched my forehead. When I opened my eyes, I noticed she was holding a wet cloth and mopping my brow. The lines in her forehead appeared deeper, concern etched into her fully made-up face, chin-length black hair styled despite the fact she wouldn't be going outside the house. She always liked to be dolled up in case someone popped round to visit.

'What are you doing here?' Sudden panic gripped my throat, which felt like it was lined with razor blades. 'How did you walk to my room?'

'Samira helped me realise I could put some weight on the cast support without toppling over. She is a genius. But it is almost midday, and I was wondering why you hadn't stirred. I came in and all your covers were off, you were still in your work clothes and your forehead was burning.' She cupped the side of my face with the palm of her hand. 'You are sick. Why don't you take better care of yourself? I see the clothes you leave the house in. Never in a scarf or a hat.'

'I'll be fine,' I said, her lecture making my head throb even more. 'I just need some paracetamol. And even if you can walk on the cast, the doctor advised you to keep weight off it, so you should be in bed, or I can help you to the sofa.' I raised myself off my pillows before wincing and screwing up my face as pain pulsed between my temples.

'You need to stop issuing orders and get some more sleep. I'm fine and know what's best for me. What do doctors know anyway?'

I was too sick to contradict her and argue that six years of medical training plus a couple of decades of experience were exactly why the doctor at the local hospital was more qualified to pass a diagnosis and recovery plan for a broken foot than she was.

Mum pushed herself off my bed and began to hobble away. 'I'm going to make you some of my special soup. That will restore your health.'

'No, Mum, please don't. You shouldn't be cooking…' But my eyelids grew heavier with every passing second. Her cast thumped against the wooden floor of the hallway as she went away, mumbling under her breath in Arabic, which she always did when she didn't want me to under-stand what she was saying. She had never taught me the language, claiming she had tried once but that I had been a difficult child to teach. And with a British father, English had been the spoken language at home growing up.

Before sleep took me under again, I reached for my phone. The message from Edoardo sat unread.

Had I been woken from a fever dream? It had felt so real, that first night I had spent with him. As my mobile dropped from my grasp, I inadvertently clicked on his name. The message popped up and before my eyelids closed, I read his words:

Of course I remember you. How could I ever forget?

–

I slept on and off for the next twenty-four hours – the pain in my head reaching unbearable heights before levelling off and moving to a dull ache. Mum had resourcefully poured the soup into a flask and brought it upstairs with several slices of buttered toast with za'atar (one of my childhood favourites) wrapped in foil and placed both items inside a tote bag that she had carried on her shoulder. Wet cloths and glasses of squash kept magically reappearing too and she made sure I took extra-strength paracetamol to alleviate the symptoms every four hours. As much as I appreciated her looking after me, I was wary of the repercussions if she overdid the hobbling around. And every visit with provisions came with a lecture about not taking care of myself as if I was still a child.

My work inbox had been surprisingly quiet, and I prayed that meant that my email had been received and dealt with. Still, I made a diary note to try and book an appointment with the surgeon to reassure him that mistakes like that would never happen again.

But I couldn't draw my attention away from the three messages I had received from Edoardo, Austin and Mateo. Curiosity got the better of me Sunday evening, and I sat up on my pillows with my laptop opened to the presentation Samira and Jena had sent through late on Friday night before this virus had rendered me incapable of lifting my head from my pillow. Upon reflection, I felt bad that I had subjected the girls to my germs at the bar.

I read through the slides Jena had obviously worked hard researching, as they contained detailed paragraphs citing various pieces of research.

The absence of serotonin in the system could cause a range of symptoms, she had written on one particular slide: decreased energy levels, sadness, feeling hopeless, mood swings, increased or decreased appetite, difficulty sleeping or sleeping too much, and cognitive symptoms such as poor memory. As I read further into what she had collated, an increased sense of doom washed over me. The recurring themes were that an absence of these molecules had a detrimental effect on your mental health. Is this what had led me to make the error in my work?

But was 'love' the answer? Surely I could just buy one of those Seasonal Affective Disorder lamps that encourage the brain to reduce the production of melatonin and increase the production of serotonin? I could also look into my budget and join a gym for a regular endorphin hit.

I clicked onto another slide in which she explained that exercise, social activities, SAD lamps and achieving goals at work can of course have the effect of producing a dose of DOSE (as she wrote it) but that they were short lived.

Love was the magic formula, apparently. She wrote:

> The simple act of touch can boost oxytocin release. Giving someone a massage, cuddling, making love, or giving someone a hug leads to higher levels of this hormone and a greater sense of well-being.

Touch. When was the last time I had felt a man's fingers on my skin? When had I last made love? Sex was different. It required less emotional attachment. If lucky, it led to an orgasm, a five-to-eight-second release, but the comedown always left me feeling flat if the guy rolled off and went straight to sleep. I rarely stayed over at someone's house in the hope of a morning cuddle.

When was the last time I had had a hug? I couldn't remember and if I had it would no doubt have been an awkward one.

Jena had written out the facts in black and white, the numbers in bold.

> A **10**-second hug helps the body fight infection, eases depression and lessens tiredness.
>
> A **20**-second hug reduces the harmful effects of stress, relieves blood pressure and ensures a healthy heart.
>
> Nirvana is reached when you hug a loved one for more than **20** seconds as it causes the release of oxytocin.

I wasn't a hugger and neither was Samira. Jena was the opposite and always flung her arms around both of us the second we met up. It made me wonder how much affection she got from her long-term boyfriend, James. They had been dating for several years and I knew she was waiting for a proposal to take their relationship to the next level.

The presentation went on to detail why both Jena and Samira thought resurrecting men from my past was preferable to turning up to sunny hotspots and opening up a dating app to try and swipe on a match. The probability of finding someone within such a short timeframe and for that interaction to lead to something meaningful was slim, they had written, whereas men who I already had a connection with had a higher probability of getting 'DOSEd' up with.

Wow. They had gone to a lot of trouble, I thought as I went through slide after slide of all my previous dates. Had I been with that many guys? I wasn't slut-shaming myself, but it made me wonder what I had been looking for with all these interactions. Why had nothing in the last few years lasted longer than a few months?

Was it because of Josh? He had been my mid-twenties boyfriend who had made me wary of diving in again; a junior doctor at the hospital with an erratic schedule, he wanted me to make the sacrifices for our relationship. I almost gave up everything to be with him – my friends, my blossoming career – because I thought I loved him but had thankfully seen the light. The next girl he dated a matter of weeks after we had broken up had been more than willing to give up her career and they were now married with two kids. I respected her choice, but it would never be mine.

My ten-year work plan had always been my driving force. But was it now responsible for my 'mental health decline' as Samira and Jena had alluded to on Friday night?

I slammed the lid of my laptop. No. I was Laila Clarke. Correction. I was *Dr* Laila Clarke. Capable. Responsible. Reliable. Organised. Flu was a blip. And if Jena and Samira were my best friends, they would understand why my career meant so much to me and that I was no fool. I knew I needed to take some time off. I knew I would head for burnout if I didn't get some proper sleep and book a break now and again. Love was *not* the answer.

Once I was on the Henderson team and they had recruited a new clinical scientist to take on those respons-ibilities I had filled in for, I would be able to plan the next year more efficiently. Mum would be recovered and back working again, helping share the bills. The way it had always been. Long ago she had persuaded me of the benefits of us living together – that one day, the Notting Hill cottage in a prime area of London would be mine. Dad had bought the place just before I was born, sinking his inheritance on a deposit after his mum passed. But it had a hefty mortgage, so helping pay it was beneficial to me, Mum would often remind me. She couldn't do that alone with her wage from working as a housekeeper. What was the point in me renting and paying someone else's mortgage? she would reason.

I clicked onto my work calendar, making a note to chat to my supervisor on Monday about the possibility of rolling forward some of my holiday entitlement. I could easily cite exceptional circumstances. Maybe then I could appease Jena and Samira by planning a girls' summer break during Jena's long school holidays.

Slipping my laptop off my bed, I picked up my phone. Curiosity got the better of me and I went to the message from Mateo.

> Querida Laila,
> It has been so long. Of course I remember you. Please let me apologise for so many years of silence. How are you? Where are you? Life has been full of many changes and many experiences and now I find myself in a remote place far from Spain, where the beauty of my surroundings breathes new life into my very being and I have begun to heal. Costa Rica is my home for the next few months and then… who knows. Please tell me how you are. It would be lovely to reconnect again. I have missed you.
> Mateo

My heart picked up speed as I read his last few words. It was a strange feeling. Memories stirred, long suppressed. My body was awash with something, but I couldn't put a name to it. Longing, perhaps? Nostalgia? Or was it a feeling of what might have been as Jena had suggested?

I shook those thoughts away and turned my head on my pillow. The past was in the past. I shouldn't go back.

Chapter 7

Geneva – fourteen years ago

The birth of the internet. It was incredible. Here I was staring at the computer of Tim Berners-Lee: the man who invented the world wide web, a British scientist who was working here at CERN, the European Organisation for Nuclear Research. He had created it in 1989 to meet the needs of data transfer between fellow scientists.

The tour guide carried on with his speech while I took in the space around me – the 450,000 processor cores and 10,000 servers inside the data centre was a sight to behold. There were cables everywhere, the constant din of machines running, scientists meeting to exchange ideas, and various other school tours awaiting their slot in front of the first ever computer. It was inspiring but I could hardly wait for the part of the tour that took in the first ever particle accelerator. That might even make me change my mind about applying to do a chemistry degree next year.

A nudge in my ribs brought me back to the present. Jena's eyes were wide, and she was cocking her head.

'What?' I said.

She leaned in with her hand covering her mouth as if she had a secret to tell and we were back in primary school and not almost in the middle of our A levels gearing up to apply to university, ready to take the next big step towards our futures.

'Ten o'clock,' she whispered. 'Cute guy alert.'

Jena nudged me again. I relented and turned to ten o'clock but didn't immediately notice anyone that stood out.

'I can't see him. Anyway, pay attention.'

'Why? You know I want to do biological sciences in the future.'

'*I'm* still undecided, so…' I pressed my finger against my pursed lips.

Once the talk finished, Jena slipped away to the head of the group, trying to find the cute boy no doubt. I reached into my rucksack to retrieve my notebook so I could write down some notes from the speech but didn't look up as I moved away and went slap bang into the back of someone, the notebook flying out of my hands.

'*Perdón*,' they said, right as I blurted, 'Sorry.'

We both reached down at the same time to retrieve the corkboard-bound book, our hands brushing. He had a threadbare bracelet hanging from his wrist. As I looked up, our eyes met. His were green mixed with brown and orange flecks. Oh no, the fact that I had noticed this meant I was staring, deeply, falling, sinking…

'*Lo siento*,' he said.

My eyes travelled down to his lips as he said those words.

'I'm sorry, what did you say?' I said, gazing into those dreamy eyes again. Dreamy? *Oh, Laila, no.*

We both stood and I noticed he was only a few inches taller than me. I, however, was above average height for my age. The guy's black T-shirt was teamed with faded jeans and a grey zipped hoodie. His hair was falling madly in all directions, that sweet spot between *I haven't seen a hairbrush in days* and *this took me hours to achieve with a tub of gel*. It was most definitely long enough on top to run your hands through.

Oh, no, no, no. Why are my hands running through his hair?

I realised then that he hadn't responded to my question and was staring right back at me. His blink rate began to pick up speed. Nerves, perhaps?

'I said "sorry" in Spanish,' he said finally, his accent thick.

'I think it was my fault. I wasn't looking where I was going.'

'Are you coming to hear the talk?' He tipped his head to the room I had exited.

'No, we just had it.' I turned to my group before realising they were nowhere to be seen. I looked around and craned my neck to see over the hordes of Spanish-speaking students that pushed past me, taking mystery green-eyed guy with them. 'Except now I've lost them,' I said with a hint of panic in my voice.

'Good luck finding them,' he said, before he was swallowed into the crowd.

'Thanks,' I murmured but he was gone. I fished out my phone to text Jena, praying there was reception in the building. Thankfully she responded instantly with her location.

After the visit to CERN, we had the afternoon to ourselves and a few of us chose to visit the Old Town and walk along the bank of the lake. The sky was the palest blue and the air the cleanest I had ever inhaled. My mind was a whirl of all I had seen. Physics was my hardest A level by a long shot. Could I imagine doing a degree in it and maybe applying for an internship here one day? I sent a quick text to Samira detailing the visit to make her jealous, but she was no doubt sunning herself in Dubai, so possibly it was us who should be jealous of her. Her parents had insisted she go back home for the Easter holidays and not attend this school trip.

The only reason why I was here was thanks to Dad. Mum had said it was an extravagant expense, but Dad had seen the merits of the trip – an 'investment in your future', he had called it. I couldn't wait to visit him again and tell him about what I had seen and heard. Our get-togethers had begun to be a little stretched out even though he had committed to seeing me once a fortnight when he and Mum had first separated a couple of years ago.

But the trip to CERN and Dad weren't the only things on my mind. When I closed my eyes, I could see *his*. They were like the specks of malachite I had seen through a microscope at school a few months ago, their botryoidal formation evident in their colour and brilliant patterns.

'Oh my God,' Jena suddenly squealed beside me, forcing my eyes open. 'I see him.' Clutching my arm ridiculously hard, she began bopping on the spot.

'Where?' I said, turning away from the water to the square.

'He's over there.' She pointed at a group of students, and I inwardly sighed that yet again I couldn't spot him.

'Come on.' She dragged me away from our classmates, in the direction of the national statue that stood proud next to the Ferris wheel.

'We are not going on *that*,' I said, trying to shake myself free from her hold.

'But he's in the queue with his mates.'

'*You* go and join them then.'

'No way, you know I'll get all tongue-tied and flustered. You *have* to come with me.'

I rolled my eyes and thought through how I could boost her confidence so she could be brave enough to do the chatting-up herself before we got to the start of the ride. The queue moved swiftly as passengers were plucked off their pods and others pushed on with precision and speed. It was only when we got closer to the group that I realised in the middle of the party was the Spanish-speaking guy I had seen earlier.

'Not *him*,' I whispered in Jena's ear. 'The one with the Nike backpack?'

She nodded enthusiastically as a ripple of disappointment flooded through me. It was an unusual feeling considering I had only had one moment of contact with him. And I was wary of cute guys after my entanglement with Alex Benedictus at the end of last year. But there was something about the green-eyed guy that I couldn't put my finger on, the desire to know who was behind those dreamy eyes.

'I met him earlier inside CERN,' I said. 'He speaks Spanish.'

She clasped her hands and an expression of pure delight crossed her face. 'If you've met him, then it won't be so weird when you get his number for me.'

It was in that moment, as we almost reached the front of the queue, that I realised she had no intention of joining me on this ride as she propelled me forward with a shove in the back and ran away.

A ruckus ensued between the green-eyed boy's group and the man operating the machine. French and Spanish words circled around me until the Swiss guy ordered me inside with a huff and I took my seat. Before he closed the pod, I was joined by one other passenger – his back to me. The capsule then jerked forward and began its ascent. I caught sight of Jena in the distance, waving wildly at me before doing a thumbs up. That's when the guy turned, and I clocked my companion.

'Oh, hey,' I said, trying to swallow away my nerves as my stomach lurched.

'Hey again.' A look of surprise was etched on his face before a broad smile spread across it.

'Um.' My voice was quivering as I desperately attempted to take some shaky breaths in and out to combat the rising fear gripping my throat.

'Are you OK?' His voice was full of concern as he twisted his body towards me.

But that only had the effect of rocking the pod and it creaked and groaned as it continued to climb.

I shook my head and grasped the metal bar tighter as the breeze whipped my hair about my face, but I dared not lift either of my hands to tame it.

'I… I'm not good with heights,' I said as nausea rose up my body. 'They freak me out.'

'Maybe you need to be distracted. That will take your mind off the fear.'

'O-K,' I said, looking wildly around as the sight of Lake Geneva came into full view, wondering how the hell I was meant to do that. I squeezed my eyes shut, not able to look at my surroundings any longer. The ride stopped and a memory surfaced of that time when I was eight on a Ferris wheel that had broken down for two hours before it was fixed, during which time I had a full-blown panic attack. That thought made my pulse rise.

'What happened?' I asked with shaky breaths.

'It's OK, it paused to let more people on.'

Right as he said those words, it carried on with its ascent.

'Hold my hand,' he said suddenly, 'and look into my eyes.'

I felt a brush of fingers and grabbed his hand tightly, my nails digging in, but he didn't try and pull it away. Slowly, I opened my eyes and blinked up at him until I met with those green irises again. Those eyes were reassuring, mesmerising.

'What's your favourite thing to do?' he asked.

'You mean like hobbies, sport?'

'Like in your studies. You're a scientist, right? That's why you're here on this trip?'

I nodded. 'Chemistry is my favourite. I love balancing equations,' I said, not quite believing I had blurted that out. It was such a nerdish thing to say.

'Me, too,' he said. 'Though I love biology just as much. Physics is my least favourite. Yeah, I know. Why did I come on the CERN trip, right?'

I smiled. 'Hadn't crossed my mind. I think CERN's an inspiring place no matter what field you might want to pursue.'

A pause. We were still ascending, and the fear was resurfacing.

'Don't break contact. Look at me.'

I did as he said and went back to staring at those malachite irises, his hair ruffling in the breeze.

'Can you balance equations in your head?' he asked.

I nodded again.

'Wow. That's impressive. How about…' He paused, trapping his bottom lip in his teeth before reaching into his rucksack with his free hand and pulling out what looked to be a chemistry book in Spanish. Maybe he was as much of a geek as I was, as I had a stack of chemistry exam flashcards back in my suitcase at the hostel. He flicked to a page and looked back up at me. 'In the release of energy during cellular respiration, glucose plus oxygen goes to carbon dioxide plus water.'

I closed my eyes and mumbled under my breath as I imagined the symbols and the numbers that were needed for it to balance. Within a minute, I opened my eyes and stared back at him. '$C_6H_{12}O_6$ plus $6\ O_2$ goes to $6\ CO_2$ plus $6\ H_2O$.'

He briefly glanced down before looking back up at me and beaming. 'Correct.'

I mirrored his smile. 'Another one,' I said, a thrill pulsating through me.

This continued several times with only one obscure equation catching me out.

It was then I realised we were at the top and had stopped again.

Placing the book back in his backpack, he squeezed the top of my hand with his other one. 'It's OK, you're safe. We've stopped again to let more people on,' he said with a glance outside the pod. 'It's… beautiful up here.' He scanned our surroundings before settling back on me and giving me a sympathetic smile. 'Just don't look down.'

I tentatively broke eye contact and took in the view. My mouth dropped open as I scanned the horizon: the Old Town stretching far and wide, the distant undulating mountains. The air was even more crisp at this height. It was a sight to behold. Then we lurched forward again and I felt my stomach almost fall out of my body.

'It won't be much longer,' he reassured. 'We'll get back to the ground before you know it.'

I breathed in deeply before exhaling loudly.

'Can I ask… if you don't think me rude, why did you come on the wheel if you're scared of heights?'

'Jena. My friend. Meant to be my best friend, though after I get off this blinking ride, I'm gonna kill her. She wanted your number but was too shy to ask.'

'Oh,' he said.

I stared intently at his face. Was that disappointment etched into it? I shook that thought away. Jena had first dibs because she had seen him before me and our friendship was more sacred than ever letting a boy get in the way of it, no matter how cute he was with the most delicious accent to match. Besides, he probably lived in Spain or even further away. That would completely rule out any kind of blossoming relationship. Online romances were not my thing. And had I forgotten my plan? Over coffee with Dad, we had picked out a list of top universities that I wanted to apply to. He had told me that affairs of the heart (as he had called them) could wait until I had got the grades to meet any offers.

'Then you must have it,' he said, removing his hand from the top of mine and reaching into his pocket for his mobile. I recited my digits with the international dial code before feeling my phone buzz in my back pocket. But I dared not answer the call because that would mean removing my hands from their safe positions.

'Thanks,' I said before realising we had reached the bottom. In one swift move we were ushered off the pod, our hands still clasped together.

An awkward moment followed when we looked down at our embrace. I pulled my hand away, feeling heat swell in my cheeks.

'I'm Laila, by the way. Laila Clarke.'

'It was a pleasure to meet you, Laila,' he said with a nod. 'I'm Mateo. Mateo Pérez.' He turned to walk away before looking over his shoulder. 'Message me,' he said, before throwing me that winning smile that made something inside me swoon. But before I could correct him and say surely he meant Jena should message him, he had already disappeared into the crowds.

Chapter 8

Numb. I was numb. Closing the door of my supervisor's office, I returned to my desk and stared at my computer screen. Her words hadn't registered, not even slightly. I stood up and hesitated, wanting so desperately to go back in there and argue my case again, but knew it was pointless.

My working life continued around me but I was frozen to the spot, no longer by the chills of flu but something more deep-seated and alarming.

An email popped up in my inbox and I sat back down, the title confirming my worst fears – *Investigation/Leave*. Beneath it was one of those internal emails announcing opportunities to further one's career. I usually gave them a cursory glance before deleting them so they didn't clog up my account, but I didn't even have the energy to do that.

With shaking fingers, I picked up my mobile and sent Samira and Jena a message. One acronym. Three letters:

SOS

An hour later, I was sat at a cafe off Euston Square, staring into the depths of an Americano. The door swung open and in flew Samira in a haze of Miss Dior, one corner of her black wrap coat draped over her shoulder, killer heels clacking on the wooden floor.

'Sorry I'm late,' she appeared to announce to the whole cafe and a few heads popped up from their laptop screens. This was eleven a.m. on a Monday in a random coffee shop. *This* was a world I didn't know existed because there had been no other world but my lab for ten years. Jena couldn't make a sudden appearance at this time of day obviously because she had classes to teach.

Samira's embrace was brief. She didn't do public displays of affection. Pointing at the guy behind the counter, she called out for a double espresso even though this was a counter-service coffee shop. But the barista nodded with a smile and said he would bring it over. She unwound her wrap and laid it on the back of the chair in front of me before unbuttoning her suit jacket and sitting down.

'Fuck,' she exclaimed, slamming her hand on the table. 'What happened?'

'It's like I told you on the phone. There's going to be an internal investigation, annual review, bad timing, forced leave etc. etc. I don't know, Samira. None of it is making any sense. I have to work out the week, make handover notes and then…' I gave a lacklustre wave.

'And that heart project thingy you were hoping to get onto?'

'The Henderson team?'

She nodded and it occurred to me I could have said any name and she would have assented.

The threat of tears pressed at the back of my eyes and I tried to breathe deeply to avoid their flow. While Samira didn't do public displays of affection, I didn't do public displays of *my life is ruined, what the hell am I going to do?* breakdowns.

'They've withdrawn my application.'

'Oh, Laila.' She reached across the table and grasped my hand, the emerald in the ring on her middle finger catching the light. It had been a twenty-first birthday gift from her parents, hand-delivered by the exclusive jeweller's it was purchased from. But deep down I knew all she had wanted on that momentous birthday was for her folks to have been there to give it to her themselves.

'Ten years of my life down the drain because of one error, albeit a pretty major one.'

'Surely that's not true. You said that boss woman was hopeful and encouraging in your meeting, that it was merely a formality, that they had no choice to put you on leave. They could have sacked you, right?'

'They can't do that until they have done a proper, thorough investigation. And there was no avoiding one because the patient's family lodged a complaint.'

'And how long will the investigation take?'

'A few weeks.' I stirred my spoon in my coffee. A pointless action because there was no milk or sugar in the cup. I needed my fingers to be focused on doing something because they hadn't stopped twitching since I left my desk.

'And these weeks represent time they have told you to take off? Forced leave?'

'Yes. Apparently, it has also come to their attention that I haven't been using up my allocated holiday entitlement, said it looked bad and sent a terrible message to the rest of the department. They wanted to make an example of me but said I could return after my break in a limited capacity, whatever that means. Regardless, they're unhappy I haven't taken any of my contracted days off already as it will be a struggle to find someone to cover my roles.' I cradled my mug in the hope that the warmth from the china would soothe the chill in my bones.

'They didn't seem to mind prior to today, overloading you with all this extra work, putting all this pressure on your shoulders.' She flicked her hair.

The barista brought Samira's coffee to the table along with two pink macarons. 'On the house,' he said, nodding at the sweet treats.

'You're too kind,' she simpered.

He beamed before retreating.

'Is that next weekend's plans?' I said with a head tilt in the direction of cafe boy.

She laughed. 'Not sure I'm done with Friday-night bar boy yet.'

'How was he?'

'Energetic,' she said with a giggle, her shoulders shaking beneath her pinstripe suit.

Her laugh was infectious, and I found myself smiling until I remembered where I was. Not at a cocktail bar on a Friday night with my girls but a coffee shop in the middle of the working day. I stared into the depths of my bitter black coffee, willing it to suck me back into the past, where capable Dr Laila Clarke would not have made such a life-altering error. Shoving the mug to one side, I sank my head into my arms as they leaned on the table.

'Oh, Laila.' I felt a pat on my shoulder. 'It will all work out. Maybe…'

She paused and I lifted my head up. 'Maybe what?'

'Maybe it's time for a change? Maybe this all happened for a reason.'

'You're beginning to sound like Jena.'

'Perhaps she is right and is the only one out of the three of us that knows what she's doing with her life, has a plan that involves not having to do everything on her own all the time. Knows how to balance a career and a proper grown-up relationship even if it is boring and suffocating.' She scooped several spoonfuls of sugar as she spat out those words. Something was up. Samira was a strict black coffee drinker.

'Hey.' I rubbed her arm. 'What's wrong?'

She stirred her coffee. 'I shouted at Rosie this morning. She said she didn't want to go to school and I told her that wasn't an option. It escalated and I snapped at her. I had an early meeting and I was in no mood for one of her little tantrums. But now I feel horribly guilty.'

'You were feeling under pressure, and I'm sure deep down she understands. Talk to her this evening. Maybe there's something going on at school.'

'She'll probably be asleep by the time I crawl in tonight. I've got work drinks that I can't get out of. That'll make me feel doubly guilty, especially after my weekend fucking cocktail-bar boy.'

'You need time to yourself too, Samira. And I thought Rosie loved spending time with your parents?'

'She does, mainly because they shower her with gifts every time. She's the only reason they come back. They couldn't even extend their stay to spend last night with me. They took the red-eye back to Dubai. But God did I need this weekend. It made me feel like a woman again. Desirable. Like I could peel off all the other layers of me and be fun and fabulous.'

'You don't need a man to validate those things. You already are fun and fabulous.'

'I know that.' She stared at her espresso but I could tell by the tone in her voice that she wasn't convinced. 'I don't think it's working out,' she continued. 'Me doing the school drop-offs. I thought I could manage it this year not needing a full-time nanny and save myself a bit of money in only needing after-school care until I got home. But it's so much more stressful for me. And Rosie keeps saying, "Larissa doesn't do it like that," and my temperature gauge goes through the roof when I think she prefers our old nanny over me. Oh, I don't know, I never thought it would be this hard, being a single parent and trying to build a successful career. But by God was the weekend fun. A chance to let my hair down. And boy could that boy find *the* spot. The best feeling.' She let a playful smirk break over her face.

'I wouldn't know,' I mumbled.

She threw a scowl at me before draining her espresso. 'You know what I'm going to say so I'm not going to say it. Instead, I'm going to go to the counter, pay for my coffee, get that barista's number and get back to work. And *you* are going to go back to the hospital and hold your head up high. You're Dr Laila Clarke, for fuck's sake. You'll get through this and figure out your next steps. I know you will.'

She blew me a kiss and in a whirl she was off.

Once she left the coffee shop, I tapped my mobile and stared at my inbox. The email beneath the spine-chilling one about the investigation, labelled *Career opportunities*, caught my attention. Scanning the attached PDF, I sat up as one event piqued my interest. A conference. A three-day cardiology conference at Berkeley in California with lectures and seminars by keynote speakers including well-renowned academics from around the world. One speaker's name stood out from the rest and when I clicked on the link, his picture popped up. Dr Walker. He looked so familiar. Reading his bio, it hit me. He had been one of my professors at NYU.

A crazy thought took over my brain and began the building blocks to a plan. What if this was a sign? Jena would see it as one and wouldn't hesitate in telling me that of course I could get on a plane and go to the conference. Yes, I had been paying the mortgage payments on the house on my own the last couple of months, but I still hadn't needed to dip into my savings. Financial independence had always been my number one objective in working so hard these last ten years, but I had been squirreling away some funds each month for a rainy day. And maybe *this* was the rainy day.

I thought back to last Friday's cocktail night. Could I take my besties' advice to restore my mental wellbeing and see the Love Intervention plan through?

There was no way I could tell Mum what had happened at work. She would worry unnecessarily, before turning her words to disappointment, followed by doubt about how we would live if I lost my job. And if I told her about what my two best girlfriends had suggested, she would be horrified. Hooking up with three guys in three weeks? No respectable woman would do that, she would insist. Mum was old-fashioned in that respect. She had always told me there had been no one else she loved apart from my father and there had been no one after he left because men were a complete waste of one's time and effort, she loved to say.

But what if I told Mum that this conference would further my career and that I had decided to take some much-needed rest afterwards? Then maybe, just maybe, I could get away with this crazy, insane plan of Samira and Jena's. It wouldn't be an out-and-out lie, more a stretching of the truth.

Because the truth was… I hadn't been able to get the idea of the trip out of my mind since those messages from Austin, Edoardo and Mateo had popped up on my phone. Feelings that had been suppressed for a very long time were suddenly bubbling beneath the surface.

Could I be open to creating a new version of myself? One that had fun sometimes, let her hair down and allowed herself to be open to pleasure and desire. After all, where had the last fifteen years of exams, dissertations, theses and lab work got me? Signed off. I needed to get back on track. I needed a break so I could come back stronger. Or maybe Samira was right, I needed to get laid. I giggled at that thought. This was so unlike me.

I opened my DMs on Instagram and saw the notification from Austin. Clicking on it, I took a deep breath and read it.

> Clarke! Major flashbacks. How are you? Come visit. I'd love to show you my vineyard.

Settling back in my chair, I stalked his profile. In most of the photos he was in various degrees of undress. Those muscles, those abs. I nibbled my bottom lip as I took in the snaps. Was he unfinished business? God, those fuck-me eyes and kissable lips. It would only be a week of fun, nothing more. I didn't believe Jena's analysis in the slightest: once a fuck-boy, always a fuck-boy and that

67

suited me fine. The girls didn't know I had first-hand experience of his bad ways.

But I wasn't in this for love as much as Jena wanted me to be. I could, however, sign on the plan's dotted line for a bit of fun, especially with Austin Bradley, who certainly wouldn't be after more. The thought of travelling to the other two destinations to reconnect with Edoardo and Mateo could be parked for a while because meeting up with them would mean having to face things in the past that I wasn't sure I would ever be ready to confront again.

Typing out a message to Samira and Jena, a smile finally broke over my face at my decision.

Five words. One declaration.

Let the Love Intervention begin.

The Love Intervention

Remit: 3 weeks, 3 guys
Locations: California, Puerto Rico, Costa Rica

*Checklist (in no particular order and with no
particular guy)*

1. *Savour a meal*
2. *Get a tan*
3. *Go skinny-dipping*
4. *Have sex*
5. *Make love*
6. *Know the difference between 4 and 5*
7. *Have a hug lasting longer than 20 seconds*
8. *Go horse-riding*
9. *Save a turtle*
10. *Fall in love*

Signed:
Laila
Samira
Jena

Not doing number ten – Laila

Yes, you are – Jena

Let her have some fun – Samira

Chapter 9

It was lunchtime on day two of my conference and I was balancing a plate in my hand as I chewed some baked salmon and baby potatoes. In between mouthfuls, I held my own among a group of international scientists specialising in cardiology, all leaders in their field.

I was back in the game. Networking. And it felt good. My feet, however, were throbbing from standing for the last hour in these heels, and I was clock-watching until I could get back to the auditorium and sit down for the next speech followed by a two-hour workshop. Thankfully I had managed to sleep again last night after forcing myself to stay awake on the flight to NYC and the transfer to San Francisco, which seemed to have kicked jet lag to the kerb.

The stopover in JFK hadn't been long enough, thankfully, to let memories of the last time I had been there spiral me into the past.

I still couldn't believe I had done it. After that bleak Monday back in London, I had kept my head down at work, trying not to get paranoid whenever my colleagues stopped talking when I entered the lab. Another clinician had arrived on secondment to take on my duties and he had spent time shadowing me on my last day before I gave him a handover file. A couple of juniors asked me about my holiday plans, and I decided to keep it simple and say I was visiting distant family in the States: an elderly relative who had taken sick, hence my sudden departure.

Mum had been a little too enthusiastic when I told her of the plans for Samira and Jena to alternate visiting. I owed them big time.

I had made reservations for next week at an Airbnb in Old San Juan that Edoardo had recommended as it belonged to a friend. To say he was stunned that I was visiting was an understatement. I had lied and said I was at a work conference in NYC, which seemed like a more plausible journey to have made to Puerto Rico. I told him the country had been a bucket-list destination for a while and that his LinkedIn profile had suddenly popped up on my feed as a possible acquaintance, which felt like fate. The lie sat heavy on my chest.

Mateo had promised me he would sort some accommodation for me in Costa Rica. He too was shocked that I was coming to visit. I hadn't divulged where I was spending the previous two weeks.

Austin and I had missed each other's calls repeatedly due to our work schedules and the time difference so had settled on sending messages instead. I said I would be free to catch up on my second evening in Berkeley. I had told him I 'happened' to hear from a mutual source that he was now living in that region. I hadn't let on that the mutual source was my two best friends, whom he had only met once ten years ago.

Back in my hotel room, I examined three possible choices of outfit for dinner tonight. What look was I going for?

Austin had messaged in the morning and invited me out for dinner at one of the places where his wine was stocked with a plan to stay at his sister's place afterwards as it was close by. I had been a little relieved. His vineyard was over an hour's drive from the university, and I had been hesitant to go to his place for our first…

Jeez, what is this? I wondered as I tossed my linen trousers and T-shirt combo onto the bed. *A date?*

I did a quick video of the other two choices and sent it to my WhatsApp group chat with the girls. Samira had changed the name of it to: *Love Intervention Is A Go*. She had of course given me many warnings about the first stop but equally had told me to have fun and see it as nothing more than a fling, should the opportunity arise. After all, this was only meant to be three possible short liaisons – three possible chances to kickstart my dating life again and get DOSEd up. Was it possible to store up these molecules for future mental health dips? Unlikely but worth a shot.

I still had lingering doubts about having a liaison with Edoardo and Mateo, but Jena had insisted that even if things didn't get physical with either of them, there were more than enough opportunities for a dose of DOSE from reconnecting with a past love and an old friend, as well as the joy of being on holiday, experiencing new cultures and different ways of life.

Jena responded to my video message first.

> Definitely the dress

She added several fire emojis.

We had all met three times prior to my departure: one pamper evening, one shopping trip and a cocktail night during which we had written the Love Intervention checklist on the back of a coaster. At Samira's favourite salon, I had been buffed and waxed, hair and nails done,

72

and I barely recognised the woman staring back at me in the mirror now that I had slipped on the dress and a pair of Samira's wedge sandals. I hardly ever looked in my long-length bedroom mirror back home in London. Work required hair to be tied back, neat clean nails and a functional wardrobe to go under my lab coat. And what was the point in ever having a facial if I spent most of my working day wearing goggles? It had been some time since I had got dressed up.

Having applied some mascara and lip gloss, I grabbed my cardigan and purse and headed out.

I stilled when I exited the hotel and saw who was waiting outside, leaning on his Jeep.

He hadn't noticed me, his gaze fixed off into the distance, arms folded. Decked out in beige slacks and a pale blue long-sleeved shirt with the top two buttons undone, he looked as I remembered him and I could feel my pulse quicken as I stepped forward.

When he saw me, he took a step back before shielding his eyes from the low-lying sun behind me. A broad smile flooded his face as he sauntered over.

Déjà vu. The feeling was so strong. His gait transported me back to that grad party at NYU, the night he first spoke to me.

'Well, well, well.' He gave a half laugh. 'Laila Clarke.'

I stretched out my hand, not knowing the correct greeting. He took it, but with a strong grip he pulled me close and kissed both my cheeks.

We both inhaled audibly at the same time and laughed shyly as we stood in front of each other, realising that we had caught each other sniffing.

'You smell good,' he said, no doubt catching the scent of cocoa butter from my body lotion.

'So do you,' I said, suddenly feeling heat seep through my cheeks.

'Fresh out of the shower,' he said, with a sweep of his hands down his body.

'Me, too,' I said with the same hand gesture.

Oh boy. That sounded *so* loaded and now images of Austin Bradley naked in a shower were crowding my mind. I needed to rein it in a little. But it was hard not to feel the tension that pulsed between us, all that pent-up desire that I had obviously sat on for ten years. Forget Mateo being the one that got away; maybe it was Austin.

He dipped his head. 'I feel lost for words, suddenly. I can't quite get my head around you being here.' As he looked up, that eyebrow-and-corner-of-his-mouth-raised expression took me back to our grad days.

I shrugged with my hands outstretched. 'I can't believe I'm here, either.'

We stood awkwardly for a few beats, his stare still intense while I rocked on my heels.

'I'm sorry,' he said, shaking his head a little. 'Where are my manners.' He turned and opened the passenger door and let me step inside.

When he drove off, the breeze from his opened window ruffled his sandy hair while we exchanged some small talk about the conference, and I babbled on about the seminars I had attended and the professors I had met. Nerves always made me talk nonsensically and without pausing for breath. Why was Austin having this effect on me? I certainly hadn't been rendered a gibberish mess on the dates I had been on over the last few years – the random matches I had made on various dating apps that hadn't got my excitement level up like Austin appeared to have done in a heartbeat. Maybe it was the accent – the soothing dulcet tones of his Californian twang.

When the car began its ascent a few minutes later, I wondered where he was taking me. My interest was piqued when I saw a board signalling we were entering the Hillside Club & Spa. He drove slowly along a path that was shaded on each side by overhanging evergreen trees until we came to a clearing and a grand whitewashed art-deco building stood in front. As we pulled into the entrance, a valet rushed round and opened my door. I stepped out to the sound of water gushing from a feature fountain in the middle of the lush, manicured grass.

When I saw the five gleaming stars painted underneath the club's sign, I was suddenly glad I had opted for a dress over my romper onesie or casual trousers and T-shirt outfits.

I noticed Austin discreetly slip a note to the valet as he took the keys before driving off. Austin ushered me ahead and I nodded at the doorman as the electric doors sprang open. I was immediately engulfed with the headiest scent of jasmine, roses and lilies. There was a serenity to the lobby, in its muted décor and furnishings, soothing scents and low hum of chatter from guests mingling in the distance.

A man in a sharp grey suit and shiny black shoes rushed forward and bowed with a flourish.

'Welcome, Mr Bradley. Your table is ready out on the terrace.'

'Thanks, Bob,' he said, that winning smile on his face again. I gave Austin another discreet check-out. His shirt was tailored, stretching over his pecs and muscles, and his tanned chest was more visible now that I was closer. Three buttons were undone, not two as I had originally spied.

'Checking me out, Clarke?' he said, and I realised then that I had lingered far too long taking in his appearance.

'Um, no not at all,' I lied, and it was met with a disbelieving eyebrow raise, his hands on his hips.

'OK, you caught me. Nice shirt. Happy now?' I smiled.

He inspected it as if it was nothing special. 'It's a throw-back to my Wall Street days. It's been a while since I got dressed up for a date.' And with those words uttered, we headed off.

A date. This *was* a date.

Out on the terrace, my jaw dropped. We were so high up that San Francisco Bay lay out before us, the Golden Gate Bridge visible far, far in the distance.

'Wow,' I whispered with my back to Austin.

The maître d' showed us to our table, which was the closest to the glass barrier, discreetly tucked behind an arch of honeysuckle, two overhead heaters providing much-needed warmth against the cool evening. Samira and Jena had obviously stretched the truth in declaring all destinations enjoyed summer weather during our British winter. That said, California was a good fifteen degrees warmer than London with an abundance of sun, so they could be forgiven for not delivering on three hot spots for their plan.

Austin pulled out my chair and I sat down, thanking him, before the gentleman offered us each a menu and placed the wine list directly in the centre of the table. It was the first thing Austin picked up.

'Do you mind?' he asked.

I shook my head. 'Not at all. My fallback is always the house white or red, so it would be nice to have someone order who actually knows what they're talking about.'

'It all depends on what your food choice is.'

I studied the menu, but my eyes bulged when I took in the prices.

'Please, Laila.' Austin's tone was soft and I looked up into those deep blue eyes as he stretched a hand over the dark wood and lightly touched my fingertips. 'I don't want to embarrass you, nor do I have any expectations for this night, but as I didn't consult you on where we were having dinner, this is my treat. I insist. And besides, my family have been regulars here for years and I can always secure a discount.' His smile broadened and instantly made me feel more relaxed.

I usually insisted on going Dutch on first dates. It was easier that way. If there had been no spark, no connection, it always seemed best to call it quits with neither party indebted to the other. But here was Austin bypassing that awkward moment at the end of the meal and taking charge. It floored me somewhat. I liked to be in control on a date. But maybe that hadn't worked out for me up until now. Maybe it was time to try a new approach and let my date take the lead.

'That's very kind of you. How about the two-course set menu A?' I said, having already checked that it was in fact the cheapest option.

'Only if we get ice cream later. I know the best place.'

'My treat?'

'Deal.' He threw me a cheeky wink, which lightened the moment.

He took a while to study the wine list and when the maître d' returned, Austin went back and forth discussing various tones and depths. I wasn't following because I couldn't take my eyes off the view. Yes, that was the Golden Gate Bridge in the distance. It was a *pinch me* moment. When I lived in NYC for that graduate year,

I had fallen in love with the city but was painfully aware that there was a whole country to explore. Edoardo and I had made plans to spend that summer after graduation doing that before things turned sour and all I wanted to do was go home, back to England.

'It's the best view of the bay,' Austin said, breaking my thoughts, 'in my humble opinion.'

'It's breathtaking. I've spent the last two days in a conference room, so it's wonderful to check out my surroundings and breathe some fresh air,' I said, inhaling deeply.

A waiter returned with a bottle of white, showed Austin the label and poured him a small amount. Austin swirled the liquid around the glass, sniffed and took a sip before nodding.

I thanked the waiter for my glass and brought it to my lips. It was light and refreshing. A cabernet sauvignon from Napa Valley, I noted as I spied the label.

'It's good, right?' Austin waited for my verdict, but the truth was I couldn't tell my chenin blanc from my chardonnay.

'It's delicious.'

'It'll go perfectly with our chicken mains and is light and easy on the palate so as not to drown the flavours of your seasonal salad.'

I smiled in acknowledgement of his analysis. 'So... when did Austin Bradley, NYU physics grad, become so interested in wine? And what happened to bring you back here?'

'How much do you already know?'

I held the stem of my glass and shifted in my seat. 'I know nothing.'

'You mean you haven't stalked my Instagram?'

I nibbled the inside of my cheek. 'I might have clicked on a few posts but you know, Insta vs reality…'

He brought his glass to his lips and paused, and it was hard not to get lost in his intense stare again. His eyes had caught the setting sun that was beginning to dip even lower and they were the palest blue. The rays also highlighted strands in his hair, longer on top and a little curlier than I remembered.

'What's on your mind, Laila Clarke?' he said. Oh boy, he had caught me staring again. Or was this his way of deflecting my questions?

I sat back in my seat and took in the view again. 'I don't know. I'm finding this all a little surreal.'

'You and me both.'

'The truth is there is a lot on my mind. I haven't stopped in… forever. And the last few weeks have been…' I paused, bringing my hands to my lap. 'Difficult for me. I needed this break, badly, but the "not working my day job" part isn't sitting right with me. It's hard to explain. Plus…' I lifted my glass. 'I'm out on a date with Austin Bradley, with this incredible view of the bay and the sun is setting. I mean, it's sunny for starters.' I laughed. 'England has been grey for weeks on end.'

'Isn't it always grey?'

'This winter has been particularly brutal, and I have been running myself ragged for weeks, months, years even.'

'Sounds familiar.' His mouth downturned and he had a faraway look.

'Something happened at work, and it's forced me to stop and recalibrate, take a step back.'

'I get it.'

'You do?'

'This is the very reason I came back here. I burned out. Plain and simple. Yeah, the money was great at my old job, I had a nice apartment on the Upper East Side but when I hit thirty, I thought what the fuck am I doing? I was existing on about three or four hours' sleep a night and chugging several Red Bulls a day. It was work hard, play hard, only it was all the time. I… began to drink a lot; it became a habit when I got home late at night. But one glass of whisky began to turn into half a bottle most evenings. I was washed out.'

He paused and a pang of sympathy welled inside me at his openness. It was almost as if we had stayed in touch, and this was one of our regular catch-ups.

'My big sister flew out to New York to see me,' he continued, 'said the whole family was worried about me. I quit not long after, cashed in my shares at a ridiculous discount but I figured it would be worth it.'

'Was it?'

He took hold of the stem of his glass and held it up to the light.

'It's a different kind of work now. It's still labour intensive what I do but there's a huge difference.' He paused to take a sip before setting his glass down. 'I get to be outside most of the time; that's one perk. I'm also my own boss, which' – he shook his head with a smile – 'is absolutely liberating. There's also a science behind the fermenting and the actual creation of the wine, which I love. Takes me back to college days. But it can get stressful and relentless looking after my grapes, so I guess that appeals to my workaholic tendencies. It's been a while since I did something special like this.'

At those last few words, he held my gaze and the look he gave made me hold my breath in anticipation. His honesty floored me and endeared me to him in equal measure. He wasn't afraid to be direct.

The waiter brought our starters and broke the moment.

'Thank you,' I murmured, to which he nodded before laying Austin's avocado tartine in front of him.

My salad was a kaleidoscope of colours and textures. I closed my eyes as I took each mouthful. When was the last time I had stopped to enjoy my food? A thought came to my mind: the checklist.

1. Savour a meal ✔

Lifting a lightly chargrilled asparagus tip, I dipped it in the mustard vinaigrette dressing and sucked it before taking a tantalising bite.

Austin dropped his fork and it clattered on his plate, breaking my sensory experience with my food. 'Sorry.' He coughed into his napkin before adjusting his position on his chair. 'It slipped.'

We carried on enjoying our starters, while I asked him about his family. They all lived close by, his middle sister in the Bay Area and his parents out in a large house with a pool in Stockton, where he grew up. Everyone loved to congregate either there or at his vineyard once a week, and it was a chance for Austin to throw a ball with his two nephews.

Our main courses arrived, and we continued our conversation over the tenderest chicken breasts with an array of locally sourced roasted vegetables with a creamy mushroom sauce. It was simply the most delicious meal I had had in… I couldn't even remember my last dinner date but I think it had been at one of the chain restaurants and clearly unmemorable. Or maybe it had been the company.

The sun had set and a waiter had come round mid-meal to light the two tealights on our table and turn up the heaters, offering me a blanket for my lap. The Golden Gate Bridge glowed in the distance, and I felt at peace as I continued to breathe in the fragrant air around me.

'So, Laila Clarke.' Austin pushed his clean plate to the side, leaning on the table a fraction. 'What are your plans for the rest of your stay?'

I wiped my mouth with my serviette and finished my mouthful. 'I'm not sure. Tomorrow is the last day of the conference. Then I need to r—' The word caught in my throat. It was an alien one to me. I didn't know how to act upon it nor believe I could embrace it. 'I need to relax.'

Austin picked up our second bottle of wine and filled my glass. 'Is there any way I could tempt you into letting me help you achieve your goal?' There was a twinkle in his eyes as he said those words.

'What did you have in mind?' I said, my voice drowned out by the thumping of my heart.

'It's a bold idea. Might I suggest the first thing you do tomorrow morning before you go to the conference is check out of your hotel. Then I will pick you up after your sessions finish and drive you to the vineyard. There's plenty of room and I can guarantee an abundance of R&R. No expectations. I promise.' His face glowed in the candlelight as he leaned forward a little more with that declaration. 'And maybe this time, you won't turn me down.'

I sat back in my chair. 'When have I ever turned you down?'

'I remember the day you did very clearly. Don't you? Our last night before Christmas recess.'

'I think you are mistaken, Austin Bradley,' I said, neatly folding my serviette and laying it next to my plate. 'I don't recall doing any such thing.'

He shook his head slowly. 'Maybe I have remembered that time wrong.'

'I think you have. And that's a very generous offer but I think I would like to sleep on it, if that's OK with you?'

'Of course. No pressure.'

Austin's words had thrown me. It was like a tunnel to the past had opened, calling me back to that day. No, Austin must be wrong. There had been only one outcome to that night. Hadn't there?

Chapter 10

'I am never going to leave this rail,' Jena declared, taking pigeon steps along the ice, a look of abject fear on her face as she grasped the edge of the skating rink tight.

'We could get you one of those penguins to lean on,' Samira said.

The trouble with that statement was that she had said those words with a smirk and Jena's face crumbled at the sight of it.

'I'm not six years old,' Jena said. 'It would be embarrassing.'

Samira sighed, twirling on the spot. 'I'm not hanging here all afternoon. I'm going to do a sweep of all these hot grads, then you can introduce me to my favourites, Laila.'

'I don't know everyone here. The invite was to anyone doing STEM classes.'

But my words fell on deaf ears as she had already skated off, doing a spin followed by a Salchow jump, causing a group of admirers to clap. She looked unbelievably glamorous in her Patagonia pink puffer and faux-fur pink headband, and she knew it.

Bryant Park ice skating rink was magical this afternoon. The golden lights of the Christmas tree at the far end twinkled as twilight began to turn to dusk. Samira and

Jena had flown in a few hours ago and I had invited them to one of the activities that the school committee had organised for the last day of the semester.

'I'll be fine, Laila,' Jena said, somewhat unconvincingly as she was still clutching the barrier for dear life. 'Please don't pity-skate with me. I think I might take a break at the next exit and watch you guys.'

'Are you sure? I don't mind, honestly.'

'Yeah, I'm sure. Go and catch up with Samira. I'll get us some hot chocolates, perhaps.'

'That sounds perfect. I'll do a couple of loops and then come and find you.'

She nodded and I skated off, pulling my beanie down over my ears and blowing hot air in the space between my mouth and my scarf. It was crowded out on the ice, and I strained my neck to try and find Samira. When I caught sight of her, she was skating backwards with a crowd of guys lapping up every word she was saying, periodic laughs causing streams of mist to float into the peerless sky.

When I turned to move to the outer edges of the rink, someone's skate caught the back of mine. My arms flailed as if that would help keep me upright, but thankfully I was met with a reassuring hold when two arms wrapped around my waist, setting me back on the ice. Turning my head to acknowledge my saviour, I looked up into the eyes of Austin Bradley.

'Thanks,' I said, my cheeks flushing with embarrassment.

'You're very welcome.' He loosened his grip.

The sudden release of his hold caused me to slip and slide again and I reached out to grab the only thing I could get a grip on – Austin's jacket. The action caught him by surprise and he had no time to adjust his footing. We both hurtled to the ground in a *whoosh*.

I yelped as a pain shot through my bottom, the part of me that had made contact with the ice first.

Austin groaned next to me. 'Jeez, Clarke. If you wanted me that badly, you could have asked me out on a date. There was no need to floor me to get my attention.'

I scrambled to stand, noticing my jeans were all wet on my backside and down the back of my legs. 'I was not trying to get your attention. You bumped into me.'

'I think you'll find I rescued you from falling before you decided to take me under anyway.'

'So not true.'

That smirk thing that he pulled every time I saw him reappeared. He was obviously trying to rile me, but I wasn't going to fall for it.

With a flick of my scarf over my shoulder, I skated off and left the rink at the nearest exit, before realising Jena was on the other side. The dropping temperature sent goose pimples over my wet legs and I shivered, my teeth clattering. Locating the nearest restrooms, I attempted to use the hand drier to dry my jeans for several minutes before returning to the rink.

'There you are,' Samira hollered from a distance. She was walking effortlessly on her blades towards me, holding three steaming cups. 'What happened to you?' she said. 'You've got a face like thunder.'

'Austin Bradley happened to me,' I said, prising one of the cups from her fingertips.

'Spill. I still haven't met him yet.'

I held the cup in my hands and the heat emanating from it spread through my fingertips and along my arms. 'He's somewhere on the ice, being an ass.'

'You *so* have a crush on him.'

'I do not,' I said defensively. Blowing steam away from the beverage, I took a sip before coughing. 'This isn't hot chocolate.'

'Of course it's not hot chocolate. Where do you think we are, back in primary school? It's a S'mores N'more Boozy Special. Thought it was about time we got our party started. We need to pre-drink before tonight. Where's Jena? Still sulking?'

'Be nice, Samira. She's still heartbroken.'

'Jeez, it's been months since he left for Oz. It's time she moved on.'

'Leave her be. She'll heal in her own time.'

'Maybe we should do some matchmaking tonight.' She took a long sip of her drink. 'How about that Spanish guy she met on that school trip, the one you're besties with.'

'Mateo? He should be here somewhere.'

She continued to savour her drink while scanning the ice. 'Why haven't *you* hooked up with Mateo?'

'Because we're friends.'

'Then why can't he be your friend with benefits? Surely that would fit in with your work schedule.'

'Because sex will ruin everything.'

'Says who?'

'Says me. And besides, I think the moment has passed. He doesn't look at me in that way. He's always goofing around in practicals anyway. Not sure where the passion would suddenly spring from.'

'Hmm,' she mused but I sensed she wasn't listening as her gaze was still firmly fixed on the rink.

'Is that for me?' Jena suddenly appeared beside us, pointing at the other cup in Samira's hand.

'It's got booze in it,' Samira declared, handing it over.

'We *are* on holiday, I guess.'

'That's more like it.' Samira beamed, nudging Jena in the arm.

Jena took a large gulp of her drink and wiped her mouth. 'Mmm, what's in it?'

'No idea.' Samira giggled and all at once I was overcome with feelings of joy as I took in their bright smiles. Our friendship had endured the highs and lows of sixth form and our university days, and here we were, thousands of miles from home, spending our first ever Christmas and New Year with each other and not with our own families.

A pang of guilt wracked me at the fact I wasn't returning home for the holidays. But the truth was Christmas hadn't been the same since my parents separated and Mum had never been a fan of the season, she'd once declared, which was why she always offered to work through the festive period.

There was only one other person I would have loved to have spent this Christmas with.

Dad.

But I didn't want to confide in Samira and Jena that I was secretly hoping he would reply to my letter and beg me to spend part of the holidays with him. They knew Mum well and had sworn they would check in on her during my year abroad and as much as I trusted them, I would never want them to be put in a position where they'd need to lie about the fact that I was desperate to reconnect with my father.

'God, I've missed you guys,' I said.

'We've missed you, too.' Jena linked her arm with mine. 'Thanks for having us here. I hope it's not a huge distraction for you.'

'It's the Christmas holidays, for heaven's sake,' Samira declared, raising her cup.

'Well…' I chewed my bottom lip. 'I will have to carve out some time to study so I probably won't be able to join you every day to sightsee, but I'll do my best.'

'Speaking of sightseeing.' Samira drained her cup and laid it on the nearest table. 'Show us this boy you have a crush on.'

'I don't know who you mean,' I said, turning away and hoping she couldn't see my flushed cheeks. She was speaking the truth though I dared not admit it out loud. And I certainly didn't want Austin to see the effect he had on me as well as a long list of other female grads, instead choosing to throw him icy stares every time we passed by each other on campus or in the lecture theatre as we both had maths classes together. I was still too embarrassed after our first meeting and simply didn't want to give him the ego boost.

'Is that him?'

I squinted to see where she was pointing to and, lo and behold, there was Austin Bradley. 'How did you guess?'

'I have a radar for guys like him.' She readjusted her headband and began to walk away.

'Where are you going?' A sudden panic gripped my throat.

'I'm going to make his acquaintance and suss out your chances.'

My mouth dropped open. 'You're not.'

Jena giggled beside me. 'This is like old times. The gang together like we're back in Yard watching the sixth-form boys walking past our bench.'

I shuddered at the memory. Sixth form had been a massive learning curve for me when it came to boys and

I'm not sure I had ever recovered from my first time with Alex and the humiliation of being one of his many conquests. That's why I had always been guarded. And that's why I knew I should be wary of someone like Austin. *Agh*. Then why did my body betray me whenever he came within six feet of me?

—

Spinning. My head was spinning. I had let Samira top up my Christmas punch cup a few too many times. The room was swaying or was that me? Every movement was taking a Herculean attempt to complete, even blinking. The pressure of the last semester had been relentless, and today felt like the first one where I had let my hair down. All my assignments had been completed so I deserved this night off. *Right?*

'He hasn't stopped staring at you all night,' Jena shouted by my ear over the thumping track of the sound system that had been set up in the dining room of my halls for the Christmas party.

'Who?' I said, my cup by my lips, eyes scanning the room in the hope I would lock eyes with Austin.

'Tall guy, eight o'clock.'

For once, I wished Jena could turn me in the right direction. I straightened my arm. 'Twelve o'clock.'

She pulled my arm down and giggled. 'What are you doing?'

'Finding the right o'clock.'

'How drunk are you?'

'On an interval scale, and not a nominal, ordinal or ratio one, with one being a little tipsy and ten being passed out, I would estimate that I am at around a seven.' I leaned into her, and she buckled.

'Woah there, easy, tiger,' she said, putting me to stand straight. 'Maybe a glass of water should be between your intervals, perhaps.'

I turned to her and cupped her face in my hands. 'I love you, Jena Hadid. You are the most caring, loyal girlfriend I could have ever asked for.'

Her head appeared to split in two and I was struggling to keep hold of it. Maybe she was right. I did need to ease off the booze. Then I remembered we were boy-spotting.

'Bearing in mind I have beer goggles on at the moment, is he a) fit and b) could you point me in the direction of him, pretty please with a cherry on top.'

Jena grasped my arms and turned me. 'Dark hair, stubble, intense eyes and phenomenal dress sense. The one in the middle,' she clarified.

There he was: the moody, broody Italian, as Alesha had once referred to him. She had tried but failed to hook up with him in the early weeks of the semester, but she hadn't minded the rebuttal as she wasn't majoring in Italian. She said he had turned her down because he had a girlfriend back home in Rome, but I wondered whether that was true or just Alesha making up for the fact that he simply wasn't interested in her.

Jena was right. He was periodically staring at me while he was talking to his two mates, who I think also did engineering. It was hard to make out faces in the low lights of the room and because everything was a little blurry. But yes, he was hot, there was no mistaking it. And even though I had never spoken to him, I knew that accent would be a big turn-on. If he was flirting, then *surely* he was single.

A slower track suddenly came on. 'I love this song. Dance with me,' I said, flopping my arms around Jena, spilling my drink all over her. 'Whoops.'

She tugged at her jumper. 'It's fine… I guess.'

Oh no, she was mad. 'You can go to my room and borrow anything you want.'

'No, it's OK, I'll go and change into something from my suitcase. I'll be back.' And with those words she was off. A couple of friends from down the hall were letting us borrow their room for the holidays so that Samira and Jena didn't have any accommodation costs and Samira had very generously used some of her frequent-flyer air miles and bought Jena her ticket as she wasn't earning enough to cover all the costs of the trip. Samira had called it a twenty-second birthday/Christmas gift. Her generosity knew no bounds.

The music swirled around me, and I closed my eyes and let the tempo throb through me, my heartbeat echoing the bass.

'I'll dance with you,' a voice behind me said and, at first, I thought I had imagined it. The words were like liquid gold, and they electrified me before arms enveloped my waist and I leaned back.

Turning in the embrace, I grasped his neck and opened my eyes. Austin's face was inches from mine as he leaned down. I let a coy smile creep into the corner of my mouth. At least I hoped it was coy.

As we moved to the beat, his body began to grind into mine and his touch flamed my insides.

'Laila Clarke, I thought this day would never come.'

'And what day would that be?'

'The one where you invite me to your room.' His hand trailed up and down my spine and my breathing became ragged.

'That would be very forward of me.'

He tipped his head back. 'God, you're such a tease.'

I then felt his hold on me slacken as he acknowledged someone else on the dance floor and threw them a wave. He leaned down and whispered by my ear. 'I'm gonna stop by your room in ten minutes.'

Before I had a chance to reply he was off into the crowd.

'What was all that about?' Samira asked, appearing by my side.

'I think tonight's the night with Austin.'

'Seriously? Are you sure?'

'I… think so.' I held a finger to my temple. My head was beginning to throb, and I began to doubt what his intention was.

Samira had one of her guarded looks. I knew it all too well: arms folded, lips pinched. 'When I was talking to him on the ice, he referred to your roommate as "hot".'

'Alesha? I mean she is hot but… yeah that is kinda an odd thing to say.'

'Be careful. Remember what happened with Alex.'

His name seemed to reverberate off the walls of the room. And in a flash, I was sixteen again at that New Year's party – making out on a bed of coats at Samira's Pimlico flat, the party pounding outside the bedroom door. I had wanted that moment to be with someone I cared about and maybe even loved but was too worried about being called a prick tease if I didn't go all the way. Instant regret had washed over me after it happened, and it had hurt too. Alex had pulled off the condom and dropped it in the bin on his way out, mumbling something like 'see ya' as he left.

Suddenly I felt a wash of nausea ripple up my body.

I ran from the room, clutching my stomach, and threw open the back door. The night air hit me like I had been doused in dry ice. Stumbling to the nearest bush, I bent over and heaved into the foliage.

Hands appeared to pull my hair away from my face as I continued to hurl and gulp in shaky, cold breaths in between projectiles. A jacket was wrapped around me with a reassuring hold on my shoulder, followed by a cup appearing in front of me. I took a sip. It was water and like a balm against my coarse throat. A tissue followed and I wiped my mouth back and forth, the tidal wave of nausea beginning to abate.

'Thank you,' I whispered finally, handing the cup back, not daring to turn around and look into the eyes of my saviour as embarrassment burned my cheeks despite the cold.

'*De nada*,' he replied.

'Mateo?' I peered up at my knight and was met with those green eyes. Even with the lack of moonlight, they were bright and soothing. 'I didn't think you would come to the party.' I clutched my arms tightly around his jacket, involuntarily breathing in the scent at the collar. It held that familiar smell of his. Every time he breezed into the lecture theatre and took his seat beside me, it wafted over me like a walk through a pine forest on a fresh winter's day.

'Are you OK?' His voice was full of concern.

'Afternoon drinking that leads into evening drinking caught up with me. I'll be fine once my stomach settles. What are you doing out here?'

'I came to say goodbye. I need to be at the airport in about an hour but I couldn't go until I had seen you. I wanted to give you…' He leaned into me and for one split second I thought he was going to kiss me, but he merely mumbled his apologies and pulled out something from his jacket pocket. 'This. It's a small Christmas present.'

The sentiment floored me. 'Thanks,' I said, taking the gift from his hold.

'You don't have to open it now. I know you are spending Christmas here with your friends and you won't be with your mum, so I thought it might be nice to open something on the day.'

That familiar, comforting smile appeared again and soothed my throbbing head.

'That's sweet of you. I'm sorry I didn't get you anything.'

'Oh, don't be silly.' He waved away my words. 'It was a spur-of-the-moment thing.'

We stood awkwardly for a few seconds, before I remembered I needed to go back to the party. Austin was waiting for me. I peeled off Mateo's jacket and handed it to him. Leaning in, I brushed my lips on his cheek. 'Thanks for the gift,' I said. 'I'll see you next year, right? Dr Walker's nine a.m. on Jan third.'

He nodded and an unreadable expression covered his face. Opening his mouth, he appeared to want to say something else, but then closed his lips tightly before uttering the next words. 'See you next year.'

He turned and walked away, and I headed back to the party.

In the bathroom along the hall from my room, I laid Mateo's gift on the counter and looked at my face in the mirror. It wasn't a pretty sight. I rinsed my mouth with water before brushing my teeth and gargling some mouthwash. I tousled my hair a little before straightening my skirt and lowering the neckline of my tight burgundy jumper.

I took some deep breaths in and out. I wasn't sixteen anymore, nor had that been my last sexual experience. This situation was totally under control despite the numbing effects of alcohol pouring through my veins. I still needed to be a little tipsy. Call it Dutch courage because there was something about Austin Bradley that excited me but also intimidated me. The truth was, I couldn't wait to take the attraction I had been battling with for weeks to the next level. I didn't need to think about what would happen afterwards. Everyone knew Austin had a reputation but maybe with me it would be different. I was also desperate to know whether the rumours about him being the best stud on campus were true.

I left the bathroom and made my way to my room. Voices could be heard from inside as I approached.

Wait. Is that a sock on the door?

It hadn't been fully closed by whoever was inside. Tiptoeing closer, I pushed it gently to create more of an opening.

I couldn't make out what they were saying but the sight of Alesha in a compromising position with a semi-naked Austin was all the evidence I needed to make me want to run far away, and to realise Samira had been right all along. I hadn't heeded her warning when she told me he had referenced my 'hot' roommate. There was no mistaking what was going on. What a fool I had been. I couldn't even be mad at my roommate because I had always told her that I wasn't interested in Austin.

Seems I had had the measure of him that first night I met him. Anger fizzed in my body at the thought I had been this close to making a fool of myself again like I had with Alex Benedictus. But alongside anger sat disappointment. The night had been full of promise and now it was over. As I swept back into the party, I picked up another cup of punch to drown my sorrows. I wasn't in the mood to find Samira so she could gloat that she had been right and scanning the room didn't unearth her. Jena wasn't to be seen either. She must've crashed after changing out of her wet jumper.

Before turning back to my bedroom, someone in the far corner of the party caught my eye. It was hard not to notice him because he was staring directly at me, a cheeky smile breaking in the corner of his mouth, his eyes sparkling with mischief as he stood alone. Maybe my night wasn't over just yet.

Chapter 11

I was embracing the plan, I told myself as Austin shut the boot to his Jeep, which now contained my suitcase and hand luggage. Of course I wasn't going to say no to his request. Why else had I contacted him in the first place? My remit had been set back in London for this adventure and I couldn't go back on it. But I wanted him to know I wasn't jumping at the chance to pack my bags and shack up with him for a few days, which was why I had only given him my answer this morning before the first seminar began. And I told him about my main condition: separate rooms. He'd laughed at that, reminding me that he had already said that's how it would be.

There was no need to bring up that night of the Christmas party again. What happened in the past was water under the bridge. A decade had passed since. And what good would it do me to mention that it had hurt me a lot to see him with Alesha – not that I had ever divulged to my roommate that I had seen them. She had met her French boyfriend merely a couple of days later before flying off to Mumbai for the holidays and Austin, as far as I could remember, had been in and out of relationships for the rest of the graduate programme.

Austin opened my door for me and I slipped into the passenger seat. He was wearing a denim long-sleeved shirt hung loosely over a white T-shirt with faded jeans. Only

Austin Bradley could get away with double denim. His fingertips were tinged purple, I noticed.

He caught me staring at them and gave me a hint of a smile as he went round to his side of the car and strapped into his seat. 'A grape emergency,' he announced, lifting his fingers from the steering wheel and wiggling them before gripping the leather again.

'Oh,' I said. 'Sounds serious.'

'I handled it,' he said.

'Literally.'

He laughed and turned to me, leaning his arm on the back of my headrest as he reversed out of the hotel car park. I got the full-on aroma from his freshly laundered clothes and a pleasant earthiness, as if he had already spent time labouring outdoors.

'I've missed your smart mouth, Clarke,' he said, raising his eyebrows before putting the gear stick into drive and heading away from the hotel. His admission set off a flutter in my stomach as I caught his intense gaze in the rear-view mirror, and I wondered when this man would stop rendering me nervous in his presence.

I took in the scenery outside the window as we worked our way out of Berkeley and onto the Richmond–San Rafael Bridge – a huge metal structure that took us into San Rafael Bay on its five-and-a-half-mile stretch east from San Francisco Bay.

'There's snacks and water in the cooler on the back seat. Help yourself.'

'I'm fine, thanks.'

'Actually, that wasn't an offer, more of a demand, though it's not my intention to be so rude.'

'Excuse me?'

'I need you hydrated and at a comfortable hunger level.'

'Dare I ask why?'

'As part of the Bradley R&R package you have signed up for, I took the liberty of booking you in for a massage with Crystal and those were her requirements before getting to work on your body. She's a friend of the family and runs a massage therapy business not far from the vineyard but also does house calls. I have work to do until the evening and didn't want you to be bored. And after you confided in me about how tough it's been at work, I thought what could be better than the most relaxing thing imaginable. Then you can join me for dinner. I'm cooking. After that...'

I swallowed hard, in anticipation of what he was going to say.

'An early night.' He laughed when he clocked my expression. 'Whatever were you expecting me to say?'

'I don't know what you mean. No expectations, remember.'

He shifted his hands on the steering wheel. 'Yes, no expectations. And hopefully you'll wake up refreshed and I can give you a proper tour of the vineyard where we will do some vine pruning, followed by a tour of the cellar and wine tasting in the evening.'

'That's thoughtful of you, to have arranged all that. I don't want to put you to any trouble if you're busy.'

'It's my pleasure and you're not. The advantage of being my own boss is I can step aside when necessary unless there are grape emergencies.'

I laughed. 'I'll be on full alert if that happens and more than happy to occupy myself if you get called away.'

We continued chatting as Austin drove away from civilisation into low-lying green valleys while I tucked into the snacks and quenched my thirst. An hour later we pulled into the vineyard, the Jeep rocking as we drove over an uneven path, higher up into the hills until we pulled up in front of a single-storey ranch house with a terracotta roof.

'*Casa mia*,' Austin announced as he pulled the gear stick into park.

He came round to my side and opened the door. As I stepped out, a cooler breeze tickled my arms and I hugged myself.

'I hope you brought some jumpers with you.'

'I have one stashed in my case.'

'There's plenty of blankets in your room if you want to use them for our al fresco dining tonight. I'll get you settled in and then introduce you to Crystal.'

Austin gave me a brief tour of the house, pointing out the large dining area adjoining the kitchen, which was sleek and modern, and the living room complete with a feature wall of exposed brick and white three-piece suite. The place seemed homely and lived in but also exquisitely decorated. At a guess I reckoned he would have hired an interior designer. He pointed to his room before showing me to mine next door. It had wooden floors, underfloor heating and splashes of modern art dotted around the pale walls, with a reading nook in one corner and the most stunning view out to the vineyard from the bay window.

I didn't have much time to gather my thoughts and freshen up before a beautiful young woman with a perky smile introduced herself to me and told me she was here to take all my cares away. After a twenty-minute consultation during which she asked me about my life, my work and my stresses, she got the room ready and plugged in a soothing backing track to a hidden sound system.

Undressing in my en-suite bathroom, I came out wrapped in a towel to a darkened room and a massage table unfolded in the centre. For the next seventy minutes, I was put into a state of pure bliss. Crystal used a cold-pressed jojoba oil on my skin and added a few drops of aromatherapy oil to a diffuser close by. Her elbows and forearms slowly sank into my body and moved towards muscle tension points that I didn't know existed, releasing knots with her touch. The wringing technique – where flattened hands and fingers were used to pull soft tissues in a treatment area in opposite directions – had the effect of releasing endorphins around my body, she told me. At the mention of the word, I thought of Samira and Jena and mentally ticked that I was getting some of my DOSE.

I slipped into a borderline comatose state by the end but managed to mumble some form of thanks and appreciation before she left. Pulling on a fluffy bathrobe I found hanging on the back of the bathroom door, I filled a large glass with water from the jug that was laid out on the dressing table and went over to the banquette in front of the window. When I opened the drapes, I was amazed to see the most spectacular sunset forming in the distance. After quickly changing into jeans and a navy silk blouse that Samira had lent me, I grabbed one of the small blankets from the trunk at the foot of my bed and wrapped it around my shoulders before stepping outside.

The peace hit me first followed by the distant rumbling of a tractor, its headlights cutting a path through the low light. It parked up as I sat down on one of the outdoor sofas that was covered with throws. The wooden deck had an arrangement of rattan furniture laid out around a glass table, with strings of fairy lights draped over the railing, the distant view of the vineyard the backdrop.

Austin stepped out of the tractor and made his way towards me. His checked shirt was rolled at the sleeves and his jeans and boots were mud-splattered.

'Hey,' he said as he stepped closer. 'How you feeling?'

'Sore,' I said with a smile and his eyes widened. 'Don't worry, it's an expected sore. Crystal is some kind of sorceress. She said it's perfectly normal that I will feel some soreness now and pain in a couple of days too and I should continue to stay hydrated.'

'I take it wine isn't included in that list of lubricants.'

'Haha, I doubt it.'

Austin came out a minute later with a tray of nibbles and aperitif wine along with a large jug of water.

'What's all this?'

'Pre-dinner snacks and the best way to introduce your palate to the flavours of dinner,' he said, nodding at the bottle of wine. He then pointed at the mud on his clothes. 'I gotta take a shower and it will take a while for the meat to marinate so dinner won't be for at least another hour or so.'

'I'm in no rush.'

He tipped his head. 'I am. I need you in bed by ten.'

And with those words uttered, he disappeared inside the house.

Why was it that everything that came from his lips sounded suggestive?

It occurred to me then that if I felt even the slightest bit uncomfortable, I couldn't escape – we were in the middle of nowhere. But the truth was, I didn't want to escape. My life back in London and the lab suddenly seemed like a million miles away.

Jena was right about the power of touch. It was healing in so many ways. I popped an olive in my mouth and savoured the aperitif. I felt open to the possibility of where this interaction was headed and let my mind run wild with the idea of ticking off number four on my checklist.

Chapter 12

Movement outside my bedroom roused me as early morning light filtered through the curtains. I stretched out and felt a twinge in my shoulder. Rubbing it away, I breathed in, and the aroma of roasted coffee beans made me moan with anticipation. I checked the time on my phone, and it was gone seven. I couldn't even remember the last time I had woken without an alarm.

Austin had kept true to his word. I had been in bed by ten last night. Alone, I hasten to add. The flirty banter had continued but mellowed as the evening wore on and we relaxed in each other's company. We reminisced about our time at NYU and Austin told me about his life in NYC post-graduation: the gruelling hours, the constant client networking and the realisation that had hit him at thirty that he wanted to get off the treadmill but didn't know how.

My clothes had smelled of woodsmoke when I'd changed last night due to the fire Austin had lit after our BBQ feast. The flames had crackled and hissed as we toasted some marshmallows and made s'mores. Once we had said goodnight and I'd showered, sinking into crisp white sheets was heaven and it was simply the most comfortable bed I had ever slept in.

I realised I hadn't updated the girls in the last twenty-four hours so sent them a quick text saying I was enjoying my stay and that Austin had been the perfect gentleman so far. Jena sent a heart emoji back while Samira sent the smirking-faced one.

Wrapped in another fluffy blanket over my summer silk PJs, I left my bedroom and followed the coffee scent, but as I got closer, a waft of something sweet and savoury filled my nose too.

The sight at the stove took me by surprise. It was Austin wearing an apron over a white T-shirt and checked pyjama bottoms, a sizzling frying pan in his hand. He shook it before letting it clatter back on the hob.

'What's all this?' I said, sliding into a chair by the kitchen table and clocking a glass of orange juice and a carafe of coffee laid beside a setting for two.

He laughed. 'What do you think it is? It's breakfast. Sleep well?'

'Like a baby.' I lifted the glass of juice and brought it to my lips. It was fresh, I noted, and the pulp filled my mouth with a juiciness I had never tasted before.

'Good,' he said as he brought over a plate filled with pancakes and another with crispy bacon on it, 'cos I need you to have a lot of energy for today. So, eat up.'

There it was again. That hidden suggestiveness lying behind his words, or maybe it was because I was on high alert to his ways that I assumed everything he said had a double meaning. In theory, I should come back with a retort telling him in no uncertain terms that I did not take orders, but for some reason, I kinda liked the idea of being told what to do.

I wolfed down a pancake with a lashing of maple syrup and took a piece of bacon between my fingertips, savouring the crunchiness and salty tang as it hit the roof of my mouth before licking my fingers in delight.

Austin observed me as he supped his coffee.

'What?' I asked, wiping my hands on a napkin, wanting to know what was going on in his mind.

He leaned forward. 'You seem different to how you were when we met yesterday. Your cheeks are all flushed, and your hair has this sheen to it.'

I laid the back of my hand against my warm skin and self-consciously patted down my hair. 'I honestly can't remember when I last had a more restful sleep. I also had a shower last night because my hair was all smoky from the fire. There were some products in the bathroom, and they smelled amazing. Hope you don't mind that I used them.'

'Mind? Of course I don't mind. May I?'

My heart thrummed in my chest as he leaned in and brought his nose close to my hair, breathing it in. I closed my eyes as his fingertips gently touched a few strands. The lightest hold and my lips parted in response. When I opened my eyes again, he was sitting back down in his chair, drinking his coffee like nothing had happened. But could I detect him smirking behind his mug?

'It does smell good,' he said, finally. 'I'll let Georgia know you like them.'

'Who's Georgia?'

'A friend and also the brand owner of those hair products. They were a gift.'

'Oh.' It suddenly occurred to me that maybe Georgia had been or was still more than a friend. Maybe even the masseuse, too. She certainly seemed to know her away around my bedroom.

I sipped my coffee, and my mind went back to the Austin I had known all those years ago in NYU. There had been a string of girls he was supposedly involved with during that Master's year and I had no doubt that when he said he 'played hard' during our evening meal at the club, that could only mean one thing. But what did that matter? Austin lived over five thousand miles from me, and I wasn't looking for a relationship with him.

'Anyway,' he said, breaking me from my thoughts as he wiped his mouth with a napkin, 'we'd better get changed.'

I nodded and dipped my last piece of pancake in the remnants of the maple syrup before shoving it in my mouth.

'I'd recommend wearing something you don't mind getting dirty and possibly a swimsuit underneath.'

Before I had time to finish my mouthful and ask him why, he had already left the table. When I heard his bedroom door close, my mind went into overdrive. What could he possibly have planned that warranted me needing a swimsuit? And the way he had said 'dirty'. I fanned myself with my napkin.

Back in my bedroom, I rooted around in my suitcase for one of the bikinis Samira had shoved into my basket when we had trawled H&M during our shopping trip. Slipping on the red one, I put on a grey T-shirt and one of my blue work shirts that I had worn to the conference, but left it unbuttoned and tied it at the waist. Pairing it with my jeans and the lace-up boots I had travelled in, I scooped my hair into a ponytail.

A half hour later, we were bending down over a vine, the tractor parked in the distance. The sun was warm on my face, but the air had a slight chill to it.

'You see…' Austin stretched his arm along the vines, 'if you had come during the harvest, these fields would be filled with part-time workers and interns all racing to get the best grapes to kickstart the whole wine-making process, but I find this period the most beautiful and the most important. It's all about timing. If we prune too early, the new buds might be killed off by a late frost. Prune too late and the new shoots are playing catch-up with the growing season.'

I nodded as he talked, taking in all his knowledge about removing woody vine branches that were at least two years old and spurs, the younger branches that were only one year old. He stroked one branch and applied his secateurs to snip a piece, placing it in the large bucket we had hoisted from the tractor.

'It's a careful balance, knowing which ones to cut and which ones to leave. But this work is crucial as it will set us up for the growing season, preventing overcrowded vines.'

'But I would have thought the more vines the better. Wouldn't that lead to more produce?'

'You'd think, right?' He snipped another offshoot with precision and great care, 'but actually grapes need plenty of room for air to circulate, which helps prevent mildew and rot.'

'How far have you pruned?' I said, holding my hand to shield the sun in my eyes as I scanned the area.

'We've done the first cut as it were, but now I like to go back and prune on a more detailed level and examine each vine.'

'That sounds very time-consuming.'

'Yes and no. It's all part of the process. And the weather is looking good for the next couple of weeks so we should start to see some buds coming forth, which will be unbelievably exciting.'

'Can I have a go?' I said, nodding at his cutting implement.

'I thought you'd never ask,' he said with a coy smile. 'It's about time you earned your keep.'

My mouth dropped open, but my expression was met with a nudge in the ribs.

I took the spare secateurs and examined the vine closely, considering everything Austin had been saying. It was hard to distinguish the one-year-old branches from the newish-looking ones. I settled upon one in particular and leaned in. As I was about to cut it, I looked over my shoulder to Austin for reassurance, but his face gave nothing away. Deciding against it, I snipped a branch that I was sure of as it had a slightly more distressed appearance.

'Perfect,' he murmured. His voice was close, as if he was whispering it by my ear. I inhaled deeply and held my breath captive for a few seconds before releasing it slowly and coming to stand.

'You're a natural, Clarke,' he said, his hands on his hips, and I blushed at the compliment.

The next few hours flew by in a flurry of back-breaking work. Intermittent light showers dampened our clothes, but we didn't run for shelter, mainly because there was no shelter nearby and because, as Austin pointed out, it would waste half the time if we kept riding back and forth to the house. I assumed this was why he told me to wear a swimsuit under my clothes. We only took a break to have lunch, which Austin had prepared and packed in a cooler – leftovers from last night. The grilled chicken and potato salad tasted even better after a hard morning's work.

By mid-afternoon, my calves ached, I was covered in dirt from kneeling and slipping in muddy patches and the coffee in the thermos flask had been drained.

'I think it's time to call it a day. Ready for the second part of today's activities?'

Only the second part? I dared not ask how many parts there were.

'Does it involve sitting down?' I smiled playfully.

'Where's your stamina, Clarke?'

I swallowed hard as I thought of one particular activity that might require stamina. Maybe Samira was right, I needed to get laid, get a release and then be able to move on. But Austin had until this point not given me any indication that our time together was going to lead to more. There had even been a comment a couple of hours ago when I said my fingers were getting tired and he had suggested that we could finish off in the morning. Another day of pruning? Surely I could rest in the hammock I had seen out in his back garden?

I sat back in the tractor, and it felt good to no longer be on my feet. It was getting a little chillier so I wrapped my arms around myself.

'Are you cold?'

'A little.'

'I know something that will warm you up.'

My mouth opened at those words. No way could that be misconstrued as something without a loaded meaning.

'But first,' he said, 'it's time to give you a lesson and then there will be a test. And there'll be no prizes if you fail.'

There was an authoritative tone to his words but at the end of the sentence he delivered one of his cocky eyebrow/mouth lifts.

We parked up in front of a large building and my breath caught when we stepped inside. There were rows and rows of barrels lining one wall and the rest of the space was filled with many different types of machinery. There was a ladder leaning against one of the larger barrels, which had red marks dotted on the side. I wondered if that had been the reason for his grape emergency that had stained his fingers yesterday.

'Wow.' There was no other word.

'Good thing you weren't here after the harvest. You would barely be able to hear yourself speak.'

'This place is incredible.'

'I love it here. This is where my scientific knowledge can best be used. There are so many different decisions a winemaker can make. And the pressure that surrounds the fermentation process is intense, depending on whether we are trying to make a white wine, red wine or rosé.'

I walked around the building as Austin delivered an in-depth, step-by-step guide to how he and his team made their wines. He talked about clusters, skins on, skins off, clarification and stabilisation and how aging was an essential step in the process, allowing wine to develop its unique flavours, aroma and style.

'You see, it all depends on my preferences.' He smiled broadly. 'I get such a kick out of making these decisions, being the boss.' He caught my gaze as he said that last word.

I took in the place as I did a three-sixty turn. 'It's impressive, Austin. You're obviously passionate about this.'

'I am.' He nodded, his mind seemingly lost in his own private thoughts. He then clapped his hands. 'Right. Lesson over. Do you think you've learned enough for a taste test?'

I stroked my hand over one of the barrels. 'Challenge accepted.'

'Come this way then, madam,' he said with a hand flourish, and I giggled before following him out of the winery and into a separate room. It was lined with cases of wine, a desk overflowing with paperwork and a tall oak table with stools placed around it.

I watched as Austin busied himself, pulling out various unlabelled bottles and some food items from a fridge before returning everything to the table with a tray of glasses. My eyes widened at the amount on the metal dish. But I assumed it would be merely a taste of all these wines and not a glass of each.

'I guess before we begin, I have to ask whether you want to swallow or spit.'

Game over. He was doing this deliberately. 'Don't think I don't know what you're doing, Austin.'

He held his hands up in defence. 'Whatever could you mean?'

'You must think I was born yesterday. You haven't changed one bit, have you?'

'You knew I was talking about the wine, right?'

'Yes, I know. But it's all those eyebrow raises and mouth twitching that you do as part of your delivery that makes me…' I stopped myself short.

'Makes you what?' His voice was lower, deeper.

I decided not to answer that as it would only inflate his ego. But why was I being so prickly? Was it the unresolved hurt rising to the surface?'

'Doesn't matter,' I said, finally. 'I am happy to *drink* the wine.'

'We got there in the end.' He laughed before reaching over the table for a silk-looking scarf.

As he leaned in, holding it up to my face, I sat back. 'What's that for?'

'With the way your mind seems to be operating, I bet you've already decided. What I wanted was to do a little blind taste testing. It's more fun and besides it's a bit of a giveaway if you can see the colour of wine in the glass.'

'Oh.'

'But you're right. I should have consulted you.'

'No, it's fine. I guess I am a little on edge.'

'You'll have to try and learn to relax then, Clarke. Your shoulders have gone all tense beneath your shirt. Was that massage's effect that short-lived?'

I breathed in and out deeply. 'I'm sorry. It's still taking some getting used to. The… "having fun" thing.'

'I must be doing something right if you've made that admission.'

'You are, Austin. You have done so much, and I am so appreciative.'

His eyes twinkled. 'Good. Then let the game begin.'

Chapter 13

The last thing I saw before everything went dark was Austin's eyes. They appeared darker in the low lights of the cabin. He tied the scarf around the back of my head, and I swallowed hard, sensing his proximity. His fingers trailed my arms gently, my skin alight at his touch.

'Relax, Laila,' he said, his voice by my ear.

'I'm trying.'

'Right.' He clapped his hands, and it startled me. 'Taste number one. Reach out.'

I did as I was told and clasped the glass and brought it to my lips.

'Woah, woah there. Remember what I said about the senses needing to be heightened first. Swirl the glass a little.'

I did a soft circular movement with my hand and hoped the liquid wasn't spilling from the sides.

'Do you remember why we do this?' he asked.

I thought back to Austin's talk. 'To enhance the evaporation of compounds, which helps to release the aroma.'

'Haha, trust you to remember the scientific reason.'

'And… something about increasing the surface area thereby exposing it to more oxygen. But I can't remember why that's a good idea.'

'You get an A for effort, then.'

'Stingy.'

'Increasing the surface area softens the tannins, thus making it taste better. So… inhale and tell me what you smell.'

I brought the glass to my face and drew a deep breath through my nose. 'Umm. Cherry, maybe, or is it black–berry? Very fruity.'

'Now taste it and tell me what you think.' His voice came from behind me and was unexpected. I could feel the heat rising in my body at his nearness.

I took a sip and moaned before taking another. 'It's delicious. Definitely cherry and maybe… is that a hint of liquorice?'

'I'm not saying anything. I truly believe everyone's taste experience can be different. What type of wine do you think it might be?'

I took some more sips and finished the glass. 'It's defin–itely your white zinfandel.'

A slow clap sounded around me. 'Impressive, Clarke,' he said, and I beamed. 'Now open your mouth.'

A breath hitched at the back of my throat. Instead of questioning I did as I was told. Something touched my lip. It was wet and slippery.

'Bite,' he said, and I did. I continued to have more nibbles and whatever it was tasted heavenly. 'It's important to clear your palate so I am introducing some of the tapas that I like to serve when I have tasting parties up at the house.'

Suddenly my mind was filled with the idea of how much fun that would be: Austin and all his friends sitting around the oak table in the living room, laughing and sharing an evening together. Living with Mum meant I hadn't taken the next step into adulthood. Nights with Samira at her flat were rare because of Rosie, and Jena's boyfriend was too much of a homebody and always complained we shrieked too much, which was why our Friday night meet-ups were in a bar or restaurant. As long as cocktails were on the menu, we didn't mind where we convened.

'It's delicious,' I said once the third piece slipped down my throat. 'Tasted like a chargrilled pepper with a hint of lemon and thyme.'

'Spot on,' he said as he gave me a couple more. I licked my lips in appreciation.

We then moved on to the next wine and, in between each bottle tasting, a different array of foods appeared including various cheeses. The appetisers caressed my lips and delighted my mouth as I was hand fed by Austin. Was it possible to tick *savour a meal* twice on the Love Intervention plan? I could feel the wine hitting hard now and whenever I got something right and Austin praised me, I giggled.

The next time he asked me to open my mouth wide, I caught his fingers in my teeth, and he yelped. I snort-laughed at his reaction.

'Austin, are you drinking as much as I am? Because anyone would think you're trying to make me drunk.'

'That wasn't my intention. You're clearly a lightweight if you are already.'

'Hey,' I said, mock offended.

'You do however have something on your…' I felt his fingers gently caress my chin and his thumb brush over my lips. 'On your mouth.'

Something reverberated deep down in my belly. A desire, a longing. It was rushing through my bloodstream.

I thought back to Jena's slides on the presentation. This was a release of dopamine. 'Dopamine and another hormone, norepinephrine, are released during attraction, especially when something feels good', she had written. I crossed my legs and readjusted my position.

'Ready for the last one?' he asked.

'Ready as I'll ever be.'

My hand reached out but inadvertently knocked into his and wetness soaked my front right as Austin exclaimed, 'Shit!'

I pulled off my blindfold and my eyes took a moment to adjust to the light. My clothes were drenched in red wine.

'God, I'm so sorry,' he said, reaching for a cloth.

I inspected the splodges on my shirt. 'It's fine. But it would be the shiraz, wouldn't it?' I looked up at him and he laughed.

He handed me the cloth, but it was pointless, the stains were already imbedded.

'Dab the marks to at least soak the moisture,' he suggested, 'and then give them to me.'

'My clothes?'

'Yes, your clothes. I need to get them treated as soon as possible.'

'Is this why you suggested the swimsuit?'

'You think this is my ruse, that I deliberately doused you in red wine so I could get you naked?'

'Who said anything about naked?' I folded my arms. 'Confess, Austin. What was your game plan?' I slipped off my stool, untying my shirt and flapping it away from me. 'You've clearly done this a thousand times: invited someone to your vineyard, done the blindfold taste test and then spilled the wine. Let me guess, you have a hot tub somewhere out back.' I stretched my neck to try and look out the window.

He dipped his head as if he'd been caught cheating. 'There is no hot tub, but I do have an outdoor shower. And it wasn't a ruse. I like having a shower outside after a hard day's work even in the depths of winter. It's exhilarating, and it's nice to go back into the house already clean. I have a storage cupboard next to it filled with bathrobes and towels so you're not cold for long.'

'Oh,' I replied, taken aback by his confession.

'And as for whether I have done this before. Some parts. But I have never let any female guest touch my vines. Except you.'

His words and proximity were sending my pulse racing. That release of molecules was setting my insides aflame. My inner seductress was waking from her long dormant period after the wine had begun to lower my inhibitions.

'Then I had better take off my clothes, seeing as I am such a special guest.'

He sucked in a breath and his pupils dilated.

Turning on my heel, I shrugged off my shirt and threw it behind me in the hope he would catch it, before untucking my T-shirt and pulling it off in one swift move.

Looking over my shoulder, I handed my top to him, and his eyes drifted over my bikini top. I stretched out my arm. 'You'd better lead the way. I have no idea where this shower of yours is.'

He clutched my things tightly, before passing by me, brushing his shoulder against mine as he went.

Outside, the cool air hit me, and my nipples hardened in response to the chill. I hugged myself tightly, lightly bouncing on the spot. Austin led me round the corner to the shower. It was positioned against one of the back walls of the house with the largest faucet I had ever seen. There were two wooden sides but apart from that it was completely open. Thoughts of Austin showering naked filled my head. He would be in full view of… well, the view was out towards the setting sun – there wasn't another house in sight – so I guess no one. It was the perfect spot for nude showering.

Oh God, Laila. Get thoughts of naked Austin out of your head.

But why? I challenged myself, knowing it was the wine talking and not sober, rational Laila, who would want to take things slower.

Austin leaned in and turned the handle. A cascade of water fell like it was Niagara Falls. Opening the wooden chest, he located a massive towel and hung it over the hook on the other side of the shower.

Soon enough, steam began to rise, and a warm mist blew towards me.

'Be my guest,' he said, ushering me towards the jets of water before turning and heading back to the house with my wine-soaked clothes.

'You're not joining me?' I called after him.

He paused and looked over his shoulder. 'You want me to?' His chest was rising and falling as he drank me in.

I slipped off my boots and socks before popping the button of my jeans and pulling them down. 'Yes,' I said, confident in my decision.

He didn't need a moment to respond. Discarding my clothes, he shrugged off his shirt and peeled off his T-shirt in two rapid moves before unzipping his jeans to reveal tight swim shorts with an unmistakable bulge straining against the fabric.

Stepping under the shower head, I flinched as the hot water momentarily scalded my skin before I let it cover my body and wash away all the stickiness of the wine and the sweat from our pruning work. Closing my eyes, I tipped my head back and let the jets of water rain on my face.

I sensed a movement behind me and knew Austin had stepped inside. A finger trailed down my arm. Turning round, we locked eyes as the water lashed down on us. Then his lips were on mine, feverishly, tongues exploring wildly. His mouth moved towards my neck, my shoulder, his hands cupping my behind, squeezing me into his hard-on. The feeling made me groan with desire.

He swept my ponytail off my neck and undid the tie of my bikini top before loosening the knot on my back and letting it fall, taking one of my nipples in his mouth, biting, caressing with his tongue, while his fingers kneaded my other breast. He spun me round and I arched my back into him. His mouth was by my ear, his breathing ragged.

'I have wanted to fuck you since the moment you sucked that asparagus tip.'

At that comment I laughed.

'God, I want you so badly,' he almost growled.

'Here?'

'Yes, here.'

'How?'

Stupid question. This was Austin Bradley. I was sure he had built this shower for that very purpose.

'First, I'm going to drive you wild with my fingers.'

Before I could respond, he had plunged his hand inside my bikini bottoms and began to caress me, softly. My knees buckled and I leaned my hands out to the side to steady myself. His fingers were like magic, the movements like he was conducting an orchestra, switching time signatures effortlessly. I could feel a pressure there rising and rising and when he suddenly removed his hand, I was left aching and wanting it to return.

With the pause, I was able to compose myself somewhat and looked over my shoulder before turning to face him.

Austin was breathing heavily and the way he devoured my body with his eyes was as if I was his favourite vintage and he couldn't wait to have a taste.

'Everything OK?' I asked, suddenly feeling a little self-conscious.

'I needed a moment. You're so fucking beautiful, I was about to lose it before I even entered you.'

Not wanting to be apart a second more, I kissed him again, more slowly this time. But when he bit my bottom lip, a wanton groan slipped out of me.

'That's it,' Austin murmured against my mouth, before breaking free from the embrace and pulling down his shorts, letting his dick spring free. He stepped out of the shower momentarily and opened the trunk before fetching something out of it. In one swift move, a condom packet was ripped in his teeth and he slipped its contents on.

He undid the ties of my bikini bottoms and kneeled a little before plunging deep inside me. It was wild, it was fun, and I let myself go as a kaleidoscope of molecules ripped through me. In the heat of the moment, the checklist popped into my mind.

4. Have sex ✔

Chapter 14

Seconds. Minutes. Hours.

They drifted by in a haze of sex, sleep and more sex. Day became night, night became day. A squeeze on my arm would signal to me that Austin was leaving his bed to go and work in the vineyard only for him to return merely a couple of hours later, his arms lifting me into the shower before more entanglements ensued. I don't think there was a corner of the house that we hadn't had sex in. He brought me coffee or juice intermittently and we feasted on tapas and wine and worked our way through the contents of his fridge. I hadn't moved beyond the four corners of the house aside from moments on the deck to gulp in fresh air. We watched movies on his big sixty-five-inch screen, binged one box set and chatted about random stuff until either sex or sleep interrupted our train of thought.

I had no idea what this was except the sweetest form of pleasure. My body ached, though. A mixture of the delayed effects of the massage, the hard labour from the pruning and all this vigorous sexual activity. When I had commented on this yesterday, Austin had immediately rolled out a couple of yoga mats. He was an expert teacher and it felt good to stretch out my sore muscles. But it was hard to completely tune out the thoughts that were racing in my head. How was this week going to end? What was

I going to say to Austin about where I was headed next? Samira had insisted I didn't tell any of the guys anything. But Austin and I had become so intimate, it seemed wrong to lie.

–

'Wake up, sleepyhead,' Austin whispered.

'What time is it?' I mumbled, my head a little foggy. In fact, what day was it?

'It's time to get up.'

The bed dipped as he sat down and I turned over, opening my eyes to his smiling face. He was smartly dressed in a white shirt and navy-blue slacks. 'Why are you all fancy?'

'My family are coming for dinner.'

I sprang up, clutching the sheet close to my chest. 'Your what?'

'My parents, two sisters, their partners and my nephews. They're excited to meet you.'

'They are? How do they even know about me?'

He twisted his hands in his lap. 'Today is usually the day we get together, but I told my folks I couldn't make it. That set off a series of events. My younger sister called to interrogate me as to why I was so busy, and I told her about you. Next thing I knew, my older sister called me and told me I had to host. I couldn't say no. They're pretty persuasive when they gang up on me.'

'Oh,' I said, swallowing away a flurry of nerves that had suddenly bubbled up from my chest into my throat. We were going from our own private affair to meeting the family in a matter of days.

'Hey.' Austin touched my shoulder, breaking my thoughts. 'You OK?'

I nodded, tucking the sheet under my armpits, the need to cover up overwhelming me as if his whole family might walk in at any second.

'Sorry, I know I should have consulted you, but you were sleeping so peacefully that I didn't want to disturb you. They're all bringing round various dishes for starters, mains and puddings so I only have to provide refreshments.'

'Who did you say I was exactly?'

'An old friend from my NYU days.' He leaned in and plumped for a quick kiss on the lips before getting up and checking himself out in the mirror, tucking his shirt into his trousers.

'A friend that you have been sleeping with for the last three days,' I clarified.

'I left out that part. Anyway, can you get out of bed? They'll be here in half an hour.'

'So bossy,' I mumbled under my breath, as I dragged myself out from the sheets.

I came into view of the dressing table mirror and his eyes widened as he drank in my semi nakedness in the reflection. 'I can show you what being bossy is like.' He turned and pulled me close, his mouth at my neck, his fingers kneading my bottom, finding their way inside the fabric of my knickers.

'But I have to get ready,' I moaned, trying but failing to not be intoxicated by this man.

He pulled back and stroked my cheek. 'I'll message them and say we're running late.'

His lips found my neck again and I pushed all nervous thoughts to the back of my mind and let myself enjoy the thrill of his touch once more.

'So, tell us all about yourself, Laila,' Mrs Bradley asked as we sat down in front of a feast of food, from vegetable lasagna and various salads to a cheese platter and another one filled with three types of bread.

I swallowed a forkful of aubergines and peppers in a tangy tomato sauce and wiped my mouth with a serviette. 'Umm, I work as a clinical scientist at a hospital in central London. My field of expertise is cardiology.' I filled them in on a typical day in my working life, the long hours, the satisfaction I garnered from helping people, diagnosing heart disease early thereby giving people a chance for a longer lifespan. As the words flowed from my mouth, it made me realise that as much as I was having fun here, I was itching to know how the investigation was going. I hadn't confided in Austin that my job was on the line.

'Wow, beautiful *and* smart,' Austin's mum said when I paused, nudging her husband, who nodded in agreement. My cheeks flushed at the compliments.

We moved on to my life outside work, any hobbies I had, and my lack of interests made me question what I was doing with my life. Cocktail night with my besties couldn't be classified as a hobby, could it? Aside from work, what else did I have?

'Austin said you're leaving tomorrow night,' his younger sister said with a downturned mouth, curling her bright blonde hair behind her ears. 'Can't you stay longer?'

'Sadly not. I have a flight to Puerto Rico. I'm visiting...' I dropped my fork as I realised I was about to blurt out who I was going to see. 'A friend,' I added hastily.

'That's a shame,' she replied. 'Maybe you'll come back and visit again? Or I know Austin would love to go back to London.'

I turned to him. 'You've been to London?'

He shifted in his seat. 'That was a very long time ago,' he said, leaning into me, his voice low, 'during my undergraduate degree.'

'Oh,' I murmured.

He cleared his throat. 'Now can we stop with the inquisition. Laila didn't sign up for the Bradley offence.'

'Speaking of offence…' And with those words uttered by his older sister's husband, the conversation turned to American football and an in-depth critique of the 49ers season. I had no clue what they were talking about when phrases such as 'tight end' and 'third and ten' were thrown around but I was relieved to have the spotlight taken away from me.

After dinner, I helped clear the table with his sisters and took the dishes to the sink, which Mrs Bradley had filled with suds, while the men cracked open some beers and went out into the back garden to start a football game with the boys.

Mrs Bradley regaled me with a myriad of tales about Austin as a child, while his sisters interjected with embarrassing stories from his middle-school days when he had a mouthful of braces and hardly smiled.

The whole setup floored me. It was like they had embraced me into their family already, as if I had always been a part of their Sunday evening meet-ups.

'Are you OK, honey?' Mrs Bradley asked. 'You've been wiping that glass an awfully long time. I know Austin likes his wine to be a specific way, but I don't think he'll mind if there are a few dull marks on his glassware.' Her smile was warm and full of kindness.

'Sorry,' I said, placing the glass in an overhead cupboard.

'I know we can all be a little overwhelming at times,' she continued. 'But can I tell you a secret?'

I laid the cloth down on the counter. Austin's sisters were out of earshot, discussing puddings at the fridge. 'Yes, please do.'

'My son has never looked happier.'

Her honesty floored me. I opened my mouth to say something in return, but the words didn't come.

'He keeps his cards very close to his chest,' she continued, 'but not this time. I know he has a bit of a reputation when it comes to the ladies. He's a lot like his father in that respect.' She giggled and her admission made me feel all layers of awkward as I imagined Austin's father as a cad back in the day. 'But when Bradley men fall for their keeper, they fall hard.'

Before I had a chance to digest what she had said and think of an appropriate response, her daughters had come over with a pavlova and wanted adjudication on whether to squirt cream on top or not. I excused myself and left the kitchen, the need for some fresh air catching me unawares.

I hugged myself tightly as the cool evening chill covered my skin. I contemplated going back inside to get a cardigan but the talk inside had my head in a spin. Austin thought I was his 'keeper'. What had he said in those conversations with his mum and sisters? This was only ever meant to be a week's liaison, a chance to act upon all that suppressed desire. But I couldn't deny that being in his company this week had been a welcome elixir. Something had shifted in my mindset, but I couldn't put into words what felt different all of a sudden. Would the girls say it was simply the repeated high of oxytocin and dopamine being released through my system? Or was it something more? Something deeper?

From the edge of the deck, I could see the men and boys down below, throwing a ball between each other, their game punctuated with laughter and merriment. I didn't grow up in a world like this. As an only child, there were no big family meals and for the last fifteen years it had been me and Mum. Before Dad left, mealtimes had been imbued with awkward silences from Dad punctuated with the occasional passive-aggressive comment from Mum and usually I couldn't wait for dinner to be over. There had obviously been cracks in my parents' marriage long before Dad left. But what I had experienced this evening was a one-eighty-degree about-turn from those dinners; the Bradleys were obviously a close-knit family and they already thought I was a part of it.

Later that evening, once pavlova, fruit salad and some of Austin's dessert wine had been consumed, the Bradleys left in one big flurry of hugs and kisses. As three large Jeeps drove off with dust in their wake, Austin's grip around me tightened and he exhaled loudly.

'Thank God, they're gone.' He spun me round and in a heartbeat his lips were on mine, and he was pulling me into him. 'I have wanted to kiss you desperately for the last four hours,' he murmured.

Sensing my lack of reciprocity, he pulled back. 'Hey, what's wrong?'

'Your mum thinks I'm your "keeper". Care to elaborate?'

He dipped his head and puffed his cheeks. 'You know what moms are like.'

I stepped away from him. 'No, not really. I have never met the entire family of someone I have been intimately involved with in one swoop, when we haven't even had a conversation between the two of us about what this is.' Irritation laced my words. Austin hadn't been entirely honest with me. This hadn't been a casual meet 'n' greet; they had been sizing me up as a potential life partner.

'You're right, I'm sorry.' He closed the space between us, curling a lock of my hair behind my ear. 'But if it's any consolation, they loved you.'

I swatted his hand away. 'I didn't realise I had to win them over, Austin. I mean the last few days have been amazing, but—'

He held a finger over my lips to silence me. 'Please, don't let there be a but.' His eyes were almost hound-dog like. 'Come on, let's go inside.' He tugged my arm gently, willing me to follow him. 'I don't want to have this conversation out here.'

Initially, I stood my ground, but his pleading look eventually softened my prickly exterior and I let him lead me back into the house.

Austin's ability to set a mood was faultless. He clicked the button for the fireplace, and it came on at the right temperature, lights dimmed, before he brought a tray to the oak table with an after-dinner drink and some amaretti cookies on it.

We sat on the floor on the plushest cushions, leaning our backs against the sofa. Austin handed me a glass and took a long sip of his as if he was steeling himself to say his next words.

'I don't want you to go.' He didn't look at me when he spoke and there was a vulnerability to him in the way his shoulders dipped forward, his head lowered.

I took a sip of my drink for courage, the strong liqueur catching at the back of my throat. 'I have to go, Austin. My life is in the UK.'

He turned. 'But you have another two weeks off work. Change your plans, stay with me. I don't want you to leave.' His hand lay on my knee, and he stroked it in a rhythmic motion, his fingertips warming my skin.

I pinched my lips, thinking through carefully what I wanted to say. 'These last few days have been amazing but we both know that our lives are very different.'

'But I love having you here. I love having you in my home, my bed, my vineyard. Have you not thought about us being together beyond this week at all?' He grasped my knee, a look of longing on his face.

I chewed the inside of my mouth as I stroked the contours of my glass. 'Coming to California was never meant to be anything more than a holiday. My job is in London—'

'And you're a phenomenally talented woman who could do wonders here, using your expertise to save lives in America. There are many organisations that would kill to have you work for them. Or…' He propped his knees up and rested his clenched hands on them. 'You could run the vineyard with me.'

I placed my glass down on the table and turned to him, steeling myself to say these words. 'Austin… I…'

'Yeah, I know. Crazy, right?'

'It's not just my job that is in London; my mum is there too. I couldn't move to America.'

'She could come and live out here. I could build a granny annexe. There's acres of space.'

I didn't know how to answer that, especially as he had said the word 'granny'. He was imagining a life not only with me in it but with kids too. My heartrate picked up speed at the thought and my palms became clammy.

Flashbacks entered my mind. The night Josh had booked a table at a top London restaurant where he announced his promotion for a job he hadn't even told me about, which was up in Manchester. I had been reluctant to go out that night because I was in the middle of exams, but he had persuaded me I needed the break. He had then gotten down on one knee in the middle of pudding to gasps all around the room and declared he wanted to make it official and for me to start a new life with him up north. He told me accommodation was included in the package and thought we could start a family straight after the wedding. I was twenty-five. When I said I needed time to think about it, we started arguing because he couldn't see why I was dithering. That's when his old-fashioned views about women came to the forefront as he believed his future wife shouldn't work and that my exams weren't that important. I felt like I had been blindsided.

'Sorry,' Austin said, breaking me from my thoughts, 'that was a bit much, wasn't it?'

I took some deep breaths to steady myself. Austin wasn't Josh. We had merely had a one-week affair, nothing more. 'Let's not spoil the end of my trip wondering about what this means and where it might be headed.'

He didn't appear appeased. His forehead furrowed and he opened his mouth before closing it.

I jumped in before we went any deeper down this rabbit hole of make-believe. 'I have had the most amazing time here, Austin, but I have never once contemplated the idea that I could live my life away from England. I'm not even sure if my skills are transferable to anything here.'

His body shifted away from me and his shoulders appeared to lock beneath his shirt.

'This is all new to me, Laila. I've not felt this way about someone before. It's like torment. I don't want you to leave.' He tipped his head backwards, as if he was trying to get inspiration from the ceiling.

'That's it,' he said suddenly. 'I'll come with you.'

'Where?'

'To Puerto Rico. We could explore the island, the two of us. Have a proper holiday together.'

My heart stopped. 'I… I don't think that's a great idea. And besides, how could you leave your work at such short notice?'

'I'm the boss, remember. I just need to make some calls.'

My cheeks burned as I attempted to pluck up the courage to say the next words. 'You can't come with me, because I'm visiting… Edoardo.' His name seemed to echo off the walls into the sudden heavy silence.

Austin shuffled backwards. 'Edoardo as in your ex-boyfriend Edoardo?'

'Well… yes. He and I dated for a few months back in our NYU days.'

'Yeah, I remember him.' His tone was full of disdain. 'How could I forget?'

'What's that supposed to mean?'

'You clearly have no memory of what happened the night of the Christmas party, do you?'

'Yes, I do. I caught you in bed with my roommate, right after you said you would be waiting for me.'

He exhaled audibly. 'That Indian girl?'

My nose wrinkled. 'Yes, Alesha. Jeez, was she that unmemorable?'

'Her name maybe, but everything else? Absolutely not. I was waiting for you that night like I said I would. Decided to make myself comfy and get settled in your bed, shirt off. Possibly a little presumptuous but hey, I was only twenty-one, horny as hell and the way you were grinding up against me on the dance floor had the blood flow down there at fever pitch. Next thing I knew she came in and practically threw herself at me, claiming someone had told her I was in her room waiting for her. She pinned me down and I laughed it off and steadied her before she made an even bigger fool of herself. I got dressed and came looking for you. Seems you had no intention of coming to your room, as I saw you kissing the face off that Italian dude.'

His words threw me. 'But… no… that couldn't have been what happened. I thought—'

'You thought wrong, or rather, you thought what you always thought of me, that I was nothing but a dumb jock womaniser.'

I hung my head. 'Look, I'm sorry, Austin. I guess I was mistaken.'

'Doesn't matter. Water under the bridge. And yeah, you're right, this was fun, real good fun, but I know what it can never be.' He stood up and dusted non-existent dust off his trousers. 'It's been a long day and I gotta get some rest because some possible purchasers are coming to the vineyard tomorrow. But I'm happy to drive you to the airport in the evening.' His monotone screamed that 'happy' was the last thing he was feeling about anything.

The coldness radiating from his body language threw a chill over my limbs despite the warm room. The heat that that had been generated from our affair was now completely extinguished. 'No, that's fine. I think I'd quite like to do some sightseeing in the Bay Area. If you could drop me off at the nearest bus station first thing, I'd appreciate it. I'll find a locker at the airport for my suitcase and explore the city.'

He nodded. 'If that's what you want.' And with those words he switched off the fire and headed to his room.

Was that what I wanted? Or did I want to say sorry – sorry for all the years I judged him, for the mistake I made, for the hurt I had obviously caused.

But it was too late. Our week-long affair was over. It was time to move on.

Chapter 15

Why don't I let them get close? Why do I keep myself guarded?

Those thoughts spun around my head as I waited in line at immigration at Luis Muñoz Marín International Airport. I had slept fitfully on the flight over to JFK before taking my connecting one to Puerto Rico after a day in which I'd wandered the streets of San Francisco aimlessly, wishing Austin was with me. He had said goodbye at the bus stop but not even waited for it to arrive. The farewell came with a brief hug, and I had half expected him to follow up with a pat on the back. After he had mumbled his apologies about needing to get back to the vineyard, I had stood there alone, a sad feeling hitting me hard in the chest. Dopamine withdrawal?

I had voice-noted Samira and Jena and told them everything, from the passionate sixty-two hours together to the evening meal with his family and the subsequent argument and cold goodbye. They had no choice but to listen to me rambling on and when their voice note verdicts came, they couldn't have been more polar – Samira claiming that he had love-bombed me and Jena declaring that it was all unbelievably romantic: the bad boy wanted to commit, to settle down, to start a family. Did I not want those things too? she had questioned. Why had I never given those thoughts even a second consideration?

Shouldn't my biological clock be ticking by now? Isn't that what everyone assumed women my age should want?

Agh. No. The way the week had ended only served to reinforce what I believed about relationships. They were hard work and needed time and commitment. Once this extended holiday was over, I would return to my old life. Samira and Jena were wrong. I didn't need love. And Samira was hardly one to talk; she didn't believe in love either. My week with Austin had only reinforced her stance on men, she had said in her voice note: that they were useful for sexual needs only.

The doors of the airport exit automatically opened and with a deep breath I stepped into the San Juan late-morning heat, palm trees swaying in the distance along the boulevard that separated the lanes of cars and motorbikes. With a new resolve to put the past week behind me, I headed over to the taxi rank. The twenty-minute journey to my destination in Old San Juan ended in a colossal jam as my driver attempted to carve a path down a single-lane road that had two-way traffic. Rapid-fire Spanish was hurled out of his window at other drivers until eventually he pulled up in front of my Airbnb. Horns hooted as I stepped outside and fumbled to find some dollars to pay for the ride. As he sped off, along with a trail of other vehicles behind him, I took in my surroundings.

It was the most colourful street I had ever seen – rows of terraced houses on either side of me, each one painted head to toe in a colour of the rainbow or a muted pastel. The luminous yellow of my building blinded me as I scanned it, shielding my eyes from the sun reflecting off it. I scrolled my inbox on my phone for the lockbox code that the owner had emailed last night, released the keys and opened up the iron gate. After hauling my case up two flights of stairs, I opened the door to my apartment. It was like I had stepped back in time. The living room was awash with ornate furniture and old masterpieces adorned the walls. A ceiling fan overhead created a small breeze and the polished mahogany table beneath it in the centre of the room had a glass top with tourist guides and maps fanned out. It was surrounded by a gold brocade sofa and two armchairs with plump velvet cushions on every seat.

As soon as I clapped eyes on the bedroom, I collapsed in a comatose heap onto the bed and fell asleep.

–

A jolt roused me. The front door to the building had been slammed shut and footsteps were thundering on the stone stairs. Voices escalated in Spanish before they muted as another door was closed. My travel clothes were sticking to me in a mass of perspiration, so I changed out of them into a vest top and shorts before heading to the kitchen. My phone informed me I had been asleep for a couple of hours and there were no messages, which only reinforced that Austin had meant what he said during our last heated conversation – that there was nothing more to say and that what we had enjoyed together was only a moment of mutual pleasure – nothing more. Number four on the checklist had been ticked off multiple times along with several meal delights but that was all.

The terracotta tiles were cool against my feet and there was a sticky note on the front of the fridge from Edoardo's friend that said:

Enjoy

Inside, there was orange juice, milk, cheese, and bottles of water. Scanning the mint-green laminate counter, I saw a loaf of fresh bread, various jams, a kettle and a coffee machine. The kitchen table had a folder with instructions on how to get a breeze going in the apartment and manuals for all the appliances.

Preparing a plate of food and a cup of coffee, I pushed open the shutters at the back of the apartment to a large balcony with two wrought-iron chairs by a table. The ground was lined with black and white checked tiles, and an abundance of lush green foliage with a scattering of tropical flowers lined the space. The freshly brewed coffee roused me while I sat and listened to the sounds of the city – distant cars rumbling along the cobblestoned road, birds chirping up above. The cheese had a tartness to it I noted, as I took my first bite, and the bread was filled with seeds and walnut pieces. It was delicious.

My phone buzzing on the table made me sit up. Wiping my fingers on some kitchen roll, I saw that it was a video call from Edoardo.

'Shit,' I cursed, patting down my hair and hoping that I looked half decent. I accepted the call, and his face filled the screen. There was an expression of disbelief on his face before a broad grin replaced it.

'*Ciao*,' he said.

'*Ciao*,' I replied.

One word but it set alight something inside me. Suddenly I was transported back to that moment I had flung my arms around him at the Christmas party all those years ago – the same look of surprise and bewilderment in his eyes.

He shook his head and mumbled something in Italian, looking up to the sky. 'I had to call to check this wasn't a dream.'

His accent made my heart hammer against my chest, and I became awash with other memories, of study dates in cafes, where his words and kisses distracted me. It was a wonder I got the grade I did but after that initial honeymoon period where I had only left his side for lectures, seminars and lab work, I had been stricter with myself and used Edoardo as an incentive to get my work completed during the day so my evenings could be spent with him.

'I'm real,' I said. 'I'm here.' I did a quick scan of the courtyard and the peerless blue sky above with my phone, hoping that would make it obvious that I wasn't in grey, old London.

He puffed out his cheeks and slowly exhaled before running his hand through his hair. 'Yes. You are for sure not a dream. I'm sorry I couldn't meet you at the airport, but I have managed to take the next few days off.'

'Oh, Edoardo, you didn't have to do that. Arranging this accommodation was more than enough.'

He tutted with a little chin tilt. 'Laila, come on, that is nothing. Organising some accommodation through a friend, it was easy.'

'Maybe. But I don't believe for one moment that that is the usual rate I am being charged.'

A flush crept into his cheeks to confirm my suspicions. 'Is it OK, though? Is it to your liking?'

'It's beautiful. But I haven't had a chance to have a proper look around. I crashed as soon as I arrived. It was a…' I paused, realising I was about to say the words 'turbulent overnight flight from San Francisco'. I had originally told him my conference was in New York and that was the reason for the trip to Puerto Rico. 'It was a tiring conference,' I said instead, 'so I can't wait to relax and do some exploring.'

'I am so sorry I cannot sightsee with you this afternoon but perhaps tonight, you are free? Would you like to have dinner with me?'

I curled my hair behind my ear. Why was I hesitating? Was it because of Austin? That was old news now. And I was committed to the Love Intervention, to reconnecting with Edoardo and maybe... even more.

'I would love that,' I said finally.

He beamed in response. 'I will text you the location later. For now, I must say *ciao* as I have to go back to work.'

I waved before the call went dead.

After I had cleared away the remnants of my lunch and returned to the courtyard, my mobile buzzed with two texts from Edoardo. The first was a Google Maps pinpoint location of a restaurant; the second was a message saying he couldn't wait to see me tonight. As I clicked on the link, I noticed it was an intimate restaurant with a small rooftop terrace offering spectacular views of the city. All the photos were of couples leaning in, laughing, kissing.

I couldn't get my heartrate to settle down. Was it wild panic that Edoardo thought this was more than a casual meeting of two old lovers? Perspiration was sticking to the back of my neck. It was muggy outside, so I went back through the kitchen and along the living room to the other wooden shutters, which completely blocked out the light. When I opened them, a breeze shot through the apartment, cooling the space immediately with the most wonderful fresh air. The view from the small balcony of the colourful colonial buildings was glorious and I took several pictures with my phone before sitting down on another outdoor chair and sending them along with a message to the girls with a request for their counsel.

Within a few minutes, Samira had started a group video call, and both their faces filled my screen.

'It's about bloody time we saw your face,' Samira said right about the same time Jena squealed before apologising to James, who was sat next to her. There were some words exchanged between them before she got up.

'I gotta go outside cos the football's about to begin,' she said. 'Hold on a sec.'

As she stepped outside, juggling her phone and her coat, it was hard not to notice the slush on the ground and the dark grey clouds above.

'Has it been snowing?' I asked.

'It's been sleeting, more like,' Samira said.

'And it's frigging freezing,' Jena said.

'Then go back inside,' I suggested.

'Nah, it's OK,' Jena said. 'James says the flat's too small and our voices reverberate.'

I decided not to challenge that statement, instead noticing that Samira was in my kitchen back home.

'How's Mum?' I asked her.

'She's good, watching a Disney movie with Rosie. The best babysitter I could've asked for.'

My shoulders dropped. I hadn't realised how much stress I had carried in them over her wellbeing, so it was reassuring to know Mum was coping.

'I've even managed to catch up on a lot of work,' Samira added.

'I thought this was your week off?'

Samira rolled her eyes. 'It's recorded as time off but there's always the expectation to keep working.'

'I can't thank you guys enough for last week – for playing tag team looking after Mum.'

'You've already thanked us a million times,' Jena said, her misty breath filling the screen. I couldn't believe I was sitting here talking to them a world away with not a cloud in the sky and the heat of the sun on my skin.

'I can't wait for half term,' she continued, 'so I can spend extended time with her. We've been swapping recipes and making plans.'

'Oh.' A dart of jealousy cut across my chest even though I knew it was wrong to feel like that. 'And James is OK with that?'

'He grumbled a bit last week, but he's decided to take an impromptu ski trip with his mates and now it's all he can talk about.'

There was something in Jena's voice that didn't sound right but I knew now wasn't the time to bring it up. She and James always set out their budgets for the year and something like a bonus trip abroad would mean having to make compromises elsewhere, so I hoped my trip – and Jena's birthday contribution – hadn't impacted things between them.

'Anyway,' Samira said, 'what's the latest with you?'

I pulled up my legs and rested my feet on the other chair. 'I have a date tonight.'

'Woohoo,' they both cried in unison.

'But I'm nervous… and I feel guilty.'

'There's nothing to be guilty about,' Jena said.

'But I slept with Austin knowing that I was going to spend the next two weeks with two other guys. And now I am about to go on a date and lie about being in another guy's bed merely two days ago.'

'Seriously,' Samira said sharply. 'Would a guy feel this way? They wouldn't give it a second thought. You had fun with Austin and that's that. You never lied to him or misled him. It's over now and it's time for part two of the plan and hopefully ticking off a few more items on that list.'

'It's time for second-chance romance,' Jena declared.

'I'm not sure I'm ready for that. The way things ended between me and Edoardo…' I trailed off as I remembered I had never been fully open to the girls about how we broke up.

I listened as Samira and Jena gave their thoughts and opinions on the detrimental effect guilt can have on one's internal system and I made a promise that I would go to dinner tonight with an open mind and open heart. The conversation then turned to what I planned to do for the rest of the day and my outfit of choice for tonight. I waved them goodbye with a multitude of thanks before sending a text to Mum saying the conference had gone well and now I was enjoying some time off touring the region. If I told her I had flown to Puerto Rico, the Spanish Inquisition would ensue. The lies were piling up anyway, so what did it matter that I hadn't told her of my travel plans? From the message I received back, I wondered if she was missing me at all. Extended chats with Samira in Arabic were delighting her and she had done a big online shop in preparation for Jena's visit, ready to cook up a storm and chat even more in her native tongue. I simply replied to say that I was glad she was enjoying her time.

Another message from Edoardo suddenly popped up on my phone. He apologised for taking any liberties but wondered if I would like a guided tour of the city. I assumed he didn't mean with him because he had said he had to work. The idea of someone organising my afternoon suddenly appealed to me. I replied yes and instantly another text came through saying a gentleman called Antonio would be ringing my doorbell in half an hour.

The next few hours were a whirl of history and beauty. Antonio had been hired by Edoardo as my personal guide. In the shaded area of various plazas, he regaled me with historical tales from the sixteenth century and pointed out the famous monuments and cathedrals as we walked around the city. I marvelled at the Castillo San Felipe del Morro and stood on the edge of the wall looking out to sea as soldiers would have done hundreds of years ago. We had several breaks, during which time Antonio let me savour the best coffee, a ham and cheese toastie and the most refreshing slushed ice imaginable. When I tried to pay for his time at the end of the tour or at least offer him a tip, he waved it away and said he had been more than compensated.

–

Early evening came and, after a cool shower, I stood admiring my image in the full-length mirror. There was something different about my appearance. I had taken the sun, that much was obvious from the smattering of freckles across the bridge of my nose, but there was something in the way my shoulders sat more squarely – my posture was straighter, too. I looked… relaxed. It was obvious I had needed a holiday but there was something about the warmth of the sun on my bare arms and legs today that had been intoxicating. I had obviously boosted my serotonin levels, I thought, remembering the slide Jena had produced on the presentation.

Slipping on one of my floral sundresses and sandals, I sprayed some perfume and grabbed a light cardigan before heading out. The sun was setting in the distance, throwing an abundance of mellow orange light across the plaza as I crossed it to reach the restaurant.

The building was painted a bright pink, and I could hear music and laughter spilling out as I approached. The waiter ushered me upstairs, through the bar and the indoor seating area, outside onto the terrace, which had string lights crisscrossing above the space. The sight of terracotta rooftops and the dome of the cathedral in the distance with the sun setting behind it took my breath away.

Edoardo wasn't there yet, and I sat down on a stool beside a tall table at the back that had the best view – a spot he had reserved. I was brought a small glass of Prosecco on the house and a bowl of olives.

Minutes slipped by as well as the sparkling drink. I pulled out my mobile to check for messages and saw a voicemail notification from Edoardo. He apologised that he could no longer make it. A pile of work had landed on his desk from his boss as he was about to leave and he was told that if he wanted to have the time off, it needed to be done before tomorrow. His words came with a multitude of 'sorry's.

A second later the waiter came with the menu and said card details had been left and that I could order whatever I wanted.

I smiled through the embarrassment of being stood up and the sympathetic expression he threw me in return made my cheeks burn even more. It was tempting to leave but I didn't want to cause a scene.

It wasn't the first time Edoardo had stood me up. I popped an olive in my mouth as I thought back to the last time he had. That event had begun the unravelling of our relationship though I hadn't probably realised it at the time. And perhaps it was one of the reasons I had guarded my heart so tightly since.

Something stirred in my mind and moisture built at the back of my eyes. I turned to the view, conscious that I didn't want other diners to think I was getting emotional over being stood up. These were memories I had fought to suppress for so long and I thought the sight of touching down at JFK airport, albeit briefly, would have triggered them, but no, it was this: being stood up by Edoardo.

Chapter 16

NYU – ten years ago – March

'What do you mean you can't take me?' I said, pressing my mobile closer to my ear as if I hadn't heard him right.

'*Mia cara*. I am sorry. I promise next weekend, OK?' There were loud voices in the background, and I knew the drinking had already begun so it was pointless begging Edoardo to reconsider driving me three hours north of here to Saratoga Springs.

He rang off before I had a chance to say anything in response. It made me wonder whether he had wanted to take me there at all. Over pizza last night in my room, he had tried to convince me that the lack of response to the letter I had sent my father meant he didn't want to reconnect. It had after all been almost six months since I had sent it. But there was something in my heart that ached at Dad's silence, and I wanted to go and confront him. I was clinging on to the idea that he had simply not received it.

None of what had happened four years ago made any sense. When I had returned from the physics trip to Geneva, Mum told me he had gone: left for America to start over. She had grown weary with my inquisition as to why and how he could leave without saying goodbye, merely asking me, 'What did you expect?' But I had chanced upon a letter from him to Mum in our letterbox during the Christmas break of my final year at UCL. She had never brought it up and I had ransacked the house looking for it again, but it had vanished much like Dad. It made no sense to me why he had tried to suddenly reconnect with Mum and not me. Our relationship had been loving, so I had thought.

I needed to find an alternative way to get upstate, but I hadn't wanted to do this trip alone.

Sitting on the steps to the school building, I pulled my jacket close. The buds lining the trees on the sidewalk were bursting to break into blossom, but a cold snap had kept them in a stranglehold. Weather warnings had been issued of a potential snowstorm in the region during the next few hours and I had been keen to hit the roads early in case.

Edoardo had originally agreed to the trip because he was going to Vermont for the weekend with his engineering friends. But now they were pushing it back until late Sunday, so he had told me, because they were celebrating something or other tonight. I wasn't listening to his excuses. Disappointment washed over me as I sank my head into my knees.

'Laila?'

I looked up into the concerned face of Mateo. 'Hey.'

'Is everything OK?'

I pursed my lips and raised my eyes to the sky, the build-up of moisture catching me by surprise. 'No, not really.'

'Would a coffee and a walk help?'

I smiled at his thoughtfulness and considered his offer. Maybe talking things through would help. 'Yeah, I think it might.'

That broad, sympathetic smile appeared, and instantly I felt calmer. Mateo bought us a couple of flat whites from the coffee hut on the corner and we began our walk around Washington Square Park. Kids ran around in the distant playground, shrugging off their coats before throwing them at weary-looking parents, and a few people had braved the chill to sit on benches reading newspapers alongside couples out on dates whispering sweet nothings in between sips of coffee.

I took a deep breath and told Mateo everything: about my dad's letter to Mum, me trying to reconnect when I arrived last summer and how weeks had turned into months with no reply. I told him that Edoardo and I had planned this trip, that I was intending to tag along with him dropping me off in Saratoga Springs before he headed further up north to Vermont. And then I told him that I didn't know what to do next.

He stopped walking. 'I'll take you.'

I turned to him. 'What?' I said, not quite believing his words.

'I said I'll take you. I have my international licence, so it is no problem.'

'What about your work?'

'What about yours?'

'All done.'

'Me, too. We're such geeks, right?'

At that I laughed and nudged him in the ribs. 'Hey, speak for yourself. I like to get ahead sometimes. And this weekend is one I had been building up to for ages, so I knew I had to have a clear schedule. Are you sure you have the time?'

'Laila, I wouldn't offer unless I was sure. There's a Dollar Car Rental place on Charles Street. I've used it before. How about we meet there in an hour?'

'But… what if he's not in?'

'Then we'll leave a note and drive back. Maybe the letter never reached him. Maybe we could ask a neighbour or something. He could be out in town having dinner. Then I don't mind driving back tonight if you don't manage to connect with him.'

'And if he's in?'

'Then it is up to you. I can book into a motel and wait until the next day or until Sunday, whatever feels best for you. I will bring some course reading with me in case.'

At his easy response, I flung my arms around him. Initially it took him by surprise, and his arms hung like dead weights but when they wrapped around my waist in return, I sank into his embrace, and it felt nice. There was the slightest movement in his hands along my back and warmth radiated in their path. But then the pressure intensified and I laid my cheek on his chest and I could feel his heartbeat quicken as if this hold meant something more. The moment caught me off guard. We were friends. Only friends, I reminded myself.

'I appreciate this, Mateo,' I said, finally breaking free from the hug.

'*De nada*,' he said. Those words took me back to when I had heard him say that for the first time: that moment when I had looked up into his eyes and felt something stir. Now was no different as I took in those kind, green eyes.

I stepped back, suddenly awkward, as if he could read my mind. We were friends, I repeated to myself, and I had a boyfriend. 'Right, I'd better get packed. *Gracias*,' I added to lighten the mood and he smiled.

The ride was traffic-free and had a relaxed air about it. Nerves were bubbling beneath the surface, but Mateo was doing a good job of distracting me from them. We laughed about one of our professors having fallen asleep during his own lecture and we shared notes on how our theses were going and tactics to manage our impending deadlines.

A little after four, we pulled up by the sidewalk next to the address I had written down from that envelope. It was a classic-style colonial house with a porch wrapped around it, a swing chair on the right of the veranda.

'I'll be here if you need me,' Mateo said, and I nodded before taking a deep breath and stepping out the car.

Taking more deep breaths in and out as I walked up the path, a flurry of snowflakes landed on my face. There were no lights on in the house when I rang the doorbell. I waited a few moments, but no one came to the door. It was then that I saw something hidden behind the bushes around the side of the house. I went closer and saw it was an estate agent's sign that had a *Sold* sticker plastered over it.

'Can I help you?'

The voice startled me, and I looked behind to see a woman with a long cardigan on, arms wrapped tightly around her waist. Her silvery hair was tied up in a neat bun.

'Umm, yes,' I said, stepping closer to beneath her covered porch. 'I was looking for the owner of the house.'

'The old one or the new one?'

I wiped snowflakes from my coat. 'Oh, I don't know. It's Victor Clarke I'm hoping to find. He's my... father.'

'What do you know,' she said, giving me a rather obvious once-over. 'I can see the resemblance. Your skin is a little darker, but it's in the eyes and those apple cheeks I can see him. Oh, we were so sad when your father told us they were leaving.'

'They?' I said, rubbing my hands together, wishing I had brought my gloves from the car.

'Why, yes, him and his husband.'

I stopped moving. Had she uttered that last word? Surely a slip of the tongue. Surely she meant 'wife'. And even then, I couldn't get my head around that concept either.

'They were the sweetest couple,' she continued. 'We've never had any gay folks living around here, but you know, this is quite a progressive town 'n' all.' Her smile broadened.

'I'm sorry, what?' I said, certain that we were talking about another Victor Clarke. Certainly not the one who had been married to my mother for sixteen years. 'I think maybe we are talking about a different person.'

'Very striking, tall, strong British accent, always wearing a cravat even in the height of summer.' She chuckled and my shoulders sagged as I realised she was most definitely talking about Dad. He had a collection of those cravats in every colour of the rainbow.

'They threw quite the party, did Victor and Gregory. But I knew your dad yearned for sunnier climes. I believe they spend the winters on the West Coast now; bought themselves a little des res in Southern California and spend spring and summer at Gregory's flat on the Upper East Side.'

I knew my mouth was moving but there were no words emanating from it.

'Wait here a minute, honey. I think I have a forwarding address somewhere in my bureau.'

She disappeared and it was suddenly hard to breathe. Dad was… married. To a man. Dad had a whole other life I knew nothing about.

'Are you OK, sweetie?' she asked studying my face. 'Here, let's sit you down.' She ushered me towards the door, but I wrestled myself from her hold, apologising profusely for the manner in which I had flinched at her touch.

'I'm fine, honestly. It was a shock, to know he no longer lives here.'

'They moved out a good six months ago now.'

'That's when I wrote to him.'

'Their mail has been piling up I'm afraid. I think they planned on coming by and clearing out the last of their things at some point. It took a while to sell the place. We haven't met the new neighbours yet, not even sure if the sale has completed.' She looked over my shoulder and saw the hire car. 'Did you travel far?'

'Only from New York City. My dad and I lost touch when he moved to the States, but I'm studying a Master's programme at NYU for a year and thought I would surprise him.'

'I bet he'll be mighty happy to connect with you when this weather turns,' she said, pulling the folds of her cardigan around herself even tighter. 'Oh yes, here's the address.' She pulled a piece of paper from her pocket and handed it to me.

I thanked her and headed back to the car. A numbness sank into my limbs as I stepped inside. Mateo didn't say anything but let me sit there in silence for a while. The shock was too great.

How could I have not known something as important as Dad's sexuality? And aside from that revelation, the fact that he had remarried. Why had he hidden everything from me? Did Mum know? Is that what that letter had been about? Nothing made sense. Dad and I had been close, I thought. I ran through the last time I had seen him in my head over and over again. He was excited for me, for my forthcoming school trip to CERN and I knew he would want to hear all about it upon my return. Pie and chips and peas. That's what we had eaten – a takeout. I had been complaining about my upcoming exams and he had told me that they were nothing to worry about, that if I had done the work, they would be easy. I had snapped at him, accusing him of not understanding how education had changed since his day. It was no longer about memorising but applying knowledge – questions deliberately written to catch a student out. Dad hadn't responded to my little outburst, merely choosing to sit in silence over what then became our last meal together.

A touch on my hand brought me back to the car. It was gentle, reassuring.

'Is everything OK?' Mateo asked.

I looked through the windscreen where snow had begun to settle. 'I'd like to go back now,' I said, drawing back my hand.

'Of course,' he said and didn't probe me further. I leaned my arm on my window and lost myself in the darkness of my mind – the cold trail of Dad's disappearance fading even further away, the revelations of a man I clearly didn't know wanting to set up camp in my brain but numbness prevailing.

An hour and a half into the journey, the weather turned dramatically. The windscreen wipers were doing their best to clear the snowfall, but the visibility was rapidly deteriorating as night-time enveloped us and the flurries escalated.

'It's not looking good,' Mateo said, leaning forward in his seat, obviously straining to see the road ahead.

It occurred to me then that we had been driving for over five hours straight with only that brief stop at Dad's old house. 'Maybe we should find somewhere to rest for the night?' I suggested. 'Have something to eat. You must be exhausted.'

Mateo's hands tightened on the wheel. 'If you're sure that's OK? I think I saw a sign for a motel up ahead.'

–

I didn't even think twice about sharing a single room with Mateo that night, him on the floor and me lying on the bed with my eyes open for hours on end. Once exhaustion took me under, the next thing I knew there was movement beside me as a coffee was placed on the side table. Mateo continued to give me space, and I appreciated it more than he could ever have imagined.

But back in the rental car, the words tumbled out. The confusion. The shock. Mateo listened and didn't comment until it had all come out in a stream of consciousness swiftly followed by an angry outburst mixed with sadness and tears. A lot of tears. He had repeatedly asked me if I wanted us to stop and take a break, but I had shaken my head.

Once Mateo dropped me back at my halls, he hugged me once more and said he would be around if I needed to talk to him again. As I walked away, I bumped straight into Edoardo. His arms were folded over his chest.

But when he saw my face, his crumpled. '*Amore*, what's wrong?'

'Nothing.'

He looked over my shoulder and it occurred to me that he must have seen me embrace Mateo.

'I went to my dad's house,' I said, feeling the need to be honest. 'Turns out he no longer lives there. Moved out to California a few months ago.'

'I am so sorry to hear that. And I am sorry I couldn't do this journey with you.'

'It's OK, Mateo took me.'

'Oh,' he said but that 'oh' felt loaded. 'You went today there and back?' he asked.

'No, we went yesterday but got stuck in the snowstorm on the return journey and had to stay over in a motel.'

At that, his nostrils flared, and he placed his hands on his hips. 'Separate rooms?'

I curled my hair behind my ear. 'No, of course not. We're not made of money. Mateo slept on the floor… *all* night. I'm not even sure why I am telling you this.'

'Because I am your boyfriend.'

'I am not having this conversation,' I said, beginning to walk away.

'No, no, no, wait, *mia cara*. I am sorry,' he said, clapping his hands together, as if he was beseeching me. 'I didn't mean it. Please, forgive me.' He held on to my elbow, a slight tug bringing me closer to him. 'I am still hungover. Let's go back to your room. We can have coffee and you can tell me all about the visit. And I will help take your mind off everything.' He stroked his thumb over my cheek. 'I missed you, that's all.'

One look at that pleading expression and I knew I would give in and brush aside his comments – or were they accusations? And once he was in my room and I was in his arms, his kisses would make me forget, his body would make me forget. And that's what I wanted, to forget.

But as I let him slip his arm around my shoulder and lead me away, uneasiness tightened the muscles of my neck at the lie I had told him.

Mateo hadn't spent the whole night on the floor. When my tears had flowed again in the darkness, I had sensed a movement in the room before my bed dipped. He had lain down beside me. Arms had drawn me close, and I had accepted them. I had only been able to fall asleep because I was in Mateo's arms.

Chapter 17

A sound roused me, but I didn't clock where it was coming from. My eyes adjusted to the light in the room and then I remembered where I was: Puerto Rico. The noise came again. It was the door buzzer. A thump reverberated through my head when I sat up, and I pushed a spot in my temple where it hurt the most. *That'll be the three margaritas catching up with me.*

Last night had turned out to be a lot of fun. A table full of Canadians had insisted I join them, and dinner turned into dancing once the tables were pushed back and the music turned up. It was gone one in the morning when they walked me home. It was one of the most spontaneous things I had done in a long time, along with making the monumental decision to undertake the Love Intervention, obviously.

Another buzz sound. 'All right, I'm coming,' I said, dragging myself out of bed. The clock on the wall showed me that it was only seven thirty in the morning.

Opening the door, I was shocked to see Edoardo standing there cradling a picnic basket, decked out in a navy-blue polo shirt, grey board shorts and sunglasses on his head.

He drank me in, and it was as if ten years had suddenly dissolved like the sand in a minute timer. I pulled up the strap of my silk pyjama top that had slipped down my shoulder and self-consciously folded my arms over my chest.

The years had been kind to him, I noticed, his strong jaw and defined Roman features even more noticeable now that he was clean shaven. The moody Italian, as Alesha had loved to call him, but he had always saved his smiles for me. And one appeared as soon as his gaze returned to my eyes.

'Eh… *scusa*, I…' he mumbled as if completely lost for words. '*Buongiorno*.' He leaned in to give me a kiss on both cheeks. 'I am sorry if I wake you. Did you not get my message?'

'No, I'm sorry I didn't. I pretty much passed out once I got home from dinner. What's all this?' I said, nodding at what he was carrying.

'A peace offering.' His mouth downturned. 'I feel so bad I stood you up last night.'

'It's fine, I understood.'

'But now, is OK, I am all yours.'

He brushed past me, and the scent of his aftershave stirred more memories inside me. In the kitchen he pulled out fresh croissants, eggs and bacon from the hamper.

'Edoardo, you didn't need to do all this. Your friend left me lots of breakfast items.'

He spied the half loaf of bread on the counter and tapped it. 'It's stale now. And *this*.' He picked up the tin of instant coffee. 'This is an insult to an Italian, which is why I brought you…' A thermos appeared from within the basket. '…freshly brewed coffee from my apartment. You are a visitor here, so it is important I show you a good time. It won't take me long to cook breakfast, maybe ten minutes. Why don't you get changed. You will need a swimsuit for what I have planned.'

Another request for a swimsuit. That thought made me think of Austin, but I pushed memories of our time together to the recess of my mind.

Back in my room, I took a shower and changed into my green bikini, teaming it with a white vest top and black shorts. A savoury aroma drew me out into the courtyard. Edoardo had a cloth on his shoulder and was laying down two plates of food.

'That smells amazing,' I said.

'*Buon appetito*,' he said with a flourish of his hands.

I slid into the chair, took my serviette, and placed it on my lap before tucking into the tastiest mushroom and bacon omelette, washed down with grapefruit juice plus easily the best coffee I had ever drunk. One shot of it and I felt the heaviness of last night's drinking session dissolve.

'Mmm,' I murmured. 'None of this was necessary, you know. I had a lovely time last night and met some nice people. It was very generous of you to leave your card.'

'It was not an attempt to buy your forgiveness, but I knew I had been put in an impossible situation and wanted to make things right. I didn't want to let you down again.'

I paused before chewing my mouthful slowly, wondering what he meant by the word 'again'. A sad expression had crossed his face and then with a slight head shake he picked up his fork.

'But now I get to relax for a few days,' he said, popping another mouthful of omelette in his mouth. 'At last.'

'You hadn't planned to take this time off?'

'No, but it was long overdue.'

'How long have you been working out here?'

'A year now. The restoration project I have been working on in La Perla is coming to an end soon, though.'

'And then?'

He shrugged. 'I am not sure. Possibly back to Italy. Moving around every year or so has been fun but there is something missing in my life.' At those last few words, he looked at me intently before wiping his mouth with his serviette. 'And you?'

'Me what?'

'What brings you here, *really*?'

The word 'really' was delivered with an eyebrow raise.

'Like I said in my messages.' I set my fork down on the plate and pushed it close to my knife, feeling heat begin to build in my cheeks. 'I've always wanted to visit here. And next week I am heading to Costa Rica.'

'Wow, nice. Any reason you chose there?'

'I have a friend who is volunteering out there and it's another bucket-list destination.' I could hear the pitch in my voice faltering but thankfully Edoardo didn't seem to notice, and he didn't probe me further. I took a last sip of juice. 'So… what's the plan?'

'I have three days to show you the whole island.'

'Is that possible?'

'I think so. Puerto Rico is a place of so many contrasts: the culture, the sea, the rainforest… I want to give you a flavour of everything. I hope yesterday showed you some of the incredible history, the places UNESCO has bestowed their favour on. Also, you can see the devastation that is still apparent around here, their need for tourism to be thriving again. I want to be able to give you a behind-the-scenes tour – something that only someone with experience of this island can give you.'

'Sounds amazing.' I beamed, wondering if we might tick any of the Love Intervention list in the process. 'Let's do it.'

Edoardo had rented a hire car for the next few days – a metallic red convertible. He said it wasn't necessary to own a car while living in San Juan because most of his time was spent in the office or on site – two locations a walk away from the apartment he was renting.

We had the top down as we left the windy streets of the old town before hitting the freeway. I tamed my hair with an updo but even then, wisps broke free. The music was blaring, and it made conversation all but impossible, but as we had headed off, Edoardo had merely said, 'Enjoy the ride,' so I did – taking in the scenery on either side of the freeway: palm trees and low-rise buildings interspersed with shops, neon signs adorning their windows. When I asked what we were going to be doing, he said one of his favourite pastimes.

We pulled into a surf shop two hours later at the end of a sandy track in Rincón on the westernmost tip of the island. Edoardo did a high five/shoulder pat combo with the owner of the eco tour company and spoke in Spanish, introducing me at one point with a sweep of his hand. The owner gave a chef's kiss and I felt suddenly shy in their presence, curious to know what they had said to each other. When we left the hut and stepped through a blanket of palm trees, the beauty of the ocean stopped me in my tracks before I noticed the waves in the distance – angry and menacing.

I felt a touch on my fingers. It was Edoardo's hand on mine. 'Don't worry, *mia cara*, we won't be going far, not after only one lesson.'

The affectionate moniker that he used to call me all those years ago gave me pause, and I slowly withdrew my hand from his touch. I opened my mouth – to say what, I wasn't sure – but Edoardo sensed my unease, and he held his hands up.

'Laila, I am so sorry. I didn't mean to say those words. They slipped out.' He dipped his head. 'I am sorry. For it all. For the way things ended between us. I didn't realise this would be so hard. Seeing you again.' He searched my eyes and I let his words settle somewhere inside me – in a place of forgiveness. But it was also a place that had other memories. Painful ones.

'I knew this would be difficult,' I said. 'For the past not to catch up with us.'

'We went from zero to one hundred when we first met, didn't we?'

'Yes, we did.' I smiled as I thought back to that Christmas party. To say Edoardo was shocked when I had gone straight up to him in the middle of the dance floor and planted my lips on his had been an understatement. We had danced and danced and kissed and kissed until the last revellers had gone back to their rooms. I was practically asleep on his shoulder at five in the morning, when he helped me back to my room and slipped out saying he was headed for the airport.

'And then at the end we crashed.' His jaw pulsed and I wondered whether he was thinking back to that day. 'Do you think we can start over?'

I studied his eyes – pleading with me to say yes – and they softened my mind to the idea of a new chapter, a desire to throw caution to the wind and see what happened next.

'I think I'd like that,' I said, finally.

He outstretched his arms. 'I am Edoardo Moretti, your surf instructor for the day. And here, on cue,' he said, spotting his friend walking towards us with two boards, 'is the equipment we will be using.'

Edoardo's friend handed one to me and explained how they were both waxed and ready to go. He also recommended a half wetsuit to protect myself from the sun that would be stronger out on the water. Edoardo helped me into it, and goosebumps rippled along my back when he placed his fingers on my skin to make sure it didn't catch in the metal zip. I thanked him and fiddled with my hair as I watched him peel off his clothes, showcasing that physique I had seen on that photo of him that the girls had included in their presentation. I had on occasion wondered whether what Edoardo and I had had only been physical. But no, we had gotten deeper than that during our relationship.

Hadn't we?

The request to start over had been shaken on, but was it that easy to forget the past? Jena had shared many second-chance romance books with me and, of course, in each one there was a happy ever after at the end.

Was Edoardo my happy ever after? Did I even believe in the concept? I gave my head a slight shake.

Much like Austin's life, Edoardo's was far from mine, and his familial home was in Italy. How would it even work between us?

Puffing air from my cheeks, I decided to park those thoughts and try and live in the moment. I was getting ahead of myself again, getting swept up in Jena's romantic ideals. Learning to surf wasn't on the checklist but it was something new to experience – something that a few weeks ago I would never have dreamed of doing. And the thought of accomplishing something new thrilled me.

I listened intently for the next half hour as Edoardo delivered basic instructions on how to lie on the board and then push myself up. We practised and practised on the sand until he declared we were ready to go into the water. He secured the safety hoop around my ankle, and we carried our boards to the sea.

We paddled and paddled until we found the right spot. Time and again, I attempted to stand on the board when I caught a wave, but kept unceremoniously falling in and inhaling a gallon full of water in the process. My nose stung and my eyes were all scratchy as I continued to go under and resurface with my hair caked over my face, spluttering water from my mouth. But Edoardo was unbelievably patient and on the twenty-second attempt, it happened.

With a heave and a spring, I was up. Crouching at first, then rising to a stand – wobbly, but definitely a stand.

'I'm doing it,' I said, in a voice laced with disbelief. 'I think I'm doing it,' I screamed.

'You are,' Edoardo confirmed from somewhere behind me, 'you are.'

I had no idea how long I was standing for. It felt like minutes, but it was probably closer to a few seconds. Losing my balance again, I toppled off, crashing beneath the wave before whooping as I resurfaced. The rush of achievement was exhilarating. But Edoardo didn't let the momentum fade. He moved from 'standing up' coach to 'riding your first wave' coach.

My arms began to throb from all the paddling but with one more effort, I finally managed to ride a wave for three whole seconds before I went under again. By this point, my head kept resting on the board in between attempts and Edoardo called it a day when he spotted me doing it.

It was like trudging through treacle as I pulled the board out from the water. Edoardo waded out behind me before scooping up my board effortlessly under his arm and laying them both on the sand next to our things. He unzipped my wetsuit and I luxuriated in the sun warming my limbs as I towelled my face.

'What?' I asked, when I caught him smiling at me.

'You're beaming.'

'That was such a rush, I loved it.' My breathing was erratic and heartrate double the normal speed. I willed it to settle but then realised that I needed to stop and take in this moment. This was clearly a rush of endorphins pumping through my system and wow, it felt good. Surely this couldn't be achieved in a gym in freezing cold England. Perhaps the endorphins were dancing with those serotonin molecules from the sun and the dopamine from having achieved something I never thought I would ever get the chance to do.

Edoardo bent down to open the cooler he had brought from the car and handed me a bottle of water. It was refreshing and I took several swigs as my pulse began to slow. He sipped his and seemed lost in thought as he looked out to see where bigger waves were swelling.

'You didn't do any surfing,' I said.

'It's OK,' he said, turning back to me. 'It was more fun watching *you*.' He nudged my shoulder with his.

'That's sweet, but you said yourself, it's been a while since you had time off. We don't have to rush off, do we? I'd love to watch you.'

He hesitated for a moment before dropping his water bottle on his towel and picking up his board. 'OK, then. *Grazie mille.*'

With a wink and flick of his wet hair, he was racing across the sand, his muscles bulging at the strain of carrying the surfboard under his arm until the water kicked up around him. Hurling himself onto his board, he paddled further and further – far further than we had been. For a moment I took in his stillness as he lay there, watching the sea behind him, waiting for the right wave to come. And then it did. With furious swipes, he began paddling back towards the shoreline until his board caught the sea's momentum and then, in an instant, he had popped up onto his board in a Spider-Man-like crouch, riding the wave as it built and surged forward. He showed so much strength and endurance, I couldn't look away. Eventually the wave petered out and he hopped off into the water before pointing his board back out to sea, flattening himself once again on top of it, and starting the process again.

A good half hour later he finally pulled himself out of the water and walked across the sand to where I was. His board shorts were sticking to his skin, leaving very little to the imagination, and as I reminded myself, I didn't need any imagination to remember what he looked like naked. He had left a lasting impression already during our passionate, sex-filled six months together. Would it be like riding a bike if we hooked up again? That thought brought a huge flush to my cheeks and I hoped to God Edoardo couldn't read the expression that was on my face and ask me what I was thinking.

His chest was rising and falling heavily as he dropped his board on the sand and flopped on his towel.

'You're pretty damn good, Mr Moretti.'

He turned and shielded his eyes from the blazing sun. 'Why, thank you, Ms Clarke.'

Something passed between us – a surge of what could only be described as pure lust – but I broke away from the intensity of the moment and hugged my knees. 'Thanks for this. It was fun.'

'You are very welcome. I love the ocean,' he said, gazing out to the surf. 'Family holidays to the coast were rare growing up in Rome, but when I came here and was introduced to this scene, I was immediately hooked. It's a huge adrenaline rush, feeling the power of the water against you. You have to respect the sea, though, as some of the other beaches further up along the coast,' he said, pointing to the left, 'can be quite dangerous. This beach is known for its kinder waves and is *perfetta* for a beginner.'

Edoardo filled me in on the times he had come here with friends, the surf contests he had entered, the late nights after BBQs on the sand and crashing in one of the many holiday rentals that lined the road on the way to the beach.

As he talked, his voice so warm with the joy these memories brought him, I couldn't help noticing an emptiness settling deep in my chest – the idea that I had missed out on this part of life. Work had taken over and where had it got me? I shivered as I realised this was the second time that thought had come to me, and pulled the towel around my shoulders. I was immensely proud of all I had achieved during my twenties but now…

'Is everything OK?' he asked.

'Hmm?'

'I think I lost you for a while. My stories are boring, no?'

'God, no. Not at all. They're making me ruminate over the last ten years. I've hardly done any travelling or worked abroad, and I still live at home.'

'If my *mamma* had her way, I too would be living at home. She loves to tell me how I would be a homeowner if I had saved my money instead of living my life so lavishly.'

'Do you think you live that way?'

'I certainly like the finer things in life but feel that now I am missing something. Do you…' He trailed his fingers in the sand. '…ever wonder what would have happened if we had stayed together?' He paused and searched my eyes. 'Those plans we made, to travel around America. Do you wonder where we might have ended up?'

'We were young, Edoardo, very young.' I hugged my knees tighter and stared out to sea.

'I know we were. And I was foolish – foolish to have lost you so easily. I let my jealousy destroy what we had and for that I am sorry.'

Sorry. A word I had longed to hear. A word that should have been spoken ten years ago. A word he had tried to tell me, but I wasn't in the right frame of mind to hear it. It not only needed to have been uttered by him, but by me, as well.

And Edoardo wasn't the only one I owed an apology to.

I had buried that day from ten years ago deep in my heart: the anguish, the shock. It had all been too great and marked the day that everything in my life changed. There had been a world before that day – one in which I dared to dream, to hope, to feel I could be anyone or anything. Then after that day, I only knew there was one path. A path I couldn't divert from.

Chapter 18

'I'm going to hit the library, how about you?' Mateo asked as we filtered out from our ten a.m. lecture into the spring sunshine.

I clutched my books close to my chest. 'I need coffee first, but I will join you later, OK?'

Last night had been a late one. Edoardo had insisted on coming round, having not seen me in almost a week. He had made a bold declaration that he was going crazy with this forced absence I had implemented because I was working on my thesis – that he would break down my door, if necessary, in order to spend only a half hour with me. I should have known that it was impossible to only spend a half hour in Edoardo's company. My body yet again had betrayed me, as I let him stay over, and sleeping hadn't been the number one activity. Aside from the obvious, we had begun the discussion of 'what next', for us, post-Master's. Edoardo wasn't ready to return to Rome nor had he begun applying for any jobs. And the truth was, neither had I, except for summer internships. I'd always had a plan. But now I was contemplating a life without one. Was that Edoardo's influence?

He had painted a beautiful picture of the two of us in an RV touring the US on the iconic Route 66, taking in the best of America. 'Sunsets, sex and seeking,' he had declared in my bed, his hands gesticulating wildly like they always did. Seeking what exactly, I wasn't sure, but he had liked the alliteration. He believed that if we could survive fourteen days in a confined space, then maybe we had something special.

Those last thoughts had spun in my head all night and for the first time, I hadn't been able to drift off with him in my single bed. Usually, I didn't mind him hogging most of it, but last night I had.

'Is everything OK?' Mateo's question broke me from my thoughts.

'Hmm?'

'I said see you later, and you kind of froze on the spot and drifted off.'

'I'm sorry. I have a lot on my mind.'

'Are you worried about your thesis?'

My phone buzzed in my pocket. It was a number I didn't recognise and I wondered if it was someone calling about one of the internship placements I had applied for.

'I'd better take this,' I said to Mateo. 'Sorry, I don't mean to be rude.' He waved away my words. 'I'll probably head to the library this afternoon; we can talk then.'

Mateo gave me a thumbs up and walked away.

'Hello?' I said as I struggled to hold the phone in the crook of my neck and carry my books.

There was a sharp intake of breath. 'Laila?' The voice sent shivers up my spine. I dropped one of my books and almost lost the grip on my phone.

'D… D… Dad?' I said, reaching to pick up the book and place the stack on the nearest step at the entrance to my halls.

'Oh, Laila. My sweet girl.'

'How did you get my number?'

'Your letter. We went back to the house. Saw it in a huge pile. My dear, dear girl. How are you?'

'I'm… I'm…' *In shock, disbelief. I had written you off. How could you stop calling? Why did you leave me and not stay in touch?* But I said none of those things. 'I'm OK.'

'I can't believe you're here, in the States. And in New York City no less. I knew you would make a success of your life without me.'

His words confused me. 'What's that supposed to mean?'

'It means I did the right thing in leaving.'

It was like a sucker punch to my chest. 'How can you say that?'

'Laila, I was a broken man when I last saw you: bankrupt, practically homeless, directionless. You didn't need that in your life.'

Those words hit even harder. Had the void created by his abandonment been easier to bear?

'You could have said goodbye, though; you could at least have kept in touch.' I gripped the rail to the steps to steady myself, the stone surface rough against my skin.

'Well…' His voice faltered. 'You found me in the end, didn't you?'

'Only because I saw a letter you sent Mum with your address on the back.'

'You mean she… didn't show it to you?'

'No, she didn't.'

He paused. Deep, measured breaths came down the line. The same deep breaths he always took when he was bracing himself to say something difficult, trying to keep his emotion in check. He wasn't one for tears nor could he ever handle seeing mine. 'There, there, don't cry,' he

173

would always utter with a pat on the shoulder when I was upset.

'Then you didn't know I wanted to reconnect?' he said. 'That's what I asked for in that letter. For us to find a way back to each other.'

No. I suddenly felt light-headed at his words. I refused to believe that us not reconnecting was down to Mum not showing me that letter. I steadied myself once more, my arm grazing against a jagged edge of concrete but I ignored the pain, my resilience that I had had to rely on for so many years strengthening me.

'You had my UK number; you could've called,' I said bitterly.

He sighed heavily. 'Laila, my sweet, sweet girl. There is so much to talk about, to share. It's no one's fault that we haven't been in touch for so long, but there are… things that I believe your mother chose not to tell you. And I accept, I should have been braver before that letter but at the time, I was in a very, very dark place, and your mother thought it best that I steer clear. It was your future that was in the balance. You were so close to exams, exams that would determine the rest of your life. I couldn't take the risk in defying her wishes.'

'But you say you're in a better place now. Why not get in touch? My A levels were four years ago.'

'Yes, but then you had your university degree to get through. I thought that once enough time had passed, that you would find your way back to me.'

Agh. This conversation was going round in circles. Why had it been my responsibility? I had suspected Mum had hidden things from me, but she wasn't a gatekeeper to all ways to reach me. I had been an adult for three whole years, after all, with a social media footprint for longer than that.

'I would love to see you now, though,' he said. 'I'm in the city; I travelled down late last night and your campus isn't far. We could meet at Washington Square Park, grab some coffee now, if you want? There is a lot I would love to talk about, about my life – things I haven't been brave enough to tell you before now.'

Should I tell him I already knew about him being married and to whom or wait until we met face to face? Of course I was OK with whatever his sexual orientation was but there was so much else I wanted clarity on. Had he ever loved Mum? Had he cheated on her? She had always alluded to there being someone else, but I was never clear on the timeline. My questioning was always met with 'It hurts too much' or 'I don't want to talk about it'. Maybe he was bisexual and not gay as his old neighbour had called him, or maybe he didn't believe in labels.

And how could he have gotten married again without me by his side? I was his precious little girl, he had always loved to tell me, but clearly not precious enough if he could so easily cut me out of his life. Still, this was it. The moment I had been waiting for. A chance to clear the air and have him in my life again because the truth was I missed him, terribly.

'OK,' I said, finally. 'I'll wait for you at the arch.'

He rang off with a simple goodbye.

How I wished we had both said a more profound goodbye.

–

I had already walked around the square two times, not being able to sit still even for a second. It was also

175

impossible for me to even appreciate the new breath of life that had been pumped into the trees around me, the foliage having come to life now spring was finally here. But the pleasant temperatures were destined to be short-lived as the brutal heat of the summer months was imminent.

A commotion made me turn. Far in the distance, a group of passers-by had congregated, before someone screamed, 'Call an ambulance!' I sucked in a gulp of air and dread rippled along my spine, but I shook myself from any doom-merchanting. Yes, Dad was late but only ten minutes. I was sure he would be here any second. Maybe there were problems on the metro.

The crowd grew and grew, and curiosity got the better of me. Taking pigeon steps closer, I approached the scene.

It was only when I dared to get closer that I could see what I had hoped against hope wouldn't be true.

A strangled scream ripped out of me and I dropped to my knees, my legs no longer serving their purpose as the paramedics arrived. An older woman rushed to my side to check I was OK, and I managed to mumble the question: 'What happened?'

She was speaking words, but they seemed nonsensical. The only ones that registered were 'collapsed,' and 'resuscitation'.

My response was trapped in my throat. I wanted to scream out that I knew him, that he was my father, but I couldn't.

As the lady helped me to stand, I asked her where they were taking him. She said it would most likely be the hospital in Lower Manhattan. That prompted her to regale me with a tale about being there one time with her elderly mother. I nodded politely but my eyes were solely fixed on my father as he was wheeled into the ambulance on a stretcher with a mask over his mouth, oxygen being pumped into him.

I tried to pull away from the woman, but her grip on me tightened. She must have thought I was about to buckle again.

'I'm sorry, I have to go,' I said with shaky breath, forcibly pulling my arm away, finally finding some composure.

The subway was crowded but I battled my way through and onto a packed train heading south. As I reached the entrance to the hospital, I found the reception and was directed to the emergency area.

'I'm… I…' *Dammit, why aren't the words forming sentences?*

The woman looked not the least bit interested and turned to her keyboard.

'Victor Clarke. I think he was brought in just now. I'm his… daughter.'

She tapped away on her computer but shook her head. 'We don't have anyone by that name registered here. I'm sorry.'

'Are you sure? I was in Washington Square Park, and he collapsed, and the paramedics came…' I realised at that point that I was shaking. Uncontrollably.

'Miss, like I said, we have no one registered here under that name. I'm sorry I can't be of any more help.'

I staggered to the nearest empty chair in the waiting room and fished out my phone. Dialling the number that had only called me a couple of hours ago proved fruitless. No ring tone, only a message informing me that it wasn't possible to connect the call.

Time slipped by. I had no idea what to do next, who to reach out to.

A gentleman suddenly rushed through the doors and gripped the counter at reception, yelling out the name Victor Gardner. The receptionist patiently listened to him before checking her computer and nodding, gesturing for him to take a seat in the waiting room.

He sat down two rows in front with his back to me, head bowed low. A minute later a doctor in full scrubs came out, wiping his forehead and readjusting his glasses.

'Gregory Gardner,' he said out loud to the waiting room.

It *was* him. Gregory. Dad's husband. Dad must have taken his name when they got married. My pulse beat wildly at multiple points in my body as the man stood up and went to the corner of the waiting room, out of earshot. The doctor's eyes were sympathetic. Taking off his glasses, he had a sombre expression on his face. Gregory crumpled at whatever the doctor had said and reached out to hold the wall for support.

No. No, it can't be true. Dad is… gone?

I couldn't bear it. I couldn't bear seeing these events unfold.

Standing up, I made my way along my row, mumbling 'excuse me's as I knocked into knees of waiting-room occupants before bolting from the hospital. I didn't want Gregory to see me. I didn't want him to know who I was and to, what…? Console each other? This man that my dad left our family unit for was grieving and I knew I wouldn't be able to handle it. Only *I* had a right to those tears.

I didn't stop walking. Once I hit Broadway, I knew if I kept putting one foot in front of the other, I would eventually end up on West 4th Street.

Endless blocks later, sweat was pouring down my back and I was struggling to get a hold of my breathing as I neared my turning. When I arrived at the Bobst Library building, I staggered through the glass doors and stopped still, the thump of my heart almost cracking against my ribcage as I attempted to take a deep breath. I searched and searched the space, my vision blurring with the threat of tears.

And then I saw him.

He was sitting on one of the black leather seats in the corner, a folder in his hands. When he looked up and saw me, he leaped to his feet. His beaming face soon turned to concern as I walked closer, before breaking into a run and falling straight into him. I sank once more into those safe arms, like they had been for me the night we stayed in that motel off I-87 south on our trip down from Saratoga.

'What's the matter, Laila?' Mateo whispered by my ear as he held me.

'He's gone,' I whimpered. 'Dad's gone.'

He didn't ask me any more questions. I buried myself in his chest, clawing at his jumper as the emotion choked me. His hand stroked my cheek tenderly, his thumb wiping away my tears. A kiss on the top of my head, a hold so strong, so powerful that I didn't want it to end, I didn't want to let go. As long as I was in Mateo's arms, I didn't have to accept the truth, that my father was dead.

'Don't let go. Please, don't let go,' I whispered.

'I will never let go,' he murmured. His hold tightened and he gently rocked me from side to side. It was soothing, it was comforting. It felt good but it shouldn't feel this good. Dad had died and all I could think about was how good this felt.

'Laila?'

The loud utterance of my name caused me to spring backwards out of Mateo's embrace.

Edoardo was standing there with his rucksack on one shoulder, clutching the strap, his other hand at his hip.

'What is this?' he almost spat out.

I didn't know how long he had been standing there and when I touched my face, there were no tears.

Swallowing to ease my parched throat, I said, 'I got some bad news and Mateo is…'

'Always there, always the one you turn to.'

My brow furrowed in confusion. What was he talking about? My dad had just *died* and my world felt like it was spinning off its axis. Edoardo didn't know that but the repetition of the world 'always' confused me.

'I don't… What do you mean, Edoardo?'

His lip pulled back in a snarl and he waved his arms angrily at Mateo and I. 'How many times must I find you in his arms?'

Finally, his words pierced through the veil of fog in my mind and his meaning became crystal clear. In place of confusion, I felt anger rise. 'It's not like that.'

'Isn't it?'

'Cut her some slack, Edoardo,' Mateo interjected. 'She needed a friend.'

Edoardo took a step forward, his stance menacing. 'And you are always around to offer her that friendship.'

'What's that supposed to mean?' I asked.

'You know exactly what I mean.'

Heat scorched my cheeks, but it was anger fizzing beneath the surface that was the underlying cause. 'That's it. I've had enough, of you and your jealousy. Mateo is a friend, that's all.'

He folded his arms across his chest and tilted his chin with a tut as if he didn't believe a word I had said. The action only had the effect of irritating me further. I couldn't bear this any longer. Edoardo hadn't even asked why I was in Mateo's arms in the first place. The scene spun around me, and I couldn't see a way out, nor could I eradicate the images I had witnessed: Dad's lifeless body being carried into the ambulance, the doctor's pained expression. I didn't want to believe it. It just wasn't fair. We were meant to meet. We were meant to reconcile. And now I was faced with yet another situation seemingly out of my control. No. Enough was enough. I couldn't endure Edoardo's petty jealousy and accusatory tone any longer.

'If you don't believe me then…'

'Then what, Laila?' he asked, coming closer into my space, his harsh voice only reinforcing my decision.

'We're through.'

Chapter 19

Sweat seeped from my pores. I swiped the moisture from my face with my forearm. My whole body burned from the exertion, but I knew it would be worth it when we got to the top. This was the El Yunque National Forest, the only tropical rainforest in the United States, and I was hiking in it.

Yesterday had slipped by with lunch at a restaurant close to where we had surfed followed by ice cream and then a return to Old San Juan in time for dinner. This meal was a more casual affair as we were both still in our beach clothes. Edoardo had taken me to one of his favourite food trucks and we had sat at one of the tables beside it and let dusk slip into evening around us as we talked about surfing and his life in Puerto Rico. When he drove me back to my apartment, there had been an awkward goodbye. I had thanked him with a kiss on the cheek, nothing more. He had said an early night was necessary for what he had planned for the next day, but I hadn't counted on it being a five-mile hike up to an elevation of over a thousand metres.

A huge effort had been needed to climb the jutting rocks and manoeuvre along narrow paths with over-hanging bushes and foliage. We walked in single file – no bad thing because the exertion was rendering me completely incapable of conducting a conversation.

Edoardo was leading but every few paces, he would check in on me and ask if I was OK or if I needed to rest or sip some water.

About halfway along the hike, he decided to take a detour to a rest spot. As we got nearer, the sound of water became more audible and when we arrived, my jaw dropped open at the sheer beauty of what was before me. This was La Coca Falls: a cascade of water, at least eighty or so feet high, dropping from the rocks into a bluey-green lagoon. There were a few tourists dotted around taking selfies and splashing in the waist-deep water but otherwise it was like we had stumbled upon a secret paradise.

My pulse thrummed beneath my heated skin and the urge to dive into the water overwhelmed me. I could also feel the endorphins pumping through my bloodstream – it was the same feeling I had enjoyed yesterday when we were surfing.

It was then that Edoardo turned to me and dropped his backpack to the ground. He tugged his T-shirt off in one swift move and pulled down his shorts, a tight pair of swim trunks beneath them. I had already seen Edoardo in this state yesterday but his board shorts for our surfing expedition had been longer and looser. Now, as his skin glistened with sweat, it was impossible not to notice how tight his trunks were. His bottom lip was trapped in his teeth. I knew that look on his face – that come-to-bed intense stare that had got me to do that when he had arrived at my dorm room all those years ago, fresh from his Christmas trip home.

He took a step forward, but I took one back before fiddling with the straps of my backpack and laying it down on the ground. Edoardo seemed ready to pull me towards him and forget the pain of the past – the misunderstandings, the anguish we had inevitably caused each other, but I wasn't so sure it was that easy.

Ten years ago, we had promised each other a summer of sun, sex and seeking and none of those things had transpired. Was this our chance to wipe the past clean with one brushstroke?

When I had spat out the words that my father was dead that fateful day, Edoardo had been contrite and offered his sympathy, but I had bolted. I shut him out completely, refusing to reply to his texts and not answering my door whenever he stopped by. Before long, he got the message that we were through and that I didn't want to rehash what had happened that day. I also began to shut Mateo out too, the feelings of guilt overwhelming me – that in my darkest hour, I had allowed myself to feel something else apart from pain and anger.

'*Andiamo.*'

The word cut through my thoughts. I turned and saw that Edoardo was in the water, beckoning me in with a flick of his hand.

I closed my eyes for a couple of seconds to centre myself. Edoardo was triggering so much in me – and the lines between regret, remorse, guilt and attraction were beginning to blur. When I opened them again and saw him splashing water onto his torso, I wondered whether there was any scope to form a deeper connection with him.

I peeled off my vest top and shorts, revealing my green bikini beneath. Gingerly, I stepped over the rocks until I reached the lagoon. The water was instantly cool on my hike-weary toes. As I waded in further towards Edoardo, he scooped handfuls and threw them at me. I squealed as the droplets hit my skin, goosebumps in their path.

He stretched out his hand to me, inviting me to move further towards the gush of water falling from above. I hesitantly grasped his fingers, then his whole hand. The roar of the water grew louder and louder as we stepped closer until we were underneath it. The world instantly disappeared as I closed my eyes, and all I could feel was the power of the waterfall against my head and shoulders. It was like a million fingertips on my skin kneading away all the deep-rooted stress and pain of the past. My scalp tingled with pleasure, and I felt Edoardo's hold on my hand tighten.

When we finally stepped out from the rush, we waded to the edge of the lagoon and dropped our hold as we positioned ourselves on two rocks to sun ourselves in the light breaking through the rainforest's trees above.

'Wow,' I said finally. 'I feel cleansed, almost like I've been absolved of...' I hesitated.

'Of what?' he said as he slicked back his wet hair from his face.

'I'm not sure.' I twisted my fingers in my lap as I slowly scissor-kicked the water with my feet. 'The past. How things ended between us.'

At those words, his jaw clenched. 'I was a jealous fool, Laila. There is nothing more to be said about that. *I* was responsible for how things ended between us.'

'I was as much to blame. Mateo was a friend, but now I can't deny that...' I swallowed away the fear of being honest about my feelings. 'That perhaps the line between friendship and more had blurred. Nothing ever happened between us, I swear to God, but... I guess if I am truthful with myself, I had thoughts...'

'But thoughts do not constitute cheating.'

'No, they don't.' His ability to be calm as we discussed the past made me realise that Edoardo had grown up; he had changed. Age had mellowed him.

And age had also been kind to him physically, I noted once more as my eyes trailed up his legs to his torso and then that strong jaw, luscious lips. But his physicality was no longer the pull that it had been. I needed more than that. And I wouldn't want anything more if it was based on a foundation of lies.

Samira's rules came to mind, but this time I didn't want to follow them. I wanted to be honest with him, tell him where I had been last week and where I was headed next. But before I could say anything, he spoke.

'I confess.' His head was tipped back, and his eyes were closed as he let the sun warm his face.

'What's your confession?' I asked teasingly.

But when he finally looked at me, I could see only sincerity in his expression.

'There has been no one in my life that has electrified me in the same way you did. I have never had a girlfriend who has truly challenged me, excited me, or filled me with more desire.'

At his admission, my mouth dropped open and body stilled. I couldn't let this interaction go on without speaking my truth. 'Seeing as it is confession time, I think I need to be honest with you, too.'

'You didn't come here from a New York conference,' he said with a raised eyebrow.

'Yes, how did you know?'

'When I came to the apartment, your suitcase was in the hallway. There was a luggage label with San Francisco on it.'

I puffed out a breath of air. 'My conference was at Berkeley, and I spent most of the week with... Austin Bradley.'

Edoardo showed no flicker of recognition.

'He was a physics major at NYU.'

Edoardo paused before realisation dawned on him and his shoulders appeared to lock.

'At the start of our Master's, I kinda had a crush on Austin. But then you and I got together. He and I lost touch after that year and last week was the first time I had seen him since. And next week, my friend in Costa Rica, it's... Mateo.'

At that name Edoardo's jaw pulsed but I was buoyed by my ability to be honest, so I carried on. 'This whole trip was instigated by my two best friends. They've been worried about me. I've been run-down recently, work has been relentless, and I haven't had a break in a very long time. They came up with a plan for me to reconnect with some people from my past, ones that I had a connection with, and it was luck that you all were on this side of the world, with an ample offering of adventure and sunshine.'

I paused. Edoardo's expression was unreadable.

'Thank you for telling me, Laila.'

He didn't probe me any further but stood up and put his T-shirt and shorts back on. I followed suit, my clothes instantly stained with wet patches, which I knew would dry once we continued our hike. Was the conversation over or should I continue, and tell him what had happened last week, be truly open and honest? Edoardo's back was to me, so I stayed quiet.

Had honesty not been the best policy? Had I *over-shared*?

The terrain grew harder as we set off into the rainforest and I noticed this time that Edoardo didn't keep turning round to check on me and I wondered if he was stewing over everything I had said.

It became harder to see as the mist of some low-lying clouds enveloped us and I began to struggle to keep up with Edoardo. Eventually he turned round and checked in on me. I told him I wasn't sure I could continue, but he held out his hand and I grasped it.

'You can do this. You're stronger than you think you are.'

His words and the way he held my gaze – steady, certain – filled me with a surge of energy: the feeling that I could not only push past the pain of my weary limbs, but also find a way to heal from the past. Once I got back in my groove, he walked ahead, and I pushed even harder to keep up.

Finally, we neared the pinnacle and Edoardo pointed out the lookout tower we were heading towards. The spiral stone stairs felt like another impossible challenge but I kept my legs moving, knowing that what awaited me at the top would be worth the aching thighs – and it was. Emerging from the tower staircase, I breathed in the cleanest air as I took in the blanket of lush green forest and trees down below on one side, only to walk around to the other side and see the sparkling ocean and colourful town stretched out ahead of us.

There were a few other tourists up here with us, but when they left, we were finally alone.

Endorphins spiralled in my system at the sense of achievement and they danced with the dopamine high from the hike. I was aware of Edoardo's arm pressed gently against mine, and when I turned to look at him, he turned at the same time. His expression was unreadable again but when his gaze fell on my lips, I touched them self-consciously.

Thoughts swirled in my head. Did I want to taste his lips again, have that tongue explore my mouth and dance with mine as it had done during our brief love affair? There was no denying that I still found him a very attractive man, but I still wasn't sure there was anything deeper there. I pulled back when another tour party came through the doorway onto the ledge, grateful for the interruption.

As the area became overrun with tourists, Edoardo tipped his head to the exit, and we made our way down the stairs before beginning our descent, conversation all but impossible as I had to concentrate hard on not slipping on the damp rainforest floor. We briefly stopped along the way to listen to the famous coquí frog and soak up the environment before making it back to the car, where I slumped, exhausted, in the passenger seat.

–

A jolt roused me, and it was then that I realised I had been asleep for the whole journey home. Edoardo had parked up on the kerb outside my apartment.

'Hey,' he murmured, and I turned to him. 'We're back.'

I stretched my arms out in front of me. 'Sorry, I guess it was all that fresh air and exercise that sent me into dreamland.'

'No need to apologise. I…' He paused, chewing his bottom lip.

'What's the matter?'

'I am so sorry, Laila, but while we were driving, I got an email from my boss – it popped up as a notification and I pulled over to read it. Unfortunately, something has come up and I am needed back at work, so I am afraid I can no longer be your guide for the rest of your stay. I have to pack and leave tonight for the city of Ponce down in the south. It's about a two-hour drive. That is where I will be based for the next couple of weeks. I am sorry.'

He had delivered that speech without looking at me and it made me wonder if that was the whole truth. 'There's absolutely nothing to apologise for. You have been an amazing host. It's been so lovely catching up.'

He nodded but avoided my gaze. Something had shifted since I mentioned what this whole trip had been about, who I had been with and who I was going to see next and his silence on the matter made me think he was still stewing over it.

He stepped out of the car to say goodbye at my door, but the embrace was brief. And with a wave from inside his car, he was off. I stood there alone trying to take in what had happened but I knew one thing for sure. It was time to call an end to my Puerto Rican adventure.

–

After a hot shower and a change into my cotton twinset, I took in my appearance in my bedroom mirror:

   2. Get a tan ✓

Was that it? No, there had been so much more I had achieved during my time in Puerto Rico but the way the interaction had ended with Edoardo had unsettled me. I curled up on the couch and switched on the TV. I didn't understand a word of the Spanish drama on the screen, but I didn't care. As I tried to focus, I could feel moisture at the back of my eyes building and building. The rush of emotion was so overwhelming that I couldn't hold back the sudden swell of tears that flowed down my cheeks.

And in that moment, there was only one person I wanted to call. I sent her a quick text to see if she was awake as it would be almost one in the morning, and a call came through almost immediately.

'Hey,' Jena whispered. 'Is everything OK?'

'Not really,' I managed to say through my tears. Then it all poured out: the time spent with Edoardo, the confession, the strange goodbye. The only part I left out was how we came to split up in the first place and how I had witnessed Dad's death.

At the end of my ramblings, Jena took a deep breath. 'Sounds to me like Edoardo couldn't handle the truth and it also sounds like you're experiencing DOSE withdrawal.'

'What is DOSE withdrawal?'

'You've experienced spikes in these molecules entering your system, and now they're gone. Your body has been through a lot over these last two weeks, physically and mentally, and withdrawal will now leave you drained and exhausted if the underlying causes of what is going on in your mind, how you truly feel about everything you've experienced, aren't addressed more deeply. And that's why you're craving more of a DOSE.'

'From what or whom?' I asked her.

'I can't answer that for you, Laila, because your adventure hasn't ended yet.'

Chapter 20

Through the crowds at Juan Santamaría International Airport, I stood on tiptoes trying to see if Mateo was there. It was close to midnight, but he had insisted on meeting me at the airport after my five-and-a-half-hour journey from JFK. As I had waited for my second flight of the day in the New York airport, a thought had fleetingly passed through my mind: what was Gregory doing now? It was an unexpected musing, and it didn't sit well with me. Meeting Edoardo had obviously brought all those memories to the forefront.

Ten years ago, Gregory had written to Mum and informed her of Dad's death, saying when and where the memorial service and wake would be. Mum had relayed the news to me over the phone. She hadn't offered to fly out and attend the funeral but thought it best I knew and that I had a right to make the decision for myself whether to attend. I chose not to let on that I already knew that he was dead. She had told me a 'friend' of my father's had informed her, and I knew exactly who that friend was.

I had travelled up to Saratoga Springs by bus and hovered at the back of the church for the service, staying far away from Gregory at the cemetery. No one appeared to recognise me, and no one approached me. I hadn't stayed for the wake, deciding to head back on the last bus back to Manhattan. And that's where I had left my grief.

Dad's last words to me had echoed around me for days, weeks, months: 'I did the right thing in leaving.' He had left to preserve my future and he wouldn't have wanted me to jeopardise my Master's programme. Success was what he had wanted for me, and that would be my focus, like it had always been. I had truly believed back then that ending things with Edoardo had been the right thing to do. I'd needed a level-headed plan and, once I returned to the UK, it was obvious which path I would take: the route to becoming a successful clinical scientist within the field of cardiology. Dad had died of a heart attack, and I wanted to have the knowledge and expertise to save others from such a fate.

A suitcase caught the back of my leg and broke my thoughts. Apologies outpoured from the owner, but I smiled away their concern.

Then I saw him. His back was to me, but I knew it was him. He was decked out in a dark grey T-shirt emphasising those broad shoulders, and green khaki shorts skimmed his knees. When he turned, our eyes met, and that familiar broad smile washed over his face. He ran up to me and swept me up in his arms, almost lifting me off the ground. I could feel the energy from his hold, and it was life-affirming.

'I can't believe you're here,' Mateo said, putting me back down before kissing me on both cheeks.

His hair was a lot longer than when we last met, almost like it had been when I saw him that first time in Geneva. His light beard made him more distinguished, his green eyes with the subtle brown and orange flecks – that I had instantly noticed when we bumped into each other in Geneva – even more striking.

'I can't believe I'm here either,' I said as he dropped his hold. 'But honestly, you didn't have to come all this way.'

He waved away my words. 'It's no problem. I got us a couple of rooms for the night at a local homestay. A freshly cooked meal and board for next to nothing.'

'At this time of night?'

'At a guess, I would say you haven't eaten well on the flight, and they know we are arriving late.' He grabbed hold of my suitcase and turned in the direction of the exit. 'Then tomorrow we can set off early for the drive to the conservation centre in Tortuguero, where I am based.'

'That sounds amazing, but are you sure I am allowed to come and stay?'

'Of course, I OK'ed it with my manager. There are many activities we can involve you in and I have also taken a couple of days off too during your stay. You can relax on the beach when I am busy or I can arrange a tour for you, whatever you feel comfortable with, whatever makes you happy.'

I smiled at his thoughtfulness before becoming awash with nostalgia for our time at NYU: early morning lectures with notes passed in secret between us, late-night study sessions at the Bobst Library until we got kicked out. His accent was as soothing as I remembered, too. The soft inflections, those gentle, rolling Rs.

As we reached his car, he loaded my things in the backseat before taking my hands in his and squeezing. 'It is so good to see you, Laila. We have so much to catch up on.'

'We do.' His enthusiasm was infectious and, in that moment, I vowed to put the past two weeks behind me. There was no bad blood between me and Mateo, no unrequited anything. We had been close friends who merely drifted apart with ten years of life to catch up on. Besides, that hug that had sat uneasy with me from ten years ago hadn't meant anything to him, so there was no need to bring up what happened back then.

The homestay was only a few minutes' drive from the airport. In that time, I glossed over my last two weeks, saying a conference had taken me to California and that I had a friend staying in Puerto Rico. Mateo didn't press me to say who that friend was, and our conversation moved on quickly to the week ahead. As our excited chatter filled the Jeep, I relaxed more and more.

We dined with several other travellers, a couple of whom had been on my flight, and feasted on *casado*, a traditional Costa Rican dish of rice, beans, tortillas, fried *plátanos maduros* and pork chops. It was all washed down with a tropical juice drink and followed by a pudding of *arroz con leche*. Spanish flowed between the hostess and Mateo and a couple of the other diners. There was an ease about him, I noticed, as he moved around the room, as if this was a second family to him. He had told me in the car that he had been here a few times on his days off when he had time to explore more of the country, and he had spent some nights too when he had been too tired to make the drive back to the conservation centre or wanted to let loose over a couple of beers.

I crashed as soon as my head hit the pillow and woke up the next morning refreshed. After another home-cooked meal – a breakfast of *gallo pinto* (beans and rice) – we headed off.

'That was fun,' I said to Mateo as we drove out of San José.

'I'm glad you think so. It's a little… rustic here. Probably not what you are used to.'

'Hey.' I nudged him in the arm, and he turned to me with a cheeky smile. 'I like rustic.'

'That's a good thing because things are going to get very basic at the centre. I probably also should have said, we have no Wi-Fi there either. Your 3G will be intermittent too depending on the weather, so now is the time to send some messages to your loved ones.'

At the last two words, he sent me a brief but searching look. Was that a subtle way of finding out if I was involved with anyone? What a silly thought. Why would he even care?

I pulled out my phone and tapped out a message to Jena and Samira, saying it was quite possible I was going off-grid for a few days, and one to Mum reassuring her that everything was fine.

'What brought you out here, Mateo?' I asked, tucking my phone into my rucksack before taking in the view of low-lying flat-roofed houses that lined the freeway. There were mountains in the distance, and the terrain was like no other place I had ever visited.

His fingers tightened around the wheel. 'My mamá passed away three years ago now.'

'Oh, Mateo, I am so sorry.' I touched his arm, and he removed one of his hands from the wheel and held it over mine, squeezing it gently. 'I knew she was unwell, and that's why you missed out on all the graduation ceremonies. I am truly sorry.'

'Thank you,' he said. 'In many ways it was a relief. It had been a long, very hard journey for her, from diagnosis ten years ago to all the treatment she endured. At the end, she knew there was little time left and refused to take on any more chemotherapy if only to prolong her life for a few months. When I left NYU, I went straight home to care for her, worked at a local laboratory in Madrid as a research scientist and spent my twenties doing that.'

'Did you enjoy it?'

'Yes and no. It was a means to keep being able to live with her and care for her, but I did not have the same passion for it that I had once hoped to find in my career. The first thing I wanted to do when she passed was travel. I went backpacking in Asia for many months, and I got involved with some local eco projects, preserving natural habitats, that kind of thing. I began a part-time marine biology Master's in Madrid after that and it sparked something in me.'

'I remember when we first met, you said you loved biology.'

'You remember?'

'Of course I remember. I was petrified of that Ferris wheel, and you instantly calmed me by getting me to balance equations so I wouldn't freak out and have a melt-down in that pod. That feels like a lifetime ago now. We were so young.'

'We're still young.' He threw me a smile. 'We have our whole lives ahead of us. I might not know where I will be this time next year, but I am excited by the possibilities.'

I stared out the window and wondered if I felt the same way. Something had stalled in my life. The unease about the investigation had unsettled me. Everything had been on course until it all appeared to melt away. And travel. There had been none until now, and I couldn't deny that the places I had seen over the last two weeks had cracked my world wide open again, and I wasn't sure how I would feel about going back to London, to my old routine.

'Is something troubling you, Laila? Are you not excited by your chosen path?'

His' question caught me off guard. I hadn't spoken much about my work to Austin except for that first night we had dinner and I realised now that Edoardo and I had been stuck in the past and he hadn't probed me about my life in England.

'I think I've reached an impasse. I messed up at work and am under investigation.' I puffed out my cheeks. It felt good to say those words out loud. Jena and Samira had been naturally supportive but their 'it will all work out' comments had left me feeling a little open to the uncertainty of it all. How on earth was it supposed to work out? It was completely out of my control. Best case scenario, I would keep my job but a black mark would forever be associated with my name and I wasn't sure I could live with that.

When Mateo turned to me there was nothing but sympathy etched into his face. 'I'm sorry to hear that. What happened?'

I went through an account of the lead-up to the incident, Mum's accident, taking on the responsibilities of a second team, the numbers that I had extrapolated incorrectly, the research team I had hoped to be a part of that was no more and the enforced leave I was told to take. I then mentioned that my friends had been worried, and that the conference in California seemed like a good opportunity to have some time off.

'Hmm. Sounds to me like you have been taken advantage of,' Mateo concluded. 'Your friends are right. This is a long overdue break, one that is very important for your mental health. Mine suffered when I cared for Mamá.'

My heart broke for him. 'I can imagine. It must have been so hard for you to be a carer and try and have a life for yourself outside of those commitments.'

'We couldn't afford a hospice, and I don't have a large family or siblings, so the responsibility fell to me. Papá lives in the south of Spain with his new family, not that he would have come to help me. But I wouldn't have changed those years I was with her for the world. And although I miss her terribly, I have no regrets. I spent that time with her not only out of duty but because she was my friend too; she gave me life, her support, and her love. Her absence still makes me cry inconsolably on occasion, but time is a great healer.'

I let his words breathe. They were beautiful and touching. I remembered the coffees we shared where we opened up about our absent fathers and mothers who hadn't remarried or found much purpose after their divorces, plus the similarities in our upbringings as only children.

'Do you like living with your mother?' he asked.

'I feel awful saying this because yours is gone, but... no, I don't. It feels suffocating at times. The house is like a noose around my neck, too. We could sell it, and it would be possible to afford something much cheaper, and then, maybe, I could do something different with my life.' I paused and sucked in a breath. 'Wow, I have no idea where that came from.'

'Maybe from your gut. Both of us have no siblings, and we feel this added pressure to be there for our parents.'

'That's true. Growing up, I always felt like I wasn't enough, and at times I resented the fact that my parents didn't have any more children, someone else for me to share the agony of the fallout from the family breaking up.'

'I used to feel the same. Like the affair my dad had was my fault. If I had been a better-behaved kid, maybe there would've been less of a strain on their marriage.'

'That's a heavy burden to carry. Do you still believe this?'

He shook his head. 'I will never understand my father's reasoning for bringing my mother so much pain, and although I felt acutely this need to be the man of the house and support her, I know I let resentment build that it became my responsibility and I wasn't allowed the opportunity to put myself first.'

'You could have still put yourself first.'

'I know but this would have brought my mother great sadness, a pain she would not have deserved. What is easier to bear, guilt or resentment?'

With a heavy sigh, I dropped my head back against the headrest. 'I don't know. The weird thing is, I thought it has always been my duty to care for and support my mother, but I don't think she's missing me at all since I left for California. I sometimes wonder whether she is waiting for me to figure my life out and tell her that I am going to do something very different, then maybe it would springboard her into action, force her to sell the house. I don't think she has ever recovered from Dad leaving her and, also…' I paused again because this was something I had not told anyone before. 'She doesn't know about what happened in New York.'

Mateo turned to me, a look of surprise on his face.

'You're the only one I ever told,' I said. 'Not about my father dying, obviously, but you're the only one who knows *how* he died, the fact that I was on my way to see him that afternoon and the revelation that he was married to a man.'

'You haven't discussed any of that with your mother?'

A bitter laugh escaped me. 'When I returned in the summer, she merely said she was sorry for my loss and that was that, and I lied and told her I hadn't attended his funeral.'

'That is such a heavy burden to carry, for both of you. If there is anything that my mother's death has taught me, it is that – and I know it sounds like a cliché – our time on this earth can be brief, too brief to have this unspoken tension between you both.'

Unspoken tension. Was that what it was? Did we both have walls built up around us? Is that why I always felt she preferred the company of Samira and Jena over me, because when she looked at me all she was reminded of was Dad and all the pain he had caused her?

'You're right,' I said finally. 'I need to talk to her, but I'm not even sure where to begin. I don't think I have properly grieved at all. When I saw that man at the hospital, Dad's husband, I suddenly felt like I was being choked, that the last few years of my life were a lie and that he was the reason. I couldn't face him.'

'Could you now? Has enough time passed?'

Mateo met my eyes for a moment, and something shifted. A feeling that perhaps I was now strong enough to face the past and begin to fully heal. 'I think so. But I haven't forgiven myself yet.'

'For what?'

'For…' I clenched my hands in my lap, focusing on the feeling of my nails digging into my skin. 'For not saving him.'

'But what could you have done?'

I closed my eyes for a beat and saw the scene in my mind. 'I couldn't do anything. I couldn't save him. I knew first aid, how to administer CPR, but I froze. He died because of me.' Those last few words escaped my mouth in a whisper and my throat tightened.

The first tear escaped and rolled down my check, the trembling in my fingers increasing as they dug deeper into my flesh.

Mateo suddenly pulled off the freeway and came to a stop outside some stores in the centre of a town – what town I had no clue. In an instant, he had opened his door and come round to my side of the car. I stepped out and stumbled into his arms.

Chapter 21

'I'm sorry,' I whispered against his neck, my tears moistening his skin there.

'Never apologise,' he said, his words soft by my ear.

He squeezed me tighter and I let his hold ease the pain.

The memory of that last hug ten years ago suddenly washed over me, and I pulled back with a jolt. 'I… agh.' I held my head in my hands. 'God, I don't know what's wrong with me.'

He stroked my arms, the movement soothing. When I finally looked up into his eyes, all I could see was empathy lying behind those green irises. 'I think I was suddenly triggered, by your hug. It took me back to that day, the guilt I felt…'

'You weren't responsible for your father's death.'

'Not just that.' I pinched my lips and nervously chewed the inside of my mouth.

'When Edoardo saw us?'

I nodded.

'I have felt bad about that day for so long too. It was my fault; I shouldn't have said those things to him. I was trying to be a good friend. You were in agony, but he was your boyfriend, and I should have respected those boundaries. And I understood why you shut me out after that. It saddened my heart so much when things could not go back to the way they were. Our friendship meant so much to me and I overstepped the mark. I too felt guilty for the way I behaved.'

I swiped at my tear-stained face, not wanting to confess that I had also felt guilty because I had loved that hold – that if Edoardo hadn't appeared, I had wanted him to lean down and kiss me, to kiss away the pain.

'You have nothing to feel guilty about, Mateo. I wasn't in a good headspace back then. God, what must you think?' I said, sniffing, keen to drag us away from the past. 'You've given up your time off to pick me up and I'm a mess.'

'Laila, I don't expect you to be anything. You're obviously still in a lot of pain, haven't had the chance to properly heal. Grieving for a lost one or a lost relationship can hit us at different times, but holding back that pain for too long can mean we never properly move on with our lives.'

I nodded. 'You're right. I think I have been running from that for a long time. Seeing you and' – I was about to say Edoardo's name but held back – 'transiting through NYC so many times over the last two weeks, it's brought it all up to the surface.'

'I can only imagine.'

'Thanks, Mateo. For being such a good friend. I've missed you.'

'I've missed you, too.' His eyes dipped and he shifted back a little. 'I know what we need.'

'What?'

'Coffee, the best coffee imaginable. It's about another half hour away.'

We hopped back in the Jeep and a lightness filled the car this time. Mateo switched on the radio and a low hum of salsa music formed a backing track as he became my private guide, the distant Braulio Carrillo National Park looming in the distance. He recounted tales of days off exploring the region and meeting the locals. There had been a rotation of volunteers at the conservation centre and lifelong friends made. It sounded like an invaluable experience and I was excited at the prospect of being a part of his world for a short while.

On a random dirt track, Mateo pulled over and stepped out of the car, telling me to wait a moment. He made his way into a nondescript building with a green tiled roof and, a few minutes later, came out cradling two plastic cups and a couple of paper bags.

I thanked him as he gave me one of each and I poked a straw into the iced drink before taking a sip. An explosion of flavours hit the roof of my mouth – sweet notes of honey and vanilla in the coffee. 'Mmm,' I murmured.

'It's good, right?'

'I think it's the best coffee I have ever tasted.'

'Locally sourced and roasted beans and a special syrup from a plant that is prevalent in this region.'

I settled back in the Jeep and listened to Mateo tell me story after story of the region, about the people he had befriended, how the work he was doing helped the local economy by drawing in tourism, the old ways of hunting the turtles and selling the eggs all but eradicated thanks to holidaymakers coming from all over the world to witness the important work Mateo and his team were doing.

As I listened to Mateo talk, I was in coffee and pastry heaven – the flaky buttery treat delighting my tongue with its sweetness followed by a hit of bitter dark chocolate every couple of mouthfuls. It was a heady feeling and I wondered whether it was because I felt at ease after sharing things that had been so deeply buried in my heart.

Jena would no doubt claim that I was getting a dopamine hit from the tyramine in the chocolate, which was the precursor to dopamine. I remembered it clearly from one of her slides.

We went off-road about ten minutes before we hit our destination. The Tortuguero National Park began to envelop us, and I held on to the bar on the inside of my door to keep myself steady as the road turned into a dirt track and we pulled up at the camp.

The team at the base welcomed me with open arms, and Mateo gave me a tour of the conservation centre, the library adjoining it and the dining hall where all the meals were served. Those places were all on one level of the wooden structure. The sleeping quarters were a floor above along with shower rooms and toilets. Mateo put my things in one of the bedrooms that had two sets of bunk beds, giving me the choice of lower or top bunk. The French pair who were also sharing the room would be leaving in a couple of days and a new rotation of volunteers would be with them at the end of the week. He apologised that he couldn't get me a bed in the women-only dorm room, but I told him it didn't matter.

Up another flight of stairs was an open roof with an incredible view of the national park down below and the Caribbean Sea on the other side. Mateo said he would also take me to the observation tower, which was another wooden structure deep in the national park with the most incredible views ever, he claimed.

As I took in my surroundings, I found it hard to believe there could be anything more beautiful than this. The squawk of birds and tree frogs mixed in with the chatter of tree monkeys and the continuous buzz of an orchestra of different insects. The sounds of the forest below throbbed with the heat that was all-encompassing at this height.

After lunch, I was put straight to work with Mateo as we went out on a hike to investigate some possible leather-back turtle track sightings. We also investigated a previous nest site to see whether a hatching had been successful or not. I helped Mateo pull aside sand to enable us to dig deep where the markings had been made. There was nervous energy amongst the group, which turned to relief when a collection of empty shells was found meaning that the eggs had hatched successfully.

Suddenly, there was a rush of excitement when Mateo whooped with delight. Having made a deeper hole with my help, he had discovered one baby turtle. As he held it in his hands, my heart melted. It was tiny. One of the other volunteers jotted down some notes and more measurements before we all followed Mateo closer to the water, where he released it. Slowly and along a haphazard path, the creature finally reached the sea, and everyone cheered, the sheer joy and giddiness of the moment contagious and I was reminded of the checklist once more.

    9. Save a turtle ✔

We headed back to camp early evening, and after dinner and a refreshing shower, I came out of the bathroom to find Mateo leaning on the balcony to our lodgings freshly showered too, his hair damp, wearing a pale-blue polo shirt and black sports shorts.

Decked out in one of my floral sundresses, my skin was glowing – a combination of a fresh tan and healthy living.

It also appeared to be fresh meat to the mosquitos around us, so I was doused in Deet spray. Thankfully, there were nets surrounding the frame of the bunk beds so I hoped that meant I wouldn't be feasted on during the night.

'Fancy a trip into town for a drink?' Mateo asked.

Since leaving the Jeep this morning, we hadn't had a second to ourselves and the thought of the rest of the night being the two of us appealed to me. 'I'd love that. Let me put away my things.'

Inside our bedroom, I stashed my sand-encrusted clothes into my laundry bag and checked out my sleeping quarters. I had opted for the bottom bunk and Mateo had kindly moved his things up to the top one. Picking up my phone, I noticed I had a single bar of 3G and checked my messages. The girls had sent back texts, Samira's one saying:

> Enjoy

She'd added the winking emoji. I replied with a snap of my sleeping quarters. Sitting down on my bed, I wrote the message:

> Think the chance of anything naughty going on are slim to zero considering there are four of us in the room.

Samira was online and replied:

Ooh, orgy! Fun!

At that I sent back a laughing emoji.

Something was peeking out from my pillow, and I reached beneath the net to pull it out. It was a navy T-shirt with the turtle conservation's logo on it. Involuntarily I sniffed the material, and memories stirred from long ago. That party, the Christmas party. The scent of Mateo's T-shirt reminded me of how he had wrapped up my body in his coat after I had chucked up my guts. He had appeared out of nowhere and saved me from the humiliation of going back inside with a puke-smeared face. I tucked the T-shirt under the pillow of the bunk above and closed the door behind me.

Mateo and I walked into town, the street lit up with string lights covering roofs of shops and restaurants. We headed to a bar in the centre as Mateo told me tales of nights out with the other volunteers.

Outdoor tables were full of tourists and locals; laughter and merriment floated into the humid night that was thrumming to a distant beat of piped music coming from a speaker attached to the tin-clad roof of our bar. Over a couple of rum cocktails, we reminisced about the early days of our Master's programme.

'I was thinking back to that Christmas party earlier,' I said, popping a few nuts into my mouth from a bowl that had been served with our drinks. 'The one at the end of our first semester. Do you remember it?'

He nodded. 'It was a wild one.' With an eyebrow quirked, he looked at me meaningfully.

I kicked his leg under the table. 'Hey, I was letting loose and I have my best friend Samira solely to blame for how the evening panned out.'

'All I remember was having to run halfway across town so I wouldn't miss my flight back to Madrid.'

'Then why did you come to the party so late?'

He stretched out his fingers before clutching his drink. 'I seem to remember I had been trying to finish an assignment that had taken me forever and couldn't leave until I had said goodbye to you.'

'I thought we had already done that earlier on in the day when I introduced you to my friends at the skating rink.'

'I wanted you to have that gift.' He ran his fingers up and down his tumbler before draining it and signalling to the barman for another round.

'I had completely forgotten about that. I don't think I ever thanked you because I had no idea why you had given me a bunch of colourful balls and little sticks. Was it some kind of game?'

'They were loose?'

'Yes.'

'Oh.' Sudden sadness pulled the corners of his lips down.

'Why, were they meant to signify something?'

He dipped his eyes, stroking his hands over his legs. 'It was meant to be the molecular formation for glucose.'

I looked at him quizzically.

'The first equation you balanced when we were on the Ferris wheel had glucose in it. I had a molecule set in my room and I made it for you.'

As realisation dawned on me that he had given me something so special and thoughtful, my cheeks flushed deeply. 'Oh, Mateo. I'm so sorry. It must have got crushed in the time between you giving it to me and me opening it. It was all broken apart when I unwrapped it. I think I was too embarrassed to bring it up in the New Year because I didn't know what they were.'

'That's OK.' He waved away my words with an awkward laugh. 'I was acting like a lovesick teen back then. When you didn't bring it up after, I figured I had overstepped the mark.'

My glass hovered by my mouth.

What did he say?

But before I could ask him what he meant, he had turned towards the barman who had brought our drinks. Draining my current one, I accepted the next glass and began to take long sips, wondering how to address his revelation.

The outdoor space suddenly filled with the sound of live music. A gentleman had sat down on a stool and was strumming a guitar, before he began humming the sweetest melody. Then a man with maracas appeared followed by a female singer decked out in a flamboyant colourful dress lined with beads.

A few couples got up to dance in the dusty area in front of the band.

That's when Mateo turned back to me. 'Do you want to join them?'

I observed the synchronised movements of the dancers and shook my head. 'I have no clue how to move like that, and I haven't nearly drunk enough to try.'

Mateo laughed and stood up. 'Oh, come on. It's salsa, there's nothing to it. Let me be the lead.'

It wasn't listed on the Love Intervention plan, but it looked fun judging by the broad smiles on people's faces and the laughter that floated into the night sky.

Mateo extended his hand to me across the table and one look into those eyes made me think I couldn't say no. I drained my drink and wiped my mouth with the napkin before grabbing his hand. We weaved into the centre and Mateo turned to me.

'OK,' he said. 'First, have both feet together.'

I looked nervously at those around me seemingly floating across the space.

'Hey, Laila, eyes on me.'

And in that moment, I was back on the Ferris wheel, staring into Mateo's eyes. They were as safe and reassuring as they had been on that ride and enabled me to silence the voice in my head telling me I would look stupid if I tried to dance.

I nodded, focusing solely on him and his instructions: left foot forward, tap the right and bring the left foot back. Right foot back, tap the left and bring the right back to position. In no time at all I was following those basic steps over and over again.

He clutched my hands tightly in the small space between our bodies as we moved back and forth before teaching me to turn and spin. Before I knew it, I was dancing salsa, and when I stopped counting in my head, I could let my body feel the music and the rhythm, my hips swaying.

I closed my eyes and was back at that party at NYU. The 'lovesick teen', Mateo had called himself. Had he been in love with me? Could that evening have ended in *three* very different ways with *three* different guys?

When I opened my eyes, I was met with Mateo's, and I ended up missing a step and falling into him.

He laughed. 'You OK?' he whispered by my ear.

I nodded. But when Mateo's hands dropped mine and landed on my hips, my breath caught in the back of my throat. The three rum cocktails were beginning to lower my defences and I placed my hands around his neck. In my wedge sandals, I was as tall as him and our bodies nestled into each other as if they were meant to be locked in this fashion.

Something stirred inside me, from the heat of his touch to the feeling of letting go of my inhibitions. My feet found their rhythm then, my head beside his, turning so my nose brushed the skin of his neck. As I inhaled his scent, my fingers threaded through his hair and gently tugged it. A moan sounded from his mouth that was close to my ear before he whispered, '*Cariño* Laila.' It was like a volcano had erupted in my chest and his words were molten lava.

The music stopped abruptly, and the space was filled with applause. We broke our hold, and I stepped back, suddenly feeling a rush of something in my stomach up to my throat.

Oh no, I inwardly moaned. Not again.

Chapter 22

Something drew me away from my slumber. Someone was calling my name. My eyes blinked open, wincing at the daylight streaming through the windows and then again as the memories of last night's antics flooded my mind. Mateo was leaning on the bed frame and I covered my eyes with my hands – acute embarrassment heating my face.

'Don't look at me,' I said.

'Laila, it's fine. Being here is an adjustment and I think it was all too much: the journey, the work and the drinking. I should've known better. How are you feeling now?'

'Whatever that concoction you gave me last night to settle my stomach has helped. The nausea has lifted.'

'Would you like to have a day off? You can rest around the centre while I work.'

'Absolutely not,' I said, lifting my head from my pillow and thankfully not feeling any thud in my temples. 'As long as I go slow, I should be fine. What's the plan?'

My words were met with yet another reassuring smile and details of how the day would pan out followed. I was glad we had moved on from discussing last night. I might have been overwhelmed by the effects of the journey and the alcohol, but I hadn't been so blinded by these things to know that my feelings towards Mateo were changing

– that I had felt something as he whispered those words in my ear and held me tight. There was an attraction that had perhaps been suppressed since that day he offered to drive me to Saratoga Springs and had hugged me tight, only I had never allowed myself to process that moment properly.

The day slipped by in a flurry of activity: helping with tourist visits, searching for turtle tracks, and marking new sightings. We had lunch with the rest of the team, and I attended a seminar in the afternoon about projects going forward. I knew Mateo was getting close to the end of his internship and wondered what he planned to do next.

We decided upon an early night so we were somewhat rested ahead of our patrol at four in the morning. Mateo took advantage of our lack of roommates and moved his stuff to the bottom bed of the other set of bunks, claiming the top one of mine had a hard mattress.

Mateo turned the light off and said goodnight. The sound of the jungle outside the window echoed around the small, wooden slatted room. The only breeze was from the fan that was rotating between the beds. Every time it moved away from my direction, I was aware of perspiration building beneath my vest top. And although I had bathed in Deet spray repeatedly, I also had a couple of bites on my legs. It was taking all my resolve not to scratch the hell out of them. Despite these uncomfortable feelings, my mind was at peace. I hadn't given much thought to what was awaiting me back home since I arrived in Costa Rica, and it made me wonder if the dopamine hit I was getting from shadowing Mateo's work was less spiked in nature and more of a constant high. I could see the effect of my help more obviously here: the smiles of tourists' faces when they saw one of the large leatherbacks making its way across the sand, safe in the knowledge that all the money they were spending on tours and souvenirs was contributing to the town's economy, enabling the local school to have some much-needed renovations after storm damage a few months ago.

I opened my eyes, the only visible light from the moon, a slice of it pouring through an opening in the curtains.

'I love what you do.' I spoke into the stillness, wondering if he was still awake.

I heard a shuffling sound and his bed creaked. 'It's amazing, isn't it?'

'It makes me wonder…'

'What?'

'If what I'm doing is what I want to keep doing for the rest of my life.'

'It's never too late to retrain.'

'But it's taken me ten years to get where I am. Wouldn't I be throwing that all away?'

'Not necessarily. A lot of your skills will be transferable, I assume, depending on what you want to try.'

'Hmm,' I mused.

'It also depends on what your motivation is,' he continued.

'All I have ever wanted to do is help save lives in some form or another – whether that was directly treating patients or indirectly working on the creation of vaccines and medicines. But I had never even thought of cardiology being my field until…' I paused as the rush of what happened that day filled my mind once more.

'Until what?' Mateo asked.

'Until that day – the day Dad died. I couldn't help him.'

'But you didn't know what he had been suffering prior to that, did you?'

'No, I didn't. But I truly believed for so long that there should have been something I could have done. I knew it was an irrational thought, but it made me question how many heart attacks could be prevented, how many lives could be saved if we had the chance to test more, look for early signs of heart disease. Our healthcare system back in the UK is pretty broken and reactive and I get so frustrated with work a lot of the time – all the hoops I have to jump through and the bureaucracy. And all it took was one error, and it could be whisked away from me anyway, with no other career possibilities to fall back on or pursue.'

'No wonder you were wrung out. That sounds like a very stressful working environment.'

'But being here, watching you work… it made me think… that maybe I don't want the life I have anymore.'

'I think being in nature is the best form of therapy. It was my escape coming here, without question. It's healing. It's helped me through my grief and there's a peace I find even in the most chaotic of moments, like when we are taking a large, excited tourist group out for a visit. I have the ability to block out all the noise once I hear the rush of the ocean, feel the sand under my toes.'

The rush of water. This had been a prevalent theme during my trip, and he was right, it *was* healing.

I wasn't sure at what point we fell asleep, who said the last word or who asked the last question, but peacefully I drifted off.

–

The lamp flicking on roused me, and Mateo's face came into view through my bleary eyes.

'Sorry to wake you so abruptly, but it's time to get ready for the patrol. And I got word that there's an incoming storm so it will be all hands on deck. You'll need waterproofs and I'll give you a special head lamp to wear over your cap.'

'OK,' I said, and a renewed strength pulled me out from the bed. Mateo put on his shorts and a T-shirt and left the room to give me some privacy.

There was a light breakfast waiting for me in the dining hall and we ate with the leader of the group, who told us that the storm was getting stronger and that it could reach hurricane status by late morning. Despite those warnings, he said our work was crucial as he suspected that one of the tagged leatherbacks was due to lay her eggs over the next couple of days and would need all the help she could get if she decided tonight was the night to give birth.

A touch on my hand startled me. Mateo was holding it and squeezed my fingers before leaning in. 'You don't have to do this with us. You can stay here safely at the camp.'

I shook my head, the adrenaline beginning to pump through my system. 'I want to do it. I want to be with you.'

As soon as the words were out of my mouth, I paused, biting my bottom lip, thinking back to how our salsa night could have ended. His thumb stroked my knuckles and the warmth from his touch eased any traces of anxiety within. All I felt was brave and capable. Not that I had ever needed anyone to make me feel this way but in this environment, with Mother Nature about to unleash her fury, I was grateful to have the reassuring touch from Mateo.

We made our way through the camp and down towards the beach. The ocean was awash with white froth, spewing angrily against the shore and the sky above peri-odically lit up with a purple flash of lightning. Rain began to fall softly before building in intensity and we knew it would be a race against time to spot any tracks before they were washed away. The team split up to cover a wider stretch of beach, but I stayed close to Mateo as I wasn't officially employed to be undertaking such tasks and he was the most senior of our group.

The head lamps and handheld torches danced in the moonlight like fireflies. This task would obviously be easier to do in daylight, but Mateo had explained that the female turtles preferred to come out in the darkness to lay their eggs. There had been a slight dip in the number recorded over the last few months so ensuring the safety of any possible birthing was crucial.

Before long, my legs were soaked, feet squelching in the wet sand and a slight chill began to cover my body beneath my thin waterproof. Then my torch settled upon a dip in the sand. Upon closer inspection, I wondered if it could be something, but the surrounding area didn't have any similar markings.

I called out to Mateo, and he came over and confirmed that it was a print. His excitable tone was infectious, and he kneeled to get a closer look before turning back towards the vegetation. His torch settled upon something further away from where we were, and it highlighted a more pronounced trail. He signalled to the rest of the team, and I became an observer to their crucial work. There, hidden beneath some leaves and debris deep in the undergrowth, was a leatherback. Mateo and another volunteer slipped on blue surgical gloves and pushed the sand away to create a trench while others checked the tag on her ear and recorded various important markings.

Then through a gap between Mateo and his colleague, I saw a glimpse of white. Mateo's fingers were softly caressing each cluster of eggs as they came out of the turtle and clicking on a counter repeatedly.

A few minutes later, he announced that there had been one hundred and sixteen eggs laid. Logbooks flapped in the escalating wind as the team raced to record everything. They helped bury the eggs as deep as they could, forming a human barrier so the turtle could make her way back into the sea. Rounds of high fives and hugs erupted between the team members but when Mateo faced me, he lifted me up in the air and spun me around with a whoop. I laughed as I tipped my head backwards and rain fell on my face.

I was exhilarated and clearly blissed out on dopamine but, more, from his hold, too. There was no denying it anymore. No matter how many times in the past I had tried to diminish its impact, it was clear that I had always felt something from Mateo's hold – from the touch on my hand to calm my panic attack on the Ferris wheel in Switzerland to the embrace he cocooned me in when Dad died.

As he put me back on the ground, I didn't relinquish my hold on his neck. His lips parted as his arms tightened around my waist, his breathing ragged, matching the rhythm of mine. With a surge of oxytocin reaching new heights, I leaned in and brushed my lips over his. The heat that rippled through our mouths electrified me and the kiss deepened, his hands clutching the sides of my face, tongues exploring.

A crack of thunder startled us and we pulled back. Mateo grabbed my hand as we made it back to camp, where I was drafted into pinning boards to the windows and securing equipment. The team leader then suggested taking some supplies into our rooms and sheltering from the storm, handing us walkie talkies for communication. All the while, I stole glances at Mateo, wondering what he was thinking and whether that kiss was nothing more than us getting carried away with the excitement over the turtle discovery.

Once inside our room, I peeled off my sopping wet jacket and took off my muddy boots and socks. My T-shirt was wet in places and my shorts and knickers were sodden too.

'Here,' Mateo said, handing me a towel in the darkness. He moved away and then I heard a clicking sound. 'The power is out.'

'I'm going to struggle to find some clothes,' I said.

'I know where my things are. Let me get you something clean and dry to wear.'

I began to shiver.

'You're cold,' he said.

'How did you know?'

'I can hear your teeth chattering.'

'I don't know why, though, it's a tropical storm not a winter one.'

'The temperature has definitely dropped. It's also probably the adrenaline still pumping its way through your system from the patrol. Not to be overly dramatic,' he added with that soothing accent of his. 'But I think we made it back in time before the full impact.'

'That's reassuring,' I said with a trace of humour in my tone.

Something soft touched my fingers and I realised Mateo was handing me something.

'I can't see anything,' he said, which I took to mean he wouldn't be able to see me get changed.

Resting the clothes between my knees, I peeled off my wet vest top and unhooked my bra. I dried my skin with the towel before slipping on Mateo's T-shirt. Taking off my shorts and knickers, I slipped on a pair of his boxer shorts.

A loud bang reverberated outside the room and I leaped forward, straight into Mateo, his naked chest the first thing my fingers touched.

'Hey, it's OK, you're safe.' His arms encircled me, and my body folded into his. 'I won't let anything bad happen to you,' he whispered into my damp hair.

How could he know this? We were in a wooden lodge, exposed to the strength of a raging storm with trees all around ready to be felled by its power. Mateo had showed me parts of downtown yesterday that had buildings with their roofs ripped apart from the last storm that had hit a few months ago.

Another flash of lightning and he held me closer. I counted the seconds in my head.

Ten seconds.

Thunder followed and the embrace tightened.

Another flash.

Six seconds.

Thunder rumbled once more and the wooden boards groaned.

Another flash.

Four seconds.

I had reached it.

7. Have a hug lasting longer than 20 seconds ✔

It was pure ecstasy being here in his arms – a feeling of belonging, safety and desire. The next gap was longer and I prayed that meant the storm was passing over.

'Can you lie with me?' I whispered into his chest. 'I'm a little scared.'

'Of course,' he said with no hesitation.

I felt around until my fingers grazed over the netting. Lifting it up, I climbed into bed and Mateo followed behind. I lay with my back against his body and his hand held on to my shoulder, the heat emanating from that hold instantly soothing.

We lay like that for seconds, minutes, his breathing calm and steady, lulling me into a relaxed state despite the rattling of the windowpanes.

A flashback to that kiss on the beach drifted across my mind. I could still feel that tingling of his lips on mine but also something carnal, a need aching to be met. But this was Mateo. My friend. And I was getting used to having that friendship in my life again and knew that if anything happened between us, it would change everything again. And what if I had misread any signals? What if that kiss was nothing more than a reaction to the heightened moment? He had called himself lovesick that night we salsa danced. Past tense.

What is he now?

But I was here for fun and adventure, right? Nothing more. That had been the plan. I still believed love was a complication that I didn't have time for. And as lovely as the nostalgic feelings of his friendship were stirring inside me, I could risk it again for something more, couldn't I? I had two best friends back home after all. They were enough.

He shifted in the bed, and I found myself pushing back into him, immediately feeling his hardness pressed against me.

I wanted to shut down the rational part of my brain – the part that said this was a bad idea. Mateo didn't deserve to be a pawn in my Love Intervention.

Let me live my life without judgement, I inwardly screamed as the idea of wanting much more with Mateo regardless of the consequences began to take flight.

Turning in his hold, I nestled myself against his chest, and his arm wrapped around me, the hold stronger, more assured.

The boards rattled harder against the windowpane, and the sound of the rain became thunderous. But I felt no fear now that I was here, lying in Mateo's arms.

With no vision, I became acutely aware of every other sense. His scent was a mixture of his deodorant and a saltiness probably from our trip to the beach. Then there was his touch on certain parts of me: my feet, my knees as legs began to shift and overlap and now my hair. He had moved his hand from my waist and was stroking my wet locks. My arms were crushed between us and the hairs on his chest tickled my fingertips, my lips achingly close to his skin.

'When I'm in your arms, nothing else matters.' At my words his hold tightened and then he laid a gentle kiss on my forehead. I melted in his embrace. 'When I'm here, I can forget the outside world. It's an escape from having to deal with anything, like it was that day, the day my dad died. I didn't want you to let go that day. I wanted to be in your arms... forever.'

It felt like the whole world paused as my words settled between us, and I waited for Mateo's response.

The next words he spoke were in Spanish. A part of me ached to know what he was saying, but a part of me didn't want to have to think, to have to process them. But now I was a hundred per cent sure I wanted him.

I let my lips brush his skin softly and a moan emanated from his mouth. My fingers roamed over his chest and down to his stomach, my left hand sliding across his hip to pull that part of him tighter against me.

Then my lips settled on his arm and moved up along his bicep to his shoulder where I kissed him. His fingers pressed into my back before brushing down the fabric of his T-shirt and finding the hem. As he slid his fingers underneath, it ruched at the back and a trail of sparklers lit on my skin as he moved his hand up and down my spine.

I threaded my fingers through his hair, gently tugging at it and his head tipped backwards so my lips had access to the underneath of his jaw and his neck. The kisses began slowly before becoming more feverish as I tasted his skin.

Mateo's breath became more laboured as our limbs entwined, generating a delicious friction. His fingers trailed along my front and up inside the T-shirt, my back arching as he touched my nipples. Light caresses in soft circles brought sighs from lips until a gentle pinch made me moan heavily with desire.

Then his mouth found my cheek until his voice whispered words in Spanish again by my ear.

'Yes,' I panted, 'yes, yes.' Though I had no clue what I was agreeing to. I knew I trusted him and that my body had never felt so alive.

Was it because we were in pitch darkness that we were allowing ourselves to feel this free, unbound by any questioning about whether this was the right thing to do or not? There was one main thing on the line here, the one thing that had prevented anything from happening in the past – our friendship.

But I didn't want to think about repercussions or the fact that I had been in someone else's bed only ten days ago or thought about rekindling an old relationship barely seventy-two hours ago; I wanted to think about nothing else apart from the need for him to be inside me, for him to make love to me.

I reached into the back of his boxers and squeezed his bottom, kneading his flesh, and in return, he tugged at the boxers I was wearing, and I helped him take them off me.

He shifted his position, and I could feel him hovering over me, as if he had propped himself up a little with his arms.

His fingers found my face then, and trailed over my open mouth, my breath hot and heavy against the pads of his fingertips. Then, when he pressed his lips against mine, he held them there while our breathing began to match, heartbeats synchronising.

Our kisses turned slow and sensual, his hand cupping my cheek as he tugged at my bottom lip, biting it gently. He clawed at the T-shirt I was wearing until it was off, and I was completely naked beneath him.

He exhaled against my skin. 'This is like torture. I want to see you; I want to drink you in.'

His lips caressed my chest lightly until his mouth found my breasts and nipples. When his body shifted lower and the torment from his tongue and his lips snaked down closer to between my legs, I began clawing the sheet, not being able to control the building up of… oh jeez, I had no idea what molecules at this point.

His fingers touched me between my legs, and slid easily between the lips, luxuriating in the wetness but when his tongue joined in, I gasped loudly, unable to control my response any longer. I dug my fingers deep into his shoulders and through his hair, tugging it tighter and tighter. This form of bliss continued as the roar from the storm grew louder, or was that my heart thundering throughout my body? There was a cacophony of noise from my moans and the storm until an explosion of lightning formed behind my eyelids as if the sky had burst through our room and bathed us in its electric light show.

I rode the crest over and over again until I felt Mateo shift his body again. His lips were on my cheek and then my mouth and I could taste my orgasm on his tongue as we kissed even more passionately.

'I want you so much,' I murmured against his lips.

'I don't have any—'

'I do,' I interrupted and hoped he didn't ask me why. I *was* on holiday after all. I detailed the exact spot where Samira had shoved a pack of twelve condoms in the front pocket of my luggage. He leaned away from me, and I could hear the rustling under the bed as he found my case and then the sound of a zipper. As he joined me back on the bed he paused, and I could hear a rip sound.

'Wait,' I said, finding the inner seductress in me, as I kissed his torso, his stomach and further down until I had him in my mouth. He growled as I pleasured his erection with my tongue and then my fingers.

'Laila, get this thing on me before I explode.'

At that I giggled, and it lightened the intensity of the moment.

'You are torturing me.' He laughed and before I knew it, we were both in peals of laughter, our bodies shaking.

'Stop, Mateo, you'll kill the mood,' I said, reaching to touch his lips, knowing that if there was even a spot of light in the room, I would see his smile, that smile that made me melt, only I had never ever let myself realise quite how much it had also made me swoon.

'There's absolutely no chance of that. I have wanted to kiss you since that first time I saw you outside the lecture room in CERN and it killed me that you asked for my number for your friend.'

I paused. 'Really?'

'Yes. And I had even engineered with my friends to make sure I was alone with you in the pod.'

I sat up a little. 'You did?'

'Yes, I did.'

'My God, I remember now, everyone was shouting, your group was arguing in Spanish, and someone changed their mind about stepping on.'

'A terribly orchestrated manoeuvre by a bunch of teenagers for a friend with a crush.'

'Oh, Mateo, that's adorable. And there I was on a mission for *my* friend, knowing full well it was me who had fallen, too.'

The words tumbled out. The oxytocin high was clearly a truth serum.

'I'm sorry,' I said, though I wasn't sure what for.

'Don't be.' His lips found mine again. 'It was worth the wait.'

I let his kisses caress me once more, softly, tenderly, then as if we never wanted to stop.

He was inside me now and my nails dug into his shoulders as I pulled him closer and closer to me so that there was no space between our bodies anymore.

I forgot what time it was, what day it was, where we were. We were hunkered down in our own private haven, lost in our own world and I didn't want the storm to end.

Chapter 23

The rain outside the window battered the wooden frame of the room and we drifted off to sleep before letting sweet kisses turn into another long lovemaking session. I was aware of Mateo leaving the bed for a while, but I was too blissed out to move and fell back asleep.

A kiss on my shoulder finally roused me, and my eyes opened to a fraction of light spilling through the curtains. The boards had come off the window and the worst of the storm had passed. Mateo reassured me that it hadn't reached hurricane strength though it might have sounded that way.

When I turned and looked at his face in the low light, my heart melted but I suddenly felt shy in his presence as I thought back to our earlier exploits and drew the sheet over my body.

'I… umm…' He hesitated. 'I need to get back to work. I'm sorry I can't stay in bed any longer. There's a lot of debris to clear up.'

'That's OK, I understand. I can help.'

'You don't have to.'

'I'd like to.'

'OK, if you're sure. I know the team will appreciate it, too. Tomorrow, I have the day off, so is there anything you fancy doing?'

I thought of the Love Intervention list and nodded. 'Yes. Yes, there is.'

–

The rest of the day passed by with a broom in my hands as we swept the storm damage out of the conservation centre and cleared the path to the main road from fallen branches and litter. It was labour intensive but very necessary as the new arrivals had been left stuck at the airport waiting for the storm to pass so they could come to the camp for their internships.

That of course meant the time for Mateo and me to be alone in the room was over. It also pointed to the fact that I was leaving here soon. What then? The third difficult goodbye in as many weeks?

Yes. It had to be that way. This experience had been life-changing but I had a job to go back to in London, at least temporarily until the conclusion of the investigation. But I also had my best friends and my mum. At that thought, I picked up my phone, but it was dead. Clearly the power hadn't been restored yet. I wasn't too worried as I had told the girls that my reception would be intermittent.

But I was anxious that there had been no update from work, and I didn't have a close relationship with any of my colleagues to warrant a heads-up on what was going on back in the lab.

Lying in the darkness again that night, it took me forever to fall asleep. It was agony knowing that Mateo was in the bunk above and I couldn't be with him. Every time the springs creaked above, I thought maybe he would climb down and sneak into my bed but knew he wouldn't want to wake the newcomers.

Mateo had told me to be prepared for another early wake-up, so my things were all laid out at the foot of my bed, ready for the day he had secretly planned but not let on about. I had merely told him to show me the best of the region and that I would like it to be a blend of the ocean and nature.

His gentle voice roused me and I got changed again in the dark before stepping outside the cabin. As soon as I closed the door, I saw Mateo leaning on the balcony. He pulled me towards him and kissed me, his hands clasping my face, before finding that space between my floaty cotton vest and my back, where his fingertips trailed my skin.

'Good morning to you, too,' I whispered.

He laughed against my mouth. 'It has been torture sleeping in that room and not being able to do this,' he said before kissing me again.

We finally broke apart and he led me to the car. He loaded it up with his rucksack and a cooler, but ignored my pleas to tell me where we were going. As he set the Jeep into drive, we made our way slowly along the path towards the main road, the only light guiding us from the car's full beam headlights.

Companiable silence filled the space between us along with a frisson of excitement. I couldn't resist leaning over and placing my hand on his knee, stroking the hairs on his leg, tucking my fingers beneath his shorts where a movement strained at the fabric. I wanted him again, badly.

'Are you trying to distract me?' he said.

'Maybe,' I said, in my best seductive voice.

'It's working.' He trapped his bottom lip in his teeth. 'But I need to concentrate on the road,' he said in a tone that made me think what he wanted was to pull over, but I behaved and pulled my hand away. 'You get all sorts of wildlife darting out of the reserve, but it'll be an easier ride once we hit the freeway.'

'How far are we going?'

'Quite some way. It's totally fine if you drift off.'

I settled back into my seat and pushed all thoughts of making love with Mateo again out of my mind for now.

'What do you think you will do once this internship is over?' I asked him.

Mateo considered my question for a while, one hand on the wheel, the other propping up his head as he leaned his elbow on the door. 'I'm not sure. Before we finished our Master's, I thought of staying in the US and had even been thinking of applying to do a PhD. And now I have a clearer idea of the field of research I want to pursue, maybe it's fate that it didn't work out first time around. I don't know. I've spent the last three years travelling, living like a nomad. It would be nice to stay put for a change.'

'In New York?'

'I guess that would be my first choice. Maybe upstate.' He shrugged. 'But I did love being in the city.'

'It was magical,' I said, though the pain that that time had caused me was still mixed up in those memories.

'Would you live there again?' he asked.

The question caught me off guard. And it was not one anyone had asked me before. I sat there considering it for a while and Mateo let me sit in that space. 'When I was at that conference in California, one of the speakers was Dr Walker.'

'I remember him. He was brilliant. A gifted orator and very inspiring.'

'I know, right?' I said, glad that he had left a similar impression on Mateo. 'We met on my last day, and he remembered me. He said he liked to keep tabs on some of his former students and had seen the work I had done in my career and told me about all the amazing projects he was currently involved in. He gave me his card and told me to look him up if I ever popped back to New York.'

'Wow. Can you imagine doing it?'

I laughed. 'Who "pops" back to New York on a whim?'

'Not a whim – to take another path, try new things, let it be the springboard to something cutting-edge and exciting, in the same way I did, realising working in a lab wasn't for me.'

It was hard not to be buoyed by Mateo's enthusiasm, but I decided to poke him at that last statement, stating that there was nothing I would rather do than keep working in a lab in London. Life there might have lost its sheen, but I knew I would get that excitement back in my life once the investigation was over and my name hopefully cleared. If I wanted to travel, then I would have to be more disciplined and organised with my time and book the days off.

I let the hum of the car's engine lull me and before I knew it, I had slipped back into slumber.

A gentle nudge woke me, and I realised the car had stopped. Mateo unclipped his seatbelt and leaned down towards me, planting a chaste kiss on my lips. I sat up and took in my surroundings. We were in a nondescript car park with palm trees and vegetation to one side and a corrugated-iron building to the other. The sky above was awash with orange and pink streaks threading through the clouds.

Mateo took my hand and the cooler and led me on a short trail out towards the beach. My breath caught at the sheer beauty of the sunrise in front of us. On a cluster of rocks, we sat down, and he opened the cooler to a feast of goodies – a flask of hot coffee, a Tupperware filled with melon and warm bread with a pot of jam.

To say I felt relaxed with this scene and the company would be an understatement.

'Where are we?' I asked before sucking the juice from a slice of honeydew.

'Paradise,' he said, holding my gaze before he leaned in and tasted the juice on my lips.

I melted into him and felt the rush of the swell behind me, adding to the rush of molecules that hadn't stopped coursing through my veins since that night I had spent with him.

'This is Cocles Beach,' he said, leaning back before sipping some coffee. As he turned towards the sea, his hair ruffled in the breeze. 'I stumbled upon this area thanks to one of the previous interns who told me all about the ranch and the important work they do.'

'Ranch?' I said, my hand hovering by my mouth, a drop of jam falling off my bread to my knee.

'I hope that was OK?' he said, swiping the condiment spill with his finger and licking it.

'It's more than OK,' I said, touching his chin, the soft bristles of his beard on my fingertips. I laid a kiss on his lips. 'You're a mind reader,' I said, thinking back to the checklist. 'I've always wanted to go horse-riding.'

After we packed up the remnants of our breakfast and stashed them in the car, Mateo took my hand and led me to the entrance, where we met the owner – Clarissa. She welcomed us with kisses on the cheeks and led us, plus another five tourists who had pulled up in two other cars, through to the stables, where we met all their rescue horses. As she told us about the history of the centre, how they had saved these beautiful creatures who were in bad shape and given them another chance in life, my heart ached for them.

The next hour was filled with basic instructions on how to horseback ride and then we mucked out the stables and got the horses ready. Clarissa suggested we all apply lots of sunscreen and mosquito spray and that swimwear was the most suitable attire as some of us would be horse swimming towards the end of the trail. I peeled off my vest and shorts and Mateo helped me get to those hard-to-reach places on my back with the factor fifty.

I squirmed beneath his ticklish fingers.

'How am I going to get you covered if you keep moving?' he whispered by my ear, and I sank back into him and sighed.

'I don't know. Maybe it would be easier if I was naked,' I said, as I looked up at him with a cheeky eyebrow arch.

He laughed before biting his bottom lip and shaking his head slightly. 'You. Are. Torturing. Me.'

'Me?' I mouthed and at that he playfully slapped me on my bottom.

The gesture caught me by surprise, but I liked it and slapped him back. He pulled me back towards him and kissed me. We were caught up in our own little world again, completely forgetting there were others with us.

Mateo helped lift me up onto my horse – Balsam – their best choice for beginners, Clarissa told me, because he had a sweet and quiet character. I stroked his long dark mane and patted his brown coat as I watched the others mount their steeds. We set off and I got into the rhythm of my horse's gentle trot and thought of the checklist:

    8. Go horse riding ✔

My last memory of being on a horse had been when Dad had taken me to the races and we had met one of the jockeys, who had let me sit on his winning steed. Dad had been a sports journalist back in his youth and had a pass to the winner's circle.

But that memory was replaced by another. Dad's compulsion to have a little flutter at the races soon became an addiction and his downfall. Vague memories of being dragged into William Hill on the high street every Saturday with the words 'don't tell your mother' were ingrained in my memory. I never knew how bad things had got until Mum told me that he had been declared bankrupt and the maintenance payments had stopped not long after he disappeared. I think that was when I had convinced myself that maybe shame had driven him away. It was also the time when I stepped in with weekend jobs during my A levels, followed by holiday jobs when I was at university. That was another reason why I knew I could never have taken that extended break touring the US with Edoardo. I had so much student debt to consider and my mum needed financial help to keep the house. I couldn't have abandoned her. She was the only family I had left.

Yet again, I found my thoughts slipping into the past and shook myself. I wanted to be present. In this moment. In my Mateo bubble. I snuck a glance behind me and was met with that smile. That reassuring but oh-so-sexy smile. If I was with him in the present, I was safe and didn't need to address the past or worry about the future, I convinced myself.

We headed off into the jungle and it was like immersing myself in a whole new world. The noise of the insects was deafening and the air humid and sticky. We spotted toucans and parrots and our guide pointed out a howler monkey and even a sloth. Mateo was always close behind or beside me, checking I was OK, occasionally handing me a bottle of water so I could stay hydrated. Despite the lack of the sun's powerful rays, the humidity was stifling and enervating.

When we reached the end of the jungle trail, we broke through a thicket and came out onto the most stunning beach I had ever seen, the sands crystal white and the sea a clear, rich turquoise. The horses' hooves padded over the soft sand, sinking into it until it became wetter and more compact by the shore.

Mateo came up beside my horse. 'Are you having fun?' he asked.

'Fun? This is incredible, Mateo. Thank you so much.' I blew him a kiss.

He beamed and threw one back to me. 'Do you think you are up for trying a trot and maybe some sea swimming?'

I nodded and Mateo spoke in Spanish to Clarissa, who smiled as she replied. Mateo led me ahead of the group and gave me some instructions on how to squeeze my legs and give a gentle kick. As if on cue, Balsam began to trot, and I squealed as my body slid a little to the side.

'You OK?' Mateo asked, lines etching on his forehead.

I managed to reclaim my previous upright position and began to relax as Balsam eased into a steady trot, and I replied that I was fine. A brief glance over my shoulder and I could see the rest of the group fading into the distance. The horses trotted around the headland, the sea splashing around my sandals until the steeds plunged their bodies in the water and it lapped around my waist. I shrieked with delight as we waded around the jutting palms and bushes and came round to the other side, the water line lowering as we reached the shore again. This stretch of beach was completely deserted.

'Will the others come around here?' I asked Mateo.

He looked over his shoulder. 'Sea swimming is not usually encouraged for beginners, but I told Clarissa I would keep an eye on you. And Balsam is a very experienced swimmer.'

A rush filled me knowing I had done something that was out of my comfort zone. *That'll be the dopamine hitting hard*, I thought.

We stopped at the edge of the forest and Mateo jumped off his horse, tying its rein to a nearby tree so it could rest under the shade of the branches. He poured some water in his hands and let his horse drink from them before offering some to mine. He cleaned his hands with a splash more and then helped me down from Balsam. His hands lingered on my waist before drawing me closer, and I wrapped my arms around his neck, our mouths merging once more.

When we finally broke apart, he swept his hand around the beach. 'The sea and nature, you said.'

'I did, and it's been amazing.' I looked out to the shore, the sun high in the sky, not a cloud interrupting it. It was hard to believe a storm had been ravaging the coast merely hours ago.

Slipping off my sandals, my toes sank into the sand. It was the softest I had ever felt and didn't burn my feet. I looked down at my body. My tan was even darker now and there were flashes of paler skin at the edges of my bikini. Suddenly, I was reminded of the checklist again.

'Fancy a swim?' I said.

'I'd love to,' he said, tying the reins of my horse next to his.

I began to jog backwards. 'Last one there is a rotten egg.'

'Hey,' Mateo said from behind. 'Cheat.' His protestation fell on deaf ears as I broke into a run, laughing as I did so.

But as I made it to the shoreline, Mateo appeared beside me, kicking the water up and around him as he ran ahead before diving into the sea. I followed in his path and when the water was waist deep, I propelled myself forward and began to swim – the warm Caribbean Sea refreshing on my sun-scorched limbs. When Mateo emerged, he flicked his hair off his face and swam over to me.

He drew me closer into his arms, and I wrapped my legs around his waist, letting my fingers trail along the water, revelling in the feeling of weightlessness.

'There's something I have always wanted to do,' I said. 'Are you sure sea swimming isn't meant for beginners?'

'Scout's honour. Is that what you say in Britain?'

I nodded then reached up to my bikini string and loosened the knot at my neck before unhooking the clasp at the back. Mateo sucked in a deep breath as his grip on my waist tightened. He brought me closer to him and my nipples grazed his chest before his hands touched them and kneaded them, the water lapping around me. I reached lower to loosen the strings of my bottoms before sliding them off and waving both items in the air with a whoop and a giggle. I wasn't drunk, but I felt high on something. Once more, I was reminded of the coaster where we had scrawled my list of things to achieve.

3. *Go skinny dipping* ✔

Mateo hadn't seen me naked in the daylight and I took this opportunity to lean backwards and float on my back, loosening my grip on him. As I looked up into the peerless sky, my ears partly submerged in the water, I felt truly liberated. Mateo came into view, his pupils dilated with desire, and he bit his bottom lip and trailed his gaze up and down my body. I closed my eyes and felt his touch then, a hold on my spine to keep me afloat so my arms could stop their movement, his fingers stroking my stomach, my chest, every naked inch of me, before lips replaced fingers.

It was heaven: his lips, his tongue, his touch.

With a twist, I pulled away from Mateo's hold and swam out further, the water so clear I could see the bottom. I stood on tiptoes and brushed my hair off my face, Mateo beaming as he swam closer.

'Thanks for the show,' he said, scooping me up in his arms and twirling me round. 'You are the most beautiful woman I have ever seen. I am so lucky that you came back into my life again.'

Something tugged at my heart as he said those words. Was it guilt? I was falling, hard and deep, and letting him come along with me for the ride, but the unspoken truth of where I had been the last two weeks was like a black hole at the end of the journey.

A movement on the horizon caught my eye. Far in the distance, bobbing in the water was the rest of the tour – their horses swimming like ours had been.

'Mateo!' I playfully slapped him on the chest. 'You liar. You said we would be on our own.'

'I said it wasn't a trip for beginners,' he said. 'Everyone else on the tour has ridden before.' He grinned wickedly, kneading my butt cheeks, and pressing me closer against his hard-on. 'Whoops, I guess I forgot you were the only first-time rider.'

I squirmed beneath his hold as I fumbled with my bikini, racing to get it back on, my cheeks flushing with embarrassment.

'Oh, you are in serious trouble now,' I said as they rode up beside our horses and waved over to us.

'I was hoping I was going to get to see you naked at some point today, so I had to deploy underhand tactics.'

At that I laughed.

When we waded out of the water, Clarissa gave us a knowing look and I turned to see Mateo coming out of the water many paces behind me, readjusting his shorts with his lips pinched, his hands concealing an obvious bulge beneath the wet fabric.

The rest of the day floated by with a group picnic and another ride back through the jungle towards base.

As we said goodbye and drove off into the sunset, I let the breeze from the open window tickle my face and dry my hair. Across the space between our seats, Mateo held my hand. But as he clasped it tighter, I turned away and an unexpected tear trickled down my face. I didn't want him to see it.

How could I make sense of all this? All I knew was that I would have to find the courage to be open and honest with him. Austin and Edoardo were out of the picture, but he needed to know that they had very much been in it merely days ago.

No. I don't want to spoil this moment. I wanted to be in my Mateo bubble a little longer.

Halfway into our journey, we stopped at a service station, and I popped into the restrooms while Mateo filled the car with petrol. But when I returned, there was a dark expression on his face.

'Everything OK?' I said, as I slipped into the passenger seat.

He nodded but his jaw was locked, eyes fixed firmly to the front. He started the engine and pulled out and didn't look my way.

My phone was glowing on the dashboard, and I reached for it. It had been charging through the Jeep's in-car USB port. I hadn't checked it in ages as there had been no service since the storm hit, but it looked like it had finally come to life.

But I stilled when I saw the twelve notifications on the lock screen that had obviously come through in quick succession once service had resumed. They were from only two names: Austin and Edoardo.

Chapter 24

'I can explain.'

'There's no need to explain.' Mateo's gaze was firmly fixed on the freeway ahead as darkness began to envelop us once more.

'But I want to because it's not what you think.'

He turned to me briefly but all I could see was a wounded look in his eyes. 'Isn't it?' There was a tremble in his voice and at the sound, my heart cracked a little.

I bit my bottom lip and stared at the screen of my mobile. One tap and it came to life. There they were. I could see what he would have seen. Austin's last message read:

> I miss you, please message me. Please.

Edoardo's most recent one merely said:

> I was a fool. I know that now.

I couldn't bring myself to see what else they had said in previous texts. The notifications had popped up one on top of each other, clearly in quick succession. My pulse beat wildly as I clutched my mobile, tapping it against my lips, wondering how I could explain myself out of this situation.

'I didn't mean to look,' he said. 'It kept pinging. One after another. I guess I thought it could have been an emergency – perhaps your mother.'

Mateo gave nothing away as to what he was thinking with his tone.

'I… I met up with Austin in California. And then… then I saw Edoardo in Puerto Rico.'

'By accident?'

I swallowed deeply, realising that I didn't want to tell any more lies. 'No, not by accident. You see, it was all part of the plan my two best friends came up with. A plan that clearly hadn't been thought through at all because I have ended up hurting three guys in the process. A plan—'

'Please, Laila.' Mateo raised his hand. 'I don't want to hear more. Do you mind if we listen to the radio?'

'Umm.' I hesitated. 'Of course.'

As music filtered through the speakers and filled the car, the conversation was shut down. And it was a good thing too. Because the truth was, I didn't know what I wanted to say. And Mateo's reaction appeared to match both Austin's and Edoardo's.

A chill settled over me. I had a checklist of things I had been meant to experience and I had almost experienced them all. But in the process of executing the plan and discovering things about myself, pushing past the pain to achieve things I never had, I had ended up hurting others along the way. The list that the girls and I had signed over a couple of margaritas back in a London bar seemed like a lifetime ago but there was one item on the list we had argued over:

10. Fall in love

Why call it the Love Intervention, then? Jena had challenged me and Samira.

I briefly glanced over at Mateo, his gaze fixed firmly ahead, hands clutching the steering wheel tightly. The smile was gone, jaw clenched. But there was a sadness to his demeanour and my heart cracked. *Agh*, I inwardly screamed. Look at the mess that stupid plan had caused.

–

We arrived back at camp as dinner was served. Slipping into a seat at the dining table, I listened to the events of the day and news of the two sightings. Tourist groups had come in one after the other as a few had been postponed on the day of the storm, causing a backlog. Mateo and I didn't have a moment to ourselves after that. Every time I tried to corner him, he would slip away saying he was needed for something or other.

That's when I decided to head out into town to have some time to myself. I had remembered getting a good signal at the bar we had gone to the other night, so I walked there on my own. Tonight, there was no band, only the soft sound of a Spanish guitar from the speaker on the roof. I ordered a tropical juice drink and let the evening breeze wash over my bare arms and legs.

The waiter placed the drink in front of me with a bowl of nuts and I thanked him then fished out my phone. Taking a deep breath, I opened all the messages.

Austin's first one merely said:

> I miss you.

It had been sent two days ago. With no reply from me, he had begun a stream of consciousness telling me he wished I was still there, wished he hadn't acted the way he had and that he should have been a gentleman and driven me to the airport. He said he had had time to think over everything and that there was no way he was going to lose me.

Am I his to lose?

Our chapter had closed. I'd moved on.

Edoardo's messages were a string of confessions. My admission about where I had been and where I was headed to had floored him and, once more, he had let his jealousy get the better of him as I had surmised. He said that he had tried to hide those feelings by going silent and running away. There had been no work trip and he felt horribly guilty about lying to me. Now he wished we had talked about it, and he asked whether I would come back and see him again. But his penultimate message made me sit up and take notice.

> I'm coming to London in a few weeks.
> Maybe we can meet again?

I let the phone drop from my grasp and held my head in my hands. This was more complicated than I first thought.

Did I want to meet Edoardo again?

I'd thought that chapter was also closed. I knew one thing. I wanted to call the girls, but it was the middle of the night in England. Fuck it. I wanted to see them. I missed them – I missed their words of advice and comfort.

It wasn't their fault that I had got myself into all these entanglements. There was only one person to blame for all of this. Me. I had willingly accepted their plan and I was a grown-up, for heaven's sake. I should have known this would happen. I had opened a Pandora's box of passion and desire and I couldn't see how I could close it.

Austin and Edoardo were willing to put aside what had happened and wanted to have something more long-term – that was the ultimate part of the Love Intervention, so why did the thought of a relationship fill me with fear?

I'm sure a therapist would say that it was easy to see why. Mum had always been quick to tell me men were a waste of time, that you always end up getting hurt. Had that been why I had kept everyone at arm's length since my time in New York?

New York.

A wash of longing hit me when the city came to mind. Mateo had asked me if enough time had passed to face the one person that possibly held the key to all these prolonged feelings of guilt – Gregory. Dad's... husband. It was a label I had never said out loud, to Mum or to the girls. Maybe it was time to change that. He was the one person that could answer all the questions I had about my father and how he had lived the last few years of his life.

I left the messages from Austin and Edoardo on read. My head needed to be clearer before I could consider them and the hurt that I had now inflicted on Mateo, all in the name of getting DOSEd up.

Back at the camp, I found him coming out of the shower room. A towel was wrapped around his waist and memories of earlier on today came to the forefront of my mind and I blushed deeply, remembering my naked display at the beach.

'I… I forgot my underwear,' he said, pointing to our room.

'Mateo, we need to talk.'

Droplets ran down his chest, glistening in the light of the outside lamp. 'Let me get changed. I'll meet you up on the observation deck. No one will be up there at this time of night.'

I nodded and made my way up the wooden stairs to the top. The air was still and muggy; the ocean rhythmically washed up against the shore then back out again in the distance. Night insects had started their evening chorus. I breathed in time to the waves, and it calmed my racing heart as I looked up into the sky where a million stars glimmered.

'Hey,' Mateo said, and I turned.

'Hey.' I clutched my hands together and squeezed. 'Mateo, I—'

'Can I go first? Please?'

'Yes, of course.' I hugged my arms and leaned back on the railing.

After taking a few deep breaths, he began. 'When you got in touch a few weeks ago, I was stunned. It stirred up the loveliest memories for me, of our time in the lab, in lectures, practicals, studying together in the library. Your friendship meant everything to me back then, but I think at the back of my mind, I had always hoped that there might be more between us one day. Misguided perhaps. But then I allowed myself to have hope when you arrived and when we… when we were together you said those things, those feelings that you also had when we first met that matched mine.' He paused, raising his eyes to the sky for a few beats. 'It was truly magical hearing that you had felt something too and yesterday when we were in bed and then on the beach and in the water...' He shook his head. 'Sometimes it is so hard to express what I feel in English.'

'I think you're doing a pretty damn good job of it,' I said with a smile, hoping it would encourage him to continue.

'I don't want to be a part of any love square.' His tone was direct but there was a vulnerability behind his words.

A love square. Is that what this is?

'It sounds to me,' he continued, 'that your heart is somewhere else, or perhaps your heart is undecided. I've been someone's second choice before, and it only ended in heartbreak. I don't think I can do that again. And besides, I care about you too much to force you into something that maybe you don't even want with me.'

He fell silent and I tried to gather my thoughts. Mateo and I hadn't spoken about the people that had drifted in and out of our lives the last ten years. I guessed that meant he had had lovers and relationships during that time while he cared for his mother. Of course he must have had, why wouldn't he? He wasn't a monk, for heaven's sake. And we also hadn't talked about the last forty-eight hours – those passion-filled hours – and what they had meant to both of us.

I needed to answer him but what could I say? I thought those first two acts of my trip were complete and after this third act, it was all over. Time to return to normality.

'It was never my intention to hurt you, Mateo, nor did I have a set agenda for this trip at all. Things happened, and I allowed myself to let them happen, for me to feel things I haven't felt in a very long time. This was never meant to be anything more than a chance at a holiday romance or two and I know I should have been more truthful about who I had spent my time with but I justified it in my head because I knew at the end of each trip I would be leaving for the next, before going home – back to my old life. But now... now things are more complicated.'

'Complicated how?'

'I...' The words got stuck in my mouth. 'I don't know how to explain.'

'It's fine, Laila. Don't beat yourself up over this. And you're right, it was fun. A holiday romance. And now...'

Now. It felt like such a loaded word. *What do you want, Laila? What is in that cold heart of yours that means you can't imagine a future with any one of these three guys?*

And then it came to me. I couldn't imagine my future because I still hadn't healed my past. It was time to rectify that. Time to be bold.

'I think you were right,' I said finally.

'About what?'

'I still carry the guilt of my father's death inside me and until that's resolved, I don't think I can give my heart to anyone. So... that's why...' The decision hit me like a tidal wave. 'I'm going to change my flight. I'm going to leave tomorrow. Head to New York and do a layover for the night before going home.'

His eyes widened. 'You're leaving?'

I nodded, confident in my words. But Mateo's expression surprised me. Did he want me to stay? Did he want us to work through things? Here he was being open and vulnerable, saying he didn't want to be part of a love square. Did he want me to stay so we could see if there was something between us to build on?

But I couldn't do that. I needed to absolve myself of what happened ten years ago before I could even begin to consider opening my heart to someone else. I owed it to Mateo, and to Austin and Edoardo, to make this decision with a clear head and, hopefully, a better understanding of what *I* wanted from a relationship.

'Yes, I'm leaving,' I repeated.

'I'm not sure how I would get you to the airport, though. I could maybe try and swap my day off—'

'Please don't worry,' I interrupted. 'I seem to remember one of your colleagues mentioning over dinner that he was heading that way to see friends. Maybe I can hitch a ride with him.'

Mateo nodded but he looked wounded – his shoulders sunk into himself. I wanted so desperately to fall into his arms again, but I couldn't, not when my mind was such a mess and especially as I didn't want to hurt him anymore by needing to be topped up with oxytocin from one of his all-encompassing hugs.

'You've been an amazing host, Mateo. I have loved this time with you, here, in this incredible country watching you work so hard to make a difference in this world. But it's time to face my demons. It's time to go back to New York.'

Chapter 25

I shivered beneath my coat – the coat I hadn't worn since that first flight from London. The temperature was below zero and a massive shock after the scorching low thirties temperatures of Costa Rica. I rifled through my case to unearth my beanie and scarf.

Was this the craziest idea I had ever had? I hadn't even let on to the girls what I was up to. Saying goodbye to Mateo at the conservation centre had been incredibly hard. The hug had been brief, and a promise to stay in touch bandied between us. But I knew that was unlikely. I knew I had screwed up any possible ongoing friendship with him despite my heartfelt plea for us to find a path towards it one day in the future.

A five-block walk on Third Avenue followed by another ten minutes on East 82nd Street took me to my destination. My case trundled over cracks in paving slabs until I reached number 514. Gazing up at the red brick apartment block complete with black iron fire escapes on every floor, I suddenly realised I had no clue what apartment Gregory lived in, the details of the address scribbled on a piece of paper by Dad's old neighbour long gone from my memory.

Dragging my case up the four-step entrance, I saw various buzzers listed for apartments A-H. Picking one at random yielded no response, nor did the second one

I chose. When I pressed the third buzzer, the main door clicked open. Inside there was an ornate mirror over a radiator and on the other wall – letterboxes. My gaze fell on the label for apartment H – Gardner. I contemplated going outside to ring the buzzer but couldn't face going out into the cold again. I blew hot air into my fingers to put life into them and began to haul my case up three flights of stairs. By the time I reached the apartment, sweat was pouring down my back. I unwound my scarf, slipped off my hat and unbuttoned my coat, laying them on top of my case's handle. Pulling up the sleeves of my grey jumper, I took in my tanned arms. My crazy journey in search of sun, sea and sex had been accomplished, but now there was another journey I needed to take – one towards redemption.

Inside I could hear the distant sound of classical music. My finger trembled as I rang the bell. The music stopped and I heard someone shuffling closer.

'Mrs Abbot, I've told you it's—' As Gregory emerged from the door opening, he clutched his chest and took a sharp breath. His other hand gripped on to the wooden frame, knuckles whitening. A brown and white dog appeared from behind his legs, his tail wagging, head cocked to the side.

Gregory took in my appearance from head to toe as if he was checking I wasn't a mirage. 'It's… you.'

I lifted my scarf off my case and scrunched it up inside my hat. 'Yes. It's me,' I said, my voice a little shaky.

'Laila. I thought I would never see you again.'

'But we've never met.'

'At the crematorium.'

I clutched my hat to my chest. 'You… saw me?'

He nodded. 'My God, where are my manners.' He pulled open the door and ushered me inside.

I dragged my case along the parquet-floored narrow hallway before turning halfway.

'You can leave your things here, if you wish, I mean, that is, I don't know if you were planning on… Oh darn.' He pushed his silvery blonde fringe off his face. 'For a retired psychotherapist, I am at a complete loss for anything sensical or profound to say.'

At that I let out a laugh, but it was hollow. This was all so surreal, I also didn't know how to act.

Gregory placed his hands on his hips. 'Tea. I think we need tea. You do drink it, right? Most Brits do, I know, but I never want to assume the stereotype is universal.'

'I would love a cup of tea. Milk, no sugar, please.'

'Coming right up,' he said with a nod.

Padding off to the kitchen with his dog at his heels, he left me alone in the main living and dining space. It was small with a wall of books on one side and a whitewashed open-brick wall on the other. Photo frames lined a circular table in the corner and an L-shaped sofa faced a small flatscreen. The coffee table was littered with books and scattered pages of what looked like essays. A red pen sat next to them.

'My marking for the week,' he said, as he brought two mugs and laid them down on the coffee table.

'You're a teacher?'

'Yes. I retired from my psychotherapy practice a few years ago now and was bored out of my brain. I saw an advert about training to be a teacher aimed at the mature student and thought why not, and I've been teaching psychology at Hunter College for going on two years now.'

I nodded, not knowing what to say as a follow-on.

Sitting down in front of my tea, I blew steam from it before laying it back down. Gregory claimed the spot on the bend of the couch. His dog jumped up to sit beside him before turning onto his back for a belly rub.

'It's… such a lovely surprise to see you,' he said, focusing his attention on tickling all the right spots of his pooch. 'If I had known you were coming, I would have at least offered you something more than tea. Cupboards are a bit bare at the moment. I was going to go to the store later, so it's a good thing you rang the bell when you did. I…' He paused and finally looked up at me. 'I'm rambling.' He smoothed his hands down his green corduroy trousers and sat forward. 'Clearly out of practice in the art of keeping quiet.'

'I didn't come for a therapy session.' My tone had an edge to it, and I didn't know where it had suddenly appeared from.

'No, of course not.'

Silence fell, loaded and tense. I hadn't thought this interaction through at all. I had come to apologise, hadn't I? I wanted to be assuaged of my guilt. Because no matter how many times Mateo had told me my father's death wasn't my fault, the idea that it might have been had lingered in my consciousness without being challenged for ten years.

My gaze fell upon a photograph on a side table next to where Gregory was sitting. Him and Dad in smart suits, holding hands, confetti raining down on them.

The walls were closing in as my heartrate increased. I thought I had come to say sorry, for being there the day he died and not saving him, but now the anger began to bubble beneath the surface of my skin – a stronger, more visceral reaction to seeing the photo of them together.

'Why him?'

'Excuse me?'

'Why my father? He left me for you.'

'That's not entirely true.'

'I was seventeen the last time I saw my father.' I blinked furiously, hot tears filling my eyes. 'Then one day he vanished. I assumed, judging by all these photographs of him, that it was because of you. Am I wrong?'

He patted his mutt, who was now snoozing beside him. 'Actually... that is probably a fair analysis. But he had very little back then. He was bankrupt, depressed and living one great big lie. A lie he had buried his whole life.'

'But he had *me*. Wasn't I enough?'

He looked briefly to the ceiling. 'I'm afraid you weren't. And the shame he felt in being such a terrible father and having to lie about his sexuality his entire life outweighed the pain he knew he would cause you if he left. But please understand, Laila, he wanted to make right by you, he wanted to make amends. It's such a tragedy that he...' He paused and fished a hanky from the pocket of his chunky cable-knit cardigan and dabbed his eyes before composing himself. 'He was waiting for you to reach out to him.'

I sat forward. 'My God, some therapist you must have been. Why didn't you tell him that was an awful burden to put on a kid? Why was it my responsibility to do that?'

'Laila, the one thing Victor told me, one of the last things he told me was that he wanted you to know the truth. That letter you mentioned to him, that had our address on the back, contained all the information about when we were moving and where we could be reached, but it wasn't the first correspondence he had sent. He had tried emailing, text messages. Your mother blocked his number, the emails would bounce back, so he knew writing was the best way.'

'Why couldn't he call *me*, then?' I said, stabbing my finger into my chest.

'He tried but it said the number was no longer in use.'

It struck me – I had changed numbers, right before I started at UCL. Mum had wanted to change to a new network. She claimed she had found a cheaper deal that involved bundling our broadband with our mobiles. I hadn't challenged her at the time because she was the one paying the bills, and as long as Jena and Samira had my new number, what had it mattered? Had Mum done that deliberately? A clean slate so Dad would be out of our lives forever?

'He should have addressed that letter to me,' I said finally, not buying these excuses. 'Then I would have read it. I would have known he wanted to reconnect, and I could have saved myself all this pain. Or he could have visited again. I haven't moved from my childhood home. I still live there. I'm almost thirty-one and I still live at home. This is the twenty-first century, for heaven's sake. There were a multitude of ways for him to make contact and it wasn't my responsibility to find him.'

Moisture was beginning to burn the backs of my eyes as I stared at the cup of tea, which was still untouched. Rising to my feet, I stood there, no longer able to have this conversation. 'This was a mistake. I shouldn't have come.'

Gregory sprang up from the sofa, unsettling his dog in his wake, who jumped off and looked up at him with a wagging tail, probably wondering if it was time for a walk.

'No, Laila. It wasn't a mistake. Your father wanted this. He wanted us to meet.'

I gave him an obvious once-over. He was taller than Dad and evidently a lot younger than him judging by the lack of deep wrinkles. But I didn't want to hear any more from this man.

'He wanted us to meet so we could become best friends and reminisce?' I said with nothing but bitterness in my tone.

He shook his head slowly. 'The last thing he said to me when he lay in that hospital bed was that he wanted you to know how much he loved you and was proud of you. He had seen you in the distance, in the park. He thought you might think he had stood you up.'

'I saw everything that day.'

'You did?'

I nodded but an uneasiness suddenly passed through me when I considered his words. 'What do you mean, the last thing he said in the hospital?'

'When I arrived, the surgeon told me that he had been put in an induced coma. The paramedics had managed to resuscitate him, but it had taken them so long and he needed an operation on the valve that had been put in six months prior to that. That's why we left Saratoga in the first place. He didn't want to recuperate on the East Coast; he wanted to have a taste of West Coast living. But we needed to return to sort things out with the house. I had wanted him to stay in California, but he insisted on joining me. And then when he saw your letter, he knew it was fate, that he had been right to risk the flight over, the stress he had clearly begun to put on his heart. When he left me that morning to come and see you, I could tell something was not right, but he waved away my concern.'

I shook my head slowly. 'I still don't understand. If he was in a coma...'

'He stabilised and they pulled him out of that state to see if his heart could withstand an operation. But it was a risk. We spoke only for a few minutes and then he was gone.' He shifted on the spot, reaching down to stroke his dog by the ear.

'I was in the hospital,' I whispered.

'You were?'

'I saw you. It's because of you that I didn't get to say goodbye to my father. It's you. I have lived with this guilt all these years because I thought it was something I could have prevented. And if I had seen him that day at the hospital I would have known and I would have had the chance to tell him I loved him too. I would have reassured him that I had no hatred in my heart towards him because that is what you say to someone when you run the risk of losing them forever. But I never got that chance. Because of you.' I pointed at him as I spat out that last word.

The room began to close in as these revelations spun in my head.

'I hate you. I hate you so much.' The words were cruel, and I knew I was behaving like a child, but it felt so good to say them out loud. 'I hate you, I hate you, I...' My arms were shaking and legs trembling. Gregory closed the space between us as if he didn't mind taking these verbal hits. 'I hate you so much,' I wailed and struck his chest with my fist. The blow had no strength behind it. My strength had evaporated as soon as he said those words: that I could have said my goodbye, but I had seen Gregory and run away. I struck him again and he stood there unmoving. His chest broadened as if he wanted to take the blow. I struck him again and again, his body solid and unyielding.

The tears began to stream, my surroundings blurring and the blows continuing until I collapsed into him, his arms wrapped tight around me, and I lost all sense of the world.

Chapter 26

I had no idea how long we stayed in that position, but I became faintly aware of being moved and a softness beneath me. Gregory had manoeuvred us to sit on the couch.

Anger, resentment, guilt. They had been buried inside me for so long. Was I now free from their torment? Did one outburst change anything?

Gregory showed no signs of shifting his hold. This was a contact I couldn't remember ever feeling from my parents. Dad had never been particularly demonstrative. He used to blame his old-fashioned British upbringing of being seen and not heard by his own parents. Mum was also not a hugger though she blamed me for that, saying I always squirmed out of her embrace whenever she tried.

'I'm sorry,' I finally whispered, turning my head a little.

'No, no,' he said. 'There is nothing to be sorry for.'

'I didn't mean to hit you.'

'Didn't you? Laila, please don't apologise for what felt right in the moment, regardless of whether I deserved it or not.'

Why did this feel so good? This openness. This warmth. I didn't know this man. But Dad had and he had loved him — loved him so much that he left his old life behind to be with him.

I shuffled out of his embrace and accepted the hanky that magically appeared in front of me. 'It's a clean one, I promise,' he said, and there was something in his smile that soothed my aching heart.

'Do you still miss him?' I asked, dabbing my face.

'Every single minute of every single day.'

'Oh.' His words were so honest, so raw.

'He loved you, Laila, and he was so very sorry that he couldn't be the father that you deserved to have in your life. And please...' He rested his hand on mine. 'Please understand that I had tried to make him see sense, that he should have contacted you long before you did, that your anger and hatred would be valid responses if he met up with you again and worth experiencing if it meant he could one day have a relationship with you. But he was too consumed with shame and guilt to see sense. He was very set in his ways and truly believed you would be a success without him in your life. And please also remember, I wasn't his therapist. I tried to reason with him, get him to see someone, but he was always so reluctant to let me pay for things, said the money would be wasted on him, that his issues ran too deep for anyone to get behind the walls he had built.'

I pulled my hand away and fiddled with a thread on my jumper, letting his words settle for a moment, so I could digest them more calmly than before. 'He was scared of me?' I asked, softly. 'Of how I would react to finding out about his sexuality?'

'He was scared of conflict, that much I know. I think he knew you were progressive enough to accept that part of him.'

'Can I ask you something?'

He shifted closer. 'Anything.'

'How did Dad identify? Your old neighbour called you both gay.'

'Yes, we both identified as gay although it took your father a while to embrace it, say it out loud.'

I nodded, but a myriad of other questions bubbled to the surface. Gregory had said Dad had lived with this lie his whole life. Had he ever loved Mum?

'He adored your mother,' he said, as if reading my mind. 'But his sexuality was something he had always felt forced to supress. He once tried to tell his parents that he felt different, but they dismissed the conversation with the notion that those feelings would pass. Marrying your mother gave him a sense of conformity that he so wanted to make work but couldn't. And that guilt over hurting her for so many years drove him to the edge. I don't think he ever knew how to be a father too.'

'That's not true. He had been a loving one until he left.'

Gregory shook his head slowly. 'Your mother always told him he was useless, so he told me. I, of course, only have one side of that story. You were quite a preco- cious child, kept everyone at arm's length, he said, hence why you were so independent, apparently, and he had convinced himself that you simply didn't need him. He said your last few visits were... difficult.'

I sat back, affronted. 'I was seventeen. And I was stressed about exams, my future. Besides, who wants to hang out with their parents at that age?'

'I know, I know. Victor was a very loving man to *me*, but I believe he wasn't very demonstrative with you.'

I thought back to my early teens, the pats on the back when I had come from school with an A grade or a commendation from the head teacher. The hugs had been brief, but who wants to be hugged by a parent when you're an adolescent? Back then, it hadn't felt like I was missing anything.

'I'm not very affectionate, I suppose,' I said, folding the handkerchief.

'Aren't you?'

'I haven't had much experience when it comes to relationships. Haven't had the time.'

'Ah.' He nodded.

'Ah what?'

'Oh, nothing.'

'It's clearly something. Are you about to psychoanalyse me?'

He held his hand over his heart. 'I wouldn't dream of it.' One eyebrow arched as he tried to hold back a smirk.

At that I smiled.

'And besides, it wouldn't be fair of me to make any snap judgements until I got to know you better, heard your side of everything.'

I stared at the wet hanky in my hands. 'Would you like to get to know me better?' At those words, his face lit up. 'I mean, we haven't got off to the best of starts but... my flight doesn't leave until tomorrow evening, so...'

He shifted his position on the sofa, so he was facing me. 'Nothing in the world would please me more.'

–

Gregory loosened Bailey's lead as we entered Carl Schurz Park and he trotted ahead. A steaming hot coffee cup was in my grasp, warming my fingers and heating my insides as I took little sips. The sky was the palest blue and the sun was heaven on my cheeks. We walked around the perimeter once before sitting on a bench, Gregory handing over one of the two croissants he had bought from the bakery where we had picked up our beverages.

'Hmm,' Gregory murmured as he pondered everything I had told him about my holiday. He had been good at asking probing questions and knew when to listen and nod. 'It *is* a love square.'

'But there's no future for me with any of them.'

'How would you define "a future"?'

'Marriage, kids,' I said before biting into my pastry, buttery flakes spilling down my chin. 'And that scares me.'

I filled him in on my relationship with Josh and the sacrifices he had expected from me in order to take our relationship to the next level.

'Is that what crosses your mind on every date you go on? "What will I have to give up for this to have a future?"'

'Yes. What's the point in allowing any emotional connection or committing to a time investment if it's wasted in the end. If what they want eventually is a relationship that will inevitably involve me giving up on everything I have worked hard for, then yes, what's the point? Mum gave up everything and look where it got her.'

'So, these last three weeks are the first weeks in a very long time that you have simply gone with your feelings of attraction and said to hell with it, these liaisons aren't going anywhere but I don't care?'

'The remit of the Love Intervention was to have fun.'

'But your friend Jena wanted you to fall in love.'

'That's because she's a helpless romantic.'

'And you're more like your other friend…'

'Samira. I guess. But I don't like sleeping around.'

'Don't you?'

At that my cheeks pinkened and I shifted my position on the bench.

Gregory laughed. 'I'm not judging, Laila, but it would seem like you have caught yourself between a rock and a hard place, excuse the cliché. Like I said, I'm a little out of practice.'

'I know the cliché but I'm not sure it relates to my situation.'

'From what you have told me, you have connected with these three men not only on a sexual level, but a much deeper one, but with each choice the outcome, at least in your mind, is undesirable because someone, yourself included, will end up getting hurt.'

'If I didn't continue with any of them, *I* wouldn't be getting hurt.'

'Wouldn't you?'

I raised my chin. 'I'm happy with my life in England. There's a lot of fulfilment in my work, I have two amazing best friends and I am part owner of a property in London in a desirable location.'

'These are all valid points. You said the Italian was coming to visit you in London. What if he was willing to move there?'

I hadn't even allowed myself to think about that idea. 'I'm not sure.'

Gregory stared out into the distance and took several bites of his croissant before taking a long sip of his coffee.

'Love is indeed complicated, Laila,' he said. 'And the language of love is even more so. You haven't had the best examples of what a good and healthy relationship looks like growing up either. Your family meals were in silence, there was no love or affection shown between your parents, no extended family.'

'That's partly why I freaked out when I had dinner with Austin's family. It was all so unfamiliar.'

'But did it feel nice?'

A shiver suddenly rippled through me, and I drew my coat closer. 'I think so. But it all happened so fast.' I clung on to my coffee cup tighter, but it had lost its warmth.

'I'm freezing, too,' Gregory announced, noticing my attempts to heat my extremities. 'Might I suggest we head back and if you wouldn't mind staying outside the store with Bailey, I can pick up some food for the rest of the day and tomorrow. That'll save me heading back home with him and then coming out again. I think we have a lot to discuss and unpick but I am beginning to lose feeling in my fingers and toes. Tourists love to romanticise New York City in the winter, but they don't realise their romantic endeavours could lead to frostbite.'

'Of course,' I said with a laugh, reaching down to tickle Bailey under the chin. 'I never had any pets growing up. Dad was allergic.'

'I know,' he said with a wry smile. 'That's why rescuing him from a shelter was the first thing I did when your father passed. I was so angry at him for leaving me that I think I initially got Bailey out of spite, but it was the best thing I ever did. Life is a lot less lonely with Bailey in it.' He stroked the side of his head and Bailey leaned into him, obviously utterly devoted to his owner. 'Come on, old boy,' he said, getting up from the bench. 'Let's walk some more.'

Hours slipped by after our shop and before we knew it, Gregory and I had shared life stories over a charcuterie and cheese board and moved into the evening with a bottle of red and a cooking session. I was sitting on a bar stool watching Gregory prepare a roast chicken, stuffing it with a breadcrumb and herb medley and sticking rosemary in it plucked from a pot plant by the window. An hour later, he pulled out the bird and the potatoes that had been roasting on the shelf below and turned down the heat on his steamed veg.

I offered to lay the table but when I reached it laden with plates and cutlery, I realised there was no space there.

'You can move the photographs to the window ledge,' Gregory said.

Removing each one in turn, I stared at the images of my late father. 'You had a happy life together.'

'Yes, we did. Your father had a wicked sense of humour, loved to challenge me over the Sunday crossword in the *Times* and also shared my love of books. We were very content in each other's company. And we both loved to travel, only... when his health began to suffer, that became harder to do. We truly believed that the valve replacement would give him a new lease of life. But it wasn't meant to be.'

I finished laying the table and brought our glasses of wine over. 'Did you ever consider meeting someone new?'

He lowered his gaze. 'I swore I would never date again. But as the years have passed, I have begun to be very lonely. But now that I work in a school, my spare time is taken up with marking and preparing for classes. And I don't think I could allow myself to go there again.'

'Go where?'

'To a place where I could get hurt again.'

I could see his fingers trembling as they lay on the counter, his head hung low, a sadness overtaking him. He was quite obviously trying desperately to hold in his emotions, but it seemed this was not something he was used to doing.

And in that moment, something profound shifted in my heart and I went over to him and hugged him.

Chapter 27

The living room light was off when I stepped inside the house. I laid my keys on the trestle table in the hallway and shrugged off my damp coat. The drizzle that greeted me as my plane landed at Heathrow airport had moved to a downpour by the time I emerged from Notting Hill Tube, and I hadn't had the energy to unearth my umbrella from the bottom of my suitcase.

My phone buzzed in my pocket. It was another message from Austin. Being with Gregory for that brief time had made me see things a little differently. He had said I should continue to be open to new possibilities. I had messaged Edoardo back and said I was looking forward to his visit and then to Austin I had said I wished we had parted on better terms, which had prompted a back-and-forth exchange of texts. He had wanted to fly out to NYC and tried to get me to change my flight, but I said I couldn't because I had work starting on Monday and needed the weekend to recover from my jet lag. He then proposed the idea of me coming back next month for a long weekend. I had to bring up cost as a very valid reason for saying no, but he had insisted that it would be a gift. I had left that comment unanswered.

This last message from Austin merely said:

> Glad you landed safely. Miss you.

'*Habibti*,' Mum said and I turned. She flicked on the hall light and gave me a long once-over. 'Look at you, my girl,' she said, her hands together as if she was praying. 'It's good to see you.'

'You, too, Mum.' I stepped closer and kissed her on both cheeks.

'You must be hungry; did you eat anything on the plane?'

'I'm fine. I didn't mean to wake you.'

'Nonsense, I was waiting up for you. When I got your message that you had landed, I knew it would take a while to clear customs and take the Tube home.'

'But I told you not to wait up.'

'*Habibti*, Laila, of course I would wait up. I haven't seen you in three weeks. Come, come, let me fix you something and we can talk. Jena and I cooked up a storm yesterday and the freezer is full of Middle-Eastern delights.'

The hallway clock ticked behind her. It was getting close to ten o'clock. I hadn't given much thought to what I would tell Mum about my trip. My messages over the three weeks had been brief but my unexpected meeting with Gregory had made me think I needed to be more open and honest with her. Just not now. I couldn't face the backlash if I told her everything.

I fiddled with the handle of my suitcase, nerves rendering me a little twitchy. 'Actually, I am wiped after my trip. Maybe we can catch up tomorrow?'

'Oh, OK, if that's what you want?' She took the folds of her cardigan and wrapped them tighter around herself.

'Except I am starting back at work tomorrow. One of my big clients thankfully didn't gel with their new house-keeper and has taken me back.'

'But what about your…' It was then that I noticed that she wasn't wearing a brace or a cast on her foot.

'Samira took me in for a check-up and it seems I was right. They only said three months as a precaution. The X-ray showed everything had healed.'

'Oh… that's good.'

'I'm glad someone finally listened to me.'

'I am sure the doctor was only doing what he—'

'Not the doctor. Samira.'

'Oh, right.'

'She's been so very wonderful to me, so kind and caring and she works so hard for her little girl. That sweet Rosie.'

'I'm glad it all worked out, me not being here.' It was hard to take the resentment out of my voice.

'Oh, don't be so defensive.'

'I'm not being defensive.'

She mumbled to herself in Arabic as she shuffled away. 'I'll talk to you tomorrow night when I get back from work and once you have rested and are in a better mood.'

With those words the conversation was over, and I quelled the irritation that was bubbling away inside and huffed and puffed as I lugged my suitcase up the stairs. I had to remind myself that I was relieved to see her well and on her feet, and immensely grateful to my best friends for doing a seemingly better job at looking after her. I inwardly sighed. There was bitterness behind my thoughts. I needed some sleep.

A chill greeted me inside my bedroom as soon as I opened the door. Mum liked to turn off radiators in rooms that weren't being occupied. I knew I was being silly, but

Samira and Jena had been using this room for the last three weeks and Jena left this morning. Could she not have kept it on one day for me? As I turned the valve, I noticed that all of my things from my dresser and bookcase had been moved. I found a couple of boxes under my bed, which contained my belongings. I had the feeling that Mum had done all this the second I departed for my trip. She would have hated that I hadn't left the room in a state fit for guests, even though they wouldn't have minded at all.

I lay flat on my bed and drifted off. Waking with a start, I realised that I was still in my travel clothes and that it was three in the morning. Tiptoeing to the bathroom, I washed my face and brushed my teeth before getting changed back in my room and slipping beneath the covers. But it was no good. My body was wracked with jet lag, and I was wide awake. Far too late to message the girls but not too late for those in a completely different time zone.

I picked up my phone. There were still no messages from Mateo. What had I expected him to say anyway? It was obvious from how we had said goodbye that our friendship couldn't carry on. That thought brought a sadness to my heart. If he hadn't discovered those messages from Austin and Edoardo, it made me wonder how we would have spent the rest of my time in Costa Rica. But then I wouldn't have seen Gregory. I only wished it hadn't had to have been a choice.

I opened the last message from Austin. Austin. Those days we spent together had been wild yet tender. And the love that emanated from his parents and sisters had given me a taste of what it would be like to be a part of a large, traditional family. Samira had been quick to claim he had love-bombed me whereas Jena had seen all of his actions as romantic. I thought back to my dissection of my California trip with Gregory, who had encouraged me to be more open to new possibilities, before typing the words:

Miss you too

Chapter 28

'Look at you.' Jena held me at arm's length begore giving me a quick squeeze. 'You look amazing.'

'The tan's fading rapidly and it's hardly the time of year to be showing off my limbs so no one will notice, but… thanks.'

'Where's Samira?' she asked, unwinding her scarf and unbuttoning her coat.

'I'm not sure.'

I scanned the pub to see in between bodies but couldn't catch sight of her. We were tucked away in a booth at the back, the low hum of punters at the bar a backing track that provided us some privacy without having to yell to be heard. This place had been chosen by Jena because it was within walking distance of her commuter station. I turned back and noticed Jena's shoulders sag a little.

'Is everything OK?' I asked.

'Everything's fine.' A smile appeared on her face, but I knew Jena well enough to know when she was faking it.

'Long week at school?'

'I guess. The kids are still in half-term mode. They're little shits sometimes. But it's mocks soon, so at least I can do some invigilating and tune out for some of the school day.'

'That doesn't sound like much fun.'

'I'm sure I'll feel better once the summer comes round.'

'That's four months away.'

She gave a half-hearted shoulder lift and the lines on her forehead creased.

'Let me get the first round in,' I said, standing up from our booth.

Jena laid a hand on my wrist. 'I don't think there will be more than one round. It *is* a school night after all.'

'My treat regardless. Least I can do after all you've done for me.'

I went to the bar and got our drinks. There was a tension about Jena, I noticed, as I glanced back at her unawares. She was checking her phone. Her shoulders were locked and as she placed her mobile face down, her fingers lightly tapped the table as if she was in a rush to leave.

Returning with two glasses of pinot grigio and a packet of salt and vinegar crisps, I placed her glass in front of her, opening the bag to share. 'Come on, what's troubling you?' I said, cutting to the chase.

Jena's lips pinched tight, and she stared at her hand before stretching out her arm and wriggling her fingers. 'I thought there would be a ring on there soon.'

'Won't there be?' I said before taking a sip of my wine. 'I thought you said the plan was to have a spring engagement.'

'That was before he decided to have his boys' holiday and cancel the one we were beginning to plan for over the Easter holidays. That was the original idea… or so I thought. An April engagement this year would have given us enough time to organise something for next summer.'

'Oh, Jena. I'm sorry. If I had known it would cause so much trouble, I would never have said yes to you coming to stay with Mum.'

'No, it's fine. I wouldn't have offered if I couldn't have done it. It's a bump in the road. Maybe he's got a secret weekend away planned during that time. Or maybe he's trying to throw me off the scent and make it a proper surprise. I mean, we haven't spoken about where our relationship is headed in a long time and when he came back from his trip, he said he wanted to do more spontaneous things. Like tonight, he said he was going out for a drink with some work friends, so I jumped at the chance to come out when you messaged. Sunday evenings are normally my marking nights, but I couldn't wait to hear all about your trip, and I didn't want to be home alone.'

I squeezed her hand. 'You guys will work things out. Maybe you should talk to him about how you're feeling?'

'God, no. I don't want him to think I am some demanding girlfriend or anything like that. If James wants to be more spontaneous, then I will endeavour to be the same. So… spill.' She took a large gulp of her wine. 'You glossed over the three weeks in your messages and your communication all but faded in the last week.'

'It was amazing, Jena. So much happened, I don't even know where to begin.'

'Should we wait for Samira?'

I checked my phone again and noticed a text had come through a minute ago. 'Rosie isn't well. She can't make it.' I began to tap out a reply.

'Poor Samira. Send her my love.'

Samira replied instantly asking if we could meet for coffee mid-week as she was dying for details of the trip. I told her I would see how the first day at work went and get back to her. The thought of going into the hospital tomorrow made my stomach churn. I was going back to limited responsibilities and the guy who had filled in while I was away would still be there. It would be hard to concentrate on my pared-down role until the investigation had a resolution.

We sipped our drinks while I filled Jena in on the visits to see Austin and Edoardo but when it came to my trip to Costa Rica, I paused before deciding to only tell her about the saving of the baby turtle, throwing up on my first night and the race to help the leatherback give birth before the storm struck.

'That all sounds wonderful but very tame.'

I soaked up a drop of wine that was falling down my glass with my finger before sucking it. 'Believe me, it was far from tame in the end.'

Jena squealed before squeezing my arm. 'I knew it. The one that got away.'

'Or rather, the one that found out the truth and went away. I screwed up. Big time.'

Jena popped a crisp into her mouth and crunched it. 'How so?'

'I wish now I had been upfront with Mateo from the start, told him where I had been and with whom while we were still enjoying all those wonderful friendship vibes. Then I could have gauged his reaction when I said what had happened with Austin had been a holiday fling, and with Edoardo nothing more than a chance to revisit the past and heal from old wounds.'

'But then you probably wouldn't have had all those wild times with Mateo, which you have conveniently not elaborated on.' She licked the salt off her fingers.

'Please don't let me have to use my imagination. The most exciting my sex life gets is doing it on the couch instead of in the bedroom.'

I laughed but again noticed there was a hollowness to Jena's tone.

'I'm waiting,' she said, tapping her fingers on the table.

'OK, OK. It was after our night patrol where I witnessed the leatherback giving birth and after we had shared the most thrilling first kiss in the rain. There was a blistering storm raging around us and Mateo and I hunkered down in our hut in the darkness, no electricity. I was a little scared.'

Jena gave me a disbelieving eyebrow raise.

'I had already seen the destruction a hurricane had caused in Puerto Rico and seen the damage to the houses near Mateo's conservation centre from the last storm, so yes, I was a little apprehensive. But also...'

'Yes?' She leaned closer, propping her elbows on the table, chin resting in the palms of her hands.

'OK, yes, I was feeling very attracted to him and the attraction had been building and building since the night before when we salsa danced in the moonlight. With no power, I couldn't see a thing and I was soaked to the bone. He gave me a towel and some of his clothes before coming and lying next to me on the bottom bunk.'

'With the others in the room?'

I choked on a mouthful of wine. 'I didn't suddenly become an exhibitionist. They had already left earlier on in the day, but we only had one night alone before the next occupants arrived.'

'Mmm, sex in the dark, heightened emotions, shackles released. The giving in to temptation and allowing your-self to be unbridled.'

I leaned back. 'That's, umm, very descriptive.'

'I like my open-door romance, and this scene could easily have been lifted from one of my friends-to-lovers/forced-proximity/one-bed romance books.'

'I guess that is what it was like. Mateo was a friend, and I knew once we crossed that line, there was no going back, so maybe it was easier to allow ourselves to be freer in the darkness.'

'Did you feel shy the next day?'

'Unbelievably so. But then we couldn't keep our hands off each other every time we were alone and...' I bit my bottom lip at the memory. 'We went skinny dipping in the Caribbean and I...'

She rolled her eyes to the back of her head and slumped on the table as if she had fainted.

'I did, he didn't. It's the Love Intervention's fault.'

'Sounds to me like the Love Intervention was the best thing that ever happened to you.'

I popped another crisp in my mouth and coughed as a sharp tang of vinegar hit the back of my throat before taking another sip of wine. 'It was until Mateo saw these messages from Austin and Edoardo. Now I'll probably never hear from him again.'

'But you thought that about the other two and look what happened.'

'Nothing *is* going to happen, Jena. I'm back in London now, about to return to work and things will go back to normal,' I said, my chin raised. 'I know how to do things in my life to get the spikes in dopamine needed to improve my mental health and I am going to incorporate more exercise into my day for those endorphins. Like tomorrow, I'm going to get off the Tube one stop earlier and walk that extra mile to work. And I thought of maybe doing some support work with the British Cardiovascular Society, helping organise seminars or volunteering my time in some way. And I will definitely invest in one of those SAD lamps.'

She nodded and carried on sipping her drink, not looking like she believed a word I had said.

My phone buzzed on the table. Another notification from Austin. They had increased in frequency since I had told him I missed him too. I turned over my phone and avoided Jena's glare.

'Sure, Laila. You tell yourself that. Going back to the way things were is one hundred per cent the best course of action plus a little extra exercise and some gimmicky lamp.'

'What do you expect me to do? They all live on another continent and one of them will probably never speak to me again.'

'And what if one of them appeared at this pub this second, declaring their undying love, what would you do then?'

I opened and closed my mouth, seemingly at a loss for words. 'Love doesn't work out like one of your romance novels, no matter what you would have me and Samira believe. I am so grateful to you both for unleashing the inner seductress in me for a few weeks, encouraging me to open my mind to new experiences, cultures and adventures, but the time I spent with Austin, Edoardo and Mateo will be relegated to the depths of my memory from now. It was certainly cathartic, and I am glad I went but my mind has to be on work now.'

'Then why are you still' – she reached over and flipped my phone – 'messaging one of them?'

I grabbed my mobile from her hold and shoved it in my handbag.

'I was being polite. There is no way I am going to let a guy tempt me away from everything I have worked hard to achieve for the last ten years.'

I dared not let Jena challenge me on what the hell I was doing still messaging Austin because the truth was, I didn't even know why myself. But the idea of an April trip, all expenses paid, hadn't left my thoughts since he had brought it up.

Jena excused herself, saying she needed the bathroom, and I took the opportunity to check my phone.

> I miss you so much it hurts, and I want to see you again. Let's talk.

Austin's words spun around in my head. Up until this point it had been messages about life and work, the vineyard, the news that his older sister was pregnant with her third. It all seemed quite innocent bar the ones where we had reminisced about one of our sessions on a dining chair, which had snapped in the heat of the moment. He had made me laugh when he said his mum had questioned why there was a broken chair stashed in his garage when she went to put some meals she had cooked in the spare freezer he had out there. Having spent time with his family, it was easy to imagine them getting together at the house again.

Could I possibly be entertaining the notion that a relationship with Austin might work? Was I seriously contemplating the idea of going back to California if the result of the investigation went against me? Austin had painted a very tempting life to me, and I couldn't deny that since he had been in touch and we had begun flirting again, I had wondered what a relationship with him would look like.

A notification popped up on my phone. It was one of those career opportunity ones, like the one that had led me to the conference in California. But this one was about a newly funded research team at my hospital that was being created. A pulse of excitement throbbed through to my core. This could be it. Another chance to put my name forward, provided of course that the name of Dr Laila Clarke was cleared.

Wow. How quickly my mind had turned back to work and my career. It was proof that my deep-seated belief about making sacrifices for a relationship was right. This was my life. And any guy that wanted to date me would have to realise that my future was here with my friends, my mum and my work.

I took a deep breath in and out. Austin Bradley had always been a charmer. I shouldn't confuse an idealised image of us together with the harsh reality of what a life with him would actually be like. We had connected on a sexual level. That's all. It had been nothing more than a wild affair. Samira's warnings about him still swirled in my mind.

Once a bad boy, always a bad boy.

Typing out the following message, I felt a surge of relief flood through me that I wasn't contemplating anything as stupid as giving up my life in England for him as I had once almost contemplated doing for Josh when he proposed to me and suggested a new life up north.

I don't think there's anything to talk about, Austin. What we had was fun, but I don't see a future for us.

Chapter 29

A warning. A warning and a request to keep my responsibilities reduced over the coming months. That was the conclusion to the investigation. I stared at the email that had come through this morning after my supervisor had called me in for a one-on-one chat. She had dismissed my request to put my name forward for the new research team, claiming timing was an issue. Best to let the dust settle – the cliché she had thrown at me.

I read the email for the third time as I waited in the cafe that Samira had suggested we meet in as it was close to her office. For once I didn't feel the need to drag her in the direction of the hospital. With my responsibilities already reduced due to the recruitment of the new clinical scientist, my first couple of days back hadn't been especially arduous and I knew that me taking a full lunch break wouldn't be frowned upon.

I should be celebrating, but there was still an unease about the situation, and I couldn't help but feel paranoid every time I walked into the lab. The meeting hadn't left me feeling even remotely warm and fuzzy about my career at the hospital. While I knew there might be positions that I could apply for at other hospitals in London, it would be hard to shake off the black mark against my name even though the investigation hadn't resulted in me losing my job.

Samira walked into the cafe with none of her usual high-energy flourish. Her black coat was buttoned up to her chin and her burgundy woollen hat was pulled low over her forehead, chin and mouth completely submerged by her matching scarf.

'When will this goddamn winter end?' she said, pulling off her leather gloves finger by finger and slamming them down on the table.

'And it's lovely to see you too.'

'Sorry,' she said, and leaned over to plant a kiss on my cheek. Her lips were like icicles on my skin. 'And sorry I'm late, too. It's been a hell of a week,' she declared.

'How's Rosie?'

'Oh, she's fine, I think. Doctor didn't find anything wrong. But she's still complaining of tummy aches. School wants me to come in tomorrow for a meeting, but they didn't say what it was about.'

'Poor thing. Hope it isn't anything serious.'

'I think there's this boy that's making her life a bit of a misery and she used a bad word in front of him or something like that. Playground drama. Anyway, what are you having?' She pointed at my paper cup that I was cradling in my hands. The barista had thought I had asked for a takeaway, and I had been too embarrassed to correct him. I popped the lid and noticed that I was down to the froth. 'It was a flat white.'

'Want another?'

'Yes please. I can't seem to kick this jet lag to the kerb.'

'I'm also starving,' she declared, clutching her stomach. 'Let me get us something to eat.'

She left the table and ordered our drinks then pointed to something behind the glass counter. The barista gave her a winning smile, but she didn't give one in return. Something wasn't right.

As she waited for our order, my phone buzzed on the table. Turning it over, I saw it was another notification from Austin, though weirdly it was a text message and not a WhatsApp. I hadn't heard from him after my last message, and I had wondered if he was licking his wounds after my rebuttal. Had I had been too blunt? Did he deserve a little more explanation as to why I didn't think we had a future?

> How's work? Do you get a chance for a break ever?

His words confused me. It was almost as if he hadn't seen my last message.

I wrote:

> I do now and again. Currently having lunch with a friend.

I included a snap of my coffee cup. The three dots appeared signifying he was writing another message but then they disappeared.

Samira returned with her coffee and slumped into the chair opposite me. It was then that I noticed the dark circles under her eyes.

'So…' she said, rummaging in her handbag for her lip balm, which she slathered across her lips. 'Tell me everything about the trip.' Her tone was flat, and it made me wonder whether she actually wanted to know about my three-week break full of fun and frolicking.

I reached over the table to hold her hand. 'Are you OK?'

'Yes, why do you ask?'

'You didn't even acknowledge the barista flirting with you and you're applying Vaseline and not lip gloss. I know the signs when you are not feeling one hundred per cent.'

She puffed her cheeks. 'Where do I start?'

'Anywhere you like.'

'Bar boy ghosted me, and cafe boy was a little too rough for my liking and keeps messaging for round two.'

'Since when did Samira Fares go back for seconds regarding the former guy and as for the latter… sounds like you definitely need to dodge that bullet.'

'I guess.' She stirred her coffee methodically, watching the froth of her cappuccino disappear.

'You guess. What's going on, Samira?'

'I think I want what Jena has.'

'A teaching job?'

'No, stupid. A…' She made a big deal of swallowing. 'Relationship.'

I laughed at her delivery but when I saw the sadness in her eyes, I dropped my smile. 'You're serious.'

'I told you a few weeks back, I'm tired of doing all this on my own. But what have I got to offer someone as a single mum of a nine-year-old?'

'You have loads to offer. You're smart, you're beautiful, you're funny.'

'But guys my age don't want to be a readymade father.'

'Have you even tried to date? How would you know? You've been going after the one-night-stand guys for ages.'

'Maybe it's a blip. Maybe I will come round and remember why I don't date in the first place.'

'Or maybe you can open yourself up to other possibilities.'

She shook her head a little and tapped her spoon against her cup, letting a broad smile break over her face. 'We're both about to turn thirty-one and all we can still talk about when we meet up is men. But my love life chat can wait until Friday-night drinks.' She blew the steam away from her cup before taking a sip. 'I want to know more about the last stop on your trip.'

'Nothing to tell. Mateo and I made love, and the following day he saw the notifications from Austin and Edoardo and thought the worst.'

'Made love, eh?'

'Don't nitpick.'

She gave me an eye roll. 'Did you set him straight about jumping to conclusions?'

'And say what? I hooked up with someone a week before I slept with you. Oh, and I met up with my ex whom I was contemplating having an entanglement with.'

'Yes. Though "entanglement" is a bit... outdated. What did you tell him?'

'He didn't give me the chance. Said he didn't want to be a part of a love square.'

'Is that what this is?'

'It's nothing of the sort.'

'But you've thought about it? You've considered what it would be like to be with each of these guys.'

We were interrupted by the delivery of our toasted sandwiches and two glasses of water. After giving our thanks, we tucked in, and I considered Samira's question as cheese and pesto danced on my tongue. It reminded me of all the times over my trip when I had stopped to savour a meal, to slow down and relish the flavours. Maybe it was time to stop seeing something like a lunch with a best friend as an anomaly and try and factor them into my life a little more regularly. That way I could avoid going back to how things were before the trip. Because the truth was, a large part of me didn't want to go back to my old life – the one of half-eaten sandwiches wilting by my desk, stale biscuits with my endless cups of coffee and tea to get me through the long hours in the lab or the ready meals I usually picked up on my way home, not wanting to burden Mum with having to cook for both of us. It was like we had been living as flatmates for years and neglecting the fact that we were mother and daughter.

'Earth to Laila.'

'Hmm?'

'You zoned out. I asked if you had thought of three different scenarios with each of these guys. A love square, as Mateo put it.'

'It would be a triangle anyway. I've only heard from Austin and Edoardo. Maybe I shouldn't have left Costa Rica early and told Mateo more about why I did the trip in the first place.'

'You left early? Where did you go?'

'I—' The words got stuck in my throat at the realisation that I hadn't told Samira or Jena about what had happened that year in NYU. 'I stayed over in New York and…'

'And what?'

I wiped my mouth with the napkin and placed it on the table. 'And I met up with my… stepfather.'

Samira's forehead wrinkled as she chewed. Taking a sip of her water, she gave a slight head shake. 'You've lost me.

Your stepfather? How is that even possible? Your mum has sworn off ever dating again.'

'I was talking about my dad's husband.'

Her sandwich dropped from her hold. 'I'm sorry, what?'

'My father had a lover when he was separated from Mum, and they ended up getting married.'

She wiped her napkin over her mouth, lost in thought. 'I don't think I am comprehending what you're saying. Your dad liked men, and he married some guy whom you visited while you were on your trip. That's a lot to take in. When did you find out about him?'

I absentmindedly pulled a strand of cheese from my panini as I thought back to that trip to Saratoga Springs. 'During my Master's year.'

Her eyes widened. 'That was almost ten years ago.'

I popped the cheese in my mouth and chewed. Ten years ago, but because of the Love Intervention that memory was now at the forefront of my mind as if it had occurred last week. 'I know. And I am sorry I never told you and Jena what happened during that year.'

'Your father passed away of a heart attack. You told us that much.'

'But I didn't tell you I was there.' The words tumbled from my mouth, my heart splintering as I recalled that fateful day, and tears began to sting at the back of my eyes.

She pushed her plate to the side and leaned forward. 'What do you mean you were there? You said he was living in California, that your mum told you on the phone he had passed.'

I braced myself to tell her the whole truth. 'When we were at university, I saw a letter that Dad had written Mum, and it had an address on it in upstate New York. I never told Mum that I had seen it and she never showed me what he had written. When I began my Master's, I wrote to him but never heard back. One day, during my spring semester, I went up there to the address and found out from a neighbour he had sold the house and that he and his husband were living on the West Coast but occasionally travelled back to the city.'

Her mouth continued to stay open as she absorbed my words. 'Shit. That must have come as a shock.'

I held the napkin in my grasp, tearing the corners off. 'It was. Then out of the blue Dad called me, May of that year, and we had arranged to meet for coffee close to NYU... He was late and then there was a commotion, a crowd in the distance, someone shouting for an ambulance. He had had a heart attack.'

I was aware of a touch. Samira's hand was covering mine and I hadn't realised it was trembling.

'I froze. I couldn't do anything. Paramedics arrived and I somehow got to the hospital, but they wouldn't give me any information.'

'But you were his daughter.'

'He had changed his name when he got married so they had no record of a Victor Clarke having been admitted. I sat in the waiting room not even sure what to do but then his husband arrived, and I fled. I couldn't face grieving with a man who I didn't know, someone I hadn't even known existed until a few months prior.'

She stroked her thumb over my knuckles, the movement measured and soothing. 'Then what happened?'

I took some shaky deep breaths in and out to avert the flow of tears, aware that we were in a bustling coffee shop and not somewhere private. 'Mum told me in a phone call that he had... died... and where they were holding the funeral. I went but stayed in the background and when I came home to London, I decided to bury that part of my life, for fear of it upsetting Mum. And I never told you or Jena because I didn't want to put you both in an awkward position where you also had to lie. You're like sisters to me after all' – she squeezed my hand – 'and I know Mum cares for you both as if you were surrogate daughters.'

'But you visited this man last week? Your father's husband.'

I nodded before letting a small smile break into the corner of my mouth. 'It hadn't been my intention at all, but meeting up with Austin, then Edoardo and finally Mateo brought that time up again and I realised that I had never fully healed from what happened, what I saw, the lies that had sat inside me and the guilt I felt for not being able to do anything when he collapsed.'

'And how was it? Seeing that man.' Those last two words were delivered with a tone of disgust.

I flinched, shocked at Samira's response. 'It was… emotional.'

She quirked a brow. 'I bet.'

'But I'm glad I found him.' I was resolute in this. I had sought redemption but had gained so much more and the healing I had begun in those precious hours spent with Gregory had been restorative and a part of me wished it had been more than a day.

'Really?'

Her responses to me talking about Gregory were beginning to annoy me. 'Yes, really.' I accented each syllable.

'What did your mum say when you told her?'

I hesitated. This was the reason why I hadn't allowed myself to get caught up in the joyous feelings that the visit to NYC had brought me. 'I haven't spoken to her about any of it.'

She scoffed. 'She's going to be pretty pissed at you, I reckon.'

'That's what I'm worried about.' I chewed my bottom lip at the thought of her reaction. Based on past history it would be an angry outburst followed by days of silence at the very least. But the fear of it breaking apart our relationship for a lot longer than that was very real.

'That's a long time to keep so much back from her. But you won't see him again, right? So, I guess it's another secret you'll have to bury.' She rummaged in her bag for her compact and did a quick check on her lips before pulling back her plate to resume eating.

Stillness came over me at Samira's easy dismissal. 'Why wouldn't I see him again?'

She looked at me like I'd lost my mind. 'Cos it would crush your mum if she found out that you had met up with him. But to then tell her you're entertaining the idea of having him in your life…' She shook her head but didn't finish her sentence, as if the mere idea of staying in contact couldn't be comprehended.

I leaned back, dumbstruck, and she noticed my expression.

'Come on, Laila. You know I'm right. And you've kept wanting to find your dad in the US a secret for a very, very long time; I don't think she'll recover from that either.'

It was as if I was suddenly having this conversation with my mother and not my best friend. She was meant to have my back and understand my standpoint. 'But he was my father.'

'And he left her with no means to support herself, single and alone with a teenager to raise. He also cheated on her. It must have been with *that man.*' Disgust once again laced those last two words.

I ignored her harsh tone but considered her words. 'How do you know about any of this?'

'Your mum told me everything while you were away, all the pain she suffered because of everything he did.' Her eyes were locked onto mine, searing in their intensity. 'And you think telling her about meeting up with his... husband will make her forget all that heartache she suffered?'

'So, lying is a better option?'

'The trip is already one big lie anyway, what's one more?'

I was struggling to wrap my head around Samira's words, her reaction to all of this, her dismissiveness of my feelings. 'I can't believe you're not on my side.'

'I'm not on anyone's side, Laila.'

'It sounds like you are,' I said hotly. 'Gregory is a lovely man. He and I bonded and yes, I think I would like to see him again.'

She scoffed again. 'Don't come running to me when your relationship with your mum blows up in your face.'

Her tone felt like a slap in the face. I was used to Samira's occasional histrionics but her reaction to me baring my soul shocked me and it made me wonder whether there was more that was bothering he than just her love-life problems. 'Aren't you being a little dramatic?'

'I'm an Arab. We live for family drama. Your dad was nothing but a cheat and a liar and he left you and your mum practically penniless.'

Samira's insistence that Dad was a lowlife was beginning to rile me. 'We got back on our feet in the end. Dad did his best, but he was tormented by various demons back then, living half a life.'

She slapped her hand down on the table and it caused our cups to rattle and a hush to descend over the cafe. 'But where was he when your mum was down to her last pound, working three jobs to support you when you were in sixth form? Off rebuilding his life with some American guy with no thought to how his daughter was either?'

'OK.' I held my hands up. 'I think you've said enough.' I kept my voice quiet, aware of the stares from other customers, but there was no mistaking my defiant tone. Samira had crossed a line. 'He was *my* father to forgive, not yours. And besides…'

I couldn't finish that sentence because something outside the glass frontage had caught my attention. Or rather someone. He was across the road clutching a large bouquet of flowers, staring at his phone before looking up and down the street as if he was checking he had the right location. It was the bright burst of pink and yellow amongst the grey of yet another winter's day that had made me take a second look. I blinked a few times. It was definitely him.

'Besides what?' Samira said, her tone impatient. But I had to park all thoughts of getting mad at her for the guilt she was piling onto me because there was another very real situation unfolding right here in front of me and not thousands of miles away.

'Austin,' I whispered. 'It's Austin.'

Chapter 30

'What's Austin got to do with anything?' Samira asked before biting into another corner of her sandwich.

'He's here, or rather he's there,' I said, pointing out the window.

'What on earth is he doing here?'

'I have no idea.'

Samira wrapped several serviettes around her half-eaten sandwich and shoved it in her handbag before draining her coffee. 'I think I'll leave you both to your little reunion.'

I reached out to grab her hand. 'No, don't leave. I don't know what to say to him. I have no idea why he's here.'

'Then find out and message the group chat later. Just…' She pinched her lips tightly and leaned in. 'Be careful.'

She scooped up her coat, hat and scarf and swept out the cafe, now walking towards Austin, who had crossed the road. Keeping her head down as she breezed past, her shoulder nudged into his and he turned as she mumbled something to him. He stole the briefest of glances before doing a double take. There was a flicker of recognition on his face, but she was long gone before he had a chance to place her. Even though it had been ten years since they had last seen each other, I wouldn't be surprised if he remembered her. Samira had that effect on people.

When Austin entered the cafe, he scanned the room before locking eyes with mine. My shoulders tensed at the sight of him. I had told him we had nothing to talk about yet here he was clearly wanting to talk.

I pretended I had only just seen him before standing as he approached, my jaw exaggeratedly open. 'Austin?'

He outstretched one arm before presenting me with the flowers.

'What's all this?' I said, the scent engulfing me as I took them in my arms.

'I believe they are arrowwood and wintersweets, so the florist said.'

I cocked my head at his cheekiness. 'I don't mean these, though they are gorgeous. I meant you, here, in…' I nodded to the floor. 'In a cafe in London.'

'I came to see you.'

'How could you possibly know I was here?'

He gazed down at his shoes before looking up at me with that eyebrow-raised, side-of-mouth smirk. 'You gave me a massive clue when you sent that picture.' He picked up my coffee cup and pointed at the sleeve, which had the logo of the cafe on it.

'That's a little… stalkerish.'

He laughed.

'It's a good thing I didn't go to any of the coffee chains, then. Did you have a back-up plan?'

'Nope. But I hoped I could plead on your mercy and that you would tell me your location seeing as I have flown five thousand, three hundred and fifty-four miles to talk to you.'

'Why *have* you flown here? Surely a phone call would have been easier and cheaper.'

Austin hailed a passing waitress and asked for an Americano. She nodded and simpered at the same time before explaining that it was counter service but that he could pay later. It reminded me of Samira and her ability to always get her way in any coffee shop she visited.

He sat down at my table and unzipped his leather jacket before cupping his hands and blowing into them. 'Jeez.' He rubbed his palms together. 'You weren't kidding about this brutal winter.'

I sat back down on my chair, laying the flowers on the table. 'You're avoiding my question.'

'I don't think you asked me one. I believe the last thing you said was phone calls are cheaper than flights.'

I exhaled loudly. 'Don't be obtuse, Austin.'

'Sorry. Tiredness. Been up for almost twenty-four hours.' He stifled a yawn. 'Yes, I am fully aware that phone calls are cheaper but your last message to me seemed to say we had nothing to talk about so I guess I feared you wouldn't take too kindly to a call. And besides, my big sister has been nagging me to take her to London for the last few weeks. She's calling it a babymoon even though this is nothing of the sort as I am her brother and she's left her husband to look after the kids. But she is a hopeless romantic and thought this would be a very swoonsome gesture – her word not mine – turning up unannounced to see you.'

I sat back. 'This is all your sister's doing?'

'Yup. You left quite an impression on my family, and they made me see I had been an ass to let you go the way I did.'

'I wasn't yours to let go, Austin.'

'I know, I know.' He waved away my words. 'But how would you feel if I told you I haven't been able to stop thinking of you every second of every hour of the day since you left, that I refuse to wash my sheets because they still smell of you, that every time I take a pair of secateurs to a bud, I wonder if you would cut it, or when I use my outdoor shower all I can think of is you and me fucking underneath it. Would that be better? Would that be OK to say?'

His admission left me speechless.

'Yeah, I figured that would be a bit much. Whoops.' He shrugged and removed his jacket, revealing a navy-blue polo-neck jumper that was fitted tightly over his chest.

The waitress brought his coffee to the table with a wrapped Biscoff biscuit and I took a moment to digest what he had said. Austin Bradley was a man that clearly didn't take no for an answer but he also knew how to deliver a convincing argument. The question was, could I be swayed?

Austin blew steam from his cup and took a sip.

'Agh,' he sighed. 'I needed this. Sorry, where are my manners, let me get you another.' He tried to get the attention of the waitress again.

I reached over to grab his arm. 'No, I'm fine.'

When he saw my grip on his jumper's sleeve, he held his other hand over it and threw me a watery smile.

Pulling my hand away, I fiddled with the bow tying up the bouquet. 'I've already had two coffees and I do need to get back to work. The downside of having been gone for three weeks is I have a lot to catch up on.'

'I thought you said in your message that you were having lunch with a friend.' He did a sweep of the cafe as if my companion would suddenly return from the bathroom.

'I was. You missed her. Samira. She had to go back to work.'

'Oh. The lady that knocked into me.'

'You remember her? She came to visit me during our Christmas break.'

'Umm, vaguely.' He pulled up the sleeves of his jumper before taking another sip of his coffee. 'You had two friends come and visit you that winter, I seem to remember. I wasn't sure which of the two she was.' He cleared his throat and tore open the biscuit packet before breaking it in half. 'If I can't persuade you to stay, when can I see you?' he asked popping the Biscoff into his mouth.

'How long are you here for?'

'As long as it takes for me to convince you we have a future.'

I rubbed the back of my neck, feeling mildly exasperated at the situation. 'Be serious, Austin.'

He inhaled deeply and ruffled his hair as he let out his breath. 'Tina and I are staying until Monday. It was only meant to be a short trip. I'm needed at the vineyard next week for a big event I'm hosting, and I couldn't get out of it. But...' He grasped my hand again. 'I am serious, Laila. I want to talk to you about everything. And I want to hear all about the rest of your trip.'

I shot him a disbelieving look.

'What? I do. I need to know which of those guys are my competition or maybe even if both of them are and when we can arrange a bout in a ring.' He was smirking again.

I folded my arms, unamused.

'Come on, Laila. Please. Let's meet. Let's have a date on your home turf.'

I turned away. 'Austin, I don't think—'

'Please.' He elongated the word, trying to catch my gaze. 'Show some pity on this crazy American who has come all this way to see you whether I was a welcome guest or not. One drink. That's all I'm asking for.'

I took in his expression, which finally bore traces of sincerity, my defences slowly crumbling. 'One drink.'

He punched the air. 'I'll take it. Just tell me when and where and I'll be there.'

'I think Friday night could be a possibility. I'll message you some details. Now if you will excuse me…' I picked up the bouquet of flowers. 'I have to get back to work.'

By the time I gathered my things and stood up, Austin was on his feet and had closed the space between us, the flowers almost crushed up against my chest and his. His hands cupped my face, and his touch had the ability to render my legs a shaky mess like it had every time his skin had caressed mine. Agh. My body had betrayed my mind, which had been resolute up to this point.

'Until Friday,' he whispered before brushing his lips over mine.

He left me dangling as he sat back down in his seat and picked up his coffee cup.

I took a deep breath and left, stopping outside the coffee shop out of view from the vantage point I'd had at that table.

What on earth had just happened? I needed some clarity on what I should do from the girls. Pulling out my phone, I went to the group chat but paused. The end of my conversation with Samira had bothered me and Austin's sudden arrival had meant we had left things unresolved, which didn't sit right with me. Spats between us had always been commonplace growing up, but this one ran deeper. And I could probably guess what she would say if I told her I had agreed to a date with Austin. Jena would no doubt declare it the most romantic gesture of the century. I was tired of them having such opposing views. Maybe it was time I figured how to approach him myself? That said, they were my best friends and if Austin and I had any chance going forward, I would want them all to get along.

That settled it. Friday night, I would plan for them all to meet without any warning. Seeing if they bonded without a heads-up would be the only way to gauge whether this dopamine-fuelled liaison with Austin could be something more.

Chapter 31

I dropped my keys on the plate by the front door at five thirty on Friday afternoon. Mum popped her head up from where she was sitting at the kitchen table.

I slipped off my shoes and walked over, opening the cupboard above the sink to get a glass before running the tap.

'Why are you so early?' she asked, rubbing her shoulder, her face furrowed. She was in her work clothes, and I guessed she must have got home from one of her clients.

I drained my glass and put it in the sink. 'I managed to finish everything I needed to, but I am going out with the girls tonight and wanted to get changed first.'

'That's nice,' she said but there was a lack of interest in her tone, and she appeared to drift off, her focus somewhere behind me.

Mum and I had been passing ships since I got back from my trip and a part of me wondered whether it was because I had been deliberately avoiding her or whether she had been avoiding me. Our catch-up last Sunday had never materialised because one of her clients needed her help last-minute in advance of a house viewing. To be honest, I had been relieved. Samira's warning to me about her blowing up in anger if I told her the truth about my trip hadn't stopped spinning in my mind.

I noticed a box opened on the table filled with photographs, a few scattered in front of her. 'What are those?'

She took off her glasses and picked them up, handing them to me. I slipped into the nearest chair and studied each one. They were a series of black and white photos with three little girls and two stern-looking adults standing behind them.

'Is that you?' I said, pointing to the little girl in braids, standing a little apart from the scene.

She nodded. 'Yes, it is.'

'Why are you looking through old snaps?'

'Your auntie Zaynab called me this morning.'

This surprised me. Mum had zero relationship with her sisters, and I had only met them when I was a little girl. There had been some feud between them all and Mum had never divulged what happened, only to say that she never wanted to talk to them again.

'Why did she call?' I asked.

The wrinkle at the bridge of her nose deepened and she tapped her glasses on her mouth. 'It seems your grandmother is unwell.'

'I'm sorry to hear that.' My tone sounded overly formal, like a polite stranger was saying the words, but the truth was I didn't know my *teta* at all. Mum had made sure of that.

'They want me to go over there.' The expression on her face was unreadable.

'Are you going to?'

'I'm not sure.' She hugged herself and stroked the fabric of her worn cardigan, methodically, up and down her arm.

'I would love to go with you, but I used up all my holiday entitlement with my trip.'

She patted my hand. 'That's a lovely gesture, Laila, but I think this is something I need to do alone.'

'When would you go?'

'Immediately. Maybe even tomorrow if I can book a flight. I'll have to email my clients first. Doubt it will go down well seeing as I have only just come back from sick leave.'

'I'm sure they will be understanding. It's your mother after all.'

'It's duty is what it is. And I will dread the visit from the moment I get there until the moment I leave.' She placed her glasses back in their case and slammed it shut.

'Oh.' Her confession didn't shock me at all. It was all very black and white when it came to her family. The absence of kin on both sides had left a gaping hole in my life and I had always accepted that. But something stirred in my mind as I studied these photos of a family that were strangers to me. A need to know why. Gregory had asked me to share more of my family life and there had been very little to tell him. I fanned the photos out on the table.

'I don't think I ever understood why it has to be that way,' I challenged her. 'You've always kept that part of your life closed off from me. I often thought it would have been nice to have had relatives, extended family that I could visit. And I have always wondered why you never moved on after your divorce.'

'You're not missing out on much,' she said curtly. 'Trust me. And your father was an only child and his parents long gone before you came into this world. Moving on?' She tutted but didn't elaborate.

'Yes, I know all that. But I also know something else.' My cheeks burned as the need to be open and honest suddenly overwhelmed me. Samira had told me that continuing to withhold the truth about the trip and what happened in the past was the best course of action, but I didn't want to live with these lies anymore. I wanted a fresh start. 'I knew that Dad's parents were long gone but I know that Dad…' I swallowed away the sudden dryness in my throat. 'I know he met someone else after you separated and got remarried.'

She blinked rapidly. 'How do you know that?' Her voice was shaky.

'Because…' I clasped my hands on the table. 'Because I went to find him. I went to find Dad, that year I did my Master's.'

Her eyes narrowed. 'You what?'

'I went to look for him and found out that he had moved to the West Coast with his… husband.'

She stood, the chair scraping across the kitchen floor. 'Don't ever say that word to me.'

'Why not?' I challenged, finally finding the courage to push back. 'Dad was gay. Yes, he left us, but he met Gregory when you were separated and—'

She slammed her hands on the table. 'That's not true. I told you: your father had an affair.'

Her dramatic outburst mirrored Samira's but I didn't want to deal with this conflict with anger in return. 'He never cheated on you, Mum,' I said softly. 'I know the truth now. Why have you let me believe that version of events for all these years?'

'You believe your father's word over mine?' She recoiled.

'No, Mum,' I said, resolutely. 'I don't believe his word because I never saw him. I never got the opportunity to see my father again because on the day I was meant to meet him, he died. I heard it from his husband. Last week.'

She took a sharp breath. 'You saw him?' She slowly sat down again. 'Is that why you went to America?'

'No, I didn't go there deliberately to meet with him. I went to have a break because I messed up at work and was put on leave, but I met with some old friends, friends that I made during my Master's, and it brought everything back to me. One of those friends suggested I go and visit him, maybe get some answers.'

'What answers could you possibly need? And what friends are these? I thought you went to a conference. You said you were sightseeing after that, not visiting friends. And forced leave?' She held her hand over her heart. 'This is too much to take in.'

The truth serum that had been injected into my system flooded my bloodstream. 'I did go to a conference, but I mainly went to reconnect with three guys I knew from my time at NYU. After California, I went to Puerto Rico and Costa Rica and then stopped in New York on my way home.'

She pinched the bridge of her nose. 'This is all too much, Laila. You never told me about trying to reconnect with your father and you've lied about this entire trip. What was your purpose in meeting these men? Why would you let one of them influence you into making contact with that man?'

I gripped the edge of the kitchen table to anchor myself in my quest to keep going with this honesty. 'His name is Gregory, Mum. And he's lovely. And these men that I met up with… they were all significant guys in my life when I was at NYU, when I *had* a life, before all of this happened, before I fell into a world of nothing but work, work, work.'

'How could you say all these things, Laila? You love your job. You've worked so hard to achieve what you have. Why suddenly are you flying halfway around the world for these men? And why so many of them?'

'It was Jena and Samira's idea. They wanted me to kickstart my love life again.'

'And that involved you tracking down *that* man.'

'No, they know nothing about Dad and his life with Gregory.'

She held her hands over her ears. 'Stop saying his name.'

'Why?'

'Because he ruined everything. You can believe what you want about when he came into your father's life, but he's lying, I know he is. He would never have left us if it wasn't for that man. We were fine without him. We were doing fine until he came along,' she spat out.

'But Dad was living a lie.'

'And? Your father accepted that. I accepted that.'

I sat back, her words confusing me. 'What do you mean, he and you accepted that?'

'I knew he was gay. I knew he wanted a different life, but I begged him, I begged him not to leave us.' Her hands began to shake. 'But he couldn't continue lying to himself and to you. He insisted on moving out, but I know it was because of that man. And then he started drinking and wasting all his money on the horses. He ruined himself and us in the process.'

'No, Mum. He spiralled because he couldn't see a way out that wouldn't end up hurting all of us. Gregory saved him.'

'You would take this man's word as the truth over your own mother's?'

'Mum, please.'

'No, don't "Mum, please" me. All I have ever done for you, and you go and throw it back in my face.' Her hands gesticulated wildly as she said those words.

'But it's not like that.'

'Then you will never see this man again?'

'It's unlikely, but I want to stay in touch with him.'

'Then we have nothing else to talk about.' She pushed back her chair again, throwing the photos into the box and slamming shut the lid. 'I'll be leaving sometime over the weekend.' With those words uttered, she picked up the box and walked out of the kitchen.

The truth was out. There were no more lies. Instead of relief, I felt nothing but sadness. I hated confrontation. My need to be honest had been thrown back at me and I felt like a little girl again that had been told off for doing something that my parent had disapproved of. And Mum didn't know the half of what had happened. That I had been there that day. The day Dad died.

Chapter 32

'Woohoo,' Jena screamed over the pulsating bass track of the bar's sound system. 'The gang back together.' She raised her glass.

'Here's to having had plenty of sun, skinny-dipping in the sea and lots of sex,' Samira said, clinking Jena's glass with a nod towards me.

I blushed at that brief analysis of my trip as I added my glass to the mix. Neither of them knew I had invited Austin here tonight but if I was even contemplating him becoming a feature in my life, then I wanted my besties' approval. I also hadn't divulged to Austin that it wouldn't be the two of us this evening and was keen to gauge his reaction when he realised it wasn't an intimate date for two. I had merely told him to meet me ten minutes after I had agreed to meet the girls. But getting served our first round had taken ages and I kept looking over to the front door of the bar in case Austin arrived on time. I was still reeling from my heated discussion with Mum but knew I had to park it as well as the spat I'd had with Samira the other day.

This Soho venue had been her suggestion. It was the opening night with an offering of two for one on cocktails all evening, so it was a no-brainer according to her, but we hadn't counted on it also being more of a club than a bar. A disco ball spun from the centre of the ceiling, and it sent a kaleidoscope of colours across the darkened room.

'It's a bit loud in here,' Jena said, stating the obvious. 'I wanted to hear more about your trip, but I don't want to lose my voice in the process of interrogation.'

'We're not here for another tête-à-tête,' Samira said, swaying her hips from side to side. 'We're here to have fun. And now that Laila has finally kick-started her love life again, we can be each other's wing-women.'

'What about me?' Jena said. 'You're not going to ditch me tonight, are you?'

'Guys, I am not on a man-hunt tonight,' I said, taking a sip of my cocktail through a straw, the rum-soaked pineapple juice hitting the roof of my mouth.

'Good,' Jena said. 'I don't want to be left alone. I thought this was going to be one of those catch-up nights, like we usually do. Didn't think guys were going to be involved.'

'Speak for yourself. Men are on my menu tonight. I had a moment of madness mid-week thinking I wanted a relationship but have thankfully seen the light. So I am back on the hunt,' Samira said, stretching her neck to scout any potential suitors on the dance floor.

'Actually, I have a confession,' I said, fiddling with my straw. 'Guys *are* on my menu tonight.'

'Yes,' Samira whooped, nudging me with her elbow. 'Now we're talking.'

'Or I should probably say one guy. I invited—'

'Austin,' Samira said, her face paling as she glanced over my shoulder.

'Yes. Is he here?' I turned and craned my neck before placing my cocktail on the nearest table. He strode into the bar much like he had that first day we met. A sea of women parted while simultaneously checking him out as he walked towards us, beaming.

'Hey,' he said, before leaning in, and planting a kiss on my cheek. His skin was smooth as if he had just shaved and a strong scent of aftershave tickled my nose.

'Hey,' I whispered by his ear before he leaned back and took me in, his hand finding mine and bringing it to his lips for a kiss as if there was no one else in the club except me and him.

'You look gorgeous,' he said, and I gave my appearance a once-over. My blue satin long-sleeved top was fitted and I had teamed it with a black skirt and tights. It was the most dressed-up I had been since that first date with Austin back in San Francisco.

'Umm, thanks, you look nice, too,' I said, nodding at his tailored shirt beneath his unzipped leather jacket and smart jeans, feeling compelled to return the compliment before remembering that we weren't alone.

'Austin, you remember…' But my voice trailed off when I realised it was only Jena that was staring at us like a goldfish. 'Where's Samira?'

'She's gone to the ladies'. I'm Jena,' she said, reaching out her hand towards Austin. 'I remember you from that Christmas party in New York.'

'Nice to meet you,' Austin said in response as if he had no recollection of meeting her at all.

'But her coat's gone,' I said, noticing that the stool beside us no longer had her unmissable red coat with fake fur collar. That's when I saw her at the exit of the bar – the flash of colour catching in the corner of my eye.

'Sorry, Austin, I need to do something. Jena here will entertain you,' I said without pausing for breath, not giving him a second to respond as I pushed past him.

I weaved my way around other drinkers, said 'Excuse me' several times and squeezed past the bouncer at the door to step outside. The cold March night hit me, and I shivered beneath my thin top, wishing I had grabbed my coat before leaving.

'Samira,' I called out to her as she raised her hand, trying to flag down a taxi. 'Samira, wait.'

Was she ignoring me? She pulled down her hand and began to walk away. I caught up with her and touched her arm. 'Samira?'

She finally turned around and there were tears streaming down her face.

'What's the matter?' I said, taking hold of her arms. 'Is it Rosie?'

She sniffed and shook her head.

'Then why did you leave so suddenly? Jena thought you had gone to the bathroom.'

'I… I couldn't face him.'

'Who? Austin?'

She hugged herself tightly and took a small step backwards, forcing me to drop my hold before giving a very brief nod.

'I know you have reservations about him, but I was hoping you would at least give him a chance. He came all this way from California to see me and I was hoping you and Jena could get to know him. Tears are a little excessive, though, don't you think?'

'Shit.' She stamped her heel down onto the pavement. 'I am the worst friend.' She sniffed.

'Why?'

'Because… because Austin and I…' She swallowed deeply and avoided my gaze. 'We… that is… we've met before.'

'I know you have. When you came to visit me in New York.'

She pinched her lips before looking skywards and sighing deeply, her misty breath floating into the chilly night. 'We've seen each other since then.'

A thought popped into my head. The meal I had with Austin's family. Something his sister had said, and he had dismissed it out of hand. 'In London?'

She nodded.

'Before my year at NYU?' I asked, as that was when Austin said he had visited.

She slowly shook her head. 'No. During it. That April. He came over to London for an internship and got in touch.'

'How did he have your number?'

'I gave it to him at that Christmas party.'

'Why?'

'Because we…' She stared down at the pavement.

Her inability to finish that sentence gave me pause to reflect back on that night. When I had returned to the party I couldn't see her anywhere. Samira never left a party early unless… 'You hooked up with him? That night?'

'We… kissed. That's all.'

I bit my bottom lip hard as the fragments of those memories began to become clearer in my head. 'You told me he was interested in my flatmate that night. And then I saw them together in my room and thought they were getting it on, only Austin told me a different version of events. He told me that someone had told Alesha that he was waiting for her in our room.' I took a step back. 'It was you, wasn't it? You told her to go to our room right after I told you he was waiting for me there. I don't believe it.'

'I was doing it to protect you.'

'Like hell you were. You wanted him for yourself.'

'That's not true.'

'Then why lie about it? Why not tell me you liked him?'

'You were a little preoccupied that night. Don't you remember?'

'I only kissed Edoardo because I was reeling from having seen Austin and Alesha in bed together and convincing myself that he liked her because you told me he did. I can't believe this.' I held my head in my hands for a beat. 'So, ten years ago, he came to London in the spring, and you had an affair and...'

Ten years ago.

No, surely not.

'Rosie. She's... He's...' I clamped my hand over my mouth, not wanting to complete any of those sentences for fear of them being true if I did. I rubbed my temples in a circular motion. 'I don't believe this.'

'Please, Laila.' She grabbed my hands, forcing them from my head. 'You can't say anything to him.'

'He doesn't know?'

'No, he doesn't. He knew I was pregnant. What we had was nothing more than a three-day fling but when I found out, I called him, and he was furious, said it would ruin everything for him and I thought it would for me too. I told him I would take care of it, only I couldn't go through with it.'

'And you never got back in touch?'

'He made it abundantly clear how he felt about things.'

My teeth began to chatter, and I was losing feeling in every extremity. 'You're going to have to tell him, Samira. Rosie will want to know one day too.'

'I know, I know. But not yet. And I don't want this to affect anything between you and him.'

I pulled my hands away. 'It's a bit late for that. Why would you even have suggested I go and meet up with him?'

She stared down at her shoes. 'Guilt. It's sat with me for far too long.' She looked back up at me, her eyes swimming with moisture. 'I knew you had a big crush on him all those years ago, and it was my fault that it never came to anything. I convinced myself I was doing the right thing in warning you off him, that only someone like me could handle him. I was selfish back then. And when Jena and I came up with our plan, I didn't have much of an argument to give her to exclude him. She was already starting to get suspicious when I started bad-mouthing him.'

'I can't wrap my head around the fact that you have kept this from us. We're your best friends.'

She folded her arms. 'You kept all that stuff about your dad a secret from us.'

'That's different.'

'They're still secrets, secrets that we have had to live with and bury deep inside us. We've clearly both kept significant parts of our life back from each other for a reason. In my case it was guilt and, for you, I guess you didn't trust us to be discreet.'

Her words were too much to take in. I turned back to the bar. There was a queue beginning to form to enter and I prayed the security guard would let me back in. I bounced on the balls of my feet, trying to warm myself. 'I have to go. I'm not sure I can process all this.'

'What are you going to say to Austin?'

I shrugged. 'I don't know.'

317

'Whatever you decide, I'll understand, but please know I'm sorry.'

Two words. But they couldn't eradicate the truths that had been spilled tonight and the fact that I needed to give them some considerable thought.

With a low wave goodbye, I turned away from her. My brain was struggling to understand what Samira had told me. I wanted to talk this through with someone but who? Turning briefly over my shoulder, I saw that Samira was gone and I pulled out my phone and began typing.

> What would you do if your best friend revealed that the father of her nine-year-old daughter was in fact the guy who flew almost six thousand miles to see you and declare he wanted a future with you when he has obviously lied about hooking up with said best friend?

Almost immediately, my phone vibrated in my hand, and I tentatively answered it.

'Gregory?'

'Oh, Laila. It's so good to hear from you. I wanted to message you or call you before now but was so worried I might have put you off with all that psychological claptrap I threw at you.'

I laughed. 'Not at all. I didn't expect you to get in touch.'

'But I wanted to. I so wanted to. Your visit has left an indelible mark on my life. It was so joyous, albeit far too brief.'

His effervescent tone made me smile and a warmth began to spread through me despite the cold.

'I can't talk for long. I need to go back into a bar and face the guy I messaged you about.'

'There is no short answer to what you wrote. I would love to hear more about it if you get the time to call me again. I am sure there is a lot more behind this tale.'

'I would like that. Maybe later this evening.'

'That would be wonderful. I'm in for the rest of the day doing some marking and planning my classes for next week.'

'Great.'

'Before you go, though, Laila, remember one thing. Trust is one of the cornerstones of any solid relationship. It allows you to be more open and giving. And in order to achieve that level of trust you need transparency and understanding as well as the ability to feel safe in someone's presence.'

His words surrounded me like I was wearing a life jacket on a stormy ride over the ocean.

As I rang off, something wrapped around my shoulders.

'You must be freezing out here,' Austin said as he draped my coat around me. 'Is everything OK?'

I turned to see Jena appear beside him, a look of concern on her face. 'Did Samira leave?'

I nodded.

'Oh…' She stepped in front of Austin with her back to him and leaned in. 'I don't want to be a third wheel,' she whispered, 'so I think I will head off. James is out tonight so I'll have some me time.'

'You don't have to—' I began before she cut me off.

'It was lovely to meet you, Austin. Enjoy London,' she said with a cheery smile before leaving.

'She's nice,' Austin said before taking a hold of my hands. 'But I'm glad she's gone.' He threw a cheeky grin as he brought my fingers to his lips.

I pulled my hands away from him. 'Austin, can we go somewhere a little quiet and have a talk?'

'Sounds ominous, but sure.'

On the corner of the street, we discovered a pub with misted windows and a laid-back vibe inside. I found a booth while Austin got some drinks in.

As he made his way back towards me, I braced myself for what I wanted to discuss with him. He handed me a glass of wine and I murmured thanks. Before I could open my mouth, Austin spoke.

'She told you, huh?'

I sloshed my drink around the rim of the glass. 'About your little affair?'

'Affair? That sounds a little illicit. I wasn't dating anyone at the time.'

'Then call it your secret. Why didn't you tell me about it?'

'I didn't know I needed to. You never talked about her when you were in California. How was I to know you were still close?'

'True. But you said you had visited London during your undergraduate course, not after.'

'Did I? Poor recollection, then. I am sure it was a slip of the tongue.' He took a long sip of his beer. 'Laila, I am not entirely sure what I am being accused of here. It sounds more like your friend was the dishonest one, not telling you what went down between us, as I assume you have filled her in on your trip to California.'

He had a point, but I didn't want to validate it.

'Here's my version of events,' he continued. 'She came on to me at the Christmas party and we kissed but that was after I saw you with that Italian dude.'

'I was lashing out after seeing you with my roommate.'

'Then that makes two of us. Listen.' He paused, reaching out to take my hand. 'I never intentionally set out to keep this a secret from you. I promise I haven't been dishonest. When I came to London that spring, I didn't know anyone except those on the internship. It was at your friend's bank, and it sort of happened. Neither of us could believe the coincidence.'

'She told me you called her.'

He laughed, yet again trying to lighten the conversation. 'I did. I didn't walk up to her desk at the bank and say, "Hey, wanna go out sometime?" I recalled she had given me her number and messaged her. I'm still not being dishonest here except for placing this interaction. But seeing as it was, what… more than ten years ago, I think I can be forgiven for forgetting some of the details. Can we move on now?'

I took in his words as I sipped my drink. How could I tell him that it wasn't only the fact that they had hooked up once in New York and then here in London but also so much more. It wasn't my news to share that he was also the father of Samira's daughter.

But there was something else that was bothering me. When Austin had bumped into her outside the coffee shop a couple of days ago, he had claimed he couldn't remember which one of my friends she was. Wasn't this an out-and-out lie?

'This doesn't change anything for me, Laila,' he said, peeling both my hands from my glass and clutching them, 'unless it does for you.'

'I don't know, Austin.' I pulled away from his grasp and shifted in my seat. 'I'm still trying to wrap my head around everything. Can I ask you one thing, though?'

'Sure.'

'Did you communicate with Samira once you went back to New York, after your internship?'

He leaned back, lost in thought. 'Yes, I think so. Can't quite recall the details but she called me. I think I told her there was no future for us. She lived a continent away and we were both crazy young. And besides, it wasn't anything meaningful. We both agreed it was a bit of fun.'

As he said those last two sentences, Gregory's words to me on the phone swam in my mind. Trust. How could I ever trust this man? His admission that he couldn't remember the details of what must have been a monumental conversation between him and Samira was telling. He had gotten my best friend pregnant. Surely that was something you wouldn't forget. And then not checking in on her after she said she would deal with it was something I also couldn't get my head around.

My phone buzzed on the table and interrupted my train of thought. It was a message from Samira.

'I'm starving, by the way,' Austin said. 'Came here straight from a matinee with my sister and I thought this was going to be an evening just the two of us with dinner. How about we get some food in?'

I nodded. 'OK,' I said, even though I was sure we had nothing else to say.

'What do you fancy?' he said, craning his neck to see the specials board.

'I don't mind,' I said, a little distracted as my mobile pinged again to remind me I had a message.

He threw me that winning smile. 'I'll surprise you. Need the restroom first, then I'll go order.'

As he left, I lifted the phone off the table and read Samira's message.

> Where are you?

I texted her my location and she immediately messaged back.

> I have been walking around the city and can't go home. This secret has weighed me down for ten years. I need to tell him.

I took in a deep breath and sent back a reply:

> Come now.

The second Austin sat down, he questioned my down-hearted expression. Before I could say anything, a flash of red appeared by our table. Austin turned, a look of bewilderment and then annoyance crossing his face.

'What's she doing here?' he said, his tone a little irritated.

I stood and picked up my things. 'I'm sorry, Austin. But you guys need to talk.'

Giving Samira's arm a squeeze, I threw her a sympathetic head tilt. I hoped she could understand the gesture. She was my best friend, no matter what truths she had spilled tonight. She was also the sister I never had. She would always come before any man, no matter what had happened all those years ago – whatever games she had played. And I knew Samira well enough to know that nothing of what she had done in the past was worth getting upset over ten years on.

Austin couldn't even look me in the eye as I said goodbye and left.

Chapter 33

'It's not the same without Samira,' Jena said as she poured a sachet of brown sugar into her cup of tea. She stirred the liquid and sighed. 'And I can't believe he asked for a paternity test. Seems so insulting.'

'I know. I think it was possibly a knee-jerk reaction. Samira had said she would take care of things when she first told him she was pregnant, but he never imagined that taking care of things meant having the baby and not telling him. Still, the fact he didn't even check in on her after that conversation they had ten years ago bothers me. Poor Samira.'

'It must be hard for her. When is she back from New York?'

'Tuesday.'

Jena and I were sitting in a cafe in Notting Hill, the first signs of spring in the air beyond the glass frontage of the coffee shop. She and I had agreed on a morning jaunt into west London instead of meeting for cocktails last night. Samira had left mid-week for a business trip and her parents had flown in from Dubai to look after Rosie. Samira wouldn't tell us what the trip was about but said all would be revealed on her return.

There was also another reason for our daytime meet-up. I had a date in a couple of hours and needed Jena's calming presence to get me in the right frame of mind.

Not a date with Austin. He and I had said our goodbyes over text before he left for California. The bombshell that had landed on his lap had been too overwhelming for him to think straight, he had told me. Confusion and anger had surfaced, and he needed a time-out to think about everything. I had told him to take me out of the picture. For good. His mask had finally slipped and I was relieved I hadn't given up my life here in London for him.

Gregory and I had video-called the night after I left Samira and Austin in the pub. I had curled up on the sofa – the house eerily quiet without Mum there – and told him everything that had happened over the last few days. Watching him with Bailey stretched out beside him was a comfort. I didn't let on about the fight with Mum. That would be the ultimate betrayal in her eyes.

'I also still can't believe you kept all that stuff about your dad and meeting his husband from us.'

I stroked my cup. 'I'm sorry.'

Jena leaped up and squeezed me tight. 'You don't need to apologise. I just wish you had reached out, shared some of your pain.'

I tapped her arm, and she released her hold, reclaiming her seat. 'It's in the past now.' Wasn't it? A secret no longer from my two besties and my mother. I should feel lighter, but I didn't.

'Tell me more,' Jena said, her eyes lighting up.

'About what?'

'The Italian stallion.'

I laughed. 'We never called him that.'

'What shall we call him, then? Mr Sexy Italian. Mr Second-Chances-Are-Always-a-Good-Idea Hottie?'

'Are they?'

She sipped her tea. 'You tell me. Enemies to lovers has stalled and I feel like we got *so* sidetracked with that affair that we didn't analyse your trip to Puerto Rico much.'

'There wasn't much to add. I felt like Edoardo and I were getting close again, healing from how and why we broke up in the first place, but as soon as I mentioned where I had been and where I was headed, he acted the same as he did all those years ago, fuelled by jealousy. But all his messages since I left were asking for another chance. And then I get the text from him last night saying he had brought forward his flight to London and wanted to meet this afternoon and I felt I couldn't say no.'

Jena leaned on her hand that was propped on the table. 'So romantic.'

'How is that romantic?'

'He clearly couldn't wait another second to see you. And he obviously has something important to say. Are you excited to see him again?'

I scooped some froth off my coffee and sucked the spoon. 'Not sure. But until I know what he wants to tell me, I will have to live in ignorant bliss and enjoy this fabulous coffee shop and my bestie's company.' I tore off a piece of cinnamon swirl and chewed. '*You* said you had some news.' I wiggled my fingers in a not-so-subtle fashion in front of her.

She batted my hand away and shook her head. 'No, there's no proposal.' Her voice was flat.

'Did you talk to James?'

'We had a brief chat when I came back from our night out, but he was too preoccupied with some new game he was playing on the PS4 that he *had* to complete. I tried to suggest we go out for a meal this weekend, but he said he had made plans.'

'Sounds a little avoidant.'

'He said to me, "What's the rush? We can go out to dinner anytime," when I said that it was a shame.'

'And that didn't appease you?'

Her nostrils flared. 'No, it didn't. Because I feel like I *am* in a rush. If we keep going at this pace and it doesn't work out, I'll suddenly find myself in my mid-thirties wondering why I'm still with someone that doesn't want the same things as me.' She shoved a piece of her almond croissant into her mouth.

'All the more reason why you need to schedule in that time to talk to him. Tell him it's important to you that you have this dinner sooner rather than later.'

She drifted off as if she was trying to absorb my words. 'I can't help thinking…' she said, finally.

'What?'

'About your trip.'

'Which part?'

'All of it. The travelling, the excitement of meeting up with your past love, the illicit affairs. It's all so… thrilling.' Her head dipped and she absentmindedly played with the empty sugar sachet. 'The most exciting my life has been in the last few years is getting a good interest rate when we fixed our mortgage last year.'

'That's no bad thing. You're investing for your future. It's what adults do.'

'I know, but it's all so safe.' She paused. 'I've been doing a lot of thinking. I love teaching and I love the kids at school even though most of them are little brats, but I want a new challenge and so…' She straightened. 'I'm thinking of taking a sabbatical and figuring out what I want to do with my life, whether I would miss teaching enough to want to go back to it or maybe try something new.'

My mouth dropped open and I reached out to squeeze her arm. 'That's huge. Go you.'

She beamed. 'Thanks. But I think James will say we can't afford it and that starting over in a new career would also put an unnecessary pressure on our finances.'

'Does he have a say?'

'Of course he does. We bought a flat together. It's more committed than marriage.' She licked her finger and picked up some croissant flakes off her plate.

'Then maybe you could both take a sabbatical. Take a mortgage holiday or rent out your flat. There are always options.' I took in her expression. She didn't seem particularly excited by my suggestions. 'Come on, Jena. What's bothering you?'

She pushed her plate away and a faraway look descended over her face. 'I want what you've had. I want someone who is willing to fly across the Atlantic to declare their intentions.'

I tipped my head back and laughed but when I saw her wounded look, I softened. 'You're serious.'

'I read romance. This is how it should play out. I want to know that James would do that for me. I want the hearts and flowers; I want to feel like there is no one else in the world he would want to spend the rest of his life with but me. We've been a boring married couple before we've even got married. Don't get me wrong, I love him, I do, but…'

'You're in a rut. I'm sure this could all be smoothed over if you talk to him. Tell him how you feel.'

'He'll laugh in my face. I mean, we live in the same country, same flat. I'm never going to have the big cross-Atlantic declarations. You get two and I will never know what that would feel like.'

'Maybe then it is time for a drastic change. You've got a spare room. He could get a flatmate and you could tell him you're taking a sabbatical: go and see the world by yourself. And if what you've got is worth fighting for, you'll both fight for it.'

Jena slipped into a trance after that and my body was awash with nerves at the impending date with Edoardo so we drank our drinks and finished our pastries with nothing more than chit-chat about work before saying goodbye, declaring that maybe we should park making any life-changing decisions until Samira was back. We were a trio after all. Even when we met up as a various combo of two of us, we always swore we would fill the third party in on what had been discussed. We had no secrets between us apart from the two monumental ones that Samira and I had hidden.

While I was glad everything was finally out in the open, there was an unease that sat heavy in my stomach. What would life be like when Mum returned? How were we meant to live together with all that unresolved pain and hurt to deal with? And work this week had been a constant stream of troubleshooting problems and issues – nothing even close to being on a cutting-edge research team. A fog had descended over my brain, and I wished I could recapture some of the feelings I had enjoyed during those three weeks.

The truth was I wanted another shot of DOSE.

–

'Laila.'

I turned at the sound of my name, the intonation familiar.

'Hey,' I said.

Edoardo took a hesitant step forward and kissed me on both cheeks, his arms wrapping around my waist briefly before putting his hands in the pockets of his black puffa jacket.

'I am sorry for keeping you waiting,' he said. 'I got held up at the London office of my company.'

'On a Saturday?'

He shrugged. 'They work all days and I needed to have the meeting today because I must leave for Rome tonight.'

I noticed a sadness in his tone. 'Is everything OK?'

'My papa, he is unwell, and my mamma called me and asked me to come and see them. I had wanted to come here in a couple of weeks and spend a few days in London. I wanted to spend some time with you. Your visit. It left an unforgettable mark. But sadly, this afternoon is now the only time I have left as my boss expects me back after my Rome visit.'

I expressed my sincerest wishes for the recovery of his dad but didn't know what to say about his admission about wanting to see me. My time in Puerto Rico had affected me too but perhaps not in the way he was hoping. And then Costa Rica had changed everything.

We walked past a coffee truck and ordered a couple of cappuccinos and decided to walk into Hyde Park. Finding a bench in front of the lake, we sat down and turned at the same time. We laughed when we realised we both wanted to say something.

'Please,' Edoardo said, 'can I go first?'

I smiled. 'Of course.'

'I was such a fool. When you opened your heart to me on the rocks at the waterfall, I was crushed. I thought you had come to see me and only me. To hear Mateo's name

331

was like a dagger to my heart. He had a part of you that I never had access to and this Austin guy...' He trailed off. 'I confess, I never told you but that night of the Christmas party, I saw you with him. You were both dancing very intimately. There was this look in your eyes. I knew you had feelings for him, that perhaps, I was maybe a...' He paused. 'A consolation prize, if that is the right expression.'

I stared down at my coffee cup, my fingers curled around it. 'That night I was very, very drunk. And seeing as we are being very honest with each other, yes, I will admit, I had feelings for Austin at that time. I was even about to act upon it, but something happened. It's complicated. But when I saw you and pounced on you...' I let out a half laugh. 'God, I am so embarrassed to remember that time.'

'No, no, don't be embarrassed.' He turned and rested his arm on the back of the bench. 'It was the most pleasant surprise when you launched yourself on me. I had been admiring you from afar for a while. When your roommate came on to me, I felt bad, but it wasn't her I wanted, it was you. And it is no matter how or why we started; we did. And it was a fun time for me, and I hope for you. But yes, knowing that you had been on your trip with Austin was like a gut punch. I assume something happened?' His eyebrows raised.

I took a long sip of my coffee, steeling myself to tell him these words. 'Yes, we got close during that time. In fact, he flew into London a few days ago.'

He removed his arm from the bench and cradled his coffee cup. 'Oh. I am too late?'

'There is no competition between you both, Edoardo,' I said, a little exasperated. Edoardo was never going to change, was he?

'I know, I know, I was only joking.' He nudged my shoulder with his but I wasn't appeased. 'Besides,' he continued. 'I know what we had was special and perhaps what we could have again could be even more wonderful.' His eyes were pleading and eyebrows expressive.

'I don't think so, Edoardo,' I said finally, keen for him not to get caught up in the idea of us any longer.

'Please, hear me out,' he continued. 'I know I need to show you some intent. We live very far apart, with only the opportunity for this snatched moment together,' he said, sweeping his hand in front of himself, out towards the lake where a few pedalos were bobbing in the water, filled with couples enjoying this unseasonal warmth. 'That is why I have made the decision to move to London, to start a new chapter of my life.'

I was stunned. 'Please don't say you're moving for me.'

'*Sì*, for you.'

'I can't ask you to do that.'

'Why not?'

'Because… because I don't even know if this is where I want to be anymore.' As the words tumbled out, they caught me by surprise. 'And I wouldn't want you making such a life change for me only to regret it.'

'But I have always liked the idea of living in London, and it is not far from home.'

'Then move, Edoardo, but not for me. What we had *was* special but I don't think we could recapture that again, and I wouldn't want you to make any life-altering decisions for some misplaced idea that I might change my mind. If England is where you want to move to, then do it for you. Like I said before, I can't guarantee I will be here.'

Had I really uttered those last few words again? London had always been my home. And I had truly believed it would be where I would spend my future too. Mum was here. My besties were here. But something had shifted.

Hadn't I been waiting for someone to put me first, to make compromises for me so I could continue my life here in England? Edoardo was offering to do what Josh and Austin weren't prepared to do, yet I still wasn't placated. I think I was coming round to the idea of a relationship but only if it was on equal footing, where goals and wants were aligned and with someone who I had a deeper connection with – someone that made me feel safe and not at the receiving end of bouts of jealousy.

Jena was waiting for her cross-continent declaration of love. I had had two and turned them both down.

Something stirred in my chest. An ache. A memory from the past. Mateo's Christmas gift. A gift that I now know had so much meaning behind it. That gesture had been quiet and unassuming and had filled me with joy when Mateo told me about it.

I tried to rub the memory away. What was the point in dwelling on it and where had it sprung from? Mateo had made it clear how he felt, and his silence since my trip spoke volumes.

Chapter 34

I lay on my bed studying the presentation Jena and Samira had made me. The Love Intervention. It felt like a lifetime ago that we had sat in that bar in Euston and discussed it, or rather that I had dismissed it out of hand.

Scrolling through all the men they had unearthed from my past and the three candidates that had stood out to them, I began to reflect on all the adventures I had undertaken. The situation with Edoardo was over. We had finished our coffees and said our goodbyes. There would be no second-chance romance. Austin's response to me telling him to take me out of the picture was met with 'I'll be here if you change your mind.'

Would I change my mind? No, I wouldn't.

The door slamming startled me. I closed the laptop lid and shuffled off my bed. At the top of the spiral staircase, I saw the top of Mum's head as she shrugged off her coat.

'You're back.'

'Laila.' Mum held her hand to her heart. 'I'm sorry, did I wake you?'

'No, I was still up. Why didn't you tell me you were coming back today?' I asked as I made my way down the stairs.

'I didn't want to be a bother. We didn't exactly say goodbye on good terms.'

I tugged at the sleeves of my sweatshirt, so they covered my hands, suddenly not even sure how to greet my own mother. 'How is Teta?' I asked, keen not to dwell on our last interaction.

'She's better.' Hanging her coat in the cupboard, she changed her outdoor shoes for her slippers. 'Or rather she claimed it was a miracle sent from God.' She raised her hands to the ceiling at that last word. 'A miracle that her sickness brought me back to the family.'

'It did?'

She nodded. 'Yes, it did.' Reaching out to clasp my hands, she squeezed them beneath my jumper. It was a brief gesture. 'Do you fancy some *ma'amoul* and tea? Your aunt packed me off with so many of those sweets that we'd best make a start before they go bad. I have some important things I want to say – words that have sat on my chest these last few days.' Her look was serious, and her eyes appeared watery.

'OK,' I said, and she shuffled off to the kitchen to prepare the brews.

Slipping into the nearest chair, I wondered if we were going to pick up from the heated conversation we had had before she left. I stayed quiet as she busied herself with the kettle.

She brought two mugs to the table then unwrapped the cellophane of the Lebanese biscuits tray and offered it to me.

We continued to sit in silence as we blew steam from our cups and bit into the butter cookies filled with dried figs.

'I want peace in my heart again,' Mum said finally. 'And you are the most precious thing to me in the world, but

I think I can finally admit, I have been the world's worst mother.'

I choked on some biscuit crumbs. 'Don't be ridiculous. You are not—'

'*Khalas*,' she said, holding her hand up to silence me, a word she used many times to indicate she had had enough. 'If I hadn't let my own pain and suffering cloud my judgement, you would have had a relationship with your father until the day he died. I robbed you of those years and that is unforgivable. Your father never cheated on me, but I always felt he cheated me of a life I wanted so badly but never had. And I should have shown you that letter; I should have given you the chance to make your own decisions about him.'

Speechless. I was speechless. But Mum had only paused to take a sip of her tea and seemed ready to say more so I didn't respond.

'I have also robbed you of having a relationship with my side of the family,' she said. 'All they ever wanted was to be a part of your life and I let you grow up an only child, with barely the semblance of any relatives to show you love and affection. I was too ashamed to tell my parents and sisters the truth of my broken marriage and thought it easier to say that he had an affair and left. It was a more palatable lie than telling them the truth about his sexuality. And I never told them of him becoming bankrupt either. They would have said "I told you so" indefinitely. That's why I have held on to this crumbling old house that has been such a burden, out of pride. Downsizing would have raised questions about why he wasn't providing for us. They already disapproved of me marrying him, but I was stubborn, single-minded and in love.'

At that last word she bowed her head and my heart broke. I squeezed her hand, still struggling to absorb what she was saying but a sense of peace washing over me, nonetheless.

'But enough is enough.' She pulled her hand from mine and took a tissue from her sleeve and wiped her nose. 'I have begun to make amends with my family, and I realised during this trip that they have always been there for me, and I want very much to be a part of their lives again. I also want you to be free, free from the burden of this house and my needs. I want you to know the excitement of love no matter if it brings you some pain along the way like it did for me. I want you to be free to explore and travel.' She finally paused and looked at me in a way that I had never seen before. It was an expression that had nothing but love at its core.

'I don't know what to say. This change of heart came from your trip to Beirut?'

She tutted. 'No, it came from your friends. Having them stay here with me made me realise we are not close, nor have we ever been close, and I regret that so much. The way they both talk about you, how much they were worried about you, your health and wellbeing...' She shook her head. 'I had failed to notice all these things, instead encouraging you to work harder, to strive for more, to be truly independent so you wouldn't end up a mere housekeeper. And clearly you didn't see me as someone you could open up to about your work issues either.'

Before I could reply again, she held up her hand. 'Please let me finish. These thoughts and words have been spinning round my brain since I got on that plane to Beirut. Yes, I was angry at you for keeping all these secrets of your trip from me and wondered how two such lovely girls could have kept the truth from me, but they did that because they are your best friends, and they would never betray your trust.'

'Yes, they are good friends. And I will be honest, I was always jealous of the relationship they both had with you – like they knew you in a way I could never hope to have.'

She held her hand to her chest. 'It breaks my heart that you think that.' She shook her head. 'Tough love. That's all I ever knew growing up and it is what I swore I would never dish out as a mother. I also let my relationship with your father distort everything. Loving him was my downfall and I think I didn't want that for you, so I kept you at arm's length so you would never have to rely on anyone else but yourself.'

Those words shook me. I had been held at arm's length deliberately by both my parents. I hadn't been a difficult child who didn't like affection and to be hugged. I had been a child who had not had her basic needs met. I lowered my gaze to the crumbs on the table and squashed them with my fingers, pulverising them into dust.

'I don't know what to say,' I said finally. Grabbing my mug, I was suddenly overwhelmed with the need to extract some warmth from it, a warmth that had been missing from my life. This was too much to process.

'There is nothing to say,' Mum said. 'I am offering you my sincere apologies, for being half a parent, or no parent at all. I can no longer apologise for your father's failings nor blame him for the part he played in your upbringing, but I wanted to tell you that I am moving back to Beirut.'

The cup slipped from my grasp and clattered on the table. 'You're what?' I said, with a shaky voice, mopping up the spilled tea with a sheet of kitchen roll.

'I want to start a new chapter in my life, one I should have taken a long time ago and I hope one day you might make that journey too to meet your extended family. Also...' She clutched her hands tightly on the table. 'I am glad you have made that connection with your father's partner. He was right. He wasn't the reason why your father left. I was. Your father was willing to live half a life, but that man made me realise that it was destroying your father in the process. *He* forced me to let him go. He gave your father the happiness he had obviously so desperately needed even if that happiness meant leaving behind his pride and joy. And I am so, so very sorry you never got to hear those words from your father himself.'

'I saw him that day,' I whispered, struggling to absorb what she had said. 'We had arranged to meet, and I saw the paramedics try to resuscitate him. I followed the ambulance to the hospital but...' The tears stung at the back of my eyes as I recalled what Gregory had told me about that day – how different that day could have been.

'Oh, Laila. What a tragic thing for a child to witness. I'm so sorry,' she said, the emotion overtaking her too, her eyes welling with tears. 'I'm sorry for everything.'

I sat rigid, not able to comfort her, my own mother, because there was so much bound up in those tears, tears that should be mine, not hers. There was too much to take in and I couldn't offer comfort. Too much hurt and too much suffering and I wasn't sure I could reconcile with the fact that she wanted to abandon me and not work to mend our relationship.

In that moment, I realised there was only one thing I wanted, one other person whose warmth I wanted to feel – whose arms I wanted wrapped around me.

I wanted that bubble. My Mateo bubble. But I didn't know how to get it back.

Chapter 35

Samira wrote:

> I have news

I replied:

> Me too

Then Jena:

> Me three

That had been the start of the conversation on our WhatsApp group chat last night and the reason why we were all sat in a dimly lit cocktail bar in Soho on a Thursday and not our regular Friday night. We all had something important to share and this was the first evening we could all meet since Samira got back from her trip.

'I'm moving to Dubai,' Samira announced, her chin and cosmopolitan glass raised.

'You're what?' Jena and I said in unison.

'I need a change. And I need to reconnect… with my family.'

Jena's eyes were glistening in the low lights of the bar. 'For how long?'

'Maybe a year, maybe two.' She shrugged before taking a long sip. 'I want to give Rosie a bit of stability. I also want to have more flexibility and freedom and the expat life out there will be fun and I will have a lot of help. I was in New York to meet with the big bosses and arrange the transfer.'

'What about Austin?' I asked hesitantly.

She twisted the stem of her glass. 'If he wants to be a part of Rosie's life, he'll know where to find me. But he hasn't messaged me since I confirmed his paternity, so… I'm not waiting around for him to do or say something. If he wants to begin to take an interest in her life, it will have to be how it suits her best.'

Her words only served to reinforce what I felt about Austin. His hesitancy to be a part of his daughter's life didn't endear me to him. Coupled with the fact that he had lied to me, I knew that I wouldn't change my mind about him. Enemies to lovers, or whatever trope Jena had declared it was, would never happen.

'Dubai,' Jena said, her eyes wide as if she was trying to process the word. 'What prompted your desire to move there? I mean, this is the first you're mentioning it to us.' Her wounded-deer look appeared.

'Your trip, Laila,' Samira said, turning to me. 'It had a profound effect. Your mum made me realise how much I was missing out on. She kept alluding to all these regrets over the family she wished she had in her life, and I think something resonated deeply. My parents have been trying to make amends for how they first reacted when I told them I was pregnant; they make all these expensive trips

343

at the drop of a hat to come over and babysit Rosie and up until now I have always believed they haven't wanted to make amends with me. Turns out that wasn't true. They couldn't get past the brick wall – the towering brick wall I have built around myself when it comes to relationships, family and even my own little girl. I will be cutting back to three days working in the office, and one day working from home, lengthening my weekend and reducing my pay, but it's a small price to pay if what I gain is familial connection. I need more of a work-life balance. I don't want Rosie to have the life I had – being shipped from nanny to boarding school abroad.'

Her fingers began to tremble, and I held my hand over hers, squeezing tightly, urging her to continue. The words had been delivered like a rehearsed speech full of conviction, but I knew Samira enough to know that they would have been incredibly hard to say. While this move might be the best for Rosie, I hoped it would be the best for Samira.

'This is the right decision for now,' she said, her voice trembling, 'but I'm going to freaking miss you guys.' At that, the tears began to flow, and in an instant Jena and I were up on our feet embracing her. We stayed that way as the tide of emotion swelled before it began to fade. But even then, we kept holding on to her.

'And we're going to miss you, too,' I whispered into her hair.

She sniffed before gently pushing us away. 'OK, OK, you two, cut it out.' Pulling a tissue from her handbag, she dabbed her eyes. 'This I expect from Jena, but you, Laila…' She cocked her head. 'What gives?'

I sipped my rum punch cocktail and was suddenly awash with a memory. Closing my eyes for a few beats, I was transported there, with him: the sound of the ocean, the scent of his skin, his touch, his arms enveloping me in a way that touched my soul as we danced salsa.

'Earth to Laila,' Jena said.

'Hmm?' I mumbled, pushing aside the paper umbrella poking out of my drink to take another sip.

'You checked out there,' Samira said. 'Want to fill us in on your news?'

'Let's hear Jena's.' I smiled brightly.

'I'm not sure I can top Samira's announcement. But…' She took a deep breath and let the air out slowly. 'I'm taking a sabbatical. A six-month sabbatical. On my own. James and I are… taking a break, a temporary break,' she added.

Samira and I exchanged looks but hers was more shocked as we hadn't had a chance to catch up with Samira after Jena and I last met.

'Umm, wow,' Samira said.

'How did James take the news?' I asked.

She rubbed her finger back and forth across the wooden table. 'Surprisingly well. His face lit up at the idea of having a bachelor pad for half a year. And he already knew which mate he was going to ask to move in.'

'Oh,' I said.

'But of course, he said he would miss me.' Her smile faltered and I could see the anguish she was battling inside. 'It will be good for us; I know it will. I asked him if he wanted to go with me, but he claimed it was the worst time of the year to miss.'

'In what way?' I asked.

'Budgeting and forecasting period at work and the start of the footie season. But he said as his team were likely to have a place in the Champions League, he could try and

345

arrange a trip out to visit me if there's a game somewhere in Europe that coincided with one of the cities I visit.'

'Hmm, sounds a little implausible,' Samira said. 'Do you have an itinerary?'

She shook her head. 'Some dream destinations, a Pinterest board of views and sites I want to see. I've OK'ed it with school and will only miss one term. They said they'll keep my job open for me if I come back, and I'll have the money I usually spend on the mortgage to use for my travel budget.'

I thought over what she had said. '*If* you come back?'

'Whoops. Slip of the tongue.' She grinned, a little too eagerly, and I wondered if Jena was being completely open and honest with us. 'What about you, Laila?' she said, changing the focus away from her.

'It's not my news to be fair, in light of your bombshells. But my mum has decided to move back to Beirut, to be with her family.'

Their eyes popped.

'It would seem your visits had a profound effect on her too – made her realise a few things. What did you guys say to her?'

Jena shrugged. 'We only cooked together, and she listened to me when I opened up about James, though she was very much of the opinion that I should dump his ass.' A light laugh trickled out of her. God, I was going to miss that laugh.

'Then it was probably my doing,' Samira said. 'We talked at length. She bonded with Rosie, and I confess... I cried, a lot. She held this space for me that I've never had with my own mother but want to. And then she opened up about all the hurt your dad caused her, the sadness she

346

felt that she didn't have this kind of interaction with her own daughter. I'm sorry, Laila.'

I let her words settle. It hadn't been my imagination. Samira and Mum's bond was strong, but it wasn't Samira's fault. 'Don't be sorry.'

'But I am sorry. I said some shitty things to you that day in the cafe. I know you've forgiven me but you're always so forgiving of everyone.'

'You're my best friend, Samira. I'll always forgive you. I'm only sad that you couldn't confide in us about what went on with Austin. That must have been a hard time for you.'

'Likewise, Laila. I can't imagine what you went through trying to find your dad, what you witnessed, the grief that you couldn't share with us.' She reached out and held her hand over mine.

'It was a horrific day,' I said. 'And it proved pivotal to everything I did with my life after that. I'm not sure I would have pursued a career in cardiology if it hadn't been for the fact that Dad had a heart attack, the feeling of powerlessness I felt.'

'What do you think you would have done instead?' Jena asked.

'I'm not sure. I had applied for all these summer internships that were based in NYC that were more research-based and Edoardo and I had talked of plans to travel around the US. I think a part of me didn't want to leave America. I loved living in New York, and one year didn't seem enough.' My mind wandered off as I thought of what would have happened if I had stayed. Being in Manhattan with Gregory for those precious hours had brought it all back to me. 'This intervention has shaken me in more ways than I could ever have imagined. I've started to

347

question whether what I am doing with my life is what I want to do going forward.'

'It's shaken us all,' Jena said. 'I don't want things to continue the way they are. Or at least I want to do something that makes me either appreciate what I have or force me into action, to live a life that brings me the kind of happiness I deserve.'

Samira lifted her hand for a high five. 'Hell, yes. And I for one want to focus on building good relationships and maybe even thinking about dating again. And you?' she said, looking me straight in the eyes.

'Me what?'

'What is it *you* want, Laila?'

The words were lodged in my throat. 'I… I think I want Mateo.'

'Knew it,' Samira said under her breath and Jena beamed.

'But Laila Clarke doesn't chase boys,' I said, my chin raised.

Samira threw her head back and laughed. 'Laila Clarke chases whatever the hell she wants. And clearly, he was always going to be the one.'

I straightened. 'How did you know that?'

'It was blindingly obvious from all you told us about your trips. Not only is there a strong friendship there at the core, there's also attraction, mutual support and respect and he's the only one of the three that doesn't have a massive ego.' Her eyebrow arched.

'But he reacted the same as the other two did when I told him about the plan.'

'No, he didn't,' Jena said. 'He took time to compose himself and to then express what he was thinking. *You* were the one who ran away. He was mature and respectful enough to tell you how he felt and that he didn't play games. He also gave you the courage to go and heal your wounds to be able to finally move forward *and* he speaks your love language.'

'My what?'

'Your love language,' she repeated. 'There are five of them: words of affirmation, quality time, receiving gifts, acts of service and the one that clearly is the way you like to receive love from a romantic partner, physical touch. You're not a hugger yet that's all you could talk about when it came to him. He speaks your love language; you just didn't know what it was.'

'My love language.' Those words reminded me of something that Gregory had told me about the language of love.

'Physical touch with Mateo gives you a place where you feel safe and loved and can be yourself,' Jena continued. 'It's magical when that happens. Being able to be vulnerable with someone, a person that will stand by you in your darkest moments, someone who inspires you to be the best version of yourself. I knew it would be friends to lovers that won through.'

'And it was obvious you had sex with Austin but made love with Mateo,' Samira said. 'The way you described it to me at the cafe that time, the intimacy obviously went deeper with your Spaniard, so yeah, Jena's right, your love language is obviously physical touch and you got that in a more meaningful way in Costa Rica.'

I processed their words. Physical touch. It was something that hadn't been offered to me growing up. It's what I didn't know I needed or wanted. But Jena was right. I felt safe in Mateo's arms. Always had.

I reached into my bag and pulled out the coaster we had scrawled on all those weeks ago:

> 4. *Have sex* ✔
> 5. *Make love* ✔
> 6. *Know the difference between 4 and 5* ✔

But then I pointed at the final point on the checklist that we had fought over. 'I think I've fallen in love.'

Jena squealed and clutched Samira's hand. Samira matched her enthusiasm with the broadest smile before they both clasped my hands – the circle of our friendship solid and unbreakable. Their love had led to this moment, to this realisation.

I loved Mateo but had I lost him forever?

'What do I do?' I whispered.

Neither of them said anything, their mouths shut tightly.

Both Samira and Jena had figured out the next steps in their lives all by themselves, without needing the validation from the group. They were making big life-changing moves and now it was time for me to do the same.

We would always be best friends. Distance would never break our bond even though the thought of not having these 'in real life' weekly get-togethers saddened me to the core. And had I forgotten the fact that my mother was leaving too? She had suggested I get a flatmate but also said she would understand if selling was what I wanted to do, allowing me to find something affordable for myself. Was that what I wanted? To stay in my current job and get a lodger?

The last three weeks spun in my mind. Sun, sea and sex had been the remit, but I had gotten so much more out of that trip than that.

And that's when it hit me, what I wanted to do.

There was only one person whom I wanted to start the next chapter of my life with. I picked up my phone, confident in my decision and scrolled to his number.

Chapter 36

Six months later

Do I believe in fate?

That's the question I had asked myself on many occasions since my transatlantic move. I was a scientist after all. I believed in facts and evidence, not the arbitrary concept that if two people were meant to be together, eventually they would find their way back to each other. But today I hoped against hope that maybe I could be a believer in such an idea.

That night when Jena, Samira and I had met where they had dropped their bombshells, it wasn't Mateo I had messaged, it was the other person the Love Intervention had led me to.

A soft growl broke me from my thoughts. Bailey was on his back, wondering why I had stopped stroking his belly. The sweet scent of pancakes wafted past my nose, and I turned to see Gregory bringing a plate of them to the dining table.

'How are you feeling?' he said with an affable smile. 'Nervous?'

I slipped into the nearest chair and lifted two pancakes onto my plate before picking up the bottle of maple syrup. 'A little. Feels like a lifetime since I've been a student.'

'You're going to love it. But that mutt is going to miss having you around, that's for sure.' Gregory lowered his gaze and I wondered whether his words were a cover – that secretly he was the one who would miss me.

'I won't be that far away,' I said, reaching for his hand. 'And we can meet for lunch sometimes.'

'I know, I know. It's been amazing having you here all summer. Promise you'll pop back now and again.'

'That's a given. I'm not leaving the States anytime soon.'

That was in part true, though a trip to Dubai over Christmas break was on the cards. Jena wasn't sure if she would make it, but I had promised her I would try and visit her at some point during her sabbatical if it fitted in with my post-doctorate fellowship at NYU.

After I had made the decision to go and spend some time with Gregory, and after our Route 66 trip in a campervan, my mind had been awash with the idea of finding a way to stay longer than the three months of my travel visa. Gregory had offered to sponsor me, which I appreciated, but I wanted to be here on my own steam. I had contacted my old professor whom I had met at the conference in Berkeley, and we had chatted back and forth about my options. It was by chance that a new programme with full funding had been set up in my field of expertise and he had told me I would be a perfect candidate for it. After a series of interviews and the backing of Dr Walker, I had been offered the fellowship. There was an element of teaching built into the programme and I was keen to gain some new skills as well as fulfilling my dream of having my name attached to a cutting-edge piece of research. A permanent position at the university was also an option after that should I wish to stay longer.

For the first time in my life, I didn't want a long-term plan. I wanted to be open to new experiences and new opportunities. The Notting Hill cottage had been rented out, leaving my options open for a move back to London in the future. Mum had been accepting of my plan to live with Gregory for the summer and had begun calling me every week. We were starting to create a new relationship between us and heal from the past. During our last call, she had even floated the idea of coming to New York to visit me, which I knew would take a lot of strength and courage on her part and I couldn't be more excited at the thought of it.

But there was also one thing I wanted more than anything, though I didn't believe in forcing it to happen, which was why I was heading to campus a day early to attend the new students' welcome party, to see if fate had played its hand.

Had Mateo decided to start a new chapter in New York City like me?

I had thought many times of calling – to tell him how much I missed him and how much I loved him. But as the weeks had gone by, I realised I would be too late anyway. His time at the turtle conservation centre was over and I had no clue where he would have decided to go after that, and a part of me didn't want to be at the centre of his decision-making process. I wanted us to be together because our paths had crossed naturally. Surely that made me a believer in something grand or, as Jena simply said, I was in love but didn't want either of us to get hurt by making such life-changing decisions for the sake of each other.

Through the dimly lit auditorium, I tried to find him. But it was pointless. It was too dark. As all the students filtered out through exits, I hung back, clocking all the new students in the vague hope that he would be here. Even at the welcome party that evening, I stood on tiptoes scanning over heads before weaving my way through the new graduate body on the off-chance. But he wasn't there.

The next day, I resigned myself to the fact that Mateo hadn't had a similar epiphany and, having met with a few graduates in the biology department, I had confirmation that he hadn't enrolled.

-

'How's everything going?' Gregory asked me as we stepped out from a cluster of trees in Central Park into the October sunshine. It was unseasonably warm enough for no jacket, so I had a cardigan on over my long-sleeved jersey dress.

This had been our meeting spot for the last few visits. It was a chance to enjoy the city and each other's company away from the confined spaces of Gregory's flat and my dorm room. Bailey loved the walks, too. Each time we came, we discovered a new favourite part of the park and today was no exception as we held our iced coffees and began our route around Turtle Pond. I had heard the shores of the pond gave the best views of the iconic Belvedere Castle and that observation I could validate.

'I'm enjoying the programme. Don't see enough daylight in between labs and research, which is why I treasure these visits.' I smiled up at him and took a long sip of my drink.

'Met anyone nice?' he asked with eyebrows raised.

'I've made some new friends.'

He tipped his head to the side.

'What? I have.'

'With any possible romantic connection?'

'I'm keeping my options open.'

He laughed. 'Why don't you call him?'

'Because...' I shook my cup and the ice cubes rattled against the sides.

'Because what, Laila?'

I took in his sympathetic expression. He had given me nothing but a safe space to share my feelings from the moment I met him.

'I'm scared to tell him I love him, scared of the compromises I might have to make for that love, scared he's moved on and I'm too late, so it's easier for me to let fate decide my hand.'

He paused and rubbed my arm before moving in for a gentle squeeze of my shoulder, his warmth soothing me instantly. He didn't need to say any more. The touch was enough.

'OK, those are just excuses. I need to be bolder. I need to tell him how I feel and deal with whatever happens.' A surge of confidence pulsed through me at the thought that I was finally going to do what I had so desperately wanted to do months ago. 'I'm going to call him.'

I handed Gregory my coffee cup and pulled out my mobile. It rang and rang until a recording asked me to leave a message. I hesitated before taking a deep breath.

'Hey, it's me. Laila. I know it's been a long time. I should have called before. I...' I was rambling. Bold declarations of love weren't something I was used to. 'I wanted to tell you...'

It was at that moment that I stopped talking, noticing something in the distance. To the side of the pond was a group of excited kids, laughing and squealing. As I strained my eyes, I could see what had got their attention: a collection of turtles, all sitting one of top of each other. A couple of harassed-looking parents were trying to keep little hands from touching them. But there was someone kneeling on the ground who had the closest access to the creatures, and he had obviously begun to speak because a hush suddenly descended over the children.

As he stood up and turned, I gasped. Shielding my eyes from the sun, I strained to get a better look.

He turned back to the turtles, lifting the baby one at the top of the pile before showing it to the crowd. It couldn't be but it was. It was Mateo.

'What's the matter, Laila?' Gregory asked.

'It is fate,' I whispered, in utter disbelief.

'What is?'

I pointed up ahead and Gregory followed my finger. He squinted before pulling out his long-distance glasses from his shirt pocket.

'Is that him?'

I nodded and Gregory whooped in delight. I leaned into him, suddenly feeling giddy and light-headed and he wrapped his arm around my shoulder as feelings of excitement and nerves gripped me tightly.

'Hey, don't be nervous,' Gregory said as if reading my mind. 'Go see him.'

Gregory's presence was like a tower of strength. He had given me more than I could have ever hoped for from a caregiver. He was the father I had always longed to have.

But Mateo… could he be the icing on a delicious strawberry shortcake from my favourite patisserie on Broadway?

I straightened, suddenly feeling buoyed. 'I'll catch up with you later,' I said to Gregory.

He waved me off with the broadest grin.

Walking closer to the crowd that had gathered to listen to Mateo's talk, I hung back, keen not to step in front of the little kids that were still in awe of the words that came from him and the sight of these glorious creatures. When the children were invited to come and pet the baby turtle, I took my place at the end of the queue.

As my turn came, I kneeled. It was then that Mateo caught sight of me and sprang up in shock.

'Sorry, I didn't mean to startle you.' I stood to face him.

His thunderstruck expression turned to one of his beaming smiles. 'What are you doing here?'

'I was taking a stroll with my stepfather and—'

'Your stepfather?' he said, a look of surprise on his face.

'Yes. My stepfather. I lived with him for a few months over the summer and I'm now in halls of residence at NYU doing a fellowship, so we try and meet up at the weekends for catch-ups.'

'That's incredible,' Mateo said, that familiar smile broad over his face. How I had missed that smile. 'I'm happy for you,' he said with so much sincerity.

'What about you?'

'I'm doing a PhD at Columbia.'

His words floored me as I thought back to that concept I had hoped would come to fruition. We had both decided to return to the city, only different parts of it.

'That's amazing, too.' I beamed back at him, clocking his Central Park-branded shirt.

'I volunteer for the Central Park conservancy at the weekend, giving talks and undertaking various sustainability projects.'

'That's incredible. And travelling?'

'I still plan on exploring the world during recesses. But I think I always knew my heart was here in this city. That year left a lasting mark on my life.'

'Mine too. But I'm not sure I would've had the courage to come back if it wasn't for you.'

Mateo opened and closed his mouth, seemingly at a loss for words. He then remembered where he was and placed the turtle back in the pond. We watched it swim away and it stirred a memory of the day he released one into the sea in Costa Rica.

He took a wet wipe from his bag and rubbed it over his hands. 'Laila, I'm sorry for not contacting you after you left. I regret the things I said to you. I desperately wanted you to know how much that time with you meant to me, that I wasn't angry about how things turned out. But I didn't want to put any pressure on you, I didn't...'

I stepped closer to him, wanting so desperately to break the distance between us and start over, but also wanting to hear his words, hear what was in his heart. 'You didn't what?'

'I didn't want to pressure you into making a choice because I realise there was no choice. You were living life, exploring connections, and feeling free to be who you are. And as much as I wanted you to be a part of my life, I couldn't tell you what was in my heart because I was scared.'

That word made me think of what I had just said to Gregory. 'Scared of what?'

'Of forcing you to choose.'

'It was never a choice, Mateo. There was never a square. There was only ever a line from me to you, only I didn't realise it at the time. And I convinced myself that not telling you this when I did have this epiphany was because if there was ever going to be a chance for us, I wanted it to be because it was the right time – that neither of us were making compromises or sacrifices to be with each other, wherever in the world it might be.'

His eyes searched mine, but his mouth remained tightly closed as if he was trying to absorb my words.

As he stepped even closer, his fingers caressed my cheek and the world dropped away around us. 'You took a chance on fate?'

I leaned into his hold and closed my eyes for a beat. When I opened them, I straightened and held his hands in mine. 'Yes and no. I did until I decided to call you just now.' I gave a half laugh. 'I guess I believed in the power of knowing that we would connect again, that our bond was strong enough to pull us back together one day but I realised today that I no longer wanted to leave that up to chance. I wanted to make it happen because I've known for a long time that if I ever got the chance to see you again, I would want to tell you how much I loved you.'

He brought my hands to his chest, his eyes welling up. 'I love you too, Laila. Always have. And I couldn't be happier that you were brave enough to try and reconnect. The first time and now, especially now.'

It was hard not to get lost in his eyes once more as I thought back to that moment on the Ferris wheel when he'd tried to calm my fear. 'The only equation I want to balance, Mateo, is the one between you and me.' At those last words I laughed. Jena would be proud of me. It sounded like a line lifted straight from one of her novels. 'Sorry, that was cheesy.'

Mateo squeezed my hands tighter before bringing them to his lips and touching them for a brief kiss. 'Not cheesy at all.'

'Wait,' I said, realising I had been completely caught up in the moment. 'I don't even know where you're placed in your... personal life.'

'I'm single,' he said with no hesitation.

'Well, then.' I smiled shyly as if I was seventeen again, but feeling very much emboldened now I was older. 'I was wondering if I could maybe ask you out on a date.'

'Hmm, it depends if you're asking for a friend or not.'

I laughed. 'Oh, it's definitely for me this time,' I said, before my lips found his.

We kissed softly before Mateo took me in his arms once more – the place I wanted to be, a place that felt like home. The rush of oxytocin flooded my body as the hold went over the twenty-second nirvana limit.

As the warmth of the sun coated my cheek, thoughts of how brave I had been to make this massive leap into a new life buoyed me and the power of Mateo's hold enveloped me. I felt well and truly DOSEd up.

Acknowledgements

The process of creating *The Love Intervention* has led me on a very personal journey of healing and has been the best form of therapy. The idea for the book all began with a hug – a very special hug from a lovely Greek guy I was dating a while ago. It was life-affirming. And after that hug, came the warmth and friendship from a special Italian guy who is also amazing at giving hugs. These interactions led me to write this novel and then to pursue a diploma in touch therapy, where I have learned that the power of touch is more far reaching than I could ever have imagined, so thank you, Kostas and Francesco, for inspiring me.

This is my fourth novel, and I consider myself immensely fortunate to have such an incredible agent in Kate Burke who has been instrumental in my writing journey. As the years roll by, Kate has become more than an agent – she's a good friend, and someone who I admire enormously. Our catch-up coffees are the most uplifting meetups I could ever wish for. My thanks extend to the rest of the Blake Friedmann team who work hard behind the scenes with all my novels.

This is my second novel published by Canelo and it's been a dream to work with the team there. My editor Emily Bedford is incredibly insightful and always takes my novels to the next level. Huge appreciation to the rest of the team for championing and working so hard on my books: Thanhmai Bui-Van, Deirbhile Brennan, Nicola Piggott, Kate Shepherd, Alicia Pountney, my cover illustrator Sophie Melissa and designer Cherie Chapman, my amazing copy editor Becca Allen, and my proofreader, Abigail Fenton.

The writing journey is a tough one and I simply wouldn't make it through without the endorsement of my author friends. Zoë Folbigg – you have lifted me up on countless occasions. Your warmth, humour and dating advice have been very welcomed and I am so honoured to call you one of my besties now. I'm also grateful for all the championing I have received from the rest of my writing tribe: Lorraine Brown, Kathleen Whyman, Lorna Cook, Emma Cowell, Emma Hughes, Sara Jafari, Carrie Elks, Jennifer Hennessy and Jo Lovett, from graciously quoting to WhatsApp groups/messages.

I love the #bookstagram community with all my heart. They embraced me from the start, have stuck by me with their love of all my novels and in my opinion, it is the best corner of social media. I appreciate all your generosity and kindness, all the posts, reviews and shares. Special shout-out to Emily Woosey for hosting my giveaways and her expert marketing advice.

To my co-parent/bestie/all-round superstar Dee Spence. Your friendship over the last few years has been incredible and I still remember fondly when we sat over coffee and fleshed out the storyline of *The Love Intervention* together. You are my rock, my confidant and I am incredibly lucky to have you in my life. My other best friends have also been towers of strength this last year: Sarah Brett, Minal Choksey, Hannah Tigg, Jan Jones, Sarah Richardson and Francesco Beccio. Big hugs all round.

Helen Kaye at Kingston Women's Centre – you have been incredible!

My writing stints and editing are always fuelled by coffee and I can either be found in 63 High Street in New Malden (my home from home, ably run by Ans, David and the rest of the crew) and 3 Apes Coffee in Raynes Park where I have penned many a chapter.

Where do I even begin to thank my Pressdee family? My mother has shown me levels of nurturing and encouragement that I never could have imagined. She's my biggest champion and has given me a roof over my head so I can keep writing. She is simply the best! My brother, sister-in-law and nieces continue to support my writing endeavours, but a special mention to my youngest niece Alex whose love and enthusiasm for my novels makes me want to keep writing.

To my girls – Miranda and Rose. I might be a writer, but I am at a loss for the right words to express how much you both mean to me. Miranda, you were the inspiration behind my heroine Laila and I am so grateful to your scientific knowledge, helping spare my blushes when it came to chemical equations. Your trip to CERN was the inspiration behind Laila and Mateo's meet-cute and I have loved talking through plot points with you and our manifestation chats also. Rose, you continue to amaze me too, from your warmth and humour to your words of encouragement that have kept me going through the writing of this novel. You're the best and I am so proud of you. I am the luckiest Mum in the world to have both of you in my life along with our furry trio – Biscuit, Flair and Eloise.

My final thanks go to YOU – the reader. For taking a chance on this book. I hope you find the levels of comfort it provided me during the writing process and that you seek out that hug from someone you love or care for after reading it. Please do get in touch and let me know what you think. I can be reached @carolinekauthor on Instagram.